THE COVEN
OF THE TALISMAN

BY
DAVID HANSELL

MAPLE
PUBLISHERS

The Coven Of The Talisman

Author: David Hansell

Copyright © David Hansell (2024)

The right of David Hansell to be identified as author of this work has been asserted by the author in accordance with section 77 and 78 of the Copyright, Designs and Patents Act 1988.

First Published in 2024

ISBN 978-1-83538-250-9 (Paperback)
    978-1-83538-251-6 (Hardback)
    978-1-83538-252-3 (E-Book)

Book Cover Design and Book Layout by:
    White Magic Studios
    www.whitemagicstudios.co.uk

Published by:
    Maple Publishers
    Fairbourne Drive, Atterbury,
    Milton Keynes,
    MK10 9RG, UK
    www.maplepublishers.com

A CIP catalogue record for this title is available from the British Library.

All rights reserved. No part of this book may be reproduced or translated by any form or by any means, electronic or mechanical, including photocopying, recording or by any information storage and retrieval system without written permission from the author.

The views expressed in this work are solely those of the author and do not necessarily reflect the views of the publisher, and the publisher hereby disclaims any responsibility for them.

CONTENTS

The Coven Of The Talisman 2

THE WITCH 5

THE SPELL 13

MRS. SMYTH 16

THE WIZARD 20

THE COVEN 26

THE SURVIVOR 32

CORNWALL 36

THE BATTLE 42

THE TALISMAN'S RETURN 48

THE CAVERN 54

THE TRAP 61

THE SHOOT 70

BETH AND CUTHBERT 80

THE INHERITANCE 90

CUTHBERT MEETS THE COVEN 97

SHOPPING 101

FROM BAD TO WORSE 104

BELLA'S BACK 109

CUTHBERT'S PLAN 111

TRICKED 113

ALL'S WELL THAT ENDS WELL 117

SCOTLAND 119

THE WARLOCK MASTER 122

THE DRAGON 124

A GREAT HONOUR	130
TOM'S RETURN	133
THE SECRET MEETING	136
A VISIT TO SCOTLAND	138
LEPRECHAUN'S GOLD	147
TOM JOINS THE BROTHERHOOD	151
THE OGRE	155
A TRIP TO SCOTLAND	158
STINKING CORPSE	162
A NEW ARRIVAL	165
ANOTHER NEW ARRIVAL	169
TROUBLE COMES TO THOMPSON	175
GEORGE HAS TO DIE	181
HOME AGAIN	192
THE RACE IS ON	196
THE BATTLE OF THOMPSON	204
THE DRAGON REALM	223
THE END OF DAY TWO	238

THE WITCH

It seemed just like any other workday, I woke up at six o'clock as usual, got to the Farm at five to seven as usual. But that's the last usual thing that happened that day. The Foreman said to go up to the forty acres by the big wood and spread fertiliser on it.

Now I had worked on the farm, in the village of Thompson, that belonged to the Major since leaving school and for most of the time I loved it. You were out in the fresh air, (although some days it was a little bit too fresh) there was always something different going on. Each season brought different plants and animals, there were rabbits, squirrels, foxes, deer, badgers and a multitude of birds.

So, I loaded up the spreader and headed up to the forty acres. Now this was by any standard a large field. It came about because of a government memo asking farmers to make better use of their land; they could grow more crops by taking out all the hedges and filling in the pits. That was back in the sixties and the Major hadn't bothered to put them back. Anyway, I digress. To get back to my tale, there I was spreading fertiliser happy as a pig in (need I finish?) when something caught my eye. It was the wood. For as long as I can remember no one had ever been able to get into the wood. It was a sinister looking place completely full of brambles and rhododendrons.

As a child all of us kids from the village had tried on numerous occasions to fight our way into the wood with no success. People in the village told a story about how in the sixteen hundreds, two sisters who were said to be witches lived in a cottage in the wood and practised magic. When the witches' trials were at their highest, it was said they sealed themselves in the wood and nobody had been able to gain entry since. The Major had said on many occasions that we must clear a path and chop down some of the old oaks. There were some huge ones visible inside the wood, that were at least four hundred years old, if not older, and must be worth a fortune, but for some reason we never got round to it.

But now there, I was looking at a gap in the brambles big enough to drive my tractor through and what looked like a pathway leading into the middle of the wood. Were my eyes deceiving me or could I just make out a small cottage farther inside the wood? My curiosity got the better of me, so I went to have a look. The closer I got to the wood the better I could make it out and when I got to the edge of the field, I could see it clearly. By this time, it was getting on towards lunch, so I decided to stop and kill two birds with one stone - first I'd have my lunch and then I'd have a look in the wood that I'd been trying to get into ever since I was a child. Only my curiosity got the better of me, so leaving my tractor behind I started to walk towards the opening. It's strange, I thought of all those times my friends and I had tried to gain entry but couldn't, and here I was just walking in. I looked at the entrance, there were no signs that anybody had cut their way in with a chainsaw, which as far as I could see was the only means of entry. It looked as if the path had always been there and in constant use.

The inside of the wood wasn't as overgrown as I'd expected. I thought after hundreds of years it would be an impassable jungle, but no, it seemed to me that there had been some pigs in there to eat the acorns, therefore, stopping any new growth of trees. This place was having a strange effect on me. I could have sworn I could hear them rooting about in the trees and I thought I saw something pig like moving in the shadows. 'Now this is stupid,' I thought as I got nearer, it can't be, but there was an old cottage, with smoke coming out of the chimney and it looked as if someone was living there, which I knew to be impossible, but there were roses around the door and what looked like a herb garden, all well weeded and cared for.

'I'm going mad,' I thought, 'there's no way anybody could have gotten in till today.'

'Hello young man,' said a voice behind me, 'I've been waiting for you. Expected more than one though. There's usually twelve witches. Times must be bad if only one wizard turns up.'

'Hang on,' I said, 'who're you calling a wizard? I'm a tractor driver.' I know it sounded stupid, but it was the first thing that came into my completely befuddled head.

'I've heard of people who drive cattle or even sheep to market, but I've never heard of a track-tor. What sort of a beast is that?' she said.

'It's not a beast it's a machine,' I answered.

By now my mind seemed to be full of treacle, all I could think of was - what's this old lady doing in a house that should have fallen down years ago, in a wood that's been impossible to enter for as far back as the sixteen hundreds?

'Are you alright young man? You seem a mite skittish for a track-tor driver, whatever that is. Now please tell me, what year is this?' she asked. It's two thousand and eight,' I replied, getting more confused by the minute. 'That can't be right, you must be mistaken,' she said, looking nearly as confused as I was, 'it's thirty-seven years too early. Oh dear, oh dear, oh dear, what can have happened?'

'Are you all right?' I asked getting a bit worried myself. 'Yes, I think so. I must find out what's happened to bring me out of the spell so early.' 'Spell?' I said. 'What are you talking about?' 'I'll explain later young man. Listen I can't keep calling you "young man" what is your name?'

'David Johnson, but you can call me David.' 'Well, David, if you could just take me to your village witch or midwife, I would be very grateful.'

Not quite knowing why I was going along with this obviously deranged old lady I said, 'The only midwife you'll find about here will be at the hospital in Norwich. As for witches I don't think there has been one around here for a couple a hundred years.' 'The last time the spell wore off was in nineteen forty five and there was a Mistress Clarke who was the witch for the village,' she informed me.

Suddenly I remembered this old woman, who all us kids were frightened of. She was a horrible old crone who used to chase us out of her orchard if she caught us picking her apples. She had the ugliest black cat, it must have been very old, because most of the creature's fur had fallen out, but she'd been dead for years. 'I'm afraid she's been dead for ages,' I told her. 'Oh dear. Who's her replacement then? I do hope she's been told about me,' she said looking very perturbed, 'only, I'm going to need her help if the spell is to continue.'

I knew I was going to regret asking this, but I couldn't help myself.

'What spell?'

'Well, seeing as you're a track-tor driver and I do need your help, I might as well tell you my story. It all started back in 1645, there were widespread witch hunts, and the people in the village were very superstitious and thought all witches were evil.'

'And you weren't,' I said. (Looking back on it now, I can't believe I went along with this old lady's obvious load of old rubbish). 'Me no, but I could see where they got the idea from. My sister, Bella, on the other hand was most people's idea of an old hag, I know we were sisters but our ideas on witchcraft differed completely. She was a great believer in spells, charms and potions, whereas I was more inclined to use of herbs, gentle persuasion and common sense to solve problems and only got my wand out as a last resort, but it will take more than common sense to get me out of trouble this time. Getting back to 1645, my sister and I were getting worried, we'd heard news from other witches that some of our kind had been burnt at the stake or drowned in their own village ponds and we didn't want to be next.

'So we gathered witches from around the local villages and hatched a plan to seal my sister and me inside the wood until it was safe for us to leave, but we only had enough power to keep the spell going for 100 years at a time. When the time was up the spell would run out and all the local witches would meet here and put the spell on for another 100 years, and so it has gone on since then. Every 100 years we would spend one day with the other witches to find out how things were, and if it was time to come back to the world, but so far every time we came back it was not safe. The last time was 1945 and there was only one witch to help with the spell and she said that there was a world war going on at the time.

'Imagine that everyone in the world at war with one another, so she said it was not a safe place for anybody at that time, witches or ordinary folk, but the trouble was one lone witch was not enough to redo the spell, so my sister and I decided that one of us would stay outside to help Mistress Clarke with the spell. Naturally she was the one to stay out and help.

'After nearly four hundred years of each other's company tempers were getting a mite strained and she jumped at the chance to leave. I knew that I would miss her even though at times I could have turned her into a frog, so we had a final meal together and at midnight we all said the incantation that locked me in the wood for another hundred years. But that doesn't seem to have been the case,' she said looking worried.

'So, David I'm afraid I'm going to have to take you up on your kind offer of help. Tell me is the world war still going on?' she asked.

'No,' I said, 'that war finished the same year you came back but there has been a war going on somewhere in the world ever since.' I felt almost ashamed telling her this. 'That's always been the case for as long as anyone can remember. It seems as if man is destined to destroy himself,' said the old lady looking sad. 'But back to my problem. I must find another witch and see if it's time to come back to the world.'

'Well, what can I do?' I enquired.

I can't tell you why, but I was starting to get taken in by this old lady and her story of witches and spells. I knew deep down that witches were like fairies, elves, trolls and pixies, only mythological creatures invented by people to explain strange occurrences in olden times before man knew better. But this was the twenty first century and all those things were no longer believed in. (Was I going to find out different?)

'As I said before, to my knowledge there are no witches in this village.' 'Okay, is there an old lady who grows her own herbs and makes salves and lotions to cure ills?'

'No,' I said. 'Well in that case is there a strange old lady who lives on her own and frightens the children?' she said.

'Only my sister in-law but I don't think she's a witch. Just downright mean,' (She'd give witches a bad name if she was), I replied. 'There must be someone who grows herbs.' 'Hang on,' I said, 'there is. We grow fields of herbs here on the farm but I don't think that the Major is a witch.' 'No,' said the old lady, 'witches are always women. Men are wizards or warlocks.' 'I should have known that. I've read all the Harry Potter books,' I said.

'Harry Potter? Who's he?' Oh no, how on earth am I going to explain to her about Harry Potter. 'Do you think he can help me?' 'No,' I said you're just going to make do with me.'

'That's alright, David, I'm sure you will come up with something.' (Oh yeah, I was sure I would).

'To start with, who's this Major and why does he grow all these herbs?' 'Well, I blame all these cooking programmes on television,' I said. 'Since they've been on, everyone's using herbs in their cooking. They are also used in shampoos, body lotion, tea and a hundred and one other things. We can hardly keep up with demand. As for the Major he's the farmer who owns all the land about here. His correct title is "Major Tony Smyth, Third Royal Anglian Regiment (retired)." His family have farmed this land for the last two hundred years. He lives in the manor house with his wife Bethany. Come to think of it she's the one who got him into growing herbs,' I remarked.

'She sounds like the type to be a witch. I think I'd like to meet and have a talk with her,' she said.

'I don't think she's into witchcraft, but she is an organic herbalist. She has a chain of shops selling health food and herbal remedies.'

The last thing I wanted to do was to take this mad old lady to meet my boss's wife and have her ask her if she was a witch.

'That sounds about right. When can I meet her?'

'Look,' I said, trying to change the subject, 'I'll have to be going back to work. I've been in here for ages talking to you and I'll never get this field done before it's time to leave off.' I was hoping to get away from this old lady before I went as mad as her. 'Don't worry, as soon as the spell broke and I spotted you coming, I said a spell to slow down time outside in case there was any trouble and we had to put the spell on again quickly.

So, although you've been in here for quite a while, it has in fact only been a few minutes outside.'

'Look, it's impossible to slow down time so unless you've got a time machine it will be two o'clock in two minutes and I will have been here for an hour,' I said looking at my watch. 'I've enjoyed our talk, but I must get back to work.'

With that I turned around and walked out of the wood, back to my tractor hoping that I never saw the mad old lady again. I had only been in my tractor for thirty seconds or so when the radio announcer said that it was time for the one o'clock news. 'No,' I thought I must have heard it wrong. It's now just gone two o'clock according to my watch. Quickly developing a splitting headache, I knew I had to do something or I'd lose my mind with all this talk about witches and spells and slowing down time.

So, I phoned my wife, 'Hello Sadie,' I said when my wife answered. 'Can you tell me the time?' 'Did you forget your watch again?' she said. 'Yes,' I answered. 'Well, it's just coming up to three minutes past one.'

'Are you sure it's not three minutes past two and you've read it wrong?'

I said hopefully. 'I can tell the time,' said my wife sounding rather miffed, 'anyway what's wrong looking at your phone. That's got the time on it.' 'Sorry,' I said feeling silly, 'it's been a rather confusing morning, I'll see you later,' I said, and hung up.

I then looked at my mobile, and looked at the clock on my tractor, they said the same time, and so unless someone had changed them without me knowing, the old lady was right.

I had to know so I got out of my tractor and headed back into the wood.

'I was hoping you'd be back. I really need your help,' she told me. 'What's going on? I've just found out that I'm an hour ahead of everybody else on the planet. Can you really slow down time, or is this some trick?' I said hopefully.

'I'm not tricking you. I am a witch and I can do magic, that includes slowing down time but only for an hour or two and if I don't find another witch soon I'll be stuck here in this century.' 'Well, why not stay?' I remarked, 'it's not so bad. We don't have witch trials anymore, in fact people don't believe in witches these days although there are still some people who claim they are witches; but they are thought of as weird,' I told her. 'There must be some. I can feel that there is magic about. Not a lot, but every time a witch casts a spell it leaves a residue of magic that other witches can feel,' she told me.

'If that's so,' I said, 'can you find where the spell was cast?' 'Yes, if it's not too far away. Though it will only tell me where and not who the witch is.'

'I understand that. But do witches cast spells near where they live?' I queried. 'Why didn't I think of that? You're right, a witch only performs magic around her home, so if I can find out if there has been a spell cast around here lately it would mean that there must be a witch in this vicinity. Now,' she said looking at me, 'if you would be so kind as to come here tonight just before midnight we can cast for the magic left over from an old spell, and also the witch that cast it.'

'Ok I'll be here.' Don't ask me why but I was getting drawn into this old lady's story of witches and spells and slowing down time. There had to be an explanation, I only hoped it wasn't that I was having a nervous breakdown.

THE SPELL

'So why can't the game keeper check his own birds tonight?' As you can no doubt tell, my wife Sadie was not in a very good mood. Tonight was her ladies' darts night and she would have to miss it, because I told her that I would be looking after the gamekeepers' pheasants as he'd been having trouble with foxes killing them. 'Why can't he look after them?' she said getting even redder in the face. 'I told you it's his birthday and his family are taking him out for a meal.' 'But it's my darts night and tonight is a big match, we're through to the semi-finals if we win.'

'I'm sorry it won't happen again, and I'll take you out for a meal tomorrow night to make it up to you,' I said, hoping it would get me out of trouble.

At a quarter to midnight, I left home, my wife having asked her mother to baby sit our two boys so she could go to her darts match. I made my way back to the wood. I half expected to see it as it always was, surrounded by brambles, but no, there was the gap, and I could see a light in the cottage window. I knocked on the door and it was opened by the same old lady that I had spoken to this afternoon.

'Come in, David, I was just getting a few herbs and other ingredients ready for our spell.' 'Our spell?' I said. 'I told you before I'm not a wizard.'

'It doesn't matter, I can do the spell but if I can channel it through you also it will be twice as powerful and we'll get better results.'

'Well ok, but where are we going to cast it?' (By this time I was going along with her completely, and when I look back on it now, I can't help but wonder if she had cast a spell on me). 'You said that there was a Mistress Clarke who lived in the village. Is there an open area near her house?' she asked.

'The house was knocked down years ago, but the field behind it is now the kids' playing fields. I don't know if that counts,' I said.

'Well, it's a start, we'll try that first.'

We must have looked a funny couple walking through the village that night, a young bloke and a short plump old lady all in black with a pointy hat. If anyone saw us, I had it all worked out, I'd tell them she was my aunt and was trying out her costume for Halloween. (I know it sounds silly but I couldn't think of anything else). As luck would have it we didn't meet anyone.

When we got to the field, she took out what looked like a bundle of tent pegs and hammered them into the ground in no particular order. It wasn't until she strung the wool between the stakes that I saw the shape of a pentagram.

'Now David,' she said, 'if you stand in the centre with me and hold hands I'll begin.'

So, there I was standing in the middle of the playing fields holding hands with a witch. It felt like holding hands with my granny, but only if my granny was four hundred years old. 'Why do we have to hold hands?' I moaned. 'We have to form a circle and because there's only two of us, by holding hands it will give me more power to cast the spell.'

'Ok,' I said, 'let's get on with it.'

She started to chant words I'd never heard before. She told me later that it was an ancient language only used by witches. When she finished chanting, the air seemed to be charged with static electricity, that shimmered in several different colours, after a few minutes they slowly faded, and she opened her eyes.

'Did you find anything? Is there a witch in the area?' Looking very pleased she said, 'Yes, there is and she has been casting spells right here on this very field.'

'That's all very well. But how does that help us? We're still no closer to finding out who it is though.' 'I know, David,' she said, 'it might seem so but a witch will always know if any spells have been cast in her area. So it won't be long before she comes looking for whoever's been using magic. You see it's very bad manners to cast spells in another witch's territory without first asking for her help or permission.' 'Do you think she will come tonight only? It's getting late and I'm in enough trouble with my wife as it was without staying out all night.'

'No David, you get along, this may take some time, she might not come for a few days, so you get off. I wouldn't want to be the cause of any trouble between you and your wife.' (I could've sworn that she had a little smile on her face when she said that).

'Right,' I said, 'I'll be off. Before I do, you haven't told me your name yet.' 'Oh,' she said 'I was hoping you weren't going to ask me that. It's Donna.' 'Hang on, didn't you say your sister's name is Bella?' 'Yes, my mother never gave much thought when naming us girls. I suppose she must have had some deadly nightshade in sight when we were born and decided to call one of us Bella and the other Donna.'

'Ok then, Donna, I'll be off, but I'll pop in tomorrow and see if you've had any luck finding anyone.'

MRS. SMYTH

Next morning, I set off for work. I had received a cold reception on returning home late the night before, and a not much warmer one on getting up that morning. To say that my wife was not pleased at having to ask her mother to baby sit at short notice, would be an understatement, so to save myself any more aggro I beat a hasty retreat.

On my way to the farm, I had to pass the wood, so I decided to go and see if Donna had had any luck finding anyone. I found her out in the wood feeding her pigs.

'Hello, Donna, how are you this morning?' I asked her. 'It's very strange not waking up and it's a hundred years later than when I went to bed but I suppose I'll get used to it if I decide to stay.'

'The reason I called this morning was that I wanted to find out if you'd had any contact with another witch.'

'It's amazing, twenty-four hours ago, you didn't even believe in witches and now here you are one day later trying to find one.'

She gave me a wry smile. 'I don't believe it myself,

I think you've cast a spell on me. It's the only explanation I can think of for me helping you.'

'No, David, it's just that you're a nice person and you don't like to see anyone in trouble. And also, you're very curious to see if there really are such things as witches and magic. But to answer your question, no, not yet. I haven't had anyone apart from you come to the wood since the spell ended,' she answered, 'I'm getting worried. I suppose as you said there are no real witches anymore. What am I going to do?' 'Something will turn up,' I said, trying to reassure her. 'I'll have to go to work now but I'll call in dinner time to see if you've had any luck.'

With that I left a rather worried looking Donna and went to work.

Two hours later as I was ploughing the ten acres, I thought I saw the Major's wife walking towards the wood. I hoped that Donna had some spell going to prevent her from entering.

The morning seemed to drag by, and it felt like lunch time would never arrive. Finally it was time to head back to the wood and see if Donna had been lucky in finding anyone. As I made my way back through the gap in the hedge I saw that Donna was not alone, the boss's wife, Mrs Smyth, was there talking to her as if they were old friends.

'Here's my helper,' said Donna, 'I don't know what I'd have done without him.' 'I hope you're not going to claim overtime for last night,' Mrs Smyth informed me. 'It would look strange on your time sheet, two hours' overtime for casting spells.'

'No- n -n no,' I spluttered, starting to panic. Then I noticed Mrs Smyth had a big grin all over her face, 'I'm sorry David, I just couldn't resist it. The look on your face was priceless.'

'If you don't mind me asking,' I enquired, 'why are you here? 'You know why. Didn't you and Donna cast for me last night?'

'You mean you're the witch for this village?' (I couldn't believe it, the Major's wife a witch). 'But you're just like the rest of us.' (Only with a lot more money, I thought).

'Did you think I'd wear black and have a pointy hat and ride around on a broomstick? This is after all the twenty first century, witches like everything else, must evolve. To correct you, though, I'm not just the witch for this village; there are so few of us these days that I must cover the entire county,' she explained.

'Well, that means I'm no longer needed so I'll be getting back to work, if you don't mind,' I said hopefully.

'Please don't go, I still need your help,' begged Donna, 'if that's alright with you, Betty?' 'Yes, I agree with Donna we still need your help. As a matter of fact, I'll have a word with my husband and tell him I need you to work with me for a while. That way we'll have you on hand when we need you.'

'First, take my Range Rover to the farm and bring the generator and my laptop back here.' 'Ok Mrs Smyth won't be long' I said. 'Please call me Betty,' she said. 'I don't know if I can do that. It would be like calling the queen Liz.' 'Well try, I'm only a farmer's wife, not royalty,' she said. 'Ok ---Betty. Won't be a minute.' When I got back and set up the generator, Betty plugged in her laptop and began surfing the net. 'What magic is this?' said Donna. 'It's called technology, it lets me contact people anywhere in the world. It might seem like magic to you Donna, but most people don't give it a second thought, I'll explain about it all later. Right now, I'm trying to contact as many witches as I can. Then if you decide not to stay, we can cast the spell to lock you in the wood for another hundred years.' After an hour of surfing the web a rather worried Betty turned to Donna and said, 'There's something very wrong. I've been on all the usual sites and nobody's answering. I've left messages on Facebook and one or two other sites. Hopefully someone will get in touch soon.'

'I thought you all met in covens, not on the internet,' I said.

'Yes, we did, but there are so few of us these days, it's the best way to keep in touch, although we do try to all meet up for Halloween or if there's anything that needs a full coven. That's why I'm worried, there's always someone monitoring the net in case a witch is in trouble. We can't do anymore till we hear from someone, so you can go home David. But if you come here tomorrow morning, hopefully we'll know more by then.'

With that I left the wood and went home to see if my wife was in a better mood (some hope). But when I arrived home, everything was sweetness and light with my wife.

'Hello love,' she said as I walked in, 'I've cooked your favourite for your tea tonight, steak and chips and apple pie and custard for afters.'

To say that I was surprised would have been an understatement. I had expected beans on toast after last night. 'I hear you're working for Mrs Smyth now,' she said. 'How did you find out about that? I only found out myself this afternoon, and what's this with the meal and you being so nice to me? This morning you we're in a bad mood, because you'd had to ask you mother for help, and were hardly speaking to me,' I told her.

'Well, I had a phone call from Betty, and she explained that it was not your fault.' 'Betty? Since when have you been on first name terms with the boss's wife?' I asked.

'We met one day while I was out for a stroll and got talking. She comes round once or twice a week for tea and a chat. I didn't say anything because you wouldn't like me being friends with the boss's wife.'

'That's silly darling,' I lied, 'you can be friends with whoever you like, but I wouldn't have thought you'd had anything in common.' 'Me neither,' she said 'but you know I've always loved gardening, and Betty grows herbs for a living. She's taught me a lot, in fact she's offered me the chance to train me to be a *herbologist*.'

'A what?' I shouted, 'there's no such bloody thing.'

'Well, you know what I mean,' she shouted back, 'Betty wants me to work for her in her herb growing business and I said yes. I'll be learning to grow, process and market the herbs. You don't mind do you?'

I knew she was getting fed up with being at home with nothing to do since our boys Brandon and Jordon had started school. 'Of course I don't,' I said. (It's funny when you look back on something, how you can see things now, that you missed at the time, phrases like "why didn't I see that" and "how could I have been so blind" come to mind). But back to the story, I didn't sleep well that night, something kept going around in my mind, something I knew subconsciously, but couldn't bring to mind.

I awoke next morning with a head full of cotton wool and a brain that refused to work at all. After breakfast I set off for the wood, wondering what the day had in store for me.

THE WIZARD

On arrival I found Donna and Betty deep in conversation, both with worried looks on their faces.

'Good morning,' I said, when they failed to notice me, 'anything wrong?' 'Yes I'm afraid there is,' replied Betty, 'things have taken a turn for the worse and I may have to call on you to put yourself in harm's way but as your employer I cannot ask that of you.'

'Look I can't just turn my back on the two of you now. Anyway I'm not doing this as an employee, I'd be helping Donna even if you hadn't turned up.' (To tell the truth driving a tractor day in and day out can get rather boring) 'And I'm not stopping now,' I told her.

'Ok,' said Betty, 'but just so you know, it may get a little dangerous before we've finished. But if you're sure, we'd be glad of your help, wouldn't we, Donna?'

'Yes,' beamed Donna, 'you've been a big help so far.'

'Good, now would you mind telling me what's going on?' I asked.

'Well, I think it's time I told the truth,' said Donna, 'I've only told you part of the story. Yes, my sister and I were escaping the witch hunters, but also, we were guarding something very important, a talisman of tremendous power. In the wrong hands it could be a very powerful weapon, and maybe even cause the end of our world.'

'What Donna means is the end of witches, wizards and magic,' Betty told me.

'What is this talisman and what does it do?' I asked.

'Well a coven of young witches came up with an idea to purge the world of all evil magic, but when they'd cast the spell, the talisman they'd imbued with all their power was capable of destroying all magic, good as well as evil, so it was decided to hide it away, with two witches to guard it, and to give the rest of them enough time to find a way to destroy it. The only trouble with that plan was that since the seventeenth century, the witch population has declined so much that it has taken all our time and effort, just to keep the wood hidden,' Donna explained. 'The problem we have now is that we don't have enough witches to destroy the talisman or put the spell back on the wood, but we must do something soon before word gets around that the wood is open, and a dark witch or wizard tries to steal it.'

'But what good would that do, if it destroys all magic, it will take theirs as well, wouldn't it?' I asked.

'There have always been some magic folk who believe that they can control it. The problem is the talisman has gotten stronger over the years, so if they were to open it now, it could wipe out all magic everywhere, in an instant. So you see it's vital we contact as many good witches as we can, as soon as possible, to help us protect our way of life.' 'If you don't mind me asking, would it make any difference if there weren't witches or wizards anymore?' I enquired.

'It's not just witches and wizards, it's all magic. Magic is everywhere, we just tap into it, it flows through everything, and it can be used for good as well as evil. You see most people use magic and don't even realise it, it gives them inspiration, and helps them write books, compose music, paint beautiful canvasses and much more. So you see it affects everyone. If it was to fall into the wrong hands, it could change everything,' said Betty.

It was then that we all realised that we were not alone. There standing in the doorway was a very old and very thin man. 'It seems, Tom, that we've found the place we've been looking for,' he said to somebody outside, 'and not a minute too soon.'

I noticed then that both the witches had their wands out, and that the atmosphere had turned decidedly frosty. 'Now, now, ladies,

Tom and I have only come to help. I detected your spell the other night, and knew that it was cast near the wood, so we came to investigate,' the old man told us.

'That's very kind of you, but if you don't mind, who are you and where is Tom?' Donna asked him. (I noticed that neither of the witches had put their wands away) 'I'm surprised you don't remember me, Donna, we used to walk out in our youth, and I thought at one time that we might even tie the knot,' the old man said, beaming at a rather confused looking Donna. 'GILBERT! No it can't be, if you were Gilbert you'd be over four hundred years old.' 'I am Gilbert and I am over four hundred years old, witches aren't the only ones who can cast spells you know. It was decided by the council of wizards that it was too great a risk to leave the guarding of the talisman to witches alone, so an elixir was brewed to keep me alive until this problem had been solved. And as for Tom, he's my apprentice,' said the wizard, 'he's been with me for ten years now.' 'Is he invisible?' said a rather sarcastic Donna.

'Tom! Why are you hiding out there?' shouted the wizard. 'There's witches in there with their wands out master,' came a voice from outside, 'it's much safer out here.'

'Get in here, will you, and show some backbone?' shouted Gilbert. 'I've told you before you're perfectly safe with me, now get in here and say hello to these people.'

Through the door came this thin gangly youth that looked as though he was ready to flee at a moment's notice. After he'd been introduced to us all, he seemed to calm down a bit.

'Now that we've all been introduced to one another,' said Betty 'what are we going to do about the talisman? We can't leave it hid here in Donna's cottage. As I said it won't be long before someone comes looking for it.'

'Just a minute, are you telling us that it's here in this cottage at this very moment?' asked Gilbert. 'Yes,' said Donna 'why?'

'It's just that something as powerful as that should emit a strong aura that we can all feel, and I don't know about you, but I can't feel anything.'

'Oh, my goodness,' cried Donna, 'he's right. I can't feel a thing. I've been worrying so much about finding other witches to help me cast the spell back on the wood that I forgot about everything else. 'I'm as bad, said Betty. 'I haven't felt anything either.'

With that, Donna rushed off into the next room, and started rummaging in a large trunk. After throwing out all its contents, she turned round to us with a look of terror on her face, and said, 'it's not here, it's gone. But how? No one's been here in four hundred years.'

'What about one of the witches that came to put the spell on the wood, couldn't one of them have stolen it?' I asked.

'No that's not possible. You see, my sister and I took turns to guard the talisman, while the other helped the witches cast the spell,' said Donna. 'What about the last time, you said that there were only three of you, 'who was guarding it then?' Betty asked.

'No, she couldn't, she wouldn't, after all these years of guarding it she wouldn't steal it, would she?' Donna asked almost in tears. 'It must have been my sister Bella, she's the only other person besides me who knew where it was. We had many arguments over what should be done with the talisman. She thought she could harness a small part of its power, and use it in bursts to enhance the spells we cast, but I said that it was too great a risk. If we were not careful it could back fire on us with catastrophic consequences. I thought it was only talk, just something to pass the time, but obviously it was not. She must have seen her chance when only one witch turned up the last time we came back, and took it. 'This is terrible,' said Gilbert. 'If she's out there and experimenting with it, and if she's managed to control it, there's no telling what trouble she's causing.

We must convene a coven, and see if we can find her, before she destroys our way of life.'

'How are we going to do that? There are not enough of us, we are only five and we need twelve to find a witch, especially one that doesn't want to be found,' said Donna.

'At such short notice I can only summon another five wizards, there must be two more witches you can call on,' said Gilbert.

'Well, there is old Mistress Webb over at Croxton, she retired years ago, but she's a tough old bird, could have one last spell left in her. There's only one other I can call upon, and that's my apprentice, if you think she will do,' said Betty, giving me a worried look.

'Ok that will have to do,' Gilbert told us. 'We'll all meet at midnight in the field that David and Donna cast their spell the other night.'

Oh god I thought, my wife is going to kill me.

'Betty, couldn't you find someone to take my place?' I begged. 'Only my wife's going to hit the roof, you see it's her sister's hen night and if she must ask her mother to baby sit again, she'll make my life hell.'

'It's alright I'm going to see her in a while and I'll tell her that it's all my fault,' Betty told me.

Not having much faith in Betty's power of persuasion, I went home later to face the music, only to find my wife still in a good mood, and not the slightest bit upset. 'I haven't asked my mother, I was thinking of giving it a miss anyway,' she told me.

'But I'll be leaving you on your own again, don't you mind?' I asked her. 'Oh, I won't be on my own, as a matter of a fact, there will be eleven other people with me.'

'What do mean, eleven other people? Where are you going?' I asked her. 'I'm coming with you sweetheart,' she said. 'Coming with me? I'm keeping watch on the pheasants again, you don't want to be traipsing around the woods with me in this weather.' She smiled at me and said, 'Oh David, haven't you worked it out yet? I'm Betty's apprentice, she's not training me to grow herbs, only how to use them in potions.'

I stood there looking at my wife of fifteen years with my mouth wide open, trying to come to terms with the fact that she was a witch, all be it, an apprentice.

'W—w—when? H—h—how?' I spluttered. 'About six months ago,' as I said before, 'Betty and I met one day while out walking and got talking about plants and gardening. She knows an awful lot about herbs and their uses. She explained how to make a salve to get rid of that nasty rash you had on your arm and one to cure my little nephew's nappy rash. Well, one thing led to another and finally she told me she was a witch, It was then that she asked me if I wanted to become her apprentice and I said yes.'

It was only two days ago that I found out there were such things as witches and wizards, now on top of that, I find out that my wife was one. 'What about the boys?' I said 'We can't leave them alone. 'It's alright,' she told me, 'the neighbour's girl is going to baby sit. My mother couldn't have done it anyway, it's her bridge night.'

'How can you be a witch?' I asked. 'Witches are old crones who live by themselves in a cottage in the woods, and they always wear black pointy hats and fly around on broomsticks.'

'This is the twenty first century darling, witches like everyone else have to change with the times.' (I'd had this lecture from Betty already). 'It does not pay to draw attention to ourselves, there may no longer be any witch trials or burning at the stake, but tell anyone you're a witch and they'll think you're two bricks short of a load, so we go about our business hoping no one notices,' my wife explained.

THE COVEN

Midnight found myself and eleven various witches and wizards forming a circle in the field that Donna and I had used two nights before.

Gilbert had indeed brought another five wizards, besides Tom. There wasn't one of them under the age of seventy by the looks of it. Gilbert introduced them to us, first two were Hamish and Alistair who were from Scotland. Hamish must have been at least twenty stone, with a smile nearly as big as his belly, while Alistair was half his size and had a very solemn expression.

Both wore what I would have expected wizards to wear, coats with mystical symbols embroidered all over them and the usual pointy hat, but only from the waist up, below the waist they both wore kilts with sporrans, from which Hamish often produced a silver flask and regularly took a long swig.

The next two were from Ireland, Dermot and Shamus. They on the other hand were identical twins, both looked more like leprechauns than wizards, (not that I'd ever met one), they wore the more traditional garb. I know I'm no expert on wizard's fashion, but Gilbert explained it all to me later.

Finally, the last wizard was from Wales. His name was unpronounceable, so we all called him Taffy. Taffy was by far the smallest, skinniest and oldest of them all. He reminded me of a mummy with all the bandages removed.

On the witches' side, first to be introduced was my wife Sadie who was by far the youngest witch, but if looks were anything to go by Mistress Web was not only the oldest witch there but the oldest woman alive.

By no means though, could anyone describe her as skinny, you could almost hear the chair complain as she sat down. But she was very alert and had eyes that didn't miss a thing; l liked her because she reminded me of my granny.

'We'd like to thank you all for coming,' Donna told the newcomers. 'Now if you'd all like to strip off we'll begin.' 'STRIP OFF,' I shouted. 'I'm not going to strip off, for one thing it's freezing.'

'Oh, come on darling, it's not that cold,' my wife said, grinning.

'What are you grinning at?' I asked. It was then that I noticed that all the others were grinning as well.

'I'm sorry,' laughed Donna. 'We couldn't resist it, the look on your face. It's all right, we don't dance around naked while casting spells, that is an old wives' tale. Now we've had our fun, back to the reason we're all here, a spell must be cast to find out the location of the talisman and who's got it.' After that we all formed a circle, the witches and I held hands, whereas the wizards, who all carried staves, held on to their own and each other's in turn. I had my wife on one side and Mistress Web on the other, and so the spell began.

Everybody except me started chanting. I couldn't join in because not being one of them I didn't know what to chant, but that was alright, as I was only there to make the number up to twelve. When Donna and I had cast the spell the other night a slight tingle ran through me. Donna said it was magical energy from the spell passing through us. If you can imagine that tingle multiplied by eleven, then that's what I was feeling. As they continued to chant a mist started to rise from the ground in the middle of the circle. From it emanated coloured lights that slowly started to form into the image of a large locket. 'That's it,' said Donna, 'that's the talisman, now we have to find out who's got it.' As the chanting continued the talisman turned to smoke and another image started to appear. This time it looked like a person's face. As it got clearer I heard Donna gasp, 'It's Bella,' she cried, 'it's my sister.'

The face in the smoke was crystal clear now and you could see a family likeness between her and Donna, the only difference being, that Bella looked as evil as Donna looked kind. The face in the smoke turned to Donna and said, 'Hello sister, I didn't expect to see you for another thirty-seven years. What are you doing Bella, you promised to guard it with me, not steal it for yourself?' asked Donna.

'You don't know how much I hated living in that wood with you while time passed us by, guarding something that held so much power and not being able to use it,' Bella shouted. 'But you can't use it without putting us all in danger,' cried Donna, 'and maybe destroying our way of life.'

Bella let out a roar of laughter. 'I'm not like you, sister, I have more faith in my power as a witch to worry about that. I know I can control it, and if not, I have gathered together coven of my own to help me. So if you don't want to go up against me and my followers, I urge you to keep well away or suffer the consequences.'

With that the image exploded with a force, blowing us all off our feet.

'Jesus,' groaned Shamus, 'that's one powerful witch. I'd not like to meet her on a dark night.' 'The only trouble is I think we're going to have to before this is over,' a thickly accented Welsh voice commented.

'Taffy's right we must find her and retrieve the talisman before it's too late,' Betty told us. 'First, we must find out why none of the other witches have answered my call for help. I know of at least twenty and none of them have come forward. The only thing I can think of is that they've been warned off, and now we know by whom.'

I had only heard part of what was being said because when we were blown off our feet Mistress Web had found somewhere soft to land - on me! By the time I'd gotten free and made sure my wife was ok I'd missed most of what was said. 'Thank you, young man for breaking my fall. Now if you would be so kind as to help me up, I would be grateful.'

By the time I'd gotten Mistress Web on her feet, the discussion on what to do next was in full swing. The wizards argued they'd have to report back to the council of wizards before continuing, the witches on the other hand wanted to start immediately and were getting angry with the others. 'We can't just go running around without a plan,' said Gilbert. 'We must consult the council and come up with a course of action before we do anything.'

Now, witches are solitary people, they usually go about things by themselves and only ask for help if it's too much for them to deal with on their own.

In the end it was decided that the wizards would report back to their council and the witches would try and find out why the others had not answered the call for help.

When Gilbert and the others were gone, the ladies and I went back to Donna's cottage. After making us all a cup of tea, Betty and Donna drew up our plan of action. In the morning I was to take Mistress Web home. On the way we would be stopping at the homes of two witches who could not be contacted. Sadie and Betty were going in the other direction to see who they could find.

As we walked home Sadie and I talked over what we'd seen that night. 'You must be used to all this, you being a witch,' I said. 'No,' she said, 'as I told you I'm only an apprentice. I've only been learning about making potions and recognising the herbs and roots that go into them, Betty hasn't let me do any spells yet, so no, to tell you the truth it nearly scared the life out of me.'

'Me too,' I told her. 'But you don't have to do this if it frightens you. I'll help them, you keep out of it, if anything happened to you, I'd never forgive myself.' 'I'm a witch, alright nearly a witch, and I'm not going to stand by while Donna and the others are in trouble.'

'I understand Sadie, but if it gets too dangerous one of us will have to drop out and take care of the boys.'

'Ok darling we'll worry about that when it happens. Now let's go home and get some sleep, we've got a lot on tomorrow and I've a got a feeling we'll need to be wide awake.'

Next morning, I swapped vehicles with Betty. We both agreed that it would be easier to get Mistress Web into Betty's Range Rover than my Ford Focus. Even with the larger car, it was a still a struggle to squeeze the old witch into the 4x4, I'm not going to tell you where I had to push to get her in, but it felt like a five-foot marshmallow. With her finally ensconced in the car we set off.

We arrived at the house of the first witch only to find it deserted. It looked as if she had left in an almighty hurry. On the kitchen table a half-eaten meal still lay there, and in the bedroom, it looked like someone had packed very quickly.

'Why would she leave without telling me?' said Mistress Web. 'We've been friends for years. Something must have frightened her very badly for her to have just left without talking to me first. I think we'd better get to the next one quick; I have a bad feeling about this.'

The next witch lived down a lane in a cottage that looked even older than Donna's. 'Be careful,' Mistress Web told me, as I got out of the car. 'I don't like it. Evil has touched this place. Help me out, I'm coming with you.'

As we entered the cottage, even I could feel something was not right. It felt at least ten degrees colder than outside, as I followed the old witch through the cottage, I noticed everything was either smashed or scattered about.

'Keep close to me, son, and don't wander off,' she told me. 'Some very powerful magic has been used in here, so stay close until I tell you it's safe.'

We searched every room and it was the same, furniture smashed, contents thrown about. As we got nearer to the kitchen it seemed to me to be getting even colder. 'Do you feel it David?' she asked me. 'Yes, it feels as if the temperature has dropped even more and the air seems charged with electricity.' Mistress Web contradicted me, 'It's not electricity, it's residue left over from very powerful dark magic.' As we entered the kitchen it became clear that this place was ground zero, it was a scene of total devastation, and there was not one stick of furniture, not one piece of crockery, not even a pane of glass left whole.

'It looks like a bomb has gone off in here. What caused all this?' I asked Mistress Web.

'Only a curse produced by the darkest of all witches or wizards could have caused this much damage. We must keep on searching, we must find out what happened to the witch who lived here.'

We searched the whole house from top to bottom and found nothing; every room had been ransacked. Whoever it was, they were obviously looking for something.

Let's get out of here David, we'd, best look outside and then you'd better take me back to Donna's. I think it best that we all stick together till we find out what's going on.'

'Ok,' I said, 'I'll give Betty a ring on my mobile and let her know what's happening.'

After talking to Betty, I went out into the garden. 'I hope Betty and Sadie are having better luck than we are,' the old witch said.

'I'm afraid not, all the witches they've visited were conspicuous by their absence. Some cottages look as though the witch had just left, but others have been ransacked.' 'It seems obvious to me that somebody's looking for something, but what?'

'I'm of the same opinion as you, David. They, whoever they are, must be desperate to find whatever it is they're looking for.'

Mistress Web suddenly froze, 'WHAT'S THAT!' she said pointing at the woodshed. I looked where she was pointing and could just make out a shoe.

'Stay behind me,' the old witch said. Normally I wouldn't let an old woman go into danger first, but she was the one with the wand and I was completely out of my depth.

As we rounded the end of the shed, I could see the body of the old witch who had lived in the cottage. I had seen a dead body before, but never one with such a look of absolute terror. 'Look at her face,' I said, 'she looks as if she was frightened to death.' 'She was killed by a death curse,' Mistress Web told me. 'You must be mad to use a death curse. It's said that every time you use one a little bit of your soul dies, until finally you're completely evil.'

'What are we going to do about the body?' I asked. 'Do we call the police? 'No, we'll take care of May, that's her name by the way. 'May Nightflower,' if you'd carry her body into the house, I'll give her the witches' last rites.'

It was easy carrying the body inside, she weighed hardly anything. Mistress Web made up her bed and I laid her on it, with her wand and broomstick beside her, then the old witch recited a prayer over the body in a strange tongue and as we left the cottage she turned, took out her wand, 'PHYRO,' she shouted. With that a blue flame shot out of the end of her wand and the cottage burst into flames.

'I think we'd better get out of here before someone sees the fire,' I said. We left and headed back to Donna's wood.

On arrival we found that the others hadn't had any more luck than we'd had. When we told them about May and how we'd found her, the room went quiet, and nobody spoke for what seemed ages.

THE SURVIVOR

After discussing the situation for an hour or more we found ourselves divided. Betty, Sadie and I wanted to find out what happened to the witches who'd left in such a hurry, and who'd killed poor May, while Donna and Mistress Web wanted to find the talisman. 'I know I'm new to all this,' I butted in, 'but I think that the two things are connected.'

'What makes you say that?' enquired Donna. 'I don't know, but let me ask you this. Has anything like this happened here before?' 'No, not in my life time,' replied Betty. 'Then don't you think it's a bit of a coincidence that witches start disappearing at the same time as the talisman is stolen?' 'You could be right,' agreed Donna. 'I suggest Mistress Web and I will concentrate on the talisman, while you three find out what's happening to the other witches.' Betty then split us up, so armed with a list of names and addresses we set off in opposite directions. We had already covered most of Norfolk, so Betty would cover Suffolk, Sadie Cambridgeshire, and I was given Lincolnshire. I kissed Sadie goodbye, told her to be careful and made her promise to ring me at the first sign of trouble.

As I set off for Lincolnshire, I couldn't help but wonder what I'd find when I got there. After an hour driving, I arrived at the first address on the list, but unlike the cottages Mistress Web and I had visited, this one was inhabited. The old lady who answered the door was a stereotype witch, tall, very thin, dressed all in black with a long nose that finished at a point, all that was missing was the wart with a hair poking out.

'YES, what do you want?' she asked me. 'I've been sent by Betty, the Croxton witch, I told her. We've had a bit of trouble, several witches have disappeared, and one has been murdered.'

'Murdered! Who?' she gasped. 'A witch called May Nightflower,' I replied. 'May Nightflower? We were both apprenticed to a witch over near East Dereham when we were young, but I haven't spoken to her in years. Who'd want to kill an old witch, it doesn't make sense, she wouldn't hurt a fly, why was she killed?' she asked.

'Mistress Web told me it was a death curse,' I replied. 'Nobody's used a death curse in at least a hundred years, why would anyone use one now?' she asked me.

'Betty and Donna seem to think that it may have something to do with the talisman,' I told her.

'The talisman? But the spell isn't supposed to finish for another thirty-seven years,' she said.

'The spell wasn't strong enough to last the full term.' I explained everything that had happened since that day I was spreading fertiliser in the forty acres. After I'd finished, she told me that she had felt that something was wrong, but hadn't been able to get in touch with any other witch, so she couldn't help me. I gave her my mobile number in case she heard from anyone.

I then drove to the next address on my list. Halfway there I received a call from Betty enquiring if I'd had any luck. I told her that I had found one witch, but she didn't know anything.

Betty told me that she'd hadn't had any luck either.

But Sadie on the other hand had found a witch called Anne, who had survived an attack by a dark witch who said she was looking for the talisman.

Anne said as far as she knew the talisman was safely hidden and protected by a spell that wouldn't finish for another thirty odd years. With that the black witch flew into a rage, saying that she was lying and threatened to kill her if she didn't tell her where it was. Anne suddenly whipped out her wand and stunned the black witch, who fell to the ground unconscious, giving Anne enough time to escape the house and hide in the wood at the bottom of her garden. From there she could see the dark witch ransacking her home. After she'd been through the whole house, she started to search outside, finally giving up and leaving about an hour before Sadie turned up.

Sadie was now taking Anne back to the wood. Betty thought she would be safer with Donna and Mistress Web.

But I was to carry on working through my list. After another two hours searching, I had not found any witches, so I headed off home, all the time wondering if my wife was safe.

On arrival back at the wood I found the cottage full now that Donna had taken in Mistress Webb and Anne, what with Betty, Sadie and I, it was getting rather crowded.

After hearing Anne's description of the black witch, it soon became clear that Donna recognised her as her sister, Bella. 'I'm absolutely certain it's her, but why is she looking for the talisman? She was the one who took it in the first place,' Donna wondered.

'I think I can help you with that,' Anne offered. 'When she was questioning me, she kept asking me if I'd been the one who stole it from her. She worked herself up into a rage, shouting that she would kill the one who'd stolen it and any witch that had helped her. It was then that I stunned her and made my escape.'

This started a discussion about who'd got the talisman and why they'd taken it. We were so engrossed in discussing the situation that we failed to notice Gilbert and Tom standing in the doorway. 'May we come in ladies?' Gilbert asked. 'There seem to be a few more of you since we were last here.' Then he turned to me, 'Hello David, how do you get anything done with all these lovely ladies present?' (Seeing as my wife was the only woman there under seventy, quite easily) 'You always were quite the Romeo,' Donna told him, 'but we've got no time for that now. What has the council decided?' Gilbert smiled, 'There's always time for romance.' But I think the look on Donna's face told him different.

After the introductions were made, he went on to tell us that the wizard council had sifted through all the information they had and concluded that Bella had taken the talisman with her when she left the wood, and since then someone else had taken it from her, but who and why was still a mystery. 'Is that all?' Donna asked. 'We've found That Out!' 'Yes,' said Betty, 'and we didn't need to go into council either.' 'And did you also find out that the talisman had been used?' asked Gilbert. 'No,' Betty admitted. 'Who used it? 'You don't mean that there's something that you witches don't know about?' Gilbert smiled and went on. 'We don't know who, but we do know it was a white witch and that she harnessed only a small part of its power, so she must be very powerful and practised. The most powerful witch that I've ever come across was Mistress Web's sister, Dorothy.' Every person in the room turned to Mistress Web. 'I haven't spoken to or seen my sister in ten years,' she said. 'We fell out when she wanted to go and study advanced witchcraft in Tibet of all places. I don't think she's even in the country, but, it sounds like the kind of thing she would do. When we were apprentice witches she wanted to learn everything, not content with just being a witch. She wanted to be the best and most powerful witch there ever was, always a loner, would never join a coven. Always one more spell, one more potion, the more she learned the more she wanted to learn, but if she is back and if it is her, then she must be a very powerful witch to be able to use only a small part of the talisman's magic.'

'It doesn't matter if it is your sister or not, we have to find this witch and fast,' Gilbert told us, 'it doesn't matter how good she is, there's a lot of dark witches and wizards looking for her and she's going to need our help before long, so if you've any idea where she'd hide, please tell us Mistress Web, because we have to find her before Bella and her coven do, because no matter how powerful she is she can't take on a black coven of witches and wizards on her own.'

Mistress Web closed her eyes and was silent for what felt an hour, but could only have been a couple of minutes, at last she opened them. 'She's at grannys, I can feel her. When we were kids, we developed this telepathy so we'd know if the other was in trouble and I can feel her. She's trying to block out anybody who's looking for her, but she's still my sister so I can feel her presence where others can't.'

'Whose granny?' I asked. 'Where does she live and how do we get there?' 'Well granny was the first witch my sister was apprenticed to. As to where she lives, she has a cottage on Bodmin moor in Cornwall, and as to how we're going to get there - by broomstick, how else?'

'By broomstick? You're not going to get me on one of those,' I shouted. 'It's alright David, only witches and wizards can fly a broomstick,' Donna told me, much to my relief. 'Betty, Anne, Gilbert and myself will fly down to Cornwall. Mistress Web is too old to fly, Sadie and Tom are only apprentices and haven't learned to fly yet, so you can drive them all down in my Range Rover and we'll all meet up when you get there.'

CORNWALL

Next morning after Sadie had talked her mother into coming over to look after the boys for a couple of days and with Mistress Web finally wedged in the back of the Range Rover the four of us set off for Cornwall. It had been decided that we the non-fliers would leave during the day and the rest would follow us that night. 'That is the only drawback with a broomstick, you can fly just during the night,' Betty told me. (The only drawback? I can think of at least a couple more).

I had Tom in the front with me, he seemed a nice lad, a bit nervous though. We got talking and it turned out that he was only nervous around women (and him not married yet). Having been brought up by Gilbert he hadn't had much contact with the opposite sex and told me he didn't understand them. I told him not to worry I'd been married for ten years and I still didn't understand them myself. Suddenly remembering that my wife was in the back, I looked in the rear view mirror and saw that she'd heard all that I'd said and was looking daggers at me, (whoops!). Quickly changing the subject I asked him how he'd come to be with Gilbert. He replied that Gilbert had taken him in when he was six, he could only vaguely remember his parents. He'd been a bit of a loner, and not made friends easily. He could recall being picked on at school by this one boy who made his life miserable with his constant bullying. One day while receiving a particularly nasty beating something happened. The other kids told him later that his eyes clouded over and he'd shouted something in what sounded like a foreign language and the boy flew across the playground and landed unconscious against the fence. There was an almighty row and he'd been expelled. Even though he'd not started it, the boy's injuries were too severe for him to remain at school.

That's when Gilbert turned up, he said that he was a teacher of children with special needs. He told Tom's parents that he ran a boarding school where Tom would receive an education, and the help he needed to control his temper. 'I think by that time they'd had enough of me not fitting in with the other kids, being a loner and my mood swings, which Gilbert told me was my frustration at not knowing what was going on and why I was feeling all these strange sensations. You see I'm unusual in so much as I wasn't born to a witch or wizard. Usually one or both your parents should have magical tendencies, that way there's always someone to guide you, but I had no one and Gilbert could feel that so he took me in and is training me to be a wizard.'

'What about your parents?' I asked. 'Do you ever see them?' 'Yes, occasionally I go back for a holiday when Gilbert's on council business, but we have nothing in common and I think they're glad when I leave.'

I must admit I felt sorry for Tom. Having two kids of my own I couldn't imagine not wanting to see them or sending them to a boarding school. 'Don't worry about me I'm very happy staying at Gilbert's. He's teaching me how to control my gifts and one day he tells me I'm going to be a great wizard.' And for the first time since I met Tom he smiled.

After eight hours of driving, we arrived at Bodmin Cornwall, just as it was getting dark. We would have arrived earlier only we had to make regular toilet breaks for Mistress Web and food for Tom. I've never known a lad to eat so much, he's nearly six-foot tall, thin as a rake, but eats more than enough for two grown men.

It was agreed that upon arriving in Cornwall we'd wait at a prearranged location for the others to arrive, but Mistress Web couldn't wait. 'Now we're here I can feel my sister's presence even stronger. We must find her before Bella and her cronies do. She can't keep herself hidden much longer without our help. We can't wait another hour or two for the others to get here, she needs our help now. I looked from Sadie to Tom, they both nodded their agreement. 'Ok then, where does she live?' I asked. She gave me a piece of paper with an address written on it, saying that this was her last home before she went to Tibet.

Thereafter, I put the address into the Sat Nav and off we went.

On arrival all we found was a fenced off garden, but no house. 'Well that proves she's here, there's a spell concealing the house and it's a very good one too,' Mistress Web told us. Sadie, Tom and myself stood looking at the garden. 'Can she see us?' Sadie asked. 'She should be able to see out, but if she doesn't recognise me she'll not let us in.'

Just as Mistress Web finished speaking, Tom shouted, 'Look! There is a door.' It was then that we noticed that a door had appeared out of nowhere and a witch stood looking out of it with a wand in her hand. 'Sissy,' the old lady called, 'is that you, Sissy?' As you may have realised it was Mistress Web's Christian name.

When a witch reaches a certain age she is called Mistress as a mark of respect. 'Yes, it's me Dorothy. I've come to help and I've brought some friends. Can we come in and talk?'

The old lady in the doorway lowered her wand and waved us in.

It seemed strange walking through a door that wasn't attached to anything, but once inside it was just an ordinary home. After the introductions had been made and a cup of tea brewed, I explained to Dorothy that some more help was on its way by broomstick and would be arriving after dark. 'I would appreciate the help,' she said 'it's getting harder keeping them at bay. I've felt them probing for me, they know I'm hidden from them and it's only a matter of time before they find me. But now you're all here there's a chance we can stop her.'

'There's four people on brooms just landed on the lawn,' Tom who'd been keeping watch, informed us. 'It's Gilbert and the others.' It's ok, Dorothy, you can let them in,' Sissy told her sister.

The old witch waved her wand and the door suddenly opened, and through it we could see a rather bewildered quartet standing on the lawn. As they got to the door Dorothy turned to her sister and asked, 'Are there anymore witches coming?' 'No that's the lot. 'Why?' Sissy enquired. 'It's just that there's another broomstick heading this way, and if it's not one of your friends, whoever's on it must have followed them here.' 'You four,' said Dorothy, pointing at Gilbert, Betty, Anne and Donna, 'hide in the garden, and when they land I'll try and stun them before they see me, but if I miss, one of you will have to stun them. Whatever happens they must not get away to report our position. If they do there'll be more witches than you can wave a wand at here in no time.' With the four hidden in the garden, they didn't have to wait long before a broomstick flew in over the trees and landed.

I could see the witch quite clearly and she had a completely different aura about her, whereas the ones I was with, felt like, kind but slightly dotty grannies, (except my wife that is). This new arrival made me shiver just to look at her. Before she could dismount, a jet of blue light shot out of the end of Dorothy's wand and just before it hit, the witch quickly ducked out of its way, but she was not quick enough to dodge the other four. One of their spells hit her in the face and she fell to the ground unconscious.

'What are we going to do with her?' Sissy asked the question that was on all our lips. 'I have a memory charm,' offered Gilbert. 'It'll only last twenty-four hours, but it will give us time to find somewhere else to hide.' Dorothy nodded, and Gilbert pointed his wand at the dark witch, a light came out of the end and bathed the witch in a red glow. After a while the light faded, and Gilbert returned his wand to his cloak.

Then we all went inside, and Dorothy put the spell back on the door, and we watched as the dark witch come round, shook her head, looked around for a while and completely befuddled, got back on to her broom and flew off.

'Before we do anything else we'd like to know what's going on,' Betty informed Dorothy. 'We know that Donna's sister, Bella, took the talisman from the wood in nineteen forty-five, and that you've got it now. What we'd also like to know is what's happened to it in between.'

Dorothy then went on to explain, 'I first learned that the talisman had left the wood on my return from Tibet last year. I'd been studying magic and learning wisdom with the yeti, a very old and mystical race. (Two days ago I didn't believe in witches and wizards and here I found out that the yeti also existed. This wouldn't be the last time that I wished I was back in my tractor, oblivious to all this). 'I hadn't been back long before I started to feel something was wrong. I went to visit some witches that I'd been friends with before I'd gone away. I found most of their homes empty and the witches I did meet were terrified of something and wouldn't speak to me.

'Finally, I came to May Nightflower's cottage and found her dead.' Upon hearing this we told Dorothy that we'd had the same experience and Anne told of her narrow escape.

Dorothy then went on to tell us that she'd continued searching until she at last came to a secluded cottage where she knew a witch lived who was said to have second-sight and was also the biggest gossip in the whole of Norfolk, if not the country.

If she didn't know what was going on nobody would. The door was opened by a very frightened witch, who'd only opened it because she recognised Dorothy.

'What's going on Mistress?' she asked. Mistress Green was short and round, but instead of her usual happy smile there was a look of total fear on her face.

'What's got you so frightened?' Dorothy enquired, following that Mistress Green recounted how for a long time there had been rumours about the talisman, rumours that it had left the wood, and how Bella was trying to gain control of its power, to make herself the most powerful witch ever.

'A witch in Fakenham tried to get us to join together and fight Bella,' Mistress Green continued, 'to try and retrieve the talisman, but I'm afraid she didn't find many to join her, but last year I heard that someone had indeed managed to obtain the talisman and was being hunted by Bella and her coven.' 'Yes I'd heard that also,' Dorothy told us. 'That is when I decided to find this person and help them guard the talisman from the dark coven.'

Dorothy went on to explain how she tracked down a witch called Flora who had the talisman in her possession. She was hiding in a large Georgian house just off Newmarket Road in Norwich, an unusual place for a witch to live because they are mainly country folk.

But apparently her family were very big in the world of mustard and the house belonged to an uncle of hers.

It took Dorothy a while to gain Flora's trust, but finally she realised that Dorothy was on her side and only wanted to help. She then recounted how she'd pretended to be a dark witch to join Bella's coven and find out where the talisman was hidden. Only to find that it had already been stolen from Bella. To prove to the coven that she was indeed a dark witch, Bella wanted her to use a torture curse on a witch they believed knew the whereabouts of the talisman. Flora knew she could never use a torture curse on an animal let alone a fellow human being, so she was beginning to panic. If she didn't perform the curse they'd know that she wasn't a dark witch and torture her and if she did, she'd never be able to forgive herself.

She got out her wand as if to perform the curse and looked around at the faces of the coven. She knew that she could expect no mercy from them and try as she might, she couldn't think of any way out of this.

But as luck would have it, the door flew open. 'We've found it,' shouted a sinister looking wizard, 'a witch near Swaffham has it. I couldn't obtain it on my own, she's too powerful for just one of us, it will take the whole coven to retrieve it.'

'Ok, throw her in the cellar,' ordered Bella, pointing to the witch who'd been lying in a heap on the floor since Flora had arrived. 'You can torture her when we get back. She may still know something, and until you do, we can't trust you,' she told Flora.

THE BATTLE

As she flew on her broomstick along with the coven, Flora's mind was working overtime. If Bella got the talisman back, how was she going to retrieve it, and how was she going to rescue the witch in the cellar? Also, how was she going to do all this without getting killed?

As she was thinking, she looked around at the others, they looked a motley crew. The coven consisted of seven witches and five wizards, and they all had the look of pure evil about them. She knew that there was not one of them who would think twice about killing her if they thought she wasn't on their side.

Bella's broomstick suddenly swooped down toward a cottage below them. Flora and all the others followed suit. They landed encircling the cottage so as no one inside could escape.

Bella shouted, 'I know you're in there and I know you've got the talisman. If you bring it out, we'll take it and be on our way, but if you put up a fight and we have to come and get it, I'll kill you in a very unpleasant way. What's your answer?'

It didn't take the witch inside the house long to make up her mind, because Bella had only just finished her threat when a bolt of lightning hit the witch who had the bad luck to be standing next to Bella. She flew through the air and landed in a heap twenty feet from where she'd been standing. Thereafter, the air erupted with a multitude of spells directed at the cottage. Flora could see that they were not having any affect; whoever was inside was a powerful witch and had placed a shield charm over her home, and whatever spells the coven fired at the cottage, none of them had any effect.

'Stop!' screamed Bella. 'She's using a shield charm, we'll never get in that way. We have to concentrate our efforts, otherwise we'll never get the bitch out. Everybody form a line either side of me and when I give the word, we all cast a spell at the door and try and blow a hole in her shield.' Flora tried her hardest to think of a spell that would reduce the strength of a spell cast by twelve wands. She thought that if she could reduce the power of the combined spell it would not be strong enough to break through the charm, but before she could come up with anything Bella pointed her wand at the cottage and screamed, 'Now!' And a stream of light shot out of the end and hit the door. Subsequently, the others followed suit one by one. The combined efforts of all the coven was having an effect on the shield charm. The doorway was beginning to glow red as the combined spells built up. 'Why aren't you helping? I thought you were on our side,' said Bella giving Flora an evil look. 'I am,' replied Flora, pointing her wand at the door and making a stream of light shoot out of the end, the difference being that Flora's was only light and not capable of inflicting any damage. But the coven didn't need Flora's help, because as she looked the shield started to vibrate, and suddenly it exploded with a force that knocked her off her feet.

'Quick,' ordered Bella, 'in the house before she can re-establish the shield. 'Don't kill her, bring her to me. I'm going to make an example of her so that no one will ever challenge me again.'

Flora had to get inside as quickly as possible to help the witch guarding the talisman. The coven went rampaging through the cottage destroying everything in their search for the talisman and its keeper.

As Flora entered the kitchen, she felt someone grab the hem of her cloak. Looking down she saw a hand sticking out from a trapdoor that must have led to a cellar. Lifting the trapdoor she saw a witch look up at her, 'Quick, in here, I need your help.' Flora climbed down into the cellar, closing the door behind her.

'How do you know I'm not one of them?' Flora asked the witch. 'Oh, I can tell you're not with the dark coven, you're here to help me. I could feel you as you flew here and knew instantly that you were here to help.

Now we haven't got long, they'll find me soon and when they do they'll kill me and take the talisman, but, it doesn't matter about me as long as the talisman's safe. What's your name?' the witch asked. 'Flora, my name's Flora.' 'Nice to meet you, Flora. My name's Doris and I only wish we'd met under better circumstances. Now this is what we'll do. I'll stay here and cause a diversion, while you escape with the talisman.' 'I can't leave you here alone with all them after you. I'll stay and help.' 'No, Flora, we couldn't hope to defeat the coven just the two of us. They are too strong, they'd kill us both and take the talisman. No you must go, and go now. There's a hidden tunnel behind the cabinet against the far wall. Once in the tunnel follow it to the end and you'll come out behind the big oak tree on the edge of the garden. From there you should be able to get to your broom unnoticed and make your escape. Whatever you hear or see don't stop. The most important thing is to get the talisman as far away from Bella and her cronies as possible.'

By now they could hear that someone was searching in the kitchen, it would only be minutes before they found the trapdoor.

Doris quickly pulled aside the cabinet and pushed Flora inside, before sealing the entrance up. Doris gave Flora a small box and told her that on no account should she open it, but, if possible, try and return it to the wood where it would be safe with Donna.

Once inside the tunnel Flora stood still while her eyes got accustomed to the dark, after a couple of minutes she could just make out a faint light in the distance and headed toward it. Just as Doris had said, she came out behind the old oak, found a broomstick that had been discarded on their arrival, but just as she was about to fly off, she heard a terrible scream emanating from the cottage, the coven had found Doris.

'Why didn't you fly straight to the wood and return the talisman?' Dorothy asked Flora. 'I tried but the coven wasn't far behind me and kept blocking my every turn, so I came here to hide while I considered my next move, and that's when you turned up,' Flora explained.

Dorothy looked pensive for a while and then asked, 'Can I see the talisman?'

'You're not going to steal it, are you?' asked a worried looking Flora.

'You needn't worry, Flora, I'm on your side. I'd just like to see what all the fuss is about.'

Flora left the room immediately and after a while she returned with a small box and gave it to Dorothy, 'Don't open the talisman,' she warned, 'it will destroy all magic.'

It looked a pretty ordinary box, just plain wood, no carving or writing on it, but it felt warm as if it was alive and Dorothy also felt a power emanating from within. Very carefully opening the lid, she saw the talisman sitting on a little red velvet cushion, it was round, made of silver with a red stone set in the middle and around the edge were engraved ancient runes. It was attached by a ring to a silver chain that also had runes engraved all over it, opposite the chain there was a catch that opened the talisman. As Dorothy stared at it she was overcome with the desire to open it, but before she could do so Flora shut the lid. 'It gets to you, doesn't it? You can feel it wants you to open it.'

Dorothy blinked as if coming out of a trance, 'Yes, I could feel myself reaching for the clasp.'

Dorothy knew then that on no account would she ever let Bella take it, even if it meant her life.

A little after midnight, it was dark enough for both witches to climb on to their broomsticks and head off in the direction of the wood. After a long talk they both agreed that it was the best course of action, the quicker it was returned to Donna the safer it would be.

Flora insisted on Dorothy carrying the talisman as she was by far the more powerful of the two. Also the coven would be on the lookout for Flora and would attack her on sight giving Dorothy a chance to sneak past unnoticed.

Dorothy argued that it would be putting Flora in too much danger, but Flora was adamant, she pointed out that the only thing that mattered was the safe return of the talisman. As they flew nearer to the wood Dorothy could feel the presence of evil. She had learned in Tibet that if she concentrated, she could sense other witches, and there were at that moment twelve near to Flora and her.

'Flora,' she called 'they're not far away, so be careful.' The words were hardly out of her mouth, when four witches suddenly appeared in front of Flora.

Dorothy swerved to the right as Flora soared off to the left taking the four with her. They had agreed that if Flora could lead the coven off, Dorothy would take the opportunity to return the talisman.

It had sounded a good idea at the time, but now it came down to it, Dorothy just couldn't leave Flora to the mercy of the coven.

As she turned her broomstick around to go to help, she saw Bella fly out of the cloud and come up behind Flora. She pointed her wand and shouted a curse, red sparks flew out of the end, and blasted Flora off her broomstick, and Dorothy knew then that Flora would be dead before she hit the ground.

'Look! There's another one,' shouted a witch pointing at Dorothy, 'maybe she's got it.'

Whereupon two of the four headed straight for her, while the others tried to outflank her. She had to escape quickly because once they surrounded her, she'd stand no chance, it was then that she remembered a spell that the yeti who'd been her defensive spells teacher had taught her.

He was six hundred and sixty-seven years old; his white fur was starting to turn grey, but he had the stamina of a yeti half his age, and a love of practical jokes. He would take Dorothy to some of the sacred valleys high in the Himalayas. There he taught her how to blend into her surroundings so no enemy could find her. He would tell her with a cheeky grin that when he had finished teaching her, she would be able to conceal herself as good as him, although he didn't need magic as the Himalayas were mostly covered in snow and he was covered in white fur. Dorothy not being covered in fur had to work hard to master the spells of concealment. At this particular moment she was glad she'd paid attention. Her best bet was to get to the trees and use the most powerful concealment spell she knew. Dorothy flew into a small wood, just ahead of the coven, dismounted and ran into where the trees were the thickest.

She could hear the coven landing all around and starting to search for her, as Dorothy recited the words of the spell, the sound of her pursuers getting louder the nearer they got. 'We have the wood surrounded, you can't escape. Save yourself a lot of pain. Give me the talisman and we won't hurt you.'

Dorothy knew Bella was lying, the moment she had the talisman in her hand, she'd kill her, 'Do you think a simple concealment charm will stop me finding you? If I'm not mistaken you learned that spell from that pompous old yeti. I had to endure two years with those smelly creatures, while on my quest to become the most powerful witch ever. I hate them, they said they couldn't teach me any of the curses I wanted to learn because they felt that I would use them on people. I asked them what the point was of learning them if I wasn't going to use them. Do you know what those stupid yetis told me? They said that the reason for learning them was so you would never want to use them, after you realised what they could do. I told them I would use them on anyone who got in my way and not think anything of it. Stupid creatures!' shouted Bella all the time working herself up into a rage.

Dorothy knew the yeti wasn't stupid, he must have realised that she was a dark witch and asked her to leave. All the time Bella had been ranting, Dorothy was concentrating on the charm, trying to make it so strong that Bella couldn't find her. As she concentrated she could feel warmth emanating from the pocket of her coat, she knew it was the talisman, she put her hand into her pocket and opened the box, she had no intention of opening the talisman, but she held it more for comfort than anything, as soon as she touched the talisman she could feel the power of it flowing through her. Rather than destroying her magic it seemed to be strengthening the charm, so much so that Bella stormed past her swearing and cursing, without finding her. By now she had worked herself up into a terrible rage, storming about throwing spells in every direction trying to find Dorothy, one hit a tree nearby, which exploded into kindling, spraying splinters everywhere.

The coven who were all frightened that a spell would hit them, were all now standing behind Bella. One brave wizard tapped her on the shoulder, 'She's not here' he said 'she must have escaped.' Bella spun around with a look of madness on her face and blasted the wizard with a curse that killed him instantly

'I give the orders around here, you do what I say, and I say, she's still hiding, and you'll keep looking for her till I say otherwise.'

Dorothy wondered if maybe she could reach her broomstick before she was found and fly away without Bella or the coven seeing her, but she knew a concealment charm only worked if you didn't move, however felt she could do anything while she had the talisman in her hand.

So, with this thought in mind, she started to walk towards her broom, expecting at any moment to be discovered and killed, but nothing happened. She could hear the coven crashing about in their search for her, when she found her broom, mounted it and flew off without incident.

THE TALISMAN'S RETURN

The room erupted as Dorothy finished her story, everybody had questions, ranging from, had she used the power of the talisman again, had she been followed, did Bella know where she was now, but it was Donna who'd asked the one question we all wanted an answer to, and seeing as her voice was the loudest, she got answered first.

'The reason I came here instead of going to the wood was that, one, I thought you were alone and didn't want to bring the coven down on you. Two, I wanted to have time to think about what had happened, and three, why had the talisman let me use some of its power to strengthen my spell, instead of destroying my magic as it was created to do.'

Dorothy went on to explain that she hadn't seen any sign of the coven since her arrival, and yes in answer to another question, she had used the talisman to conceal the cottage they were now in. She went on to tell them that she'd been very careful in her dealings with it, in case the last time was just a fluke.

'You haven't opened it have you?' asked Donna. 'Definitely, not,' Dorothy replied, 'so far all I've done is hold it, but just before you arrived, I was thinking about opening the talisman.' 'Why would you do such a thing?' Betty demanded. 'Well I was feeling a bit threatened and as far as I knew it was just me against the coven, so I wondered if maybe I could cast an even more powerful charm with the talisman open. The one I used while hiding from Bella felt stronger than any I had cast previously, so I thought that if I opened it and held it I'd be invincible,' Dorothy told us. 'It's a good thing you didn't, there's no telling what might have happened,' Gilbert said, shaking his head. 'We don't yet know why it's emitting this power. It was created to destroy dark magic, not to make white magic stronger, so until we find out what's going on that thing stays in its box.' After another hour's discussion it was decided that we had to get the talisman and all of us safely back to Norfolk. Once back in the wood it could be protected.

The memory spell Gilbert had cast on the dark witch would wear off in twenty-four hours and this place would be crawling with Bella and her coven.

I would take the Range Rover and my passengers back at first light after I'd gotten some sleep, which was the easy part of the plan. They were still arguing the rest when I nodded off.

When my wife Sadie woke me at first light there were just the four of us that came by car left. She informed me that the others had taken off in the night and were heading back to Norfolk. With any luck they're already back in the wood. 'What plan did they finally come up with?' I asked.

Tom told me that they'd decided that Dorothy would keep the talisman and fly in the lead, and the others would follow close behind. Dorothy had flown to Cornwall with a concealment charm hiding her so she was going to try the same thing. Only this time she would try and conceal not only herself but the others as well.

It was a very quiet start to the journey back home, all of us hoping that Dorothy and the others had arrived home safely. After we'd been on the road an hour or so Betty called us on her mobile to say that they'd all arrived back in the wood without incident. Dorothy's concealment charm had worked beautifully. It was so good that they had flown within fifty feet of a dark witch and not been detected.

Our trip back was also uneventful, apart from the usual stops for the toilet for Mistress Web and food for Tom. Once back in Norfolk we headed straight for the wood after first dropping Sadie off to check on our boys and get some sleep; it had been a long two days, and we were all feeling the strain.

As we drew nearer the wood Tom said he thought he could see someone hiding in the bushes and as we got closer a man stood up. 'It's alright, I said, 'it's only a twitcher. We get a lot of them this time of year.' 'What's a twitcher?' asked Tom. 'You must have led a sheltered life,' I told him 'they're fanatic birdwatchers. When a bird not native to Great Britain is spotted, twitchers from all over the country suddenly start to appear. The rarer the bird the more twitchers you get.' Only, I had a feeling there was something strange about this one, but nothing I could put my finger on. By the look on Tom's face, though, he had the same feeling. 'Morning,' I called as we got nearer, 'doing a spot of bird watching?' 'Yes, I'm looking for a greater crested thrush. You haven't seen one, have you?' 'No, what does it look like?' I asked. He started rummaging about in his coat pocket. 'I've got a picture of one somewhere.' But before he had a chance to get it out, Mistress Web waved her wand out of the window and stunned him. 'David, put him in the back and we'll take him with us, we can question him once we're in the wood.' Tom and I complied with Mistress Web's wishes and placed the twitcher in the back of the car. As we were lifting him a wand fell out of his coat. 'I thought there was something wrong about him when I first saw him,' I told Tom. 'Yeah, me too,' he replied.

As we drove through the gap in the hedge that led to Donna's cottage, the air seemed to shimmer. Donna informed us later that Dorothy had placed a selective concealment charm on the wood. It would only allow good magic through. That way there was no need to keep lowering and raising it when we left or returned. 'If it only allows good magic in or out, how come we just brought a dark wizard in with us?' I asked.

The wizard sat tied to a chair now fully conscious with a look of pure hatred on his face. Dorothy told me that the reason we'd been able to bring him through the charm was due to the fact he was unconscious at the time. Gilbert had been questioning him for at least an hour, and it was obvious we'd get nothing out of him. 'What are we going to do with him?' Donna asked Gilbert. 'We can't keep him tied up here indefinitely, we can't kill him and we can't let him go.' 'Why can't we kill him? The coven would have killed me and not thought twice about it. It's no more than he deserves,' cried Anne.

'We know what you've been through, but that would make us as bad as those we're fighting against,' said Donna, laying a soothing hand on Anne's shoulder. 'Put him in the cellar, he'll not escape once I cast a spell on the door,' Dorothy boasted.

We'd noticed that she'd changed since we first met, she now had this look of a drug addict, the more she used the talisman, the more she wanted to. Betty nodded to Tom and me, to do as Dorothy said, so untying him and grabbing an arm each we dragged the wizard down to the cellar where Dorothy locked him in with a spell. 'You'll not be getting out of there in a hurry,' she shouted at the wizard.

As Dorothy, Tom and I returned from the cellar, Donna suddenly stunned Dorothy. 'What did you go and do that for?' shouted Tom and I as we dived for cover, both wondering if we were next. 'It's alright boys,' said Donna trying to calm us. 'I had to stun her, it was the only way we could get the talisman away from her. I knew she wouldn't give it up willingly. I don't know if you lads have noticed but Dorothy has become addicted to the power of the talisman, the more she uses it the more she wants to. We had to get it away from her before it took her over.'

'Well, it seems to me that whoever uses the talisman is going to become addicted.' 'Yes, David, I agree, and that's why you must take it,' Donna informed me. 'Me! Why me! I'm not a wizard, I wouldn't know what to do with it.' Donna went on to tell me that it was for that reason that I was the ideal person to keep the talisman, even if I got the urge to use it, I wouldn't know how. Donna handed me the box and made me promise never to open it, and not to tell Dorothy I had it.

Moaning was heard coming from Dorothy, she was waking up from Donna's spell and not looking very happy. 'Who stunned me?' she asked. 'It was me,' Donna admitted, 'you were getting addicted to the power of the talisman, so we had to get it away from you before it took you over.' 'Who's got it now?' Dorothy asked. 'That's not important, we have to concentrate all our efforts on finding a way to stop Bella and her coven getting control of the talisman, even if it means destroying it,' said Donna, 'but first we must make certain the wood is secure. Also we must ensure that there's no one on the outside that Bella can ransom for the talisman. David, you have to get Sadie and the boys away in case they're targeted, and Betty, your husband could also be used against us.'

I immediately phoned Sadie and told her to take the boys to Uncle Bert's for a few days. She argued she wanted to stay at first, but once I'd brought her up to date, she soon saw the wisdom of getting as far away as possible. 'Why aren't you coming with us?' she pleaded. I told her that I couldn't leave the others, because if Bella got hold of the talisman nobody would be safe. I didn't tell her that I was the new keeper of the talisman though.

Betty told us her husband was away at a demonstration of new farm machinery in Wales and wouldn't be home for a week, so with Sadie safely with Uncle Bert in Weymouth, that meant there was nobody left that Bella could use against us. 'What do we do now, wait and let Bella make the first move?' I asked. 'No, first we have to find a way to destroy the talisman,' Gilbert answered. 'That way nobody will be able to use it.' The discussion continued for ages. After a while I nodded off and had the strangest dream. 'And what do you think, David?! David, wake up,' shouted Donna. 'Sorry I must have dropped off.' 'That's alright it's been a hectic couple of days, we're all a mite tired, we've been talking for hours, and we still can't decide on a course of action, and we thought you not being one of us might have a fresh outlook on our problem,' said a very worried looking Donna. 'What about the cavern, there may be an answer hidden inside?' 'What cavern?' asked Donna. 'You know, the one beneath the cottage. 'It's vast, you must have been down there.'

'David, I've lived here for over four hundred years, and my father and mother lived here and grazed pigs in the wood before that, so I can promise you there is no cavern beneath us, or we'd have known about it.' 'Well I can tell you there is, I've seen it, it's huge, it goes on for miles,' I insisted. 'David how can you have seen it, when you only found me a few days ago? And most of the time since you've been off somewhere like the rest of us.' 'I don't know Donna, but since I woke I've had this feeling that the talisman passed on some of its secrets to me while I slept.' 'How can that be? It's a spell, it's not aware of its surroundings, it's just there to be used,' Donna informed me. 'That was four hundred years ago,' I told her, 'and in that time it has evolved, it's now aware of the trouble it's caused and wants to help.'

'I think you've been imagining it. If there's a cavern under us how do we reach it?'

I know it was a dream, but it seemed so real, suddenly I got to my feet and walked through to the kitchen, moved the table to one side, pointed my hand at the floor and shouted, 'REVEAL!' The flagstones started to lift and stack themselves in a pile at one side of the kitchen, the earth underneath sank down to reveal a large cavern, the flagstones then started to form into a staircase leading downwards.

'How on earth is it that you can perform magic!' 'I don't know, Donna, but since my dream I've had the feeling that I've become part of the talisman, or perhaps it's the other way round, I don't know.'

'Give me the box please,' Gilbert asked, 'I want to check something.' Handing him the box, I enquired, 'What are you expecting to find?' Opening it Gilbert looked at the talisman and said, 'The box felt cold when you gave it to me, and now it's open I feel no magic at all coming from the talisman.' 'That's not possible,' cried Betty. 'Where's it gone?'

Gilbert and the others turned and looked at me. 'I haven't done anything, it's been in my pocket the whole time, and I haven't taken it out once.' 'We're not accusing you of anything, the talisman has obviously chosen you.' 'Why me?' I asked. 'I'm not a wizard.'

'That could be why, it must not want any witch or wizard to have that much power, so it went into you.' 'But I don't want it in me. How does it know that I wouldn't use its power for evil?' I asked Gilbert.

'I don't know, but it must trust you, to put so much power at your disposal. Have you any idea what it wants us to do now?'

'I should imagine it wants us to go into the cavern, it's only a guess, but I can't think of any other reason for me to open this entrance.' 'That's enough sarcasm from you, young man,' Donna scolded me.

THE CAVERN

As a child my parents took me to the caves at Cheddar Gorge. Although beautiful they were nothing compared to the size and splendour of the cavern, it was immense, I could hardly make out the other side.

'How could something so big be beneath my home without me knowing?' questioned Donna. 'I watched my father dig the footings when he added extra rooms on as our family got bigger, there was no sign of any cavern then.' 'That's because it wasn't there,' I explained. 'The cavern was built by the talisman. You see, over the last four hundred years the talisman has grown stronger, it's been feeding on all the residue left from spells cast by witches and wizards all over the world, particularly those cast in the wood. Eventually it grew too big for the locket the witches had originally placed it in, so it made this cavern to expand into, only the original spell stayed in the locket.' 'How come you know all this?' Betty asked me. 'The talisman told me in my dream.' 'It spoke to you?' she asked. 'No, not in so many words, it showed me how it became aware of witches and wizards, and their desire for power. At that time it didn't know the difference between good and evil, it knew it had to gather more knowledge so as to decide what to do. By the time the last spell concealing the wood finished, it had made its mind up to stay hidden as long as possible. But as we all know that didn't happen. After Bella stole it, the talisman knew it had to find someone it could trust to stop its power being used.'

'Did it tell you why it chose you to be its keeper?' asked Betty. 'The talisman doesn't talk to me in words, but I got the impression it picked me because I was neither a witch nor a wizard. I have no knowledge of spells and curses, and do not want the talisman for myself.'

I couldn't tell them everything the talisman had shown me, it still didn't trust anyone who had the power to use it. It felt very strange having this, I don't know what you'd call it inside of me, it was no longer just a spell, it had evolved, into what, I wasn't sure, but I was sure of one thing and that was that I had no chance of getting rid of it until this was all over.'

'Ok David, seeing as you're in charge, what are we looking for down here?' Gilbert enquired. 'I haven't got the foggiest idea, Gilbert, but whatever it is, it's this way,' I told him, heading off into the cavern. We walked for what I guessed had been ten minutes. By now I thought we must be under the forty acres, the walls and the roof of cavern were emitting a coloured glow that looked like static electricity, but I knew that it was magical residue left over from all the spells collected by the talisman. As I explained before it had grown too large for the locket it was placed in originally, and had built this cavern to hold all the knowledge, spells, curses, and charms it had collected over the last four hundred years.

'We're here at last, I told them.' 'Oh good,' groaned Donna. 'It wasn't that far; it can't be more than a mile.' 'You ten here young man,' puffed Donna, 'you wait till you're nearly five hundred years old and see if you can do better.'

I quickly changed the subject. 'There's something here, I can feel it, 'REVEAL!' I shouted, pointing my hands at the wall. Suddenly an alcove appeared out of nowhere, and inside it was a larger version of the box Dorothy had brought. On opening it we found seven smaller versions of the talisman. 'There's one for each of you, but don't worry about getting addicted like Dorothy, they're nowhere near as powerful as the original, but they will make your spells stronger and help us defeat Bella.'

'Are there any weapons or other devices down here that we can also use?' asked Tom. 'Not as far as I know. Whether the talisman will reveal anything else to me, we'll just have to wait and see.' After we'd walked back through the cavern, we climbed up into Donna's kitchen. The journey back seemed to go a lot quicker. Everybody including Donna and Sissy, the two oldest witches seemed to have a lot more energy, which I put down to them wearing their lockets.

When the last of them had climbed out, I waved my hands over the opening and the flagstones re-formed themselves back into the kitchen floor. 'I see you didn't even have to say a spell to close the entrance to the cavern, you must be becoming at one with the talisman.' 'I think you're right, Donna, I don't feel as though it would make me do anything I wasn't happy with. It's becoming part of me, but I'm not being taken over. I can still say no if I disagree with what it wants to do.'

'I only hope you're right, I've grown fond of you and wouldn't want anything to happen to you.' 'Don't worry Donna, I'll be alright.'

'David, there's a witch standing at the edge of the wood,' called Tom. He'd been keeping an eye on what was happening outside, and had suddenly noticed her there. 'Well, we'd better go and see what she wants then.' we all went down to the entrance. You could tell at once that she was one of Bella's coven, the witch had an aura of evil about her. Dorothy said, 'I'll open the entrance, but keep an eye out in case there's more than one of them.'

'That's a very good concealment spell you have there,' the witch sneered. 'If we didn't already know, you we're in there, we'd never have found you.'

'That's all very flattering, but what do you want?' called Dorothy.

'You know what we want, hand over the talisman and nobody will get hurt.' We could all tell by the look on the witch's face that she was lying. As soon as Bella had her hands on the talisman, she'd use it to settle a few old scores, starting with everybody who'd had anything to do with the taking of it.

'You can tell my sister that we're keeping it, and she knows she isn't strong enough to take it from us.' 'Bella thought you'd say that Donna, so we found something to change your mind. Have you someone in there by the name of David? 'Yes,' I told her. 'I'm David.' 'Do you know where your wife and children are at this moment?' 'Yes, far away from your clutches' Not far enough, I'm afraid. You see we took a trip down to Weymouth and brought them back. Poor old uncle Bert tried to stop us taking your family, and paid for it with his life. So now you realise we have them and we're prepared to exchange them for the talisman. You have an hour to bring it to us or you'll never see your wife and children again.'

Immediately, she turned and walked away and left me worrying about what to do, how was I going to rescue Sadie and the boys without giving Bella the talisman. I thought they would be safe with Uncle Bert in Weymouth. If I'd have known they'd kill him, I'd never have put him in so much danger. I knew there would be time to mourn him later, but now we had to come up with a plan to rescue my family. 'I can't give her the talisman,' I told the others. 'I am the talisman, it wants to stay part of me, and I've grown used to sharing my body with it.' 'Look David, it's out of the question giving you to Bella, even though you're now the talisman, she could still use the power within you. You're not a wizard, so you wouldn't know how to fight her.'

'I have a cunning plan,' Gilbert told us. (If I'd hadn't been so worried about my family I'd have called him Baldric). 'Tom, fetch the box the talisman was in originally and give it to David.' On his return he handed it to me. 'What am I going to do with this? 'As soon as Bella opens it she'll see that it's empty, that's why you must take the locket off and put it in the box.'

After the talisman had entered me the stone in the locket had stopped glowing and the box no longer felt warm. Gilbert went on. 'If my hunch is right, the box again feels warm, and if you look inside, I think you'll find the locket's glowing.'

When I opened the box, I found he was right, the locket did indeed glow and the box felt warm. 'It's because of its proximity to you, he said and hopefully it will convince Bella that it is the true talisman.' 'How's that going to save my family, as soon as Bella realises, we've tricked her, she'll kill all of us.'

'By the time she realises what's happening, you'll have produced a concealment charm and escaped back to the wood. Once you're safely back here, we can start to formulate a plan to bring an end to this siege.' Gilbert sounded so sure of my ability to bring this plan to fruition; I only wish I had his confidence. So, with the others behind me I walked to the entrance of the wood with the box in my hand.

This time it was Bella who stood waiting for me. 'I see you've come to the right decision. Good, now hand me the box.' 'No,' I said, 'not till I've seen my family. I said 'I could kill you where you stand and take the box. NOW! Give it to me.' 'No! You can kill me, but how do you know that this is the real box? 'Let me see my family and I'll give you the box. If it's not the real one, you can just kill me and you'll still have my family to bargain with.' At once she turned to one of the coven, who had appeared out of nowhere and said 'Bring me the bitch and her brats.' I could tell by her remark that Sadie and the boys had not behaved. From behind a tree one wizard dragged my wife forward. She looked as if she'd been treated badly, her face was swollen and she had a black eye, but she still had a look of defiance about her. Another wizard dragged my boys along, swearing.

I haven't mentioned much about my boys, that's because until now they have not been part of the story, but now it seems that they were in the thick of it. My eldest, Brandon was kicking the wizard in the shin every second step, while his brother, Jordon was kicking him on the other step; the wizard looked as if he'd be quite happy to see the back of them. 'There!' Bella shouted. 'Now! Give! Me! The! Box!' The wizards holding my family were just too far away for me to reach them. Somehow, I had to get closer. 'Here!' I shouted, and threw the box in the air, there wasn't one witch or wizard who hadn't got their eyes glued to the box as it sailed through the air, giving me the time I needed to reach my family and produce the concealment charm. (But I think it had more to do with the talisman). 'Don't make a sound,' I whispered to the boys. I had one clinging to either leg, Sadie had her arms around my neck.

'Ok, now hold hands and we'll get away from these bad people,' I told the boys.

With my arm round Sadie and the boys holding hands we ran back to the wood and safety. In the meantime, Bella was the first of the coven to reach the box. She snatched it out of the air with a look of triumph on her face, not knowing that I had left the talisman back at the cottage. Even though the talisman was part of me, the original spell was still in the locket, and I couldn't let her get her hands on it.

'Kill them!' she screamed, that was the first time any of them had noticed we were gone. 'They're gone,' cried one of the coven. Bella spun round and pointed her wand at the two wizards who'd been holding Sadie and the boys. 'Where are they?' she spat. 'All you had to do was stop them getting away and you couldn't even do that.' Bella turned to the rest of the coven, leaving the two wizards lying dead on the ground. It had been so quick that half of the coven hadn't even seen them killed.

'NOW! Find me a way into that wood or some more of you are going to suffer the same fate as those two. The talisman's mine and nobody's going stop me having it.'

While Bella was ranting and raving at her coven, my family and I arrived back in the wood, everybody crowded round wanting to know if Sadie was fine and to meet the boys. Brandon and Jordon, although not wizards, they were already weaving their magic on the witches. 'Aren't they sweet!' cooed Donna.

'I could just eat them up,' said Anne. Betty and Sissy were also not immune. It's strange how, even the hardest old women can become pussy cats when two young boys turn on their charm.

While the boys distracted the witches, I made sure my wife was ok. 'Was it rough, darling?' I asked Sadie. She broke into tears, 'They burst in while we were having tea. Uncle Bert tried to fight them off, but Bella killed him with a smile on her face. Luckily the boys had been dragged out and hadn't seen him killed. 'I just lost it and attacked Bella. She must not have seen me coming, because I was on her before she could stop me, but before I could do any real damage a wizard pulled me off. I have never seen such a look of hatred as the one Bella gave me. I honestly thought she was going to kill me, but luckily one of the coven yelled, "Bella we need her alive". At that the look of madness left her, and she came right up to my face and spat, "If I didn't need you I would kill you and your brats very slowly and very painfully".'

"Bring them",' she ordered. As she started to turn away, she stopped, turned round, and punched me in the face. "If you or your brats are any trouble I'll kill you, and use your kids to get the talisman".'

After telling me this, my wife burst into tears again, I put my arm around her telling her that she'd been very brave, and I was proud of her.

And she had nothing to worry about; it would all be over soon.

'What I want to know is how on earth you got us away from the coven without any of them seeing.' 'Um, well, there's something you should know.' 'Oh yes, and what would that be?' she asked. 'I'm the keeper of the talisman, it chose me to carry it, and while I was asleep it became part of me.' 'Is it controlling you?' 'No, Sadie, I can feel it inside me, but it's only there until it has learned enough to make its own decisions. In the beginning it wasn't aware of anything, it was only a spell to be used by others where and when they desired, but after a hundred years it became aware, though with no understanding of what was good or evil. It knew it had to learn more about its purpose and who had cast it.'

'Sadie, I think the boys are ready for bed,' Anne called, and when we looked over, both were fast asleep, one on Betty's lap and the other on the lap of a rather uncomfortable looking Gilbert. 'I think Brandon's taking a liking to you.' I couldn't help but smile at Gilbert's obvious discomfort, 'I've not had a lot of contact with children, but they seem nice boys.' As Sadie and Betty carried them up to Donna's spare room, the rest of us sat down to discuss our next move. After three hours of discussion, even with Sadie and Betty re-joining us, no decision had been agreed on. 'I don't know about you lot but I'm completely knackered, hopefully I'll be able to think better after some sleep,' I moaned.

THE TRAP

I awoke after a night's sleep, in which the talisman had communicated its plan for the capture of Bella and her coven.

'Morning David.' I opened my eyes to find Donna waving a bacon sandwich under my nose. 'Thank you, Donna, I'm starving.' I then realised that it had been twenty four hours since I last ate anything. 'This bacon sandwich is the best I've ever tasted,' I admitted. 'It should be, it's been well hung.' 'What do you mean?' I asked. 'Well, the pig this bacon came from is at least four hundred years old. You see, my sister and I butchered it just before the first spell to conceal the wood.'

This information didn't stop me finishing my breakfast, getting dressed and going downstairs. With the boys playing outside, the rest of us sat round the kitchen table. 'Have you any ideas after your night's sleep?' Betty asked me. 'Yes, the talisman wants us to lure the coven down into the cavern. Once down there we'll have a better chance of defeating them, the power of your lockets will be enhanced, giving us the advantage.'

'I know I've only been away a day or so, but what cavern and which lockets?' asked Sadie. 'Sorry darling,' I apologised. I then brought my wife up to date with what had been happening in her absence. When I had finished she looked astounded, it was after all a lot to take in. When she left, her husband was just an ordinary tractor driver, now she'd returned to find him sharing his body with this very powerful magical entity.

'What about the boys?' she asked. 'If you're going to lure them down into the cavern, then they'll have to come through this house. What if Bella finds them?' 'Don't worry, Sadie, I'll ask Donna to place a very strong protection spell on the spare bedroom, you and the boys will be perfectly safe in there, and I think if you look in the box that we found in the cavern, which had been empty, after the others had taken theirs, you'll find three more lockets, one for each of you. They'll be your insurance in case anything goes wrong.

'Now we know what the talisman wants us to do, all we must do now is figure out how to achieve this.' It was Donna who finally came up with a plan. She would call her sister and tell her we wanted to discuss the situation, to see if we could come to a solution that would benefit each side. 'Bella's not going to want to talk. All she wants is the talisman,' argued Dorothy. 'Yes, I know that she'll be plotting how to double cross us, how to sneak her coven in here when we're not looking,' explained Donna. 'That's what I'm hoping will happen, and when they rush in, all they'll find is the hole in the kitchen floor and think we've retreated into the cavern. Once they follow us down the stairs, we'll have the advantage.' 'That's all very well, Donna, but if you're out there all on your own, what's to stop Bella killing you and then rushing in?' 'I think I can help you there,' Dorothy offered. 'When I was studying with the yeti, they taught me how to project my image, and I'll teach you. It shouldn't take long now we've got the lockets to enhance our power. We will not have enough time for you to master the spell completely, but with the two of us working together I think we can fool your sister.'

'All I want to know,' this from Gilbert, 'is when we've got them all down in the cavern, what happens then?' 'Good question,' this time Betty, 'we're just country witches, all we know is everyday magic. Simple spells, nothing strong enough to defeat dark magic, look all you have to do is stun them.' I could feel the fear rising in them, they'd never had to go up against dark magic before and it was making them nervous. 'The talisman will protect you, that's why it gave you the lockets.'

Having finally calmed them down, I took Sadie and the boys up to the spare bedroom so Donna could seal them in. Sadie was nervous, but Brandon and Jordon were happily playing on their game boys, so after kissing them all, I headed back downstairs. With the rest of us all down in the cavern, we spread out and tried to find somewhere to hide. Dorothy and Donna sat down and held hands. They were trying to project Donna's image. Above them, the air shimmered and a picture of the entrance to the wood started to appear. 'Now Donna, concentrate on the entrance and try to see yourself standing there.' Dorothy was walking her through the spell, and it seemed to be working, because Donna's image started to appear, faintly at first, but as time went by it became more solid. 'That's it, Donna, you're doing great. Now you've got to project your voice. I want you to call Bella and when she comes I want you to tell her we want a truce to try and resolve our problem.' 'Bella,' she called. 'Try again, and this time louder.' 'BELLA!' This time Donna's voice filled the whole cavern, 'WE NEED TO TALK!'

Suddenly Bella appeared at the entrance, 'Why don't you open the door in the charm sister, as a sign of trust?' 'Ok Bella, but no funny stuff.' As soon as the entrance to the wood was open, Bella and her coven, who had suddenly appeared out of nowhere, rushed into the wood. 'Give me the talisman now or die.' 'You always were the predictable one, Bella. I knew once I'd opened a door in the charm, you'd come charging in shouting threats and demanding the talisman. Well if you want it you'll have to kill us all to get it.' 'No problem sister, that had been my plan all along.' Suddenly Bella's wand was in her hand, and a beam of red light shot out the end, straight at Donna. If Donna had really been standing there it would have killed her before she could react, but as it was, it just passed harmlessly through her image.

Underground, Donna and Dorothy were thrown apart by the force of the spell. We all went to help the two witches up, but Donna just sat there with her head in her hands. 'Come on Donna,' I called, 'we all need to get in position before they get down here.' She took my hand and pulled herself up. 'Thank you, David. I know Bella, she wants the talisman badly, but I never thought she'd kill her own sister to get it.'

I looked at the old witch and saw tears streaming down her face. I knew there was nothing I could say that would be of any comfort, so I left her to her grief.

Meanwhile up in the wood, Bella, discovering she'd been duped had flown into yet another terrible rage. 'My sister is not that good a witch, she couldn't have cast that powerful a spell without help. Search the house and wood. Bring anyone you find to me, don't kill any of them until we find the talisman. We may have to torture some of them to find out where they've hidden it.'

Without delay, the coven split into two groups, one went off to search the wood, while Bella led the others to the cottage. 'Start with the downstairs,' she ordered. 'If they're not found, we'll try the bedrooms. 'Bella!' a shout came from the kitchen, 'come and look at this.' Upon entering Bella saw the hole in the floor with the steps going down into the cavern. 'Well, that wasn't there when I lived here. Call the others in from the wood, I think we'll need the full coven when we descend into whatever this is.'

Donna, having had a good cry, was now back to her old self. 'David it's all very well, luring Bella and all her followers down here, but once down the steps they'll spot us straight away.' 'Not if we're invisible,' I told her. 'David, I may be four hundred years old, but I still have not mastered the invisibility spell.' 'Yes, Donna, I know that, but you've never had the talisman to help you. It's linked to the lockets you all wear and will help increase the strength of any magic you perform.' 'What are we going to do when we've lured them down here?' asked Sissy. 'They'll kill us in an instant, but I know I can't take a life and I think I speak for the others as well.' 'Don't worry, we will not be killing anyone,' I told them. 'The talisman has it all worked out. 'All we must do is stun them and it will do the rest. Now spread out, they'll be down here any minute.'

With everybody in position and concentrating on the invisibility spell we waited for our visitors. The talisman must have been transmitting its power to the lockets, because as I looked at her, I noticed Donna was fading, becoming transparent, and finally disappearing. When I turned, the others, they had almost disappeared, and as I watched they also became fainter and one at a time faded out completely. All we had to do then was wait to spring the trap.

'We can't go down there, it's obviously a trap.' This I imagined was one of Bella's cronies. 'Get behind me, you coward, I'll go first if you're frightened.' At once, Bella came down the stairs, her wand held out in front, waiting for us to spring a trap. After a lot of bullying and threatening, the coven was all standing at the bottom of the steps. 'Now spread out and find them, they must be in here somewhere, and if you find the talisman, bring it to me at once.' Fanning out in all directions, they went about their search. And even though everybody was invisible, I knew exactly where they were, the lockets linked all of us with the talisman. I could feel the others and I knew they could feel me, it was as if we all had a telepathic connection. I knew for instance, that a wizard was only about ten feet away from where Anne stood. To confirm this a ray of light shot out of nowhere, the wizard was blasted off his feet and landed in a heap twenty yards away.

Following that, all hell let loose, spells and curses were thrown in all directions, none at any specific target, just on the off chance that they would hit someone. The others following Anne's example started to stun any of the coven that came near them. Soon the air was full of spells being cast by one side or the other, but none of those cast by Bella and her coven had found any of the hidden witches or wizards. We were so far untouched, but it would only be a matter of time before the coven struck it lucky and hit one of us. But now we were winning, one by one the coven was being stunned.

Total panic had gripped Bella's followers; they were running around, throwing spells and curses left, right, and centre. 'Stop!' screamed Bella. 'They're using an invisibility spell. Everyone form a circle. They may be invisible, but when they cast a spell, sparks will fly out of the end of their wands, so when you see them, aim at that spot,' Bella told them. Before I could warn the others, Sissy threw a stunning spell at the witch standing next to Bella. Almost before it hit the witch, Bella had cast a killing curse at the spot where she'd seen the sparks. Two things happened within a millisecond. One, Sissy's spell hit its intended target, two, Bella's killing curse found Sissy. Both witches were blown off their feet, the one next to Bella only stunned, but there was no way Sissy could have survived. I had been told that a killing curse was the most powerful curse performed. Donna informed me only the darkest of witches and wizards ever used it. It was said that every time you performed one, a small part of your soul dies, until finally you're nothing left but pure evil.

As I looked at Sissy, who was now visible, I noticed she was still breathing, but unconscious. I knew I had to get to her before Bella realised she wasn't dead. 'Now you saw what I did, keep your eyes open and do the same,' yelled Bella, by which time I had reached Sissy and covered her with my invisibility spell. As I carried her away I could feel her move in my arms. Somehow the locket she wore had protected her partially so the curse had only knocked her out. 'Is my sister alright, is she hurt?' I heard Dorothy's voice in my head. I knew Dorothy hadn't spoken to me. I could only assume that we were able to communicate telepathically. 'She's only stunned,' I answered. 'Can the rest of you hear me?' I thought. One by one the others confirmed that they too had the telepathic link. This made our fight a lot easier. 'From now on we must be very careful when we stun any of them. First we need to make sure none of the coven sees the discharge from our wands. Also, as soon as you cast a spell move to one side so as not to give them anything to aim at.' But before we could put our plan into action, Bella called a truce.

'No more spells, I want to talk to my sister. Donna, I know you're here, I can feel your aura.' 'Yes, I'm here despite your efforts. You tried to kill me.' 'Sister, it was done in the heat of the moment. I didn't mean it,' lied Bella. 'Mean it or not, I would still be dead.'

Bella, 'Can't we talk face to face?'

'What do you think David?' I heard in my head. 'We must find out all we can about what she intends to do. Don't let on that the talisman is part of me, let her think that the locket you're wearing is the original one, and we'll all be watching out for anyone casting spells while you're visible.' 'Alright sister, but no tricks,' shouted Donna.

Donna started to appear just in front of her sister. I was studying Bella, trying to foresee any act of treachery, and I knew the others were keeping a watchful eye on the rest of the coven, but so far so good. 'That's a neat trick, sister, you'll have to teach me that one.' 'Sorry, Bella, but you must have this (holding up the locket) to master that spell.' Bella's eyes were drawn to the locket. Thinking it to be the talisman, 'I see you have recovered the talisman that I so wrongly stole. I don't know what came over me, but now I see the error of my ways.' 'You never were a very good liar, Bella. I know you want it badly, your eyes have not left it since I reappeared, but you can't have it. It's too powerful for one person.' 'If it's too powerful for one person, how come you've got it?' Bella screamed. 'But she hasn't got it, I have,' I said, becoming visible next to Donna. 'You!' Bella said with a look of total hatred on her face. 'Yes,' I said, 'my name's David and I'm the keeper of the talisman.' 'You! You're not even a wizard, how can you be the keeper of something so powerful?' 'Oh I didn't volunteer, the talisman chose me for exactly the reason you said. I'm not a wizard and I don't have any magical knowledge, so it thought that I'd be the ideal person to be its keeper. I, unlike all of you, would not be tempted to use it.' 'What do you mean, 'thought'? It can't think, it's only a spell.' 'I'm afraid you're a bit behind the times, Bella,' I informed her. 'The talisman has become aware it grew too big for its locket and built this cavern to expand into. You wanted the talisman, you're standing inside it.' Bella pondered for a minute. 'So, let me get this straight, the talisman's now a thousand times more powerful, and all I have to do is kill you to become the keeper.' Well that's not the outcome I'd intended. I thought once I'd explained things to Bella, she'd realise she couldn't win, but I'd had the opposite effect. Now she wanted the talisman even more. 'Haven't you been listening, Bella, we're too powerful, you can't win.' I'd hardly gotten the word "win" out, when I was blasted off my feet by a spell from Bella.

I have never felt so much pain before in my life; I lay on the floor of the cavern writhing in total agony. All around a fire fight ensued, spells and curses were being exchanged. I must have passed out, because when I came round it was all quiet.

'What's going on?' I asked. 'Oh thank God, you're alright, we were worried we'd lost you too.' Betty sat on the ground next to me stroking my head. 'What do you mean, "lost me too"?' It was then that I could hear someone crying, looking in that direction, I could just make out someone sitting next to a body. 'Who is it?' I asked. 'Gilbert,' Betty told me. I asked her to help me up, it took a bit of doing, but I finally managed to get to my feet.

Betty went on to tell that after I'd been hit by Bella's curse, a full-scale battle ensued. 'It soon became clear that Bella and her coven were no match for us. They went down one by one until only Bella remained. She had somehow managed to get behind Gilbert. By then curses were having no effect on us. 'It was as if the talisman was soaking up all their magic and turning it against them. We were all visible by then, having no need to remain hidden, so Bella had to resort to brute force and stabbed Gilbert in the back with her wand. She then stole his locket and fled back up the stairs, with all of us throwing spells at her.' 'Why didn't you follow?' I demanded. 'We can't let her get away.' 'We tried,' Donna explained 'but now she has the power of the talisman. Gilbert was dead and we feared you were also. We didn't know if we were strong enough with two of our number gone to take Bella on. Every time one of us tried to climb the stairs to the kitchen she'd throw a spell down at us. Now she's sealed the entrance and none of us can open it.'

'Ok everybody, listen up,' taking command, I gathered all of them together and gave out orders. 'Donna, you and Betty, find some way of tying up those of the coven you've stunned. Anne and Sissy see if you can get Tom away from Gilbert's body, and Dorothy, give me a hand to drag Gilbert's body up against the wall of the cavern.' Anne and Sissy had a hard time getting Tom to leave Gilbert, but finally they succeeded in taking him to one side. His sorrow now turning to anger, he wanted to kill the witch who'd murdered the closest he'd come to having a father. Neither of his real parents had ever wanted him, but Gilbert always was kind and gentle toward him, and Tom had come to love the old wizard.

As Dorothy and I lifted Gilbert into a sitting position against the cavern wall, we saw Bella's wand still sticking out of his back. 'She must have taken his wand as well as his locket,' Dorothy commented. 'We can't leave it in him. No, it is evil just like its mistress, we have to remove it,' I said as I pulled it out of his body. 'This must be destroyed, it's been used to kill more than one person, so it can't be allowed to fall into the hand of any dark witch.'

As we stood there with the wand, trying to think how to destroy it, we heard a cracking noise coming from the wall, and a hole appeared suddenly. It was about thirty centimetres in diameter and went in at least a metre. I knew the talisman wanted me to put the wand in the hole, so I inserted it in as far as I could reach, the hole then closed up until all that was left was the bare wall. 'It'll be safe in there,' I told Dorothy. 'No one will ever be able to retrieve it now.' Having dealt with the wand we then turned our attention to Gilbert.

With him leaning against the wall, we all gathered round to pay our respects. As we all stood there saying our goodbyes, the wall seemed to turn into liquid and flow out of both sides and around Gilbert's body, enclosing him like a large pair of hands and dragged him into the wall. If you looked carefully you could just make out his shape under the surface. He was now entombed in the cavern and would be a part of the talisman forever.

'What now?' asked Tom.

'Now,' I said 'we take care of Bella and the coven, once and for all.'

'I don't think you have to worry about the coven. Betty and I have made sure that they'll be no more trouble,' Donna pointed to the heap of bodies lying tied up on the cavern floor. 'That will do for now,' I told them, 'but we'll have to find a more permanent solution later. First we have to find a way out the cavern.' As if the talisman was listening, the floor in the kitchen opened and the tiles turned into steps coming down from above. As the last step touched the cavern floor, we heard a chilling scream coming from above.

I knew at once that it was my wife. Before the others could stop me I was up the stairs and into the kitchen before anyone else had moved. I didn't know what I was running into, but I didn't care, all I knew was that my wife and kids were in terrible trouble and needed my help. I ran out of the kitchen and up the stairs to the bedroom where I'd sealed my family in. As I reached the landing, I saw that the door of the bedroom had been blown off its hinges. When I looked in I saw Sadie lying on the floor, with blood pouring from a cut on her forehead. 'Are you alright darling?' I asked. 'She's got Jordon,' she cried. 'She said she'll exchange him for the talisman. She's outside the wood, she said you have an hour to bring out the talisman or she'll kill him.' I took out my handkerchief and pressed it to the cut on her head, then turned to Brandon and told him to keep the pressure on his mum's cut, and I would go and get his brother. He and his brother would fight, but let anyone hurt one and he had to take on the other as well. 'Ok dad I'll take care of mum,' he said trying to be brave. As I reached the bottom of the stairs, the others were coming out of the kitchen. I explained what had happened, and asked Donna to look after Sadie

THE SHOOT

When the remainder of us went out, we found Bella standing in the field just outside the woods, with her arm around Jordon. 'Only one of you,' yelled Bella. I told the rest to stay where they were and I started to walk towards Bella. 'Didn't I just kill you?' she sneered. 'You'll have to try harder next time, I'm not that easy to kill,' I taunted her. 'Enough of this, have you got the talisman?' she shouted. 'Believe it or not I'm the talisman.' 'You're trying to fool me. I know what the talisman is. After all, I helped to protect it for four hundred years. You've been trying fool me, by all of you wearing copies of it to put me off the scent.' She was now working herself up into one of her famous rages, 'You even made this child wear one.'

'I'll try and explain it to you again,' I told her. 'The talisman has grown over the years, and it has become aware. It built the cavern to grow into, and has been collecting spells and magical knowledge, trying to decide whether to wipe out good, evil, or all magic.' 'I don't believe you,' she shouted, 'you're trying to trick me again. Spells don't become aware, they're just spells. Now I want the talisman, and if I don't get it, you'll have one son less.' 'Don't give it to her dad,' Jordon called. 'It's ok son,' I told him. 'I'll soon have you free.' It was then that I realised that neither Jordon nor I had spoken a word, it seemed that we had been communicating telepathically. I found out later that both Brandon and Jordon were in the future going to become powerful wizards. It was then Jordon came up with a plan. 'Dad, get ready.' Promptly he kicked Bella in the shins. When she let go of him, he dived to the ground and rolled to one side. 'Little sod,' shouted Bella, drawing her wand she aimed it at Jordon, 'I'll teach you, you little swine.' But before she could fire off a curse, Jordon had reached me, and I stood him at the back of me. 'I'll just have to kill you first and then the brat,' she spat at me. I must have been the only person to ever have been hit with a killing curse twice in one day without being killed.

I then felt my boy tap me on the back. 'Dad, she's got the locket.' When I looked, I saw that Bella did indeed have Jordon's locket. 'If what you've told me is true, then I have two pieces of the talisman in my possession, and I'm feeling more powerful than I have ever felt in my life, so all I have to do is kill all the others and take their lockets, to be strong enough to destroy you and get all of the talisman's power for myself.' The others had obviously heard all that Bella had said, and decided to make sure that didn't happen. As one they rushed forward to do battle with the dark witch. Letting out a blood curdling cackle Bella turned and ran, throwing spells over her shoulder in all directions, more to slow down her pursuers than hit anyone. 'I'll form another coven, and come back in force, kill you all one at a time until I control the talisman, then I'll be the most powerful witch that's ever lived,' she cackled.

'You have to stop her before she gets away, or none of us will ever be safe again,' I shouted, but because of their ages, only Tom was keeping up with Bella. She could see that the young wizard was gaining on her, so she turned and faced Tom. He only had a second to dive to one side, before a killing curse hit the spot where he'd been standing. This gave Bella time to think, she knew she couldn't out run the young wizard, and her broomstick was back in the wood. She had to find some way of speeding up her escape, and then it came to her. As a child she and Donna could never master a spell their mother had tried to teach them. It was a transfiguration spell that turned the person who'd cast it into a bird or an animal, but maybe, just maybe, with help of the two lockets she now had around her neck, she'd be powerful enough to pull it off. What animal, she couldn't decide, but as she raced across the field, several pheasants flew up in front of her. 'That's it,' she thought. 'Even if they see me turn into one, they'll never know which bird I am.' As she ran along, she recited the spell that she could never master as a child, but now with the help of the lockets it was working.

Right in front of our very eyes, Bella turned from a running woman, into a pheasant. Taking off she headed straight for the flock of birds.

Tom ran after her throwing stunning spells at her, but after a minute she was completely hidden among the other pheasants. 'Damn, damn!' swore Tom, 'She's got away.' By then the witches and I had caught up with Tom. 'She's going to be twice as hard to catch, now she's got two lockets,' Donna said aloud what the rest of us were thinking. 'She may not have got away yet,' called Betty pointing to the far side of the field. 'There's my husband and some of his friends having a pheasant shoot, and Bella and the rest of the pheasants were heading straight for their guns.'

At that very moment eight twelve bore shotguns fired one after the other. Not every gun found a target, at least two missed, and there were more than six pheasants in the flock. Bella was ecstatic when she realised that the spell she'd tried so often to master as a child and failed at every attempt had worked. As she soared off into the sky, Bella noticed several other birds off to the left of her. 'That's great,' she thought. 'I'll hide in among them, that way no one will be able to hit me with a spell, 'and I will be long gone in no time. Busy in her attempt to escape the witches behind her, she failed to notice the line of guns until it was too late.

The pheasant on her left suddenly exploded in a mass of feathers, it was then that she realised, she'd flown into a line of guns, all intent on shooting her and every other pheasant in the sky.

Bella didn't know what to do, if she turned back into human form, the fall would kill her. If she kept on flying, the same fate would befall her, the only thing to do was to try to spoil their aim, by flying low and weaving about. What Bella didn't know was that the person behind the gun would take any bird doing that as a challenge and try their hardest to shoot it.

That's exactly what the Major did. He'd seen this pheasant fly in a pattern that they didn't normally use, and decided to try and shoot it. As he fired he could have sworn that something sparkly was hanging around the pheasant's neck. It was a tricky shot, but he knew he'd hit it, when it suddenly fell to the ground. He signalled Suzie, his favourite hunting dog to, 'Go fetch.' She ran off at a furious pace to retrieve her master's bird.

After the birds had flown over, Betty, Tom and I ran over to see if Bella had managed to slip past. 'Hello dear,' Betty greeted her husband, 'I thought you were in Scotland till tomorrow.' 'I came home early, the weather was atrocious. All we did was sit around in the hotel playing bridge, so I packed up and came home early. You weren't about so I phoned some friends for a last minute pheasant shoot.'

At that moment, Suzie came back with her bird, stooping to pick it up the Major let out a cry of amazement. 'Well I've seen everything now,' the major exclaimed holding up the bird. Around its neck hung two lockets, 'I'll take them,' Betty told him, taking the lockets off the bird. 'Is this to do with, you know what,' he whispered to his wife. 'You don't have to whisper,' Betty told him. 'They, pointing to Tom and me are a part of, you know what.' 'Oh well, I'll leave you to it, whatever it is, you're doing, and get back to my shoot.'

'Poor soul,' said Betty, shaking her head, 'He can't come to terms with the fact that I'm a witch, and pretends we're just a normal married couple and that witches are not real.'

As we walked back to Donna and the others, Tom asked Betty, 'Does this mean that Bella's gone forever?' 'To be honest Tom, I don't know. She was in possession of two very powerful magical lockets, we just have to hope that it's the last we'll ever hear of her.'

There were some loose ends we had to deal with, first on the agenda, was Bella's coven, they were still tied up in a heap on the floor in the cavern. 'Has the talisman any idea what to do with them?' Anne asked me. 'Yes,' I answered, 'first we'll get them all to their feet.'

With them all now conscious this was not too hard. 'Now stand them all against the cavern wall.' Once we had the group of witches and wizards up against the wall, 'Nobody move,' I told them. 'You can't just kill us,' cried one of the witches. 'Why shouldn't we?' I asked. 'You'd soon kill us if the tables were turned, but you needn't worry, we are not as evil as you.' I could feel that the talisman had come to a decision, watching our fight against evil, it had decided to come out on the side of good.

As we watched, the cavern wall flowed out and around the coven, exactly as it had Gilbert. Turning to me, Donna asked, 'What's happening, it isn't killing them, is it?' 'No Donna, the talisman's just taking away their ability to use magic. After it's finished, they will no longer be able to cast spells or curses, they will in fact be ordinary people.'

As I was explaining this, the wall opened and the coven were free. 'Now you know what the talisman has done to you,' I told them, 'you'll never be able to use your magic to hurt people again. It has left you with enough magic for one last flight on your broomsticks, so go home and try and do no harm to others. We will be keeping an eye on you. Any more trouble and we may not be so generous in the future.'

The next on the list was, what were we going to do with the lockets? 'The talisman wants everyone who has a locket to keep them,' I told them. 'It feels that there is an awful lot of evil magic out there, it wants us to form a coven to fight it.' 'Why doesn't it just destroy all dark magic?' this from Sissy. 'There must be a balance of good and evil in the world,' I explained. 'You can't have one without the other, even the most decent person has evil thoughts sometimes. It's being good that stops him or her acting on them. So if you destroy all evil, you destroy some good as well.' As we talked we left the cavern and went back up into the kitchen.

Sadie and the boys were sitting around the table being taken care of by Dorothy. 'I've made the boys some chips and tended to Sadie's cut.' I thanked Dorothy. Sadie still looked a little shaky, but the boys were fine, give them a plate of chips, and they forget about everything, apart from eating.

I then explained to Sadie that we were going to form a coven to fight against dark magic. 'Who's "we"?' she asked. 'Everybody with a locket, I told her. 'Not me, or my boys,' she contradicted me. 'Ok love,' trying to placate her, 'I've seen the boys' future, and they are going to be famous wizards. 'My boys are not Harry Potter,' she shouted at me. I finally convinced her that the boys being wizards was inevitable. 'Well then, I'm resigning,' she said. 'I've had enough of being hit, threatened, and terrified, and if the boys and your futures lie in magic, then there must be someone in the family who is ordinary. If for no other reason than to give the boys some sort of normal childhood.' I smiled at her, 'I don't think that anyone's going to be taking them on any dangerous missions. They must learn all about their gifts, and how to use them wisely.'

Donna who'd been listening to our conversation, put her hand on Sadie's shoulder and told her, 'Sadie, my dear, I'll take on the boys' education, nothing bad will happen to them, I promise you. I'll always watch over them, and if there's anything you're not happy with, just come and see me and we'll sort it out.'

'So, Donna, 'you've decided to stay with us in this century. I'm glad, I'd miss you if you decided to lock yourself back in the wood.'

'I couldn't do that David, I've made a lot of new friends, and even though it's got a bit hairy at times, I've never felt as alive as I do now. So yes, to answer your question, I'm staying here, somebody has to guard the cavern and put flowers on Gilbert's grave.' The old witch looked as if she was going to burst into tears. 'I know he was an old womaniser, but we were once very close and nearly got married, so I can't leave him down there all alone.'

'I must tell you all something,' I said, turning to our coven. 'Gilbert's now a part of the talisman, his life force, or soul, or whatever you call it has been absorbed. And now forms part of its consciousness, so if you each consent to wear the locket and become part of this coven, you will all eventually be absorbed into the talisman upon your demise.'

All the witches, after a lot of discussion came to the same decision. They would all join the coven and fight dark magic. Sissy (or Mistress Web as she now wanted to be called ('It's a sign of respect, to call a witch of my age Mistress,' she told us), said she felt fifty years younger since she'd been wearing the locket and even if it meant fighting the occasional dark witch, it was worth it to feel that young again.

The others, for various reasons agreed with Mistress Web.

The only thing left was, what were we going to do with the last two lockets (now that Sadie had quit and Gilbert was dead) that did not have anyone to wear them? 'We need to find two witches, or wizards,' I told them. You could see that the witches were not too happy with any wizard other than Tom joining their coven.

But I knew there had to be a certain number from each group to balance the talisman's power, I would bring that up later, when I had worked up the courage. Fighting Bella and her coven again would be a piece of cake, compared to trying to persuade this group of witches to let a few wizards into their coven. So I left them discussing who they were going to ask to wear the lockets, and took my family home.

As we walked out of the wood and down the lane to our home, I pondered on how my life had changed over the last few days. I'd gone from being an ordinary farm worker to the keeper of the most powerful magical spell on earth. Going back to driving a tractor would seem very boring after that. 'Dad, am I a wizard, can I do magic?' Jordon asked. He must have been listening while we were discussing his, and his brother's future back in Donna's kitchen. 'Dad,' this time it was Brandon who asked. 'Can we have a broomstick each?' 'And when do we get a wand?' Jordon butted in. My wife gave me that "you sort this out, look".

On arriving home, I phoned Betty on my mobile and asked for a few days off, to take my wife and boys down to Weymouth to sort out Uncle Bert's funeral. She said, 'Yes,' so we packed up and had a few days away from magic, witches and all that it involved. Once we'd gotten settled in the hotel, Sadie and I sat the boys down and had a long talk, in which we explained about the lockets and the talisman and how they were never to tell anyone about witches, wizards or anything they'd seen in the wood. Both boys promised to keep it a secret and never experiment with their lockets. But at breakfast next morning, I noticed that both boys were no longer wearing them, instead Brandon had on a necklace of wooden beads, and Jordon was wearing what looked like a black lace with a little sponge bob square pants attached. 'Didn't I explain to you last night that you must never take the lockets off?' 'But dad,' Brandon corrected me, 'we are wearing them.' 'Yeah,' Jordon said, 'we couldn't go around with those naff old things hanging round our necks, so we changed them.' 'What happened to, "we promise not to use the power of the lockets"?' I asked. Both boys grinned and said, 'Sorry dad.' I had a feeling that this would not be the last time we'd be having this conversation.

Uncle Bert's funeral was very well attended, it looked as if half of Weymouth were there. Afterwards a man in an old-fashioned frock coat, handed me a white envelope. It was from Uncle Bert's solicitor informing me he'd be in touch soon, regarding the will.

On our return to Norfolk, I made my way to the wood, where I discovered the lockets had found two new owners, Mistress Web had returned to her cottage with her sister Dorothy, Anne had also returned to her home, and Betty had gone back to the farm, only Donna and Tom remained. 'David you're back, come on in and meet the new members of our coven,' Donna welcomed me. 'I think I've met them before, haven't I?' I asked as I went forward. And shook hand with the wizards. I remembered them from the coven we'd formed to cast a spell to find the talisman.

'It's Hamish and Dermot, isn't it?' I asked. 'What are you doing here?' 'Well, Tom persuaded the witches to accept a couple more wizards into the coven,' Hamish told me. And I could feel the talisman agreed with their decision.

'David! David!' I could feel Donna's hands on my shoulder shaking me, it was like I was coming out of a very deep sleep. Slowly I became aware of Donna's frightened face. 'You went into a trance,' she told me. 'You were gone for twenty minutes. One second you were talking to Hamish and Dermot, the next you were gone. What happened?' 'The talisman wanted to communicate with me, it doesn't feel that a non-magic person should be its keeper, and it has also come to a decision about you, Tom.'

'Me?' asked Tom. 'Yes you. Give me your locket. The talisman doesn't want you to have it anymore.' 'But I haven't done anything wrong, have I?' 'No Tom, it's what you've done right. You're going to be the new keeper of the talisman.' 'Me! Why me?' cried Tom. 'It feels that it should be within a witch or a wizard, and you're the one it's chosen. You are by far the youngest, and basically, it trusts you.' 'It will be a full-time job, but one that the talisman and I feel you're up to, so how about it? Do you want the job?' 'Yes,' Tom accepted. 'In that case all that's left is for us to swap. You give me the locket and you get the talisman.' Tom took off the locket and as he handed it to me our hands touched. It felt like electricity passing from me to Tom, but I knew that it was the talisman. I felt that I'd still have a small part of it, if I wore the locket. 'The talisman wants me to tell you, "Thank you, for allowing it to share your body",' Tom told me.

Thereafter, I took my leave and hoped I was returning to my quiet life, on the farm with my family. But as I walked back home, I saw a pheasant circling the wood. I wondered, 'Had we seen the last of Bella?' I had this feeling that even if she was gone for good, some of her evil may have lingered on.

Albert Stone

Albert Stone crept through the trees that bordered the Stanford battle area. The battle area comprised of four or five villages, once inhabited by hundreds of families, a large estate with a splendid manor house, plus seventeen thousand five hundred acres of farmland. The whole lot had been commandeered by the ministry of defence in 1942 to train the troops for the Normandy landings.

Albert lived in the village of Thompson. Well, to say that he lived in the village would not be accurate, he lived in the last house as you left Thompson heading towards Watton. He was for all intents and purposes a recluse, but most of the villagers just thought of him as a "miserable old sod".

He had once been a very successful farmer, happily married, with two children. There wasn't any event, party or dance they hadn't been involved in. Everybody thereabouts liked him and his wife, and adored his children. But all that changed one cold and frosty December morning, while he was driving his family to Norwich livestock market to buy some sheep for his farm. It was going to be a day out for all of them. After the sale they were going to go into

Norwich to do some shopping, then Albert was going to take the girls to the cinema while his wife went and had her hair done, but unfortunately things didn't go as planned, because while driving there, a lorry came out of nowhere and smashed into their car killing his wife and daughters. The police said that it was nobody's fault. It had been a particularly hard frost that night and there was nothing the lorry driver could have done to avoid the crash.

Albert had survived, but the loss of his family had changed him. He could no longer stay on the farm that held so many happy memories, so he sold up, keeping only the old gamekeeper's cottage for himself. The anger over the loss of his family had turned him very bitter, to the point where he hardly spoke to a soul. The villagers who had once been his friends were now met with a wall of silence, all efforts to get through to him were unsuccessful. Finally the villagers gave up and left him to his grief.

As he crept along, he kept his eyes open for pheasants. He often poached on the land belonging to local farmers, who didn't take kindly to him killing their birds, but most had known him all their lives, and were devastated by the death of his family, and so consequently made allowances for his behaviour.

Albert wasn't worried that he was trespassing. He could hear that the Major and his cronies were out shooting, so what did one more gun matter? He wanted a pheasant for his tea and it didn't matter to him who it belonged to. At that moment he spotted a pheasant flying towards him. This one had obviously evaded the shooting party. Taking aim he fired, the bird stopped in mid-flight, as though it had hit a brick wall and dropped to the ground, dead. Having marked in his mind where the bird had fallen, he proceeded to retrieve it, which he stuffed into a canvas bag and started for home.

'DAVID, can I have a word with you?' I heard Donna call from the wood. 'Oh no, what have the boys been up to now?' I thought.

I'd been happily ploughing away on the forty acres, when the plough jammed. Getting out to clear the blockage I'd been waylaid by Donna. Fearing the worst, I headed off to find out just what trouble my boys were in this time.

After our victory over Bella and her dark coven, and the formation of the coven of the talisman as we were now called, Donna had taken on the task of teaching Brandon and Jordon about magic each day after school, so as to prepare them to become wizards. That was three months ago and I don't think she quite realised what she was letting herself in for when she volunteered. Even without magic they were a handful, but now they had their lockets, that made them part of the talisman, and they knew that one day they'd become wizards, so there was no stopping them.

Donna had learned a lot in her four hundred years, but nothing had prepared her for my two boys. 'What have they done this time?' I asked 'They're no trouble, they're always good for their auntie, Donna.' That I found hard to believe. 'No I just called you over to tell you that I've heard from Tom.' Tom was the young wizard who had taken over from me as the keeper of the talisman. After the death of Gilbert the wizard who'd raised Tom when he was abandoned by his own family, and whom he had come to love as a father, he went completely to pieces. To help him get over this Dorothy had suggested that it might do him good to go to Tibet to study with the yeti.

Being as it was, time for my tea break, I followed Donna back to the wood to hear Tom's news. After making me a cup of tea and a bacon sandwich, she gave me the letter from Tom to read. He had arrived safely and was getting down to his training with the yeti, who would be his teacher for the next four years. It was lovely to hear from the young wizard, there were also a couple of pages from Dorothy, who'd accompanied him to Tibet.

After spending a month with her sister, (Mistress Web) they'd both agreed that it would be better if she moved out. Having two witches in one house, was the equivalent of two cooks in the same kitchen, sooner or later one had to go. So, Dorothy jumped at the chance to return to Tibet where she'd once studied. She knew from experience that they'd be the ideal ones to help Tom get rid of all his pent-up emotions and focus on becoming a more balanced and enlightened wizard, and judging by their letter, being in Tibet was having the desired effect. Tom seemed more at ease and was enjoying himself. Thanking Donna for the tea and bacon sandwich and for letting me read Tom and Dorothy's letter, I went back to work.

BETH AND CUTHBERT

Uncle Bert and Auntie Olive hadn't had any children of their own. Auntie Olive had died when I was young, and for a long while he'd lived on his own, and then one day his life changed completely when he met Cuthbert. Cuthbert wasn't his real name, he'd been christened Cuthbert by a girl called Beth. You see what Uncle Bert didn't want anyone to know, was that Cuthbert is a troll (well, half troll, half human), in fact he's the very last troll.

Now trolls are not what you might call friendly, history tells us that trolls have a liking for humans, (for lunch that is). It is also written, that if daylight ever touched their skin, they would immediately turn to stone. But being half human, Cuthbert was different from all the other trolls. He could go out in daylight, and he was a vegetarian, (well, sort of).

Cuthbert's story starts a few hundred years earlier when trolls roamed the countryside spreading death and destruction wherever they went. Gorgo was by far the most feared troll ever, and he laid waste to whole villages. A call went out to all brave men, a huge reward was offered by king Ralf to anybody who brought him the head of Gorgo. From knights on horseback to the lowliest serf, all answered the call and set out to kill the troll and claim the reward. Of those who set off on this quest, most did not return. The knights fared better then the serfs, not because they were braver or more courageous, but simply because a horse can retreat quicker than a serf. So Gorgo had his fill of serfs while the knights retreated.

The king was at his wits' end. He'd sent out what amounted to an army, to capture one troll, and out of those only a handful had returned. Of those none were unscathed. Force hadn't worked, but maybe magic would. He sent out a petition to all wizards, warlocks and witches. If any of them could rid him of this scourge, they could name their own reward.

He'd blamed magic for every bad thing that had happened in the kingdom, turning the people against magic. So consequently, not one witch wizard or warlock replied, but there was one witch, named Beth who hated king Ralf more than the others, decided to go and kill the troll and claim the reward. She was fed up living in her old cottage, with a roof that let water in every time it rained. So, filling a bag with enough clothes and provisions for two weeks she set out to find and kill the troll.

After searching for a week, all she'd found so far were empty villages, long abandoned. On the ninth day of her search, she came across a village that had only recently been attacked. After an hour or so of searching, she was about to give up when she heard someone moaning in the rubble of a house nearby. On closer inspection she found a woman hiding under what was left of her bed.

The woman told Beth that an enormous troll had come into the village as everyone was sitting down for their evening meal. She had only survived because she'd gone down to the cellar to fetch her husband some ale to drink with his evening meal, when a wall had collapsed trapping her in the cellar, and by the time she'd finally dug herself out the whole village had been destroyed and all the villagers had either been killed or taken by the troll.

Beth didn't have to be a master tracker to see where the troll had gone. He'd left a trail that even a blind man could follow, so after first making sure that the woman would be alright, Beth set off along the trail after the troll. She knew trolls liked to live deep in the forest, where the sun couldn't penetrate.

Moving about, she wondered for the umpteenth time since finding the village destroyed and hearing the woman's story, whether she really needed the reward or if she could live the rest of her life in her damp and draughty cottage. At least she'd be alive, she told herself. 'I can't stay there another hour, I have to kill the troll, that's the only way I'll have any sort of life.' (Reading this you might be thinking, she's mad, how can one young witch kill a bloodthirsty troll, let alone cut its head off and carry it back to the king. To find out read on.) As evening approached Beth knew she'd have to find somewhere to hide, it would be madness to go up against a fully-grown troll at night, when they were at their strongest. Finding a tree with branches that she could get comfortable on, she settled down for the night, knowing she wasn't far from the troll's cave, and also that she would have to kill him in the morning. She found it almost impossible to sleep. Out of the corner of her eye she noticed a light shining through the trees in the distance. It looked as if somebody had stopped for the night and had lit a fire. 'What an idiot!' she thought, 'don't they know there's trolls in this part of the woods? Against her better judgement she climbed down from the tree and went to warn the fools before the trolls found them.

As she approached, the view of the fire was blocked by a wagon. She thought it funny that there was no horse grazing nearby. The reason for this soon became clear. As she came round from behind the wagon she stopped dead in her tracks. There in front of her was the horse being spit roasted over a large fire, and sitting on a fallen tree was a troll. It was nowhere near as large as Beth had imagined, but it still looked big enough to eat Beth and still want afters. All she had thought about was the reward, but now with the troll sitting no more than twenty feet away, she realised that it was going to be a lot harder than she'd thought. She decided to hide under the wagon and wait till dawn, hoping that the sun would rise catching the troll unawares and doing the job for her.

Before long a far bigger troll appeared. 'You'll never grow up to be a big strong troll like me by eating that rubbish,' he shouted, pointing at the horse roasting on the spit, 'it's humans we trolls eat, not bloody horses.' And to prove his point, he held up the sack that was wriggling in his hand. Beth knew at once that it contained the last of the villagers. 'I'm taking these home for my breakfast,' the big troll informed his smaller companion, 'there's enough in here for both of us, if you want.' 'I can't eat humans,' the little troll told him. 'That's why you'll always be a runt,' he said kicking him. 'I'm half human myself,' the little troll explained, 'it would be like eating my mother.' 'Well,' shouted the big troll, 'what's wrong with that? I ate mine, and very tasty she was too.' He went on to explain that it had been one of the coldest winters that any troll could remember, and there had been a plague among the humans, so there was a shortage of food. 'It was either eat my mother or we both starved, so while she was looking for two straws to draw so as to decide who would eat whom, I crept up behind her and hit her over the head with a tree. She was a wonderful mum, lasted me all winter.' 'Well, I don't care,' shouted the little troll, 'I'm not eating human beings, and that's final.'

As the two trolls continued their argument, Beth lay under the wagon. Her task had suddenly been made twice as difficult. One troll was bad enough, but two (well one and a half) was even harder. At that moment the large troll jumped up. Sniffing the air he nudged his companion, 'I can smell a human.' 'Well of course you can, you just brought back a sack full of them. 'No, not them, they're all male. This one's a girl, and she's close by,' he said sniffing the air. 'You search over there and I'll search this way.' Beth was hoping that the troll's sense of smell wasn't that good, and that the sun would rise before they found her. The trouble was, that the large troll had a very keen sense of smell, and found her long before that. 'She's under the wagon,' he shouted to the little troll, 'you go around to the other side and frighten her. Then when she comes out my side I'll grab her.' 'Can't we just leave her?' the runt pleaded. 'You can't still be hungry after all the humans you've scoffed tonight.' 'Do as I say, or I'll eat you instead.' The runt didn't want to harm the girl, but he was terrified of Gorgo, he'd had so many beatings off him in the past, and he didn't really want another, so reluctantly he did as he was told. When he looked under the wagon, he saw a very pretty but frightened young girl looking back at him. He knew at first glance that she was a witch, and that Gorgo would torture her before killing her.

Trolls had always hated witches, none more so than Gorgo. There had been a long running feud between witches and trolls for hundreds of years, and each would kill the other on sight. But the runt knew in his heart that he couldn't let Gorgo catch such a lovely young girl.

'When I roar,' he whispered, 'you scramble as fast as you can between my legs and make a run for the forest. It will soon be morning, and he won't follow you in daylight.' Not knowing why, but Beth trusted the little troll, she smiled at him and nodded her head in agreement. With that smile she stole his heart, and from that moment on it was hers, and he would love her for eternity.

Everything went as planned. As he roared as loud as he could, the young witch crawled between his legs and sprinted for the woods, 'Quick runt,' shouted Gorgo, 'she's getting away.'

The troll was in a terrible rage as he tore off after the girl, he swore all kinds of harm would befall the runt if she got away. As he drew level with the runt he swung an almighty blow at the little troll's head, but the runt was too quick for him, and ducked under Gorgo's blow. As he thundered past the little troll stuck out his foot and tripped Gorgo up. He knew it wouldn't be long before he was back on his feet, and when that happened he'd be one dead half troll.

No one in their right mind got between a troll and his next meal, so if he was going to survive he knew he would have to do something quickly. Reaching into the wagon, that had previously belonged to a blacksmith, he picked up a large, heavy anvil and brought it down on Gorgo's head, with as much force as he could muster. It wouldn't kill him, but he would be unconscious long enough for them to escape.

'Why did you help me escape?' called Beth, who'd been watching from just inside the wood. 'Aren't trolls supposed to kill and eat humans, especially witches? I'm not your everyday, run of the mill troll. My mother was a troll and my father human, the other trolls told me that she'd been exiled from the tribe in shame.' Smiling at him Beth said, 'That may go some way to account for your size and your aversion to eating people. Well, whatever the reason, I'm very grateful for your help, because if not for you I'd have been a troll's breakfast. But before we go any further, my name's Beth, what's yours? The little troll shuffled his feet and looked embarrassed, 'I haven't got a real name, all the trolls just called me runt. As names went it was apt, if not a little rude.'

Beth had heard that trolls were at least ten foot tall, but this one couldn't have been more than five. 'Well,' scolded Beth, 'I'll not be calling anybody who's just saved my life, by that name.' Runt started to get agitated. 'Can we discuss that later? Right now we have to get as far away from here as possible, before Gorgo wakes up.' They set off along a path that would take Beth back to her cottage. 'What were you doing in the woods all by yourself anyway?' he asked. She then explained about the king's reward for the head of the marauding troll, and how she was fed up with being a poor witch who lived in a leaky cottage and never had any money. All of a sudden Beth became aware of the sun shining through the trees. 'It's morning and you're standing out in the sunlight, why haven't you turned to stone?' she enquired. 'I've always thought that it had something to do with me being half human,' he told her. 'I've always been able to go out in the sun, but I had to be careful. The trolls already thought that I was strange. If they'd ever found out that sunlight didn't harm me, my life wouldn't be worth living.'

Beth's brain was starting to work overtime. She thought that if Gorgo had still been unconscious when dawn broke, he would have been turned to stone. If that had indeed been the case, she was in the ideal position to retrieve his head, take it back to the king, and claim the reward. She realised it would be an almost impossible task for her alone, she had no horse, or donkey to carry the troll's head. Now that it was stone it must have weighed more than her, it was then that she realised that she needed runt's help if she was going to succeed. She had stopped walking by now, and was turning over in her head what she was going to do next.

Runt turned to her with a puzzled look on his face and asked her if she was alright. 'Yes,' she answered. 'I was just wondering, do you think Gorgo would have woken up before the sun rose?' 'No, no way, he's granite now,' runt told her. 'Why do you ask?' She gave the little troll one of her most disarming smiles, and said, 'I was hoping that I could talk you into helping me take his head back, so I could claim the king's reward. Please runt, I'd be ever so grateful,' 'I'm sorry, but I just can't keep calling you runt. It's not nice, oh I'm used to that. The trolls have always called me that.' Getting very irate, Beth told him, 'Well I'm not a troll, and my father brought me up to have manners and not to be rude to people, so I'm going to call you Cuthbert, after my favourite uncle.' The little troll liked that, it would make a change from runt. 'So Cuthbert, are you going to help me?' asked Beth. He knew he'd do anything she asked of him, since the moment he'd first set eyes on her, he was her slave.

Cuthbert smiled a knowing smile. 'There's no need to take Gorgo's head back to the king. If it's treasure you want, there's a cave stuffed full of it, not far from this very spot. It belonged to Gorgo, but he no longer has any need of it.' Beth looked puzzled. 'I thought trolls had no use for money.' Cuthbert told her that she was right, trolls had no need for money. 'They just took anything they wanted, but Gorgo had a liking for shiny things, so while out destroying villages, and killing humans, if by chance he came across any shiny objects, he brought them back to his cave.'

Hearing about a cave full of gold made Beth forget about the troll's head and the king's reward. 'Can we go and see it?' she asked. 'And can I really have all the treasure for myself?' 'Well, I have no need for gold,' smiled Cuthbert, 'and there's nobody needs it more than you, Beth.'

So they set off down the track into the forest. 'First we'll have to go back to the clearing, and get the wagon. It's the only thing big enough to hold all the treasure.' 'That's all very well,' Beth told him, 'but the last time I saw the horse that pulled the wagon, it was on a spit being roasted over a fire.' Cuthbert just grinned at Beth, 'What do you need a horse for when you've got me?'

On their arrival back at the clearing, Beth could see that Gorgo had not regained consciousness before dawn, because there next to the wagon was a large troll shaped boulder. 'I'm glad he's dead,' Cuthbert said. 'He made my life unbearable.' After emptying the wagon, Cuthbert placed Beth on the driver's seat, and getting between the shafts, headed for the cave. Even though he was only half the size of a fully grown troll, he could still pull the wagon with ease, eventually arriving at the cave.

Entering the cave Beth found it to be damp and cold, all around were piles of bones. At the back of the cave, she found a hundred or more heads piled up on top of one another, like a monument to Gorgo's appetite. She tried not to think of them as once being alive. Pointing to the pile Cuthbert told Beth, 'He called them his trophies, said he wouldn't happy until he'd filled the whole cave with them.' Beth pulled a face, 'That's disgusting, even for a troll.' Cuthbert disagreed, 'Not one as evil as Gorgo.' Waving for Beth to follow, he set off down a side tunnel. Unable to see where she was going, Beth took out her wand and said, 'ILLUMINATE.' The end of the wand glowed and lit up the tunnel. 'That's better,' she said, 'now we can see where we're going.'

It hadn't worried Cuthbert one bit, being a troll, he could see perfectly well in the dark.

After a while they came to the end of the tunnel. 'There's nothing here,' exclaimed a very disappointed Beth. 'You witches aren't the only ones who can perform magic,' bragged Cuthbert. Out of his pocket he took a green stone. Beth had never seen a stone like it before, and made her mind up, that at a later date she was going to find out just what it was that enabled this troll to do magic.

Holding the stone up to the wall, he shouted 'OPEN.' Almost immediately, the stone began to glow. As the glow grew in intensity, the wall started to shimmer, Beth watched in awe as the wall slowly began to fade to reveal even more of the tunnel. 'Follow me,' called Cuthbert.

'It's not far.' And true to his word, not more than twenty yards later they came to a chamber. Beth pointed her wand into the chamber to get a better look. The sight that met her eyes astounded her; there was gold stacked from floor to ceiling, not only strong boxes full of coins, but gold plates, cups, statues and jewellery. Not everything that glitters is gold, or so the old saying goes, and it was apt in this case, because Gorgo had brought back anything that sparkled, whether or not it was valuable; if he took a liking to it, it went into his collection. The next few days were spent sorting the rubbish from the treasure. Even after discarding all the worthless junk, Beth ended up with a wagon full of gold. Now that it was full, she wondered if Cuthbert would still be able to pull it. 'No problem,' he told her.

So, with Beth back up on the driver's seat, he set off at a pace that the horse would have had trouble keeping up with, they arrived back at Beth's cottage in no time. Cuthbert had dragged the wagon for a whole day without rest. Beth felt guilty, she'd ridden all the way, and even fallen asleep for part of the journey, while poor Cuthbert had done all the work. Helping her down, Cuthbert asked Beth, 'Have you got anywhere to hide all this?' pointing to the treasure. 'Oh dear,' Beth replied, 'I hadn't even thought of that. There isn't anywhere. I haven't even got a cellar.' 'No problem,' he reached into his coat and brought out the green stone that he'd used in the tunnel. 'Come with me,' he said. Leading Beth into the kitchen, he pointed the stone at the floor, and muttering under his breath, as he recited a spell, or that's what Beth thought it was.

The flagstones lifted up into the air and stacked themselves against the far wall. As she watched a hole started to appear, eventually turning into a large cellar, big enough to hold all the gold. Once this was all finished, a flight of stairs appeared leading down into it. Cuthbert put the stone back in his pocket. Beth stood there astounded. 'What on earth is that stone?' she asked. 'I've never seen anything like it.' 'It's very rare, not many of them about, got this one from my mother, the other trolls would have cheerfully killed me to get their hands on it, but I know I can trust you not to tell anyone.'

He had never told another soul about the stone, let alone what it was, but he trusted Beth, so he made up his mind to tell her all about it. 'It's an eye from a lava troll.' 'A WHAT?' Beth had never heard of a lava troll. 'I think you had better put the kettle on as this may take a while.

Beth had to put on two kettles and a saucepan full of water before she had enough for Cuthbert's pail of tea, it had to be a pail, as a cup wasn't anywhere near enough to satisfy Cuthbert's thirst. So with a pail of tea in one hand, and a loaf of bread, cut in half and a whole jar of Beth's homemade jam spread in the middle, in the other, he settled down to tell Beth the story of the stone, and how he'd come to own it.

Millions of years ago when trolls first appeared on earth, they were very different from trolls today. As the name suggests, lava trolls evolved inside volcanoes, they didn't eat humans as trolls do today, mainly because there weren't any humans about then. They lived on granite and other igneous rocks. Lava trolls were placid and intelligent creatures, they live in harmony with their surroundings, unlike trolls in Beth's time. They loved going out in the sunlight, their only enemy was the cold. Coming from the inside of a volcano, they were semi liquid, so if they got too cold they would die, eventually it would be the cold that killed them off. Several million years ago there was an ice age that killed off all the dinosaurs. 'What are dinosaurs?' Beth interrupted. 'That's another story,' Cuthbert told her. 'Now getting back to the lava trolls,' giving her a look that said "no more interruptions", 'as the earth cooled over the following millennia, a few lava trolls managed to survive inside some of the still active volcanoes, but just as the climate changed, so the lava troll evolved into trolls as they are today. Over the following millions of years, the lava trolls that had died began to erode, and every thousand years or so, an eye from one of them is found. For some reason the eyes didn't turn to stone like the rest of the lava troll, and it was discovered that they could be used for magic. My mother told me she'd found this one while fishing in a stream one day. She never did explain to me why she'd given up eating humans, but after she'd fallen in love with my father, I don't think she could bring herself to eat another. Well, as I said, she was fishing, and she'd just caught this huge pike. As she reeled it in, she noticed something sparkling in the water nearby. Forgetting all about the fish, she dropped her rod and went in search of whatever it was that was shining in the water. She'd intended to take it back as a gift, to my father, but on retrieving it, she realised just what it was she'd found. For some reason the eyes of the lava troll had turned to gemstones, just like emeralds or diamonds, but unlike the other gems, the troll's eyes had magical properties. She knew she'd have to hide it, because if the other trolls ever got their hands on it they'd cause havoc amongst the humans.

Hundreds of years later, my mother by now a very old troll, called me to her cave and gave me the eye, under strict orders never to let the other trolls know of its existence, and that's how I came to have the eye,' he said holding up his pail. 'Anymore tea, and maybe another sandwich, please?'

Beth smiled at the little troll, she was becoming very fond of Cuthbert. You could never, even in a good light call him handsome, but he was kind, and Beth could see that he had feelings for her. After another pail of tea (sadly he'd had the last of the bread, so no more sandwiches) Cuthbert set about unloading the wagon and stacking all the treasure in the cellar. When at last the wagon was empty, he showed Beth the spell that replaced the flagstones, hiding the cellar. 'Now only you know, how to get to your gold,' he told Beth. 'What are you going to do now?' she asked Cuthbert. 'Well I hadn't given it a thought. I can't go back to the trolls, even if I wanted to, and if the humans see me they'll kill me on sight.' Beth's heart went out to the little troll, he didn't really fit in anywhere. 'Why don't stay here with me? I've got plenty of room, and I could do with the company.'

So Cuthbert stayed, they lived in the little cottage for the next sixty years. Beth often thought of the treasure sitting underneath their kitchen floor, but they never touched a penny of it. Cuthbert had transformed her cottage, he'd repaired the roof, replaced the windows, and had even installed an inside toilet, something unheard of in those days. Eventually Beth grew old, and her hearing and eyesight were failing her, but Cuthbert still loved her as much as the first time he'd seen her, cowering under the wagon, and when she died of extreme old age, he was devastated. He could no longer live in the cottage where they'd both been so very happy, so opening the cellar for the first time in over sixty years, Cuthbert filled a bag with as much money as it would hold. He set off to see the world. After all he was only a young troll of three hundred years, so he decided it was time for an adventure.

THE INHERITANCE

'There's a letter for you from Weymouth,' my wife called to me as I came in the door, 'it looks official.' 'I'll read it later,' I teased her. We'd earlier had a letter from my uncle Bert's solicitor, to say that I'd been named as a beneficiary in his will, and that he'd write to me later to inform me of the date of the reading, so I could attend. I knew Sadie was getting excited at the prospect of us coming into some money. I could see by the expression on her face that she couldn't wait for me to open the letter, but, I was going to drag this out as long as I could. 'If you don't open that letter, I'll-- I'll hit you over the head with this saucepan,' she threatened me. 'Ok, calm down, darling,' not wanting to find out if she meant it or not, I picked up the letter and read it. 'What does it say?' she demanded. 'It seems that I'm the only beneficiary.' I couldn't believe it, I knew that I was uncle Bert's favourite, but to be left everything shocked me. 'I'll have to see the Major and ask him if I can have a week off, because the reading of the will is in two days, and I have to be there.'

Next morning found Sadie and me ready to set off for Dorset. I'd explained to the Major about the reading of the will and he said it was alright for me to have a week off to sort things out.

Sadie had suggested that we turn it into a second honeymoon, so with that in mind, we asked Donna if she could have the boys with her while we were gone, knowing that when we arrived back, the boys would have been thoroughly spoiled.

On our arrival at Weymouth, we booked into a very nice hotel and relaxed for the rest of the day. After breakfast next morning I set off for the solicitor's office. Sadie had gone off shopping, I knew that by the time I'd received the inheritance, she would have already spent it. At exactly ten o'clock I presented myself at Jenkins, Cartwright and Jones, solicitors. The door would not have been out of place in a Dickens novel, it was large, painted black, with a huge brass knocker in the form of a lion's head. It didn't get any better, when it was opened by a very tall, very thin lady, in a long black dress. She'd look right at home in a black and white horror movie, I thought to myself. I then explained that I'd come for my appointment with Mister Jenkins. I was then finally allowed through the door, and she escorted me down the hallway. 'Stay here,' she ordered me, and disappeared into the office with "Jenkins" in gold letters on the door. 'Mister Jenkins will see you now,' she said on her return.

Now, I'd seen some bizarre sights since I had first met Donna and joined the coven of the talisman, but the sight that met my eyes as I walked into his office, beat them all hands down. Sitting in a leather bound chair, behind a large oak desk, was Mister Jenkins, I've always thought of solicitors as not quite human, but I'd never seen anything as strange as the one sitting in front of me now. I noticed that he was scrutinising me as hard as I was him. 'You're a wizard,' he said with a look of fear on his face. 'No, it's a long story, I do belong to a coven, but I'm not a wizard, but never mind me, what are you?' I asked. 'Before I answer, I want to know if you mean me any harm.' I assured him that I would not harm him in anyway. Hearing this he relaxed, 'I believe you. Now tell me, what it is you see when you look at me.' I looked at him, and saw a small wizened creature, it looked almost human, well part of it did. 'Not that I've ever seen one, but your appearance makes me think of gnomes.' 'GNOMES!' he shouted, going red in the face, 'we are nothing like those vile smelly creatures.' Obviously I'd hit a raw nerve, I apologised hastily, and thankfully he calmed down. 'I'm a Gargoyle,' he admitted. 'But, they are stone figures found on churches,' I blurted out. He smiled at me and continued, 'Gargoyles are a very old race, we have been around for thousands of years.' (It seemed to me that every creature I've met since meeting Donna has had a life span of hundreds of years, and we humans only have our four score and ten). 'One of the reasons we've survived so long is our ability to shape shift, we blend with you humans by taking on your form. Occasionally we've been seen in our natural state, hence all the statues of us, but all we really want to do is live out our lives in peace. Tell me, if you're not a real wizard, how come you can see me as I really am?'

I don't know why, but I trusted this Gargoyle, so I told him about Donna, the talisman and everything that had happened since my first meeting with the old witch. Looking at me puzzled, he asked, I still don't understand how you came see me in my true form, if you're not a wizard.

Showing him the locket, I said, 'Maybe it has something to do with this. I'll just take it off.' With the locket now in my pocket, I saw a man of about sixty sitting behind the desk. 'If you don't mind me asking, why did you think I was going to harm you when we first met?' 'In the past there had been some wizards who thought they could take our shape shifting powers from us. This usually ended with the death of the unlucky Gargoyle, so you can understand my nervousness.'

I promised him that I would not tell another living soul about what he was. He thanked me and said, 'Now for the real reason you've come, the will.'

Over the next hour he informed me of everything that I had inherited from Uncle Bert. 'The last item in the will is the house. It's a very large house overlooking the quay. In today's market it would be worth over a quarter of a million, but,' he added, 'here is where your problems start. You see, Uncle Bert had a lodger, and according to the will, he can live there rent free, for as long as he likes.' This came as a shock, because Sadie, the boys and I had stayed at Uncle Bert's quite a few times over the years, and there had never been any mention of a lodger.

I had hoped to put the house on the market, as soon as we'd cleared everything out of it, but this sitting tenant could be a problem.

'What am I going to do?' I asked Mister Jenkins. 'I was hoping to sell the house and get back to Norfolk as soon as possible. He pondered for a few moments, before he replied, 'As I told you earlier, your uncle left you seventy thousand pounds in his will. Why not offer this sitting tenant some money to move out? If he is in agreement, get him to sign this paper waiving all rights to the property.' With the paper in my hand, I said goodbye to the solicitor and took my leave.

Arriving back at the hotel I found Sadie in our room. Apparently she couldn't concentrate on shopping, (now there's a first) so she came back to await my return. 'WELL, what did Uncle Bert leave you in his will. Are we rich?' The barrage of questions went on for another five minutes, before she ran out of breath. When I could finally get a word in edgeways, I told her all about my visit to Mr Jenkins, and about everything I'd been left. (I never mentioned a thing about him being a Gargoyle). Sadie looked worried, 'This sitting tenant might be a problem. I think maybe the solicitor's right, we should offer this person some money to leave. I'll go and see this Cuthbert T Roll this afternoon,' I told her. Sadie looked at me with a puzzled expression, 'That's a funny name, are you sure it's right?' 'Yes love, it's written here,' showing her my copy of the will. 'Mr Cuthbert T Roll', Sadie grinned, 'it looks more like troll to me,' (as they say, there's many a true word spoken in jest). I smiled back at Sadie. 'Whoever or whatever he is, we have to persuade him to move,' I told her putting on my coat. 'I'll go and see him now.'

I left the hotel and walked along the promenade, until I found the side street that led to Uncle Bert's house. As a child I had enjoyed our family holidays in Weymouth. You could wade out at least a hundred yards from the beach, without the water rising above your waist. There is an old fort up on the Nove where we would play for hours, imagining we were soldiers fighting off the invasion of Weymouth by hordes of pirates.

But the best place of all was Uncle Bert's house. To a young boy it was a magical place, with rooms full of treasure, that he told me he'd brought back from one or other of his voyages to many a far off place. As I got older I came to realise that he was in fact a collector of all things to do with the sea, but he was also a brilliant story teller, he had never been on voyages to far off places, but as he told his stories, he could make you believe that he'd fought pirates and battled sea monsters. All the treasure he had in his house, he'd actually bought off sailors whom he'd met on the docks, but they helped him convince us kids that he'd done all the things he told us about.

It felt strange standing at Uncle Bert's door, knowing that I would not be seeing his smiling face when it opened, so putting my childhood memories behind me, I knocked on the door. It opened to reveal a plump, but cheerful looking old man, (to describe him as plump would be an understatement) he was no more than five feet high, but at least five feet wide. 'You're late,' he said, looking me up and down, 'you're not the usual bloke, what's happened to Mike? Come to that, where are my pizzas?' he quizzed me. 'I think you've got the wrong person,' I told him. 'I'm Bert's nephew, I've come to talk about the will.' Just as I'd finished talking, a pizza delivery moped pulled up. 'Sorry I'm late, Cuthbert,' the lad shouted as he dismounted, 'had a big order come in and we're shorthanded today. To make it up to you, I'll knock off the delivery charge.' After paying the lad for the pizzas, Cuthbert invited me in. 'You don't mind if I eat my lunch? Only I hate cold pizza.' 'If you've got company, I can come back later,' I offered. 'What makes you think I've got company?' he replied. 'Well, it's the fact that you've just taken delivery of four fifteen-inch pizzas.' 'Oh that's just my lunch.' Watching Cuthbert eat pizza was an education. I didn't look at my watch, but it couldn't have been more than five minutes later, when he let out a huge belch. 'I love pizza,' he beamed with a look of pure ecstasy on his face. 'I'll make us a cup of tea,' he called back as he disappeared into the kitchen. A few minutes later he came back with a mug of tea for me, and what looked like a pail with a handle riveted on the side for him.

'Have you been to see Mr Jenkins yet?' he enquired. 'Yes, I went this morning, for the reading of the will.' 'I like Jenkins, I've always got on with Gargoyles,' Cuthbert admitted, 'and as Gargoyles go he's one of the best.' I was flabbergasted. 'How come you know about him?' I asked.

'I've been friends with Jenkins for at least a hundred years, knew his mother and father before him, as a matter of fact they're both up on the roof of a church on Portland.'

Here we go again, I thought. Someone else who's been around for hundreds of years. I suddenly realised that I hadn't put the locket back on since leaving the solicitors' office. Now I could feel it pulsating in my pocket, like a mobile phone. Ignoring Cuthbert for a moment, I took it out of my pocket and hung it back around my neck. I looked at him again, expecting to see a different form in front of me, but no, he looked the same as he had before I'd put it on. 'Were you wearing that when you met Jenkins?' he asked. 'Yes,' I admitted. 'Bet that was a shock, seeing him in his true form. Not many of you wizards ever get to see a live Gargoyle, they try their hardest to keep out of your way. Had a lot of trouble with your kind in the past.' 'Hang on a minute,' I complained. 'Everybody I've met today is under the impression that I'm a wizard.' 'Well, it could have something to do with the fact that you're wearing that,' he said pointing to the locket, 'it's obviously a very powerful magical talisman, and something like that would only be worn by a wizard.' 'In this case, it's being worn by an ordinary human being who's been made an honorary wizard,' I informed him, and for the second time that day, I found myself telling a complete stranger all about how I'd come to join the coven of the talisman,(I hate that name), and its fight with Bella and her coven.

Cuthbert relaxed, 'I understand now. There was talk a year ago about a new evil that had just surfaced, but we could never find out any more about it. Then all went quiet.'

I told him that it was Bella and her coven that had killed Uncle Bert and kidnapped my wife and sons. 'Bert told me that Sadie and the boys were coming down for a visit, so as I always did when he had company, I went to stay with a wizard friend of mine over on Portland.' 'Now you know all about me, what's your story? I get a feeling from the locket that you're not entirely human.'

After making me a another mug of tea and himself another pail full, he settled down to tell me all about Gorgo and the trolls, and how he'd come to meet a young witch named Beth, and after Beth's death, he'd travelled to so many places, met so many strange creatures and interesting people that it would fill a book, (maybe one day I'll write a book entirely about Cuthbert, but I digress). He finally finished with him meeting Uncle Bert and coming to live in Weymouth.

'So, my wife was right, you are a troll. What a day! First I meet a Gargoyle and now I'm drinking tea with a troll.' 'I'm only half troll,' he corrected me. 'Sorry half troll, still it's turned out to be one hell of a day,' I confessed. 'But now to the real reason I'm here, I went on to tell about my uncle's will and the clause that affected him.' 'Yes I know, Bert told me.' 'Is this going to be a problem for you?' he asked. 'Well, we were hoping to put the house on the market and head back to Norfolk.'

I then made him an offer of some money to help him find somewhere else to live. 'I don't need the money,' he said, 'it's just that I've been very happy living here with Bert, but now he's gone the house seems so empty.' 'I'd move out tomorrow, if I had somewhere to go.' 'Why not come back to Norfolk with us? I'm sure we could find you somewhere nice to live. You'll make lots of friends, and I'm sure my boys would love to meet you. So how about it?' I don't know if it was that I felt sorry for him, or if the talisman had something to do with it, because I could feel the locket vibrating, and that usually meant that it had something planned. Making up his mind, Cuthbert said, 'Yes, I'll come and live in Norfolk.'

The next two days were taken up clearing out the house, sending all the items we weren't going to keep off to auction, and loading everything we were keeping into a van we'd hired. Having someone who had the strength of a troll to carry all the heavy furniture on his own was a great help, and speeded up the move no end. Right from the start, Sadie and Cuthbert got on like a house on fire. 'He's so cute,' Sadie gushed. He was just like a little puppy following her everywhere. If Sadie adored him, I knew that Brandon and Jordon were going to love having a troll to play with.

Cuthbert was sad to leave Weymouth, but his local pizza shop was devastated; they'd lose half of their business with Cuthbert gone.

With Sadie driving our car and me in the hire van, we set off early the next morning. Cuthbert went with Sadie in the car, along with four of the biggest flasks we could find, full of tea, and also four fifteen-inch pizzas, just in case he got peckish.

CUTHBERT MEETS THE COVEN

'He can stay with me,' offered Donna, 'until he finds a place of his own.' We were sitting in Donna's kitchen. Having introduced Cuthbert to the coven, we had just arrived back, and were greeted with the news that Mistress Web had died peacefully in her sleep. I liked Mistress Web, shelive life to the full and didn't take crap from anyone. 'We have all met here today, to find someone to join the coven in place of Mistress Web,' Donna informed me. 'We now have a locket with no keeper, and that makes us vulnerable, so we have to find someone quickly.' 'What about Cuthbert? He'd be just the person,' I said. 'Sorry David, but we already have one member of the coven who's not of the magical persuasion, we can't afford another.' 'Well in that case Cuthbert's ideal,' I told her, 'because he's half troll.'

Total panic gripped the room. All of a sudden it was full of witches with their wands out, and all of them pointing at Cuthbert. 'Calm down, ladies,' I begged, 'he's not going to hurt you.' 'What do you mean bringing a troll here?' Betty demanded. 'Yes, trolls are nasty vicious creatures, and they eat humans,' Anne screamed. Cuthbert smiled and the tension evaporated, 'What David said was right, I'm only half troll, and I've never eaten a human in my life, and even if I was so inclined, how could I bring myself to eat such lovely ladies as yourselves? (The initials B. S come to mind). Stepping in between Cuthbert and the witches, Sadie tried to shield him from the wands still pointing at him, 'Don't harm him,' she pleaded, 'he's the kindest and gentlest person I've ever met.' I was happy to see the witches lowering their wands.

'Now, Donna, why don't you put the kettle on, and Cuthbert will tell you all about how he came to be a vegetarian? Then you can make your minds up to whether or not you want him to join the coven.'

Cuthbert had insisted on bringing his pail, so we'd stopped off at a supermarket on the way home and bought a thousand teabags, and twelve litres of milk. After hearing his story, the coven looked ashamed and embarrassed. Donna took it upon herself to apologise for the coven's behaviour early. 'I'm ever so sorry, we heard the word "troll" and just panicked, but as I told David earlier, we need someone who can perform magic.' 'Oh, you mean like this?' Holding his hand over the table, he looked at me and winked. 'RISE,' he commanded, all of a sudden, the table started to rise up off the floor. 'I never knew trolls could perform magic,' Donna admitted. 'They can if they've got one of these,' Cuthbert answered, showing her the eye. The whole coven, and that includes myself, wanted to know what it was and how he'd come by it.

So, after Donna had made him another pail of tea, and this time even found him a large sponge cake, he settled down to tell us his story.

None of us were aware of the figure lurking outside, listening to everything we'd been discussing.

Albert Stone had been spying on the goings on at the cottage, ever since he'd found out that the wood was accessible. Like the rest of us lads, he'd grown up never being able to gain entry. But one day while out, he'd stumbled across the lane leading into the wood. Thinking that it would be an ideal place for a spot of poaching, he decided he'd have a look around. Imagine his surprise when he found out that he wasn't the only person in there. There was an old cottage, with an old lady living in it, so without our knowledge he'd been spying on us ever since. At first he thought we were all loonies, but over the following months Albert had witnessed a lot of things that he just couldn't understand. He now realised that instead of a bunch of loonies, we were indeed a coven of witches and wizards, and that magic did exist, and it could be very powerful, 'and now there's a troll,' he mumbled to himself as he set off home.

Brandon and Jordon had a new friend. Sadie had taken Cuthbert home to meet the boys, while Donna and the others were making their minds up about whether to allow him to join the coven. Before leaving I'd cast my vote in his favour, and had high hopes that they'd allow him to join. Cuthbert was great with the boys. After a few minutes I knew they'd be friends for life. 'Are you really half troll?', asked Jordon. 'Have you ever eaten anyone?' butted in Brandon. 'Don't ask such personal questions,' scolded Sadie. Cuthbert smiled, 'It's alright, how are they ever going to learn if they don't ask questions?' I could see that it was going to be hard work stopping them from telling all their mates about their new friend the troll, who'd just move into the village. But I was happy they'd taken to him, not that I had to worry, because with his ever-present smile and his happy disposition, who wouldn't?

At that moment my phone rang. It was Betty, summoning us back to the cottage. With us now all seated in Donna's lounge she informed us that they had come to a decision regarding Cuthbert. The boys had insisted on accompanying us back to auntie Donnas. Before Betty could say another word, Brandon piped up, 'We want Cuthbert to join.' 'Yeah, he's our friend,' Jordon added. 'The boys knew that their auntie Donna couldn't refuse them anything. 'There's no need to get yourselves upset,' Donna told the boys, 'we've all voted to admit him into the coven. That's if he wants to join.' Turning to him she asked, 'It's up to you, would you like to become a member of the coven of the talisman?' Cuthbert grinned, 'Yes, I'd love to, but there's a couple of problems I want to sort out first, the first being I have to find somewhere to live.' 'I know you said I could live here Donna, but there's something about this cottage. I've not figured it out yet, but I have this feeling I wouldn't be happy here.' Almost in unison, the boys shouted, 'You can live with us.' 'Yes,' agreed Sadie, 'we've got a spare room.' Realising that if I said no, I'd appear the baddie, I gave in and went along with my family's wishes. 'Well, that's one sorted, what's the other problem?' He looked at us rather sheepishly, 'Is there a pizza shop nearby that delivers?' Sadie laughed, 'No but we have a large chest freezer that we can fill with frozen pizzas.' 'Well, in that case, I accept.'

Donna turned the handing over of the locket to Cuthbert, into a full scale ceremony. I would have been very embarrassed, if it had been me, but Cuthbert loved all the attention. He'd spent most of his life living on his own, or with no more than one other person, and now here he was with a room full of people, who didn't see him as a troll to be feared.

With Sadie leading the way, the boys either side of Cuthbert, and me bringing up the rear, we headed back home. I was just realising, that having him live with us was going to cost me a fortune. How on earth were we going to afford to keep him in pizzas and teabags? We'd only been back at the house for five minutes, when we heard a loud noise from upstairs.

'Dad, dad, come quick,' Jordon shouted from the top of the stairs.

The boys had taken Cuthbert up to see his bedroom. On entering the room I found Cuthbert lying in the wreckage of his bed. 'What happened here?' I asked. 'He wasn't jumping on it,' Brandon blurted out. (In the past I'd had to tell the boys off for jumping on their beds). 'I didn't think he had,' I replied. 'The bed I had at Bert's was reinforced, after it collapsed a couple of times,'

Cuthbert admitted. On inspection, I found the bed broken beyond repair. 'I'm afraid you'll have to sleep on the mattress tonight, then we can go into Norwich and get you a new one tomorrow.'

SHOPPING

'A wise choice sir, it's from our exclusive range.' I could see the prospect of a large commission coming his way, by the gleam in the salesman's eyes. 'How much?' I asked fearfully. Giving me a look of sheer contempt, he replied, 'When one's talking about the solid oak Chippendale suite, the last thing one mentions is money.' We had been in this rather posh furniture store in Norwich for about an hour, trying to find Cuthbert a new bed. We'd tried all the usual superstores, with no luck. At the last place the assistant nearly had a heart attack when Cuthbert sat on his sturdiest bed and it creaked ominously. 'I think sir would do better to try this shop,' handing us a card with an address of another shop written on it, 'they cater for people with special needs,' he said looking at Cuthbert. So that's how we came to be in this overpriced, up market emporium.

'Yes and when one's expected to pay for said suite, it's the first thing one asks,' I told him. He could see his commission disappearing before his very eyes, so he decided to try a different approach. 'What sir has to realise is, the craftsmanship that goes into this piece of boudoir furniture is second to none, and not only that, the oak it's made of comes from renewable sources.' 'As I said earlier, how much is it?' I insisted. Finally giving up any hope on the elusive commission he informed us that it was 'Only, two thousand pounds.' Before my brain could come up with an answer that I could put in print, Cuthbert told the sales assistant, 'I'll take it.' The gleam was back in his eyes. 'I'll just go and fill out the paperwork.' With the pushy salesman out of the way, I explained to Cuthbert that we didn't have that sort of money. 'If I was to max out my credit cards, I'd still be a hundred or so short.' 'I don't expect you to pay, you and your family have been so kind, but I'm in a position to pay my own way.' To emphasise this, he pulled out a wallet. Like everything else about Cuthbert it was oversized, it had more in common with a suitcase than a wallet. Opening it he showed me the contents, 'Do you think there will be enough here?' there looked at least ten times more money than what he needed. 'Oh yes, Cuthbert, I think there's more than enough there.'

The salesman returned with the paperwork and a date when the bed would be delivered, 'There's a six week wait on this bed, it's a very popular model.' Cuthbert was having none of it, as far as he was concerned, he had bought the bed in the store, and he was going to take it home. Explaining that it was only for display had no effect on Cuthbert. It was his bed and he was going to take it home. Finally the owner was summoned, he told Cuthbert the same as the salesman, and Cuthbert told him that he was taking the bed home one way or another. Before things got out of hand, I decided to intervene. 'Gentlemen please, I'm sure we can come to a mutually beneficial agreement. Cuthbert, show them your wallet.' All argument stopped after seeing inside the wallet, and finally it was agreed that Cuthbert would pay two thousand pounds for the bed, and another five hundred for immediate delivery. 'I enjoyed that, let's go shopping.'

Over the next three hours, we shopped, I say 'we', all I did was carry Cuthbert's bags. He bought the boys a games console, Sadie an expensive pair of earrings, and me a new laptop. I told him he didn't have to buy us anything, but he said that he was just showing his gratitude for all we'd done for him.

While we shopped, I brought up the topic of the money and where it had come from. I learned all about Gorgo, and Beth, and how they'd taken the treasure and stored it under her cottage, how after Beth's death, he'd taken some of the gold and gone off on an adventure. 'It wasn't until I met Bert that I had any need for the gold, in the past I'd worked for my keep. Over the years I've done everything, from working on a farm to being a bodyguard for a king, but Bert persuaded me to turn the gold into money and open a bank account. That's where Mr Jenkins came in handy, He has a friend who's an antique dealer, and another who's a banker. Between them they sold off all my gold coins and deposited the money in an account they'd opened in my name, after first deducting their commission, that is.'

It took a weight off of my mind knowing that Cuthbert had his own money, his pizza bill for one week came to almost half my wages. 'What about you?' I asked 'Isn't there anything you need?' 'I could do with some new clothes.' Looking at Cuthbert I had to agree, he was wearing his usual brown corduroy trousers, check shirt and a green jumper that had seen better days. It had more holes than a golf course. Thinking back, I couldn't ever remember him wearing anything else.

We then visited every gentlemen's outfitter, large clothing outlet and supermarket in Norwich. Cuthbert tried on all styles, from plus fours and tweed jackets, to casual wear, and everything in between. Although he looked smart in a lot of the clothes he tried on, he didn't like any of them. 'I'm hungry, let's get something to eat,' Cuthbert suggested as we came out of the last clothes shop in Norwich. I took him to the market across the road from city hall. Having only seen him eat pizza, I asked him if he'd ever eaten fish and chips, 'I don't eat anything living, but I'd love some chips.' Some chips? Eight portions later, Cuthbert was back to his old self, giving up on finding any clothes that he liked.

We set off through the stalls to where we'd parked the car 'I like them.' Turning round I saw Cuthbert pointing to a stall that sold the gaudiest clothes I'd ever seen. By the time I'd got there, he already chosen three pair of Bermuda shorts and several Hawaiian shirts, the colours so bright, that they could damage your eyesight if you looked directly at them. 'Don't you think they're the most dashing clothes you've ever seen?' he asked proudly. 'Well, I can honestly say that I've never seen anything like them.' With Cuthbert looking very pleased with his purchases, we set off back to Thompson.

'Why on earth didn't you stop him?' Cuthbert had proudly shown Sadie the fruits of our shopping trip, and had gone to hang them in his wardrobe. 'You said he'd looked very dashing in them,' I countered. 'Well I didn't want to hurt his feelings,' Sadie returned. 'They are a bit bright,' I mused. 'Bright! I had to put my sunglasses on just to look at them. I knew it was a big mistake letting you go with him.' My wife's humour improved when Cuthbert gave her the earrings he'd bought for her. 'They're gorgeous,' she said, giving him a kiss on the cheek. If possible, I think he blushed even brighter than his shirt. 'I—I'm glad you like them,' he stammered. The boys loved Cuthbert's new clothes nearly as much as their games console. 'Can we have a shirt like Cuthbert's?' asked Brandon. 'No I want a pair of shorts,' Jordon demanded. 'We'll see,' Sadie told them. "We'll see" usually meant "over my dead body", but it would be enough to keep the boys quiet for a while.

FROM BAD TO WORSE

'You look worried darling, is anything wrong?' Sadie had seen my face as I walked back into the room after answering the phone. 'That was Donna, she wants you me and Cuthbert to go down to her cottage at once.' 'What about the boys?' she asked. 'Donna asked if we could leave them at home. She said she had something important to talk to us about, and that it doesn't concern the boys.' So, we left them playing on their new games console, with a bedroom full of their friends, knowing they'd be alright for hours, and went to Donna's.

I couldn't help but worry. Donna's voice on the phone sounded frightened. What I had no way of knowing was that Donna had answered the door an hour earlier, to find Albert Stone standing there with his shotgun pointing at her. 'Inside, and don't try anything,' he threatened her. 'You're Albert, aren't you? Why are you pointing that thing at me?' 'I know what you are, I've been watching you lot for months.'

Albert Stone reached over and tipped the fruit out of the bowl that stood on the table. 'Now take off the locket and put it in here,' he ordered, 'and also your wand. Don't try anything or this gun might go off. Now,' pointing to the phone that Betty had, had installed, along with the electricity to make Donna's life in the cottage more tolerable, 'I want you to phone all those who are in your coven, and get them to come here as quickly as they can, and don't try and warn them. I'll be listening.'

The closer we got to Donna's cottage, the more certain I was, that something was not right. Sadie and Cuthbert had the same feeling.

Just as we arrived, Betty pulled up in her car. She'd also gotten a call from Donna, as had Annie, who was in the passenger seat.

'Donna asked me to round up as many of the coven as possible, but I'm afraid that Annie was the only one I could find at short notice.' Betty and Annie admitted that they too had a feeling that there was something wrong.

'I think we'd better go in, but keep your eyes open for trouble.' The others followed me up the path and into the cottage.

On entering the lounge we found Donna sitting in her chair looking worried, and on the other side of the room stood Albert Stone with his shotgun pointing at us. 'What the hell's going on Albert?' I asked. 'Why are you here? 'Shut up,' he barked back, 'do as I say and we will all come out of this in one piece.' Turning to Betty he demanded, 'Where are the rest of the coven? 'This is all I could get at short notice,' she answered. 'Where are your children?' looking at Sadie and me for an answer. 'They are at home playing with their friends,' I told him. Pointing his gun at Sadie, he ordered, 'Go and get them.' 'No. I'll not bring our children anywhere where there's guns.' Looking at her face he knew there was no way she'd get the boys. 'Ok, you don't have to bring them, just their lockets. Now go,' he shouted. Sadie looked at me for advice, I nodded 'Do as he says.' Sadie left to get the lockets, having been warned not to try and get help. 'Right, while we wait for her to return, I want all of you to take off your lockets and put them in this bowl, along with your wands.' 'I don't have a wand,' Cuthbert told him as he dropped his locket into the bowl. 'No, but you do have a magic stone, put that in as well.'

'Are you trying to trick me? These are not your kids' lockets, they're just something you got out of a junk shop.' Albert Stone had gotten very upset at seeing the boys' lockets, they would change the appearance of them nearly every day. Brandon's was in the form of a web, as his favourite film at the moment was Spiderman, and Jordon had gone back to sponge bob square pants, who he said reminded him of his brother. 'They are the real thing,' Donna told him, 'if you let me have my wand back for a minute, I'll show you.' 'Ok, but no tricks.' Donna waved her wand over them and they turned back to their original shape. 'There, putting her wand back in the bowl, 'back to normal. Now what do you want from us?' 'I've been reading all about witches, wizards and all things magic. One book in particular, said that with enough power, it would even be possible to bring back the dead.'

'You think we can bring your family back, don't you?' Sadie asked. 'Yes, I can't live without them, so you're going to bring them back for me.' 'We're not powerful enough to bring back the dead, even if we wanted to, we're only country witches,' Betty tried to reason with him. 'I know you're not, but he is,' pointing to Cuthbert. 'What makes you think that I'm any more powerful than them?' Albert smiled, but there was no humour in it, 'I've seen what you can do with that stone of yours, and I'm thinking that if you use that together with the lockets, they will magnify its power enough to bring back my family.' Cuthbert sighed, 'I know how you feel, I'd give anything to have my Beth back, but it's just not possible.' 'Well you'd better hope for David's sake that it is.' He turned to me with sadness in his eyes, 'I'm sorry David, there's just no other way.' I knew what he was going to do, but I was powerless to stop him. 'NO,' cried Sadie, she had also realised his intention.

It was as if someone had pushed me very hard in the chest, the pellets had reached me before the sound of the shot. It was as if time had slowed down. I was lifted off my feet, and thrown across the room. Almost at once Sadie was at my side, with my head on her lap. I knew she was talking to me, but I could hear nothing. It felt strange, but I had no fear of dying, just extreme sadness at not being there to see my boys grow up. All I could see now was Sadie's face, the rest of the room was in darkness, but as I tried to hang on to life, even that started to fade, until finally only black.

'You've killed him, cried Sadie. 'Yes, I'm sorry, but it was the only way to make him help me.'

Albert Stone had tears in his eyes as he looked at Cuthbert, 'he's your friend, 'take the stone and the lockets, and bring him back to life.' Cuthbert scooped everything from the bowl and knelt beside Sadie, 'I don't know if I can do this,' he told Sadie. He could see the grief in her eyes as she looked at him. 'Please try,' she begged.

(I'll let Sadie take over telling the story for a while, on account of me being dead at the time). Cuthbert lifted David's lifeless body up onto the table, and with the lockets in one hand and the eye in the other he held them over the gaping hole in David's chest, a blinding white light enveloped both of them, and seemed to go on for hours, but was probably only a few minutes. All the while I was praying it would work, then all of a sudden the light faded, and when I looked there was no gaping hole in David's chest and no sign of blood. 'He's sleeping.' Cuthbert looked completely drained, it had taken a lot out of him. 'Will he be alright?' I asked. 'Yes, he's sleeping now, he has to get his strength back, but he'll be his old self in no time.'

'I knew you could do it, now bring my family back,' Albert Stone demanded.

Cuthbert sighed, 'It was only possible to bring David back because his soul hadn't left his body. Your wife and children have been gone too long, they've moved on. 'You're lying,' screamed Albert, 'how many more do I have to shoot before you do as I ask.'

I had heard stories of people who'd had near death experiences, they all mentioned a bright white light, (it's me again) and how you had to go toward it. The only trouble was that instead of being in the distance, it was totally enveloping me, and I could hear Sadie's voice asking 'if I'd be alright, and Cuthbert answering 'yes,' then I must have passed out. When I eventually woke, everybody seemed to have forgotten about me and were concentrating on Albert Stone. 'What's going on?' I asked. I then went from being totally ignored, to the centre of attention in two seconds. Sadie flung her arms around me, and cried into my neck, 'I thought I'd lost you.' 'What happened?' I asked, still a bit groggy. I'd never known my wife to dislike anyone, but she had a look of hatred on her face as she pointed to Albert Stone, 'He killed you,' she accused. 'If it hadn't had been for Cuthbert, you'd still be dead. You were lucky David, your soul had not had time to move on.'

'Another few minutes and I would not have been able to bring you back,' Cuthbert looked completely drained, it had obviously taken a lot out of him.

Wanting answers, I turned to Albert Stone, 'Why did you shoot me?' For a moment I could see deep sorrow in his eyes. 'I'm sorry, but I had to prove it could be done. I miss my family so much, and I want them back.'

Then, suddenly his face changed, the look of grief was replaced with a look of pure evil, it was as if a different person was standing there. Pointing his gun at Cuthbert, he ordered 'You're coming with me, and if you try anything, I'll kill the old crones.' Turning to the witches he warned them not to try and rescue Cuthbert. 'The world would be a better place with a few less witches and one less troll,' he snarled as he left.

I sent Sadie home to fetch me another shirt, it gave me the willies wearing one with a big hole in the middle and covered in my blood. The witches and I sat around Donna's kitchen table talking over what had just happened, and how we were going to rescue Cuthbert. 'Couldn't we convene the coven?' I asked. 'No that would take too long,' Donna replied, 'now we have two wizards in the coven, things take twice as long to get done. They have to report back to the wizards' council before making any decisions. 'No we're on our own.' Donna noticed that Betty seemed deep in thought. 'What's the matter, Betty love?' Shaking her head, Betty replied, 'I've known Albert for twenty years, and he's always been the nicest and the most gentle person, I've ever met. That wasn't Albert Stone, there's no way he'd ever shoot another human being.' 'I think you're right. Did anyone else notice the look of sadness in his eyes when I first spoke to him?' I asked the others. 'Yes, I did, now you mention it,' Anne recalled. 'Then his face seemed to cloud over, as if there were another person who'd taken over.'

Donna sat back in her chair, and sighed, 'And I know who. It's Bella.' 'It can't be Bella, we all saw her change into a pheasant, and then get shot, didn't we?' I said looking around at the others for conformation.

BELLA'S BACK

Albert Stone had taken Cuthbert back to his cottage, and tied him to a chair. 'Who are you?' Cuthbert asked. 'My name's Albert Stone.' 'No, not you, I'm talking to the one sharing your body with you, the one who's making you do all this, as at Donna's?' Albert's face changed from sad and deeply unhappy, to cruel and nasty, 'You're very clever for a troll.' 'Half troll,' Cuthbert corrected him. 'Yeah well, if you don't do exactly as I say, you'll be a dead troll.' 'As much as I love sitting here being threatened by you, don't you think things might go a bit easier if you told me what it is you want.' 'What I want,' snarled Albert, 'is a body for my Consciousness. I had to take over this one when mine was destroyed, but I'm sick to death of his constant whining about how he misses his family, so, you're going to get me a body of my own.'

Suddenly it came to Cuthbert, 'You're what's left of Bella, aren't you?' 'I've heard about you.' 'Nothing good, I hope. I thought I'd escaped. I'd stolen two of the lockets, and they had made me powerful enough to perform spells that I'd never been able to do before. I'd changed into a bird and was making good my escape, when somebody shot me. Luckily there were other birds flying close by.That enabled me to transfer my life force to one of them, and get away. But then there I was, stuck in a dumb bird. Then this fool shot the bird and ate it, so finally I was again inside a human body. Not that that was much better, I couldn't do magic. I made this body go and look for my wand. I'd dropped it when I turned into a bird, and it was still there. But even with a wand, it was no good. This body has absolutely no magic in it. What I need is a witch's body, and you're going to help me get one.'

Cuthbert knew he could not help Bella, she was bad enough before, but this time she'd have not only seven lockets, but the eye of a lava troll as well. ('No,' he thought, 'there's no way I'm letting that happen.') 'If you think I'm going to kill somebody, so you can have their body, you're sorely mistaken.'

'I've never known a troll as squeamish as you.' 'Half troll,' he told her. 'OK, but you needn't worry your, little "half troll" head about it. The witch I have in mind has only just died. All I need is for you to go and fetch me her body.

Her soul has had time to move on, leaving me with an empty vessel to inhabit.' Cuthbert looked horrified. 'You want me to go and dig Mistress Web's body up and bring it here, so you can take it over?' 'Yes,' she/he smiled. It was strange for Cuthbert, he was looking at a man and talking to a woman. 'Then when I'm back in a witch's body, and have seven lockets and your stone to boost my power, I'll be invincible, nobody will be able to stop me getting the talisman, and becoming the most powerful witch ever. Now go and bring me the old hag's body or I'll start killing your friends.'

CUTHBERT'S PLAN

Donna was working herself into a frenzy. 'There's no way we're going to desecrate a witch's grave, especially Mistress Web's, and especially not for that evil sister of mine,' she said, glaring around, daring one of us to disagree. Betty put her arms around the old witch. 'Nobody's suggesting that we give her what she wants, but we have to find a way to get her out of Albert Stone. If we go charging in there, she's just as likely to kill him out of spite. No, what we need to do is find a way to make her leave Albert voluntarily.' 'That's all very well, Betty, but you know as well as I do that the only reason she'll leave Albert is if we give her Mistress Web's dead body,' I added.

'Well in that case we'll give her just what she wants.' Everyone in the room was totally astounded by Cuthbert's remarks. Donna glared at him. 'If you think you're going to dig up a witch and give her body over to that evil sister of mine, you'll have to do it over my dead body.' Cuthbert smiled at the old witch. 'It's alright Donna, no one's going to be digging anyone up. I have an idea how we can resolve this.' Turning to Betty he asked if he could borrow her mobile phone, then he excused himself and went out into the garden.

Ten minutes later he returned, looking pleased with himself, 'It's all sorted, there'll be a coffin delivered here within the hour.'

Betty looked as confused as the rest of us, when she asked, 'What good's a coffin without a corpse?' 'You'll see,' was all Cuthbert would say. Drawing him to one side, I asked him whom he'd phoned. 'I thought my old friend Mr Jenkins might be able to help, and sure enough, he put me in touch with a friend of his in Norwich, who's agreed to do all he can to help us stop Bella.' It then came to me who, or what this person was. 'When you say friend, don't you mean Gargoyle?' 'Well let's just say that Mr Jones is not your run of the mill undertaker.'

True to his word, Mr Jones arrived in his hearse, complete with coffin that looked as if it had just been dug up. On being introduced to him I came to the conclusion that Gargoyles had absolutely no imagination. If you remember my description of the solicitor from Weymouth, Mr Jenkins, then I have to tell you that Mr Jones could have been his twin - the same black suit, the same drawn features, the same look, of being one step away from a corpse.

Now that Cuthbert had everything he needed for his plan, we all sat around the table with a cup of tea, while he filled us in.

TRICKED

'It's about time, I was beginning to think that I would have to kill an old crone or two to get you to do what I wanted.' Bella snarled at Cuthbert as he entered Albert Stone's cottage, 'Have you got the body?' she enquired 'Yes, it's back at your sister's place.' 'Why didn't you bring it?' she demanded. 'Well, there are one or two things we need to sort out first, like what's going to happen to me after I transfer your consciousness into the witch's body. I imagine that you will kill all of the coven of the talisman, and take their lockets. Will you also kill me for the eye of the lava troll? If that's the case, you can find someone else to help you.' Bella could tell by the look on Cuthbert's face that he meant it. 'If you keep out of my fight with the coven, I'll not harm you, and you can keep your magic eye. After I've gotten all of the lockets and the talisman, nobody will be strong enough to defeat me,' she boasted. 'Ok, so you won't kill me and I can keep my magic eye, but somehow it doesn't seem enough for all my trouble.' Bella stared at the half troll trying to fathom him out. 'I heard you had been made a member of their precious coven. Aren't you on their side?' Cuthbert's smile changed to a sneer. 'I needed somewhere new to live, so I thought that I'd stay here until something better came along, and I've got a feeling that you're it, so here's my proposal. I'll help you defeat the witches and get the lockets, if you let me join your coven.'

Albert Stone's face took on the look of pure evil, but even though the face was Albert's the look was all Bella. 'So it seems we're seeing your troll half at last. You have a deal, if you help me get what I want, you can be the first member of my new coven. But if I get the slightest inkling that you're trying to deceive me, you're dead. Now go and get me that body,' she demanded, but Cuthbert shook his head. 'That would be a bad idea. I've been thinking, I don't believe it would work here. The transfer has to be performed somewhere that holds a lot of magical energy, and the best place around here would be your sister's cellar. It's full of power from the talisman, it would be perfect.' 'The only problem is that it's also the home of the coven of the talisman, and I can't see my sister letting us use her cellar,' Bella sneered. Cuthbert continued, 'That won't be a problem. You see your sister and her fellow witches have gone to a meeting of the wizards' council. Now they've allowed wizards into the coven, there has to be a discussion before they take any action.' Bella laughed, a cruel laugh, 'That's the trouble with wizards, they have to have a meeting to decide if they need to blow their noses.' Cuthbert was getting impatient. 'Yeah, whatever, but it means we're free to use the cellar undisturbed.'

So half an hour later Cuthbert and Albert Stone/Bella entered Donna's cottage. 'Remember what I told you, I may not be able to use magic, but I still have control of this old fool's body. That includes the finger on the trigger of this shotgun.' As if to prove the point, Albert aimed its barrel at Cuthbert. Ignoring the remark he used the eye to open the entrance to the cellar. Still not fully trusting him she insisted on Cuthbert going first. 'It's got bigger since I was down here last, it must be all the new spells the talisman has learned.'

Bella was almost drooling at the thought of being able to use all the knowledge and spells stored in the cavern. 'Don't you think we ought to get you into a body, before the witches return?' This little troll was beginning to annoy Bella. He was far too cocky to be a member of her coven. What she needed from her followers was blind obedience, and she didn't believe she'd get it from him, so she'd already made her mind up to kill him as soon as she no longer needed him.

It was then that she spotted the coffin lying on the floor not far from where she now stood. Marching over to it, she could see the body of Mistress Web inside. 'I never realised what an ugly old crone she was, but she'll do till I can kill a younger witch and take over her body.' Turning to Cuthbert, she ordered, 'I'm ready, transfer my consciousness into this old hag, and let me warn you, if you try anything I'll jump back into this old fool and make you sorry you were born.'

Ignoring her threat Cuthbert told her to stand up against the wall of the cavern. 'It will amplify the power of the spell and make the transfer easier.' Holding out his arms in the direction of Albert Stone, Cuthbert started to chant a spell in a troll dialect that Bella didn't understand, but before she could say anything, she started to float out of Albert's body and glide across the cavern toward the coffin. Bella was so intent on the fact that she would soon be in a magical body once more, that she failed to notice the wall of the cavern extend out and around Albert Stone, fully encapsulating him in a bubble. 'As soon as I have full control of the body, and I have the lockets back from that annoying troll, I'm going to take great pleasure in killing him very slowly.' She was still savouring that thought, as she hovered over the body of Mistress Web. Something strange happened, the body in the coffin started to shimmer, it changed in shape from an old lady into, she couldn't believe her eyes, now instead of an old witch, lying there was A BLOODY GARGOYLE! She knew then that she'd been tricked, witches had tried for centuries to take over the bodies of Gargoyles, hoping to use their shape shifting ability for their own ends, but though many had tried, none had succeeded. The Gargoyles had the power to turn themselves to stone and thereby blocking the witch's entry, she also knew that it would be no good trying to take over the troll's body while he had the eye, so that left Albert Stone. She'd have to return to him. 'Once I'm back inside that old fool, I'll make that troll sorry he was ever born,' she swore to herself as she floated back the way she came, the only problem being, that he wasn't there anymore. Bella started to panic, she knew she only had a few minutes to find another body to enter otherwise her spirit would move on. Cuthbert could just make out a small black cloud floating across the cavern heading for the entrance. Realising that it was Bella, he knew her only hope was to escape to the village and enter someone else, so he closed the entrance trapping her in the cavern. Bella was terrified, her consciousness could only survive for a few minutes out of a body, 'I'm going to die,' she thought, and then she thought of all the evil things she'd done in her life, and she knew that there was only one place her soul would end up. As Cuthbert watched, the black cloud started to fade, until it had gone completely.

Albert Stone sat in Donna's kitchen. After making sure that Bella was truly gone, Cuthbert extracted him from his bubble in the cavern, he was having a hard time coming to terms with the fact that he'd shot me. 'I'm ever so sorry, David, I couldn't help myself.' I told him for the fifth time that it wasn't him, Bella had taken control of him, but it didn't help, in the end Betty cast a spell that sent him into a deep sleep.

'What was that?' Donna nearly jumped out of her seat. 'Oh that would be Mr Jones dragging his coffin out of the cellar,' I told her. 'He's in a bit of a hurry, it frightens him being around so many witches.' Cuthbert went to help Mr Jones carry the coffin, while I explained to the witches who and what Mr Jones was. The ladies insisted that he stay for a cup of tea, so they could thank him properly. Mr Jones calmed down when the witches turned on the charm. 'There must be some way we can thank you,' Betty asked. 'I was glad I could help. She killed a friend of mine in Dorsett just before she killed your uncle Bert,' he told me. 'Luckily his wife and children were visiting friends at the time, otherwise she would have wiped out the entire family. Now you come to mention it, there might be something you could do for me.' 'Anything,' offered Anne. 'That's very kind of you, but what I need is somebody who's not a witch or a wizard or come to that, any magical creature. What I need is a human who's prepared to watch over the Gargoyle mother and her two daughters. You see, Gargoyle children do not have the ability to shape shift until they're about fifty.' He must have noticed our puzzled expressions. 'Let me explain, we Gargoyles have a different measure of time than you humans. We live for hundreds of years, so to us being fifty years old only makes us the equivalent of you being a teenager, so I need to find somewhere that they can live until they reach the age where they can shape shift, but it has to be somewhere that they'll not come into contact with other humans.' 'I'm sorry, I don't know anyone who would fit the bill,' Betty apologised. Donna and Annie admitted that they also knew of no one.

Cuthbert gave them a knowing smile, 'Leave it to me, I've got just the person.' He then promised Mr Jones he'd contact him soon, then left, leaving us to ponder who he had in mind.

ALL'S WELL THAT ENDS WELL

'You want me to what!' Albert asked. Cuthbert had gone to Albert Stone's cottage to see if he was ok, and had asked him if he would take care of the Gargoyle family. 'As I told you, there is no way to bring your family back. I can feel that their loss hangs heavily on you, and I know that taking care of this mother and her daughters will be hard, but you'll be doing a good thing, and who knows, it might even help you come to terms with your own loss. Just think about it, that's all I ask.' Cuthbert left, Albert promising he'd give it a lot of thought.

I saw Albert Stone wandering around the village over the next week or so. But, unlike other times, he wasn't carrying his shotgun, and he looked as if he was trying to make his mind up about something.

'What the hell's going on now?' Sadie had just jumped out of her seat, after hearing a loud crash coming from the boys' bedroom. 'It's Cuthbert, I told her, 'He's playing on the WII with the boys.' 'Sorry,' came a voice from upstairs. Just then a knock came at the door. 'You see who's at the door and I'll sort those three out,' Sadie said as she disappeared upstairs. I opened the door to find Albert Stone standing there, 'Is Cuthbert here?' he enquired. 'Yes, and I have a feeling that he'll be down here very shortly.' As if to prove me right, he appeared on the landing, looking as though he'd just gone through one of Sadie's telling offs. I'd seen the boys with the same expression on numerous occasions, after misbehaving.

'Cuthbert you've got a visitor,' I called. I think Albert realised that Cuthbert was in trouble, because he asked if he could have a word with him in private. A relieved Cuthbert led him out into the garden. 'What have you been up to?' Albert asked, looking at Cuthbert rather sheepishly. He explained how he was playing tennis with the boys on the WII when he got a bit over enthusiastic and demolished the wardrobe. 'Enough of me, how are you doing Albert?' 'I've had some bad days, when I think about what that witch made me do. She played on my loss. Deep down I knew that my family had gone, but she convinced me that I could have them back, it made me easier to control.'

Cuthbert placed his hand on Albert's shoulder, 'You have nothing to reproach yourself for. She was a very strong witch, there was nothing you could have done.' Albert nodded. 'You may be right, but there is something I can do for the family you told me about. My wife was left an island off the coast of Scotland by her father. I myself have never been there, but she used to spend her summers there as a child. Apparently nobody lives there, but there is still the house that they stayed in, and about five hundred sheep. I'm sure it wouldn't take much to make the house habitable. It would be ideal, nobody goes there, except twice a year, at lambing, and at shearing time, so the girls would have the run of the place, and, I think the peace and quiet would do me good.'

SCOTLAND

Two months later and I was now on loan to Albert Stone. I was still employed by the Major, but over the last few months, first I'd been helping his wife Betty and now I was working for Albert. Only this time I found myself working on an island off the coast of Scotland, along with my wife Sadie, my boys Brandon and Jordon, and Cuthbert. At first it was very uncomfortable. The first week we lived in tents until we'd repaired the roof of the house. Now it was a lot more comfortable, the house was finished, and we were presently mending the stone walls of the pastures. 'Dad, dad, the boat's coming,' shouted Jordon from the cliff top. Brandon who'd been helping me with the wall, shot off down the path to the beach, I followed at a more sedate pace, and I arrived just as the boat pulled alongside the small stone jetty.

The captain looked relieved to dock. He'd never had so many strange people on his boat before. Albert had gone to the mainland the day before to meet the Gargoyle mother and her two girls and bring them back to the island. The mother looked to be in her thirties, but being a Gargoyle she might have been hundreds of years old. Her two girls were each holding one of her hands, it was impossible to see their faces as they were both wearing black cloaks with the hoods pulled up to obscure their features. Also on board were the entire coven, minus Tom, who was still studying with the Yeti. Hardly had the last witch climbed out of the boat, when the skipper put it in reverse and headed back to sea, shouting that he'd be back in four days to pick us all up. I could see by his face that he wasn't looking forward to returning. 'He seemed a mite nervous,' Anne remarked. 'I'm not surprised. Did you witches have to wear your pointy hats and carry your broomsticks? And you wizards, did you have to wear your cloaks and carry your staves?' I asked. 'Yes we did,' answered Donna. 'We're here to place magical charms and spells on this island, to make it safe, so the Gargoyles can live here undetected.' 'I'm sorry,' I apologised, 'but do you think it's wise to draw attention to yourselves?' 'Oh you needn't worry about him, we told him that we were all going to a fancy dress party to celebrate the house being lived in again,' Betty explained. 'Somehow, judging by the look on his face as he raced back out to sea I don't think he believed you,' I told her. The Gargoyle mother suddenly became agitated. 'Where are my girls?' Looking around, I saw them and my boys running across one of the fields, playing tag. Pointing them out to the mother I told her that they'd be alright, my boys would take good care of them. 'That's amazing, it's the first time I've seen them play since their father was killed.' I suggested that we leave them to play and went up to the house.

After the coven had cast their spells, it was safe for the girls to take off their cloaks. All anybody sailing by would see, would be two young human girls playing. At first Brandon and Jordon were full of how they were learning to perform magic, and how one day they'd be wizards. It took the boys down a peg or two when they found out that they weren't the only ones who could do magic, although the girls (who we'd found out were called Opal and Jade) couldn't shape shift, that didn't stop them being able to cast spells. Brandon found this out when he was in a particularly boastful mood, Opal turned his hair bright pink, and would only turn it back when he agreed not to be such a big head. Finally, the day arrived when it was time to leave, Albert was settled, he had fallen in love with the girls. Even though they were dark grey in colour and looked like two stone statues, he said that they reminded him of his own girls.

Albert was now a changed man, since arriving on the island. He now had a purpose, a new direction, something to get out of bed for, he couldn't stop thanking us for giving him this new life. The Gargoyle mother, whose name was Safire, invited us all back in one year for a holiday. By that time the girls would have mastered the art of shape shifting, so Albert and she were going to turn the house and barns into a bed and breakfast, and they wanted us to be their first guests.

As we all climbed aboard the boat to take us back to the mainland, the skipper still didn't look as though he believed that we'd been to a four-day fancy dress party, but he did seem a little less nervous, now that there were some people who were dressed in ordinary clothes. On the mainland we said our goodbyes, and all went to our various homes.

Donna had decided to stay on in this century because, she now had made so many friends and, so she could instruct my boys in the ways of magic.

Cuthbert had bought himself a cottage in Thompson, which made the owner of the local pizza takeaway very happy.

It was nice to be back on the farm driving my tractor. The past few months had been rather hectic. I was just hoping that now Bella was finally gone, that I'd seen the last of evil witches, but I suppose I knew deep down that I was only kidding myself.

All went well for six months, then all hell let loose.

THE WARLOCK MASTER

The young wizard was very pleased with himself.

He'd successfully killed a Gargoyle and stolen its ability to shape shift.

The Warlock Master would surely let him join in his quest for the source of all dark magic, now he'd stolen such a useful power.

He'd never fitted in with other wizards, they could feel that he would easily be lured toward dark magic. Some had tried to help him rid himself of his dark side, but they soon came to realise that he was destined to turn out bad, and he had. He had just killed and had not felt a second's worth of remorse, in fact he felt elated. Ever since he'd been approached by the Warlock Master, he'd at last felt he belonged. He was free to let his evil side out, no longer would he have to suppress the urge to perform dark magic.

As he waited for the Warlock Master and his disciples to arrive, he looked around the cave where they'd arranged to meet. It was just a plain old cave, but if the Master was pleased with the power that the young wizard had stolen, he'd be initiated as a disciple, and allowed to go with the others back to the Warlock Master's castle. It was said to be hidden from view by a powerful concealment spell, and only those who'd been initiated into the brotherhood could find it.

Just at that moment the air in front of the young wizard started to shimmer. Suddenly five figures appeared out of nowhere. Four were young wizards like himself. He could not make out any features of the fifth person, who he guessed was the Warlock Master. He was wearing what looked to be a monk's habit, with the cowl pulled over to conceal his face.

'**WELL YOUNG WIZARD,**' the *Warlock's* voice filled the cave '**WHAT POWER, HAVE YOU GAINED?**' The young wizard's confidence evaporated. 'I-I killed a Gargoyle a-and stole his power to shape shift,' he stammered.

When the Warlock spoke again it was in a quiet voice that was ten times more menacing, '**You killed a Gargoyle did you, and stole its power? Show** *me?'* the young wizard tried his hardest to shape shift, but try as he might he could not.

'If you had bothered to learn about Gargoyles, before you just killed one without knowing what you were doing, you'd have found out that a Gargoyle's power dies with it. 'B-but I had its power, I changed into a witch just to make sure,' the young wizard blurted out. The Warlock Master's voice *was now barely audible.* **'In that case, it was still alive and must have died later, taking its power with it.'**

The young wizard realised that he'd been tricked. 'If it was impossible to steal a Gargoyle's power, why did you put it on the list? he shouted. The Warlock master sneered, **'I put it on the list, to weed out idiots like you. If you had come to me and said that it couldn't be done, or if you had picked one of the other tasks that were achievable, I would have welcomed you into the brotherhood. As it is, you know too much to be allowed to leave here alive.**

Taking a step backwards, the Warlock raised his arm; a ball of fire appeared in the palm of his hand. 'Please,' begged the young wizard. 'I won't tell anyone about you or the brotherhood,' but just as he got the last word out, the Warlock threw the ball of fire that hit him in the chest and quickly spread out to envelop his whole body. The young wizard's screams filled the cave, until suddenly they were cut off as he exploded into a million pieces. The brotherhood all covered their faces to escape the flames, and when they looked a few seconds later, all they could see was a small heap of ashes.

'Let that be a lesson to you all, the same fate awaits anyone that disappoints me.'

THE DRAGON

'I've been dreading this day, ever since I'd found out that my boys were going to become wizards.'

I could understand my wife Sadie's concern, she herself had become an apprentice witch, before all the trouble with Bella, her coven, Uncle Bert's murder, and her and the boys' subsequent kidnapping, not to mention me being killed. (Luckily Cuthbert was on hand to bring me back to life). She was very nervous of anything magical, so you can understand her trepidation on the day that our two boys. Brandon and Jordon, both received their first wands.

'It'll be alright,' I tried to comfort her. 'Donna won't let them try anything dangerous, and Cuthbert said he'd keep an eye on them also.' 'Cuthbert! Cuthbert!' My wife glared at me. 'Are you completely daft, he's as bad as they are. Look what happened last time we asked him to look after them.'

The boys had talked him into teaching them a spell, but it backfired, and it blew up the chicken house. 'He was ever so apologetic afterwards,' I said, trying to calm her down before she went into one of her tirades, about how it was all my fault that we'd been dragged into this world of witches and magic. She always failed to mention that she was an apprentice witch herself before it all started, but to be honest, I could see her point.

When someone's looking after your children, (especially grandparents) you expect them to come home hyped up on too much sugar, or to have been fed all the wrong foods.

What you don't expect is to come home after a lovely night out, to find that your babysitter had conjured up a dragon that went on the rampage and set fire to one of your boss' haystacks. But that's exactly what happened when Cuthbert was left in charge of the boys. Although it wasn't all his fault. My boys are not the little angels that Sadie would have everyone believe. They had found, that if they worked together, they could persuade almost anyone to do their bidding, and most of the time, that person even believed that it was their idea.

This evening Sadie and I had gone to see **Madness**, Sadie's favourite group, who were playing at the Norfolk Show Ground, a big open-air venue just outside of Norwich. It was a lovely summer's evening. Cuthbert had taken Brandon and Jordon for a walk in the countryside around our home. The boys were bored so they asked him what it was like when he was growing up. He told them about the trolls and how they hated him because he was different, (he was half the size of an ordinary troll) and how after the death of his beloved Beth, he'd gone in search of adventure. He told them of all the magical creatures he'd met on his journey.

'Which one was the scariest?' Jordon asked. 'It must be the giant that captured me one night as I sheltered in his cave to escape a terrible storm.

He was going to eat me, but I wiggled out of my bindings, and turned him to stone with the eye.' Cuthbert had this magic jewel, the eye of a lava troll, which he used to perform spells, just as a witch would use her wand.

The boys loved to play with the eye, they could feel the magic in it, but not having any troll blood, they couldn't use it. 'What was your favourite?' 'Now that's an easy question to answer, Brandon, it's got to be dragons. They were the most beautiful creatures ever, so graceful in flight, such noble animals.' Jordon gave him such a look of disgust, 'But they ate people.' Cuthbert smiled at him. 'That's the way of the world, all things must feed on something. You two don't worry about the poor cows, when you're eating your burgers.' 'That's different,' Brandon argued, 'cows aren't people.' 'Are there any left?' Jordon asked. 'Not in this world, they were all banished to a realm where there are no humans.'

Cuthbert told how when man started to become the dominant force on earth, he wanted to rid the world of anything that threatened that dominance. 'So, a great meeting was called, and all magic folk were invited. Together they came up with a plan to rid the world of the likes of dragons, trolls, and giants, and any other creature that was a threat to man. 'It was the biggest coven ever convened. It needed to be, for they were going to conjure a magical realm where all the unwanted creatures could live. Like all great spells, it didn't go quite to plan. Yes, they rid the world of dragons, but some of the trolls and a couple of the giants were hid deep underground, so were unaffected by the spell.'

'Why didn't they just cast the spell again?' asked Jordon. 'Well, you see they couldn't, because after it had gone so well, or so they thought, each faction had their own idea on what to do next to create the perfect world.

The wizards wanted magic restricted to only men, the witches as you can imagine weren't very happy with that, it nearly came to violence, and in the end they all went their separate ways.'

'I'd love to have seen a dragon.' 'Yeah me too,' Jordon agreed with his brother. 'Is there any way we can go to their realm and see them?' Brandon asked. Cuthbert shook his head. 'I'm afraid not. That was one of the main laws built into the spell. No humans would ever be allowed to cross over to the creature's realm.'

The boys could tell by the look on Cuthbert's face that he was hiding something from them.

'But there is a way we can see a dragon, isn't there?'

Cuthbert looked at Jordon and then back to Brandon, he knew he could never hide anything from them, it was as if they had the ability to read his mind. 'Well there is a way, but it's far too dangerous, and your mother would kill me if anything happened to either of you.'

When the boys wanted to, they could give people the impression that butter wouldn't melt in their mouths, while the whole time plotting something naughty.

'But uncle Cuthbert, you're better at magic than any witch or wizard.'

The words coming out of Brandon's mouth were coated in honey.

Jordon carried on in the same fashion, You'd never let any harm come to us, 'and we'd love to see a dragon, if only for a minute.' Then in unison, 'Please, Uncle Cuthbert.'

Cuthbert knew when he was beaten. 'Alright. But only for a minute.'

He took the boys to the forty acres; explaining that it would give the dragon enough room to fly around, without doing any damage.

The forty acres had been sown with wheat that had been harvested the week before, so there was nothing for the dragon to destroy.

Cuthbert made them stand behind him until he'd finished the spell, ***'from time and space I call to thee, dragons appear before us three.'***

He knew the boys were looking at him. 'I know, it wasn't a very good rhyme, 'but it was the best I could come up with on the spur of the moment.'

Suddenly, bad rhyming was the least of their worries, because in the field, about a hundred yards away there appeared a mini tornado. It gradually grew bigger until they could feel the wind tugging at them from where they stood. Then as quickly as it arrived, it disappeared leaving a cloud of dust and leaves in its place. As the dust settled, they could just make out a large mass, which took on the shape of a dragon.

'You did it, Uncle Cuthbert,' Brandon shouted excitedly. 'That's so cool, I wish I could conjure dragons.'

Jordon was jealous. All he had managed so far was turning a twig into a stick insect, which he considered a complete waste of time, as even when he succeeded, it still looked like a twig.

But there in front of his brother and him was a dragon, a real live dragon that had been conjured out of thin air by a half troll, his uncle Cuthbert.

Not only that, his aunties Donna, Betty and Anne were witches, and his brother and he were training to be wizards, he loved magic.

The only thing that annoyed him was that he and Brandon were not allowed to tell their friends about any of it.

As the boys and Cuthbert watched, the dragon flapped his wings and took to the air. 'This shouldn't be happening. I only intended for you to see it, not for it to pass into our world.'

As they watched, the dragon flew in a circle as if looking for something. Finally spotting them, it made a beeline for their position.

'Stand close to me,' Cuthbert told the two lads. Holding up the eye, he muttered a spell and immediately they were surrounded by a transparent shield.

'We'll be safe in here,' Brandon tugged on Cuthbert's coat. 'We might be safe, but what about everybody else?'

Just then the dragon soared over top of them, letting loose a bust of flame that completely enveloped them. They were unharmed under the shield, and apart from it getting a little hot, they felt nothing.

Cuthbert let out a sigh of relief, 'I told you I'd protect you.' 'That's all very well, but who's going to protect that,' said Jordon pointing to a large haystack on the edge of the field.

The dragon was heading straight for it, still belching fire. Cuthbert held up the eye, **to my words you must heed, return home with all speed.**

The Dragon started to shimmer, slowly it grew fainter, until it finally disappeared, but not before setting fire to said haystack.

'Wow that was great; we got to see a dragon up close.'

Jordon wasn't as excited as his brother. 'Yeah, now I know what a burger feels like on a barbecue.' 'Look boys I think we'd better get out of here.

If we're found near a blazing haystack people are going to think we started it,' Cuthbert told the boys.

'The dragon started it, not us.' Jordon looked at his brother. 'And who's going to believe that? We tell them a dragon did it, and they're going to think we're mad.'

Nobody else saw what happened that afternoon; the fire brigade put it down to vandalism, the boys thought that they'd got off lightly. That was until their mother overheard them talking about how Cuthbert had conjured up a dragon for them, and how it had set fire to the haystack.

Sadie had grounded them for a month, and banned Cuthbert from looking after the boys, until he could show her that he could be trusted not to get them into trouble.

That was two months ago, the boys had served their grounding, and Sadie had finally forgiven Cuthbert. But back to today, now she had something more to worry about. Today is the day when Brandon and Jordon were going to receive their first wands.

'It'll be alright, they've learnt their lesson,' I tried to put Sadie's mind at ease, but all she would say was, 'We'll see.'

The boys had run ahead and were already at Donna's when we arrived.

They weren't the only ones. Sadie and I had thought that it would be a low-key affair, just Donna, Betty, Anne, Cuthbert and the two of us. But no, apparently it was a big occasion for a young wizard to receive his first wand. There were representatives from each magical community, Dermot and Hamish, on behalf of the wizards, (who were also members of our coven) two witches, Mistress Darkcrow and Mistress Holly (whom we'd never met before) Mr Jenkins on behalf of the Gargoyles, and the smallest person I'd ever seen. I found out that his name was Shamus O'Brian, and he was there on behalf of the leprechauns. He looked exactly as you'd expect a leprechaun to look.

He wore brown corduroy trousers, a plaid shirt and an emerald green waistcoat. On his head he wore a black hat with a large silver buckle on it, and in one hand he carried a shillelagh, and in the other, a cauldron full of gold nuggets, which he gave away for luck.

Donna coughed, to get everybody's attention, 'I'd like to take this opportunity to thank you all for coming here today. It's a rare occurrence in these days of science and technology to find any young boy who wants to become a wizard, so to find two, and brothers at that, is truly special.' The boys looked terrified, they thought all that would happen would be that their auntie Donna would give them their wands and that would be that.

But now they found themselves surrounded by a room full of magical folk, the majority of whom they didn't know. 'We are gathered here today,' Donna continued, 'to welcome these boys to the magical community, and to endow them with good luck.' She smiled and nodded toward the leprechaun, who took off his hat and bowed, his head nearly touching the ground. 'But we can't start yet, I'm expecting a very special guest, who should be arriving any minute now.' As if it had been staged, there came a loud knocking at the door. 'That will be her now,' she announced, heading to the door.

A GREAT HONOUR

Although Donna has been alive since the sixteen hundreds, most of that time she'd slept under the spell that concealed the wood, where she and her sister Bella guarded the talisman; that is until Bella stole it.

So, in fact she is only in her fifties. But the woman who at that moment was walking through the door, looked as if she had been alive for all those years, without any magical help. I've seen anti-wrinkle cream advertised on telly, but this woman would need a tanker load. Although her body looked decrepit, I could see by the twinkle in her eyes, that she had all her faculties.

'I'd like to introduce you all to Mistress Hazel, she is the oldest of our order, and the greatest witch ever to have lived.'

Mistress Hazel raised a hand to stop Donna. 'Enough flattery. Are these the young men who wish to become wizards?' Brandon and Jordon tried to hide behind their mother, but realised there was no escape.

Coming forward, Brandon held out his hand, 'V-very nice to m-meet you, he stuttered. 'Yeah, me too,' said a not so brave Jordon, still trying to get behind his mother.

The old witch shook Brandon's hand. 'Very nice to meet you,' she said, then turning to Jordon, she waved at him to come forward. 'It's alright young man, I'll not hurt you.' Jordon warily came and stood beside his brother. Turning to address the assembled guests she said, 'I'd like to thank you all for coming here on this auspicious occasion. Not only have we two brothers, who wish to become wizards, that is a rare thing, currently, when people have moved away from magic, but they are already part of one of the most powerful covens there has ever been.'

Turning back to the boys she asked, 'Do you have your lockets on?' Both nodded. 'Show me.' The boys looked at me. 'It's alright,' I told them. 'She's one of us.' On hearing that, they both pulled their lockets out of their t-shirts. The old witch looked surprised. 'I'd imagined they'd look somewhat different from this.' 'They do, I informed her. The boys thought they looked a bit girly, so they changed their appearance. Change them back for the lady.' 'Oh dad, do we have to?' they complained in unison. 'Just till after the ceremony, then you can change them back.'

They both said, 'REVEAL' and their different necklaces, Brandon's a wooden one with a carved eagle in the middle, and Jordon's, a black shoelace with a silver J on it, turned back to the smaller versions of the original talisman.

'That's more like it,' the old witch smiled. 'How do you change the appearance of them without wands?' she asked. 'We don't know, we just think what shape we'd like, and it just happens,' Jordon told her.

Mistress Hazel turned to Donna, 'It seems these boys are far ahead of where they should be at their age. I think that even without their lockets they would still become great wizards, but with them they will be even more powerful. You will have to keep a very close watch on them, and at the slightest hint of any dark tendencies, you will have to take the appropriate action, do you understand?' Donna nodded. 'Good, now where are the wands?' Betty handed Mistress Hazel an ornately carved wooden box.

The old witch opened it; we all craned forward to get the first look at the boy's wands. 'Now Brandon and Jordon, before you receive your wands, do you solemnly swear to only use them in the service of good, and never against innocents?'

In one voice the boys replied, 'We do.' 'Then step forward one at a time to receive them.' Brandon held out his arm in front of his brother, 'Eldest first,' he said, and went to get his wand. Jordon looked as if he was about to fight his brother to be the first but decided against it.

'There you are young man,' handing Brandon his wand, she cautioned him, 'you are only allowed to use your wand under supervision. You must never tell anyone who isn't in the magical community about it, or that you're to be a wizard. Do you so swear?' Brandon looked very serious 'I do.' Once Jordon had taken the same oath, the ceremony turned into a party, which went on till late into the night.

Long before it ended, Sadie had taken the boys home to bed. As the party wound down, Mistress Hazel called for quiet. 'I have put off speaking of this until now, because I didn't want to spoil the boys' day, but there is something very bad brewing. Rumour has it that a new evil force, even more deadlier than Bella, is emerging. I charge you all to be wary and to report anything you learn to either the council of wizards, or to myself. Please be vigilant, and may good magic be with you.'

On my way home, I decided not to tell Sadie or the boys for the time being, until we knew exactly what we were up against, there was no point in worrying them.

TOM'S RETURN

The next day saw me muck spreading on the ten acres; I had just finished my third load and was heading back to load up again, when I noticed Sadie walking down the lane toward me. 'Hello darling,' she said when I stopped the tractor, 'I'm going to see Donna. Cuthbert told me he'd seen a young man talking to her this morning.' 'What's so strange about that?' I asked. 'Nothing, but from the description he gave me, it could have been Tom.' 'That can't be right,' I told her. 'Tom's studying in Tibet for the next two years.' 'I know David, but I have this feeling that something's not right, I can't explain it. I've had it since the day of the boys' party, so I'm off to see Donna, and see if she knows anything.' Forthwith she set off down the lane.

'I was right, it was Tom,' were the words that greeted me as I walked in the door after work. 'Did you see him?' I asked. 'No, he'd left before I arrived. Donna was in tears. She wouldn't tell me anything. Only that it was indeed Tom, but said she wanted to see you when you got home.'

So, after promising her, that I'd explain everything upon my return, I set off down to Donna's.

The old witch looked upset when I walked into her cottage. 'Hello David, good of you to come.' 'No problem, I told her. How can I help?'

Donna looked as if she was going to burst into tears at any moment, 'I had an unexpected visitor today.' 'Yes, I know,' Sadie said. Donna suddenly looked very fragile.

'He came to tell me that he no longer wished to be the keeper of the talisman or to be a member of our coven.' I was shocked, Tom had been so proud to have been chosen by the talisman to be its keeper.

'Did he say why?' I asked. Donna shook her head. 'All he said was that he had something to do, and he couldn't do it as the keeper of the talisman or as a member of the coven. He seemed so distant, not the Tom we know.'

Just then I heard singing coming from the kitchen. 'Who's that?' I enquired. 'Oh that's Shamus. Mr Jenkins and Shamus have both decided to stay on for a day or two, so they could pass on some of their knowledge to the boys. In the past wizards have not been very friendly towards Gargoyles and leprechauns, what with trying to steal their powers and so forth, they thought that if they could get two young wizards from a powerful coven on their side, it might go a long way toward stopping anymore attacks on their kind.'

Still singing, and carrying two platefuls of what looked like curry, Shamus O'Brian entered from the kitchen. 'Oh sorry, Donna me darling, I didn't know you had company. 'Well if you hadn't been singing so loud, you'd have heard him enter,' Donna teased the leprechaun. 'You remember David, don't you?'

Holding out his hand as he came forward, 'Yes, we met at the ceremony, 'you're the boys' father, a fine pair of lads you have there, you must be proud of them.'

I shook the Leprechaun's hand, and thanked him for his comments about my boys. 'Think nothing of it me lad. Do you like curry?' I told him I did. 'Good, I made enough for three, but Mr Jenkins doesn't like spicy food. You'd think someone who can turn himself into granite would have a stronger stomach, but his loss, is our gain. Here, you two tuck into this, and I'll get myself some from the kitchen.'

I gratefully started on the curry, Sadie had taken the boys over to her mother's, I'd told her not to bother to make me anything to eat, I said I'd get myself something after I'd seen Donna. So all I was looking forward to, was a pizza that we had in the freezer, left over from when Cuthbert stayed with us. This was a lot better, one of the best curries I'd had in a long while.

As if reading my mind, Shamus said, 'You seemed to be enjoying that.' 'Yes, it's lovely. Did you have it delivered?' I asked him. 'No lad, I cooked it myself,' he boasted. 'Shamus is a brilliant chef, he cooked me very tasty paella last night.'

I think Donna was rather taken with Shamus.

'Don't think me patronising, but they are not the dishes I'd expect a Leprechaun to cook.'

Shamus smiled at me, 'You're right, but contrary to folk lore, we don't just eat potatoes. We Leprechauns are quite the connoisseurs, we love good food and fine wines. I have trained under some of the best chefs in Europe.'

Twenty minutes later, having finished our curries and a tasty strawberry cheesecake that Shamus had also made, Donna and I got back to talking about her visit from Tom.

'Didn't he give you any idea what he was up to?' Donna shook her head, 'No, all he'd say was that it was very dangerous, and that he had to do it on his own.' As I looked at the old witch, I had the feeling that she was holding something back.

Covering her hand with mine, I asked, 'That's not all, is it?' Donna shook her head, 'Tom said that you were not to be given the talisman this time.'

I was shocked, 'I had been the original keeper of the talisman, and I'd thought that it would revert to me if ever Tom gave it up. Did he say why he didn't want me to have it back?' I asked.

'It wasn't him, the talisman wanted to go to Cuthbert, Tom thinks it needed to go to someone with powers.'

Walking back from Donna's, I pondered over all that she'd said. It seemed strange to me, why had the talisman chosen Cuthbert to be its keeper, and not Donna, or even Betty or Anne? Apart from Donna and myself they were the longest serving members of the coven.

On my right as I walked back home was a small wood. I noticed two figures standing just inside. Upon my approach they stopped talking and the younger of the two walked off into the wood. Getting nearer I recognised the other as Cuthbert. 'Hello David, been to see Donna?' he asked. 'Yes,' I answered, 'she told me of the visitor she'd had today. That wouldn't have been the same person you were just talking to, would it?

I could tell from his expression that something was not right. And as if to confirm my suspicions he said, 'I'm sorry David, but Tom swore me to secrecy. All I can tell you is, that it's very important, very dangerous, and he must do it alone.'

THE SECRET MEETING

'So young wizard, you wish to become a member of the brotherhood, do you?' Tom looked at the hood of the Warlock Master and tried to make out his features, but all he could see was blackness. No! it was more than blackness, if you shone a light into blackness, you would be able to make out what was there, but Tom believed that if you were to shine a light at the Warlock master's face it would show only black.

'Yes, I would,' he answered the Warlock. *'But aren't you a member of the coven of the talisman,'* the Warlock sneered. Tom laughed, 'Not anymore, I quit. Got fed up with all that. We are a coven for good, and we protect the innocent crap. I want to do as I please. If I stay in the coven, I must play by their rules, and I'm no team player. Not only that, if you wear the talisman, they know everything you're doing and thinking. Well I've had enough, I want to learn dark magic and be taught it by the best.'

The Warlock Master studied Tom for several minutes, *'If you're to be accepted into the brotherhood, you must prove yourself to them and to me. There are tasks you must perform. Here,'* he said holding out a gloved hand, containing a scroll.

Tom took it. *'When you have completed any one of the tasks on the list, cast the spell written on the bottom of the scroll, and I will arrange to meet you here. If you have completed it to my satisfaction, you will be initiated into the brotherhood. Fail and it would be unwise of you to appear'.*

As if to signify that the meeting was over, the Warlock Master shimmered into nothing, leaving Tom standing alone in the cave.

'Well, is he for real?' asked Simon Grey, head of the brotherhood, as the Warlock Master appeared in front of him. *'I couldn't tell, but he's hiding something. If he has some agenda other than joining us we'll soon know, that is why I made it so that whoever attempts any of the tasks on the list must kill to complete it. It's impossible to get any of the powers from the creatures with them alive.'*

At that very moment, a worried Tom was reading the list of tasks given to him by the Warlock Master 'What am I going to do?' He thought, he'd have to perform some feat of powerful magic to be deemed good enough to join the brotherhood, or at least to be taken for training.

A VISIT TO SCOTLAND

Donna's cottage was the scene of another meeting. It had been in full swing for an hour before I arrived. 'Sorry I'm late,' I apologised. 'What's going on?' Looking round at their faces, I could tell that this wasn't a social gathering. 'I received a phone call from Albert Stone this afternoon. He wouldn't say why, but he wants us all to go to the island as soon as possible,' Donna explained. 'I told him we would be there in a day or so, but he said we needed to be there sooner, and that it was very important.'

It suddenly became bedlam in Donna's cottage, everybody had their own idea as to how we were all going to get to Scotland, some weird, some downright dangerous, all totally unachievable. As the noise reached a crescendo, everybody stopped talking since a loud banging threatened to burst their eardrums. Turning to the source of the noise, we saw that it was Shamus the Leprechaun banging on the doorframe with his shillelagh.

'I've been listening to your ideas, and have concluded that none of them will work. For instance, you can't all fly up there on broomsticks. Some of us haven't got them, and if you will forgive me, some of you that have, are too old to make such a long journey. And some of the other ideas are so farfetched that they are not worth considering. So, there's only one way for us all to get there quickly, and that's by rainbow.'

Donna looked puzzled. 'What do you mean, by rainbow?' Shamus explained that it wasn't a real rainbow, it was a teleportation spell invented by the Leprechauns. It incorporated the colours of the rainbow to hide the fact that it was a spell; humans would think nothing of seeing a rainbow, so Leprechauns could move about freely without being noticed.

Shamus answered everybody's questions, such as does it hurt, how long will it take to get to Scotland, and are there any side effects. After he'd answered their questions to everybody's satisfaction, we went out into Donna's Garden where Shamus made a big show of casting the spell, (more for showmanship than anything I thought).

A small ball of light appeared out of the ground in front of Shamus which grew to the size of a large beach ball that shot into the air, arcing across the sky leaving a rainbow behind it. Turning to Donna he bowed, 'Ladies first.' She looked worried. 'What do I do?' she asked. Shamus said, 'Just walk into the rainbow and before you know it, you'll be on the island.'

Donna walked into the rainbow, it was as if one second, she was there and the next she was gone, 'Ok who's next?' Shamus asked.

It was the strangest sensation I'd ever felt, as I walked into the rainbow. It was like I'd been sucked up in a giant hoover. Only to be deposited seconds later, on the lawn outside the farmhouse on the island just off the Scottish coast, which had become the home of Albert Stone and the Gargoyle family he'd agreed to care for.

Albert was there to greet me. 'David, so glad you could come at such short notice.' After shaking my hand, he led me into the farmhouse, I thought Donna's cottage was full on the night the boys received their wands, but that was nothing compared to the amount of people (and I use the term "people" loosely) who were crowded into Albert's lounge.

Albert must have read my mind. They started to arrive about two weeks ago; it was about that time we named the island.

'The local authorities said that if we wanted mail to be delivered here, we would have to give it a name, and seeing as we were going to open a bed and breakfast here, we thought it a good idea. We decided to call the island Haven. As well as registering the name with the local council, Safire wanted to name the island magically. She cast a spell so that all magic folk would know it as place of good magic. That's when they started to arrive, and there's been a steady stream ever since. We've got witches, wizards, Gargoyles, and Leprechauns, there's a Unicorn in the barn, and an ogre in a cave down by the shore.

'When I agreed to help protect Safire and her girls, I didn't expect to have to protect half of the magical community as well.' Albert looked worried, 'I'm not equipped to deal with any dark wizards that come looking for our guests.'

Safire coughed to get everybody's attention, 'I'd like to thank our friends from Norfolk for answering our call for help so quickly. For those of you who do not know these folks, let me introduce to you some of the famous (famous?) coven of the talisman.'

It seems that our exploits battling Bella and her coven were common knowledge among the magical community. So, as you can imagine, it took quite a while to be introduced to all of Albert and Safire's guests.

Which comprised of three wizards, the oldest being Oswald Greybeard, the middle aged one, Marcus Brownbeard, and the youngest (only about thirteen) Simon Nobeard. Apparently all the wizards in their coven (except that is for young Simon) were very proud of their facial hair.

The witches' contingent consisted of two young girls, who had only just become witches. They introduced themselves, the short chubby one being Evangeline Mead and her twin sister who was the opposite, at least two feet taller and thinner than some skeletons, was called Adriana.

The Gargoyles grudgingly gave their names. I could tell by their demeanour that they still had a distrust of witches and wizards. The four Gargoyles were called Sandstone, Limestone, Granite and Marble. (Gargoyles turned to stone when they died, so consequently they took their names from the rocks into which they would eventually turn). The Leprechauns on the other hand were very friendly and eager to meet us.

But first there came the family reunion, one of the Leprechauns turned out to be Shamus O'Brian's brother Michael, the other, their cousin Liam Delaney.

In the half an hour it took us to meet the witches, wizards and Gargoyles, the Leprechauns had conjured up a feast of food and drink off to one side, and we were now tucking into platefuls of food and tankards full of their most favourite ale.

'Sorry to break up your party gentlemen, but we have important things to discuss,' said a rather disgruntled Safire. 'You carry on lass, we've nearly finished. You see it's an old Leprechaun tradition. We never leave the table till all the food and drink has gone,' Michael O'Brian smiled.

Giving them the "whatever" look, Safire started to tell the rest of us the story of how they came to have a house full of magical beings.

'It started the day after we'd named the island "Haven". First to arrive was the Unicorn. Every morning Opal would go out to feed the chickens and collect the eggs, she came running in saying that there was a large horse with a pole sticking out of its head in the barn. Albert and I went with Opal to see for ourselves. 'It--- it's a Unicorn,' he stammered. 'Where did it come from?' he asked.

'Having no idea, myself, I couldn't answer his question. But after making sure it had plenty of hay and water, we left it in the barn, deciding to phone you to see if you could shine any light on its appearance. But before we could call you the others started to arrive. Apart from the Unicorn we had room for them all in the house. It's a bit cramped, but we manage.

'The last to arrive was the ogre. Even if we'd had no guests, I would never allow such an obnoxious thing into our house. Ogres are not the most pleasant of creatures,' Safire explained. 'They are neither good nor bad, they're just ogres, they never seek the company of other races unless they want something, usually they'll try to steal it. If this cannot be achieved they'll try to con it out of you. You cannot trust an ogre, you cannot befriend an ogre, your best course of action is to have nothing to do with them.'

Safire told us that the ogre had found a cave down by the shore, where he caught fish and ate them raw, preferring to keep himself to himself.

'But why are they here?' asked Donna. 'I was getting to that,' replied, Safire. It seems that there is a new evil emerging. A powerful Warlock out there is gathering a following of young wizards, all of whom must prove themselves by killing and stealing a power from a magical creature.

And I think my husband was the first to be targeted.'

'What makes you think that?' asked Donna. 'Correct me if I'm wrong,' interrupted Betty, 'but doesn't a Gargoyle's power die with it?'

Safire nodded. 'Yes, but that's not a well-known fact, only someone who's made a study of us would know that.'

'I think I may be able to help there,' the offer coming from Oswald Greybeard. 'We've been keeping an eye on this warlock. He first came to our notice after the death of Safire's husband, we could not understand why anyone would want to kill a Gargoyle.'

Turning to Safire he said, 'I know what you're going to say, and yes in the past there has been some bad feeling between our races, but wizards are more enlightened in this new millennium, we try to live in harmony with other magical folk, although, even we draw the line at ogres. But getting back to the point, we found out from a young wizard whom the Warlock had tried to enlist into something he called, "the Brotherhood".

He had been given a list of creatures and their powers, he was to choose one from the list, kill them and steal their power.

'On the list that the young wizard scanned, were the names of the three wizards you see before you now.' He pointed to himself and his two companions. 'Also on the list were two witches, who had to be twins,' he looked in the direction of Evangeline and Adriana.

'Yes, we heard that, that's why we came.' 'Also,' continued Oswald Greybeard, 'a leprechaun, a Unicorn, an ogre, plus several others that the young wizard could not remember.

'It seems that the Warlock is gathering followers, but they must be very powerful themselves, hence the gathering of other creature's powers.

I fear also that he makes them kill to take them, so as to turn their souls dark, only then can he make them do his bidding without remorse.'

'What is he planning to do?' Anne asked. 'We don't know,' admitted Oswald.

'I do,' said Cuthbert. 'He's trying to find the Dark Wizard's spell book.

'But that's just a myth!' Oswald shook his head, 'I'm afraid it's not, Donna, we have been spreading the rumour about, that it's just a bedtime story for young wizards, but in fact it's true.

'Years ago, in our arrogance we decided to compile two books - one the book of good spells, the other the book of dark spells. Almost as soon as we had finished, we realised that the book of dark magic was too dangerous to be read by anyone.

'So, the wizard council decreed that it should be destroyed, but we soon found out that something with that much dark magic inside could not be harmed by any amount of good magic. Hence, it was decided to hide it away deep in the earth, and guard it with powerful spells and charms. That was three hundred years ago, and all those who knew the whereabouts of the book are long gone.'

Another hour of talking, no one else had anymore to add. They all knew that there was evil coming, and they were in some way part of it.

Getting Cuthbert on his own at last, I asked him the question that had been nagging me.

'How come you know what the Warlock Master is looking for?' Cuthbert apologised, 'Sorry David, I'm sworn to secrecy. If it got out people we care about would be in danger, so you're going to have to trust me, but there will be a time when I need your help. I hope I can count on you to help me and not ask too many questions; all will be revealed if we succeed.' 'And if we don't,' I asked. 'Well then it won't matter because we'll all be dead.'

Leaving the rest behind, Shamus gave me a lift back to Norfolk by rainbow.

Donna and the others were staying, to up rate the spells and charms they'd previously placed on the island to protect the two Gargoyle girls.

They were also adding a new spell to ward off anyone practising dark magic.

'Where have you been? I've been worried sick.' Sadie had come home with the boys, to find that I wasn't anywhere in sight. 'We walked down to Donna's thinking that you'd be there, only to find that you'd all gone off somewhere.'

I told Sadie all that had happened while she was gone. She sighed, 'I was hoping after the coven had dealt with Bella and her cronies, things would get back to normal, but then again, what is normal for the mother of two young wizards!'

I tried to reassure her, 'No one's going to harm you or the boys, there are enough witches and wizards around here not to mention a half troll, who are more than capable of stopping any number of warlocks who might wish harm on the boys or you.'

The next day was Saturday, Brandon and Jordon were both very excited. I'd told them we were going to the island for the girls coming of age ceremony. 'Can we go on our broomsticks?' Jordon asked. Sadie immediately vetoed that idea, 'No you can't. You've only been flying for a week. Besides how do you think your father and me are going to get there? 'We could give you a lift,' Brandon offered.

'Thanks, but we've got a far quicker way, anyways you can bring your broomsticks with you,' I told them.

So, an hour later we all gathered in Donna's Garden, the boys gripping their broomsticks, and looking forward to flying all around the island, also I suspected, showing off in front of the girls.

Not that Sadie and I were empty handed. Shamus, having had the cottage to himself, had spent the whole night cooking for the party planned to celebrate the girls' coming of age.

We were loaded up with sausage rolls, quiches, cakes, and a whole selection of delights. Bearing in mind there were also several witches and the girls' mother, likewise preparing for the party, I didn't think anyone would be going hungry.

We stepped out of the rainbow to find everything in full swing.

Four trestle tables were set up on the lawn, and on top were the brightest and most colourful tablecloths, piled high with a large assortment of food, to which Shamus added his offerings.

The girls looked lovely in their party dresses. Albert and Safire had bought them, on one of their rare visits to the mainland.

Coming of age was a big milestone in a Gargoyle's life, it was the time when they could take on human form, and no longer needed to be concealed by spells. If they chose, they could live as a human until they reverted to the stone from which they had evolved.

Safire called for order, 'I'd like to take this opportunity to welcome our friends who have come to celebrate my girls' coming of age. Please step forward my darlings.' The girls, still in their Gargoyle form, came nervously to stand facing their mother.

The next part consisted of Safire asking Opal and her sister, Jade a series of questions in the Gargoyle language, and the girls giving the appropriate responses.

'Now for the benefit of our guests who don't speak Gargoyle,' Safire reverted to English, 'Have you made your minds up? Do you wish to stay in your natural form? Or do you want to take on human form?' Opal, being the oldest, spoke for both, 'We've had a long talk and decided we'd like to take on human form.' Safire and Albert looked relieved, 'Good. In that case there's something I'd like you all to see. If you'll all please follow me to the barn.'

It took a minute for my eyes to become accustomed to the dark interior of the barn after the bright sun of the garden.

But when they did, I saw the most beautiful creature, it was pure white, and out of its brow grew a long-twisted horn.

I felt Sadie grip my arm. 'Is that a unicorn?' she asked. Brandon butted in 'Yes, it is mum. Donna has been telling us all about them in our magical creature's lessons.' 'Yeah,' Jordon took over from his brother, 'we've learned about dragons, trolls, giants and ogres so far.'

Safire smiled at the boys, 'Did you know that unicorns have the purest souls of any creatures; there has never been an evil unicorn. They are the personification of good, which in part has led to their decline. We are very lucky to have one here today, as they play a big part in the Gargoyle coming of age ceremony.'

Safire approached the creature with great respect, 'Would you be kind enough to allow me a tiny piece of your horn for my daughters' coming of age spell?'

The unicorn nodded very slowly. 'Thank you, you are most kind.'

It was then we all noticed the knife in Safire's hand. 'What's she going to do? asked Jordon. Donna smiled, 'There's no need to worry. Safire's only going to take a small amount of the unicorn's horn to use in the spell that will change the girls' appearance.'

As we all watched she scraped the blade over a tiny area. When it moved, I could see dust falling from the horn, which Safire collected in a golden bowl that she held in the other hand.

After she'd finished, she bowed to the unicorn, 'Once again I thank you.'

We left the barn and continued the ceremony out in the garden thereafter. Afterwards the change in the girls was amazing; they'd gone from being the two grey Gargoyles who we'd grown fond of, to two pretty, thirteen-year-old human girls.

The change in the girls was what we'd expected, what we hadn't expected though was the change in the boys. Before the ceremony they'd all been mates. Brandon and Jordon had been showing Jade and Opal all the spells. Quickly our boys and the Gargoyle girls had become good friends.

In a time when people let things like colour, race, and any number of other reasons stop them getting along, it was nice to see our boys making friends and getting on so well with other species.

Gargoyles, they took in their stride, but it seemed that thirteen-year-old girls were another matter.

Suddenly both Brandon and Jordon were tongue tied. 'Y-you -look very pretty,' stammered Brandon. Jordon stood behind his brother with his fingers down his throat making gagging noises.

The boys finally got used to the girls' new appearance, and half an hour later they were back to their old selves.

LEPRECHAUN'S GOLD

'It's a pied wagtail. Can you see it boys? It's lovely,' Cuthbert had just taken up bird watching, and as with every hobby he'd tried since returning from Scotland, he'd thrown himself into it wholeheartedly.

After coming to live in Norfolk, Cuthbert had tried to fill his time with various hobbies, such as photography, although most of his photos consisted of a shot of his thumb obscuring the lens. Cooking, that is, until Sadie banned him from her kitchen. And line dancing, where he was asked to leave after one incident when he got carried away and demolished half of the dancers in one foul sweep.

We were hoping that ornithology would be less strenuous and have a calming influence on him.

'It's a bird, Uncle Cuthbert, there's millions of them flying around,' Jordon was feeling bored.

He and Brandon had been dragged out of their lessons with Donna to accompany Cuthbert on one of his bird watching safaris.

Brandon was of the same opinion as his brother. 'This is boring,' he begged, 'please can we go back to our lessons now?' (Something I could never imagine my boys saying). 'Yeah Donna was just going to teach us a concealment spell.' Jordon smiled to himself, 'That will be very useful when mum comes looking for us to do our chores, we'll be able to hide until she's gone.' But Cuthbert wasn't listening; he was staring through his binoculars at one part of the wood. 'Uncle Cuthbert, did you hear what we said?' asked Brandon.

Still looking through his binoculars, he muttered, 'Ok you boys get along back to Donna's, I'll see you later.'

With that he got up and walked off in the direction of the wood.

'I thought it was you,' Cuthbert told the person standing just inside the trees. 'I take it you need my help.' Pulling off the hood that covered his worried face. Tom sighed. 'Yes. I'm in a bit of trouble this time, I don't know if even you can get me out of it.' Walking over to a fallen tree and sitting down, Cuthbert patted the trunk next to him, 'Come and sit here and tell me. What's troubling you?'

Tom sat down beside the half troll and gave Cuthbert the list that the Warlock Master had given him.

I must collect one of the powers, and if you know anything about those creatures, you'll know that the only way to do that is to kill its owner, and that is something I could never do. Tom had confided in him, that he was on a mission for the wizard council, he was to infiltrate the Brotherhood and find out where the book of dark magic was hidden and get to it before the Warlock Master.

'I take it that's the whole idea, you must be prepared to kill otherwise you're no good to him.'

Tom looked lost. 'Now you see my dilemma? I can't take a power back to him, because I could never kill.'

'You may not have to,' smiling at him, Cuthbert patted Tom on the back, 'if I can find where Beth and I used to live, I have just the thing hidden in the cellar.'

'Will it still be there after all these years?' Tom asked. 'I think so. Witches' cottages are usually handed down from one witch to another, so with a bit of luck I'll be able to locate it.'

Tom looked sceptical. 'What if the Witch who lives there has found it and sold it?'

Cuthbert smiled, 'No witch would ever be able to break the spell that I put on the cellar, and unless the cottage has been demolished it's still there.' Cuthbert left Tom in the wood, after first turning an old hut that had once belonged to a gamekeeper into somewhere fit for Tom to hide until he got back. On the outside it still looked as ramshackle as always, but on the inside, it had everything he'd need for a few days.

Cuthbert came through the door at such speed, that he knocked me off my feet. 'David, have you got a map of England?' he asked picking me up 'Yes,' I replied and 'if you give me a minute for the room to stop spinning, I'll look for it.'

Later with the map spread over the kitchen table I asked, 'What exactly are we looking for?'

'Beth's cottage,' he replied. 'How are we going to find that? There isn't a logo that says witches' Cottage anywhere on the map.' I told him.

Getting the eye of the lava troll out of his pocket he waved it over the map. 'There is if you know how to find it.'

'I've found it,' he said pointing to a Witches' hat symbol that had appeared next to the name Thompson. 'It's here, but the only Witches' cottage anywhere near to Thompson is Donna's,' I told Cuthbert.

'Oh, what a fool I am.' The look on his face told me that something had just clicked in his brain. 'How could I, have been so dense?' he said slapping his forehead. 'Deep down in my heart I knew, that was why I couldn't take Donna up on her offer of a room when I first arrived.'

'What are you talking about?' I asked. Getting very excited, he grabbed me by the shoulders. 'The cottage where my Beth and I lived, and where I buried all of Gorgo's treasure, is the very same cottage that Donna is now living in.'

I didn't like lying to Donna like that, why couldn't have we just told her. Cuthbert and I had lured her away from the cottage by saying that the boys needed help with their history homework, and seeing as she had lived through the period they were learning about, it had sounded plausible.

'We can't tell anybody about this until it's over, it's safer that way.'

As we talked, we climbed down into the cavern under Donna's kitchen.

'If there's a vast treasure down here, how come we've never found it on our other visits?' I asked.

'When the talisman expanded into the cellar, it must have pushed everything in here to the wall, and as it got bigger the walls got farther and farther away.

'So, if you would start here and go clockwise, I'll go in the other direction. If you find the treasure, give me a shout, and if I find it, I'll do the same.'

After half an hour searching, I'd found nothing. The cavern had grown even larger than the last time I was here, it didn't seem possible that a ceiling that vast could hold itself up.

But then it wasn't very long ago that I didn't believe in witches and wizards, let alone Gargoyles and Trolls, but now, I class some of them as my friends.

'David, I've found it,' Cuthbert called from somewhere on the other side of the cavern. 'I can't see you,' I shouted back, 'keep calling and I'll head toward your voice.' ***'My girlfriend is a big fat troll, I loved her from the start, her eyes are like big cesspools, and her breath smells like a fart.'*** (This I found out later was the first verse of a Troll love song). I carried on walking until I found Cuthbert, who was still singing at the top of his voice. 'You can stop now I'm here,' I told him as I approached.

He said there were only ten more verses to go, but I persuaded him to save them for another day.

Muttering to himself about some people not knowing a good song when they heard it, he led me to the biggest pile of treasure that I'd ever seen. (Not that I'd seen many, in fact this was my first one). 'WOW! That's a lot of gold and jewels,' I said, 'they must be worth millions.' 'All this is my Beth's, she never touched any of it after we brought it here, as it had cost so many lives, and she wouldn't have been happy spending it. So, we left it down here and got on with our lives.'

'So why are we down here now?' I asked.

'There's something here that can help young Tom out of a muddle.' After a few minutes searching he'd found what he was looking for.

'Here we are,' he said holding up what I knew from my dealing with Shamus to be a Leprechaun's pot of gold.

I thought it was almost impossible to part a Leprechaun from his gold. He said, 'It is, but the owner of this pot had the misfortune to appear at the end of his rainbow at just the exact moment that Gorgo came around the corner.'

TOM JOINS THE BROTHERHOOD

It looked just like any other cave, but Tom had a bad feeling about this one. Something evil had taken place in there, but he put that out of his mind. He was there to meet the Warlock Master and the Brotherhood.

Hopefully he'd persuade them to let him join, and then he'd be able to find out just where the book of dark magic was.

'I hope you've got something better for me than the last young wizard that tried to join the brotherhood.' Tom spun round; there behind him stood the Warlock master, he'd appeared out of nowhere.

'Why? What happened to him?' asked Tom.

Even though he couldn't see under his hood, Tom knew that the Warlock was smiling. 'Oh he's still about here somewhere, or what's left of him is. And you will be keeping him company if you haven't brought me something good.'

Tom tried to look confident. 'Will this do?' he asked, pointing to the Leprechaun's pot of gold.

Holding out a gloved hand, the Warlock ordered, *'Give it to me.'*

His voice echoing around the cave, 'Hang on, not so fast, you promised me that if I collected a power for you, I'd be allowed to join the brotherhood.'

'And so, I will, I always keep my word.' Tom thought to himself, 'Yeah, only as long as it suits you.'

'You'll forgive me for wanting to check that it's real, before going any further.' Tom handed over the pot.

'I don't know how you did it, but this is a real pot of gold from a Leprechaun'.

'That's my secret,' Tom told him. The Warlock Master pulled a wand out of his robes. Tom thought he'd gone too far by refusing to say how he'd come by the gold, but the Master waved it at the wall of the cave and muttered a spell. Almost immediately a portal appeared.

'Follow me.' Tom knew that the doorway led to the master's lair, and if he entered, he'd be completely alone. Neither Cuthbert, David nor any of the coven could help him, but he had to find out what they were up to, so he walked through and hoped he was good enough to stop the Master and his Brotherhood alone.

Almost immediately after entering the portal Tom found himself standing on a beach. When he turned round all he could see behind him was a cliff, the portal had disappeared. He had a feeling that he'd been here before, and when he looked out to sea, he recognised the view.

There just out to sea was a structure called Durdle Door. He remembered one summer when Gilbert, the old wizard who had raised him after his parent disowned him and wanted nothing more to do with him, when they found out that he had magical powers. He'd taken Tom on holiday to Dorset, and Durdle Door had been one of the places they'd visited.

It jutted out from shore, a piece of the cliff that hadn't been eroded since the bay had been formed one hundred and forty million years ago.

In the middle there was a hole that formed the shape of a door with the top rounded. At the time Tom thought, it was a magical place; he imagined that there was another world on the other side.

He was about to find out that his childhood daydream was correct.

'Are you coming, or would you like to do a bit of sunbathing first,' the Warlock sneered.

Tom turned toward the voice and found the Warlock standing next to a rowing boat.

'Get in,' he ordered. Tom climbed into the boat, the Warlock got in and laid the end of his staff in the water. The boat shot off as though it had an outboard motor and headed straight for Durdle Door. As they came closer, Tom could see through the opening to the sea beyond.

Just as the boat was about to pass under the arch, the warlock took a wand out of his pocket and pointed it at the hole in the cliff, and shouted, **Give me passage,'** the air seemed to shimmer, just like the air in hot climates, and as they passed through, the air around Tom felt charged with static electricity, but he knew it was magical energy from a spell of some sorts that had been placed on Durdle Door.

'Death to all wizards,' came a voice from somewhere nearby. Tom turned toward the shout. There outside a cave in the cliffs stood the most disgusting creature Tom had ever seen.

It was short and vastly overweight. (For a human that is). And it was covered in boils that oozed puss everywhere.

'Whatever sort of creature is that?' asked Tom. **'Ignore it, it's only an ogre. I was going to kill it, but it's just not worth the effort.'**

Tom had never seen an ogre, he knew that Albert and Safire had one living in a cave on their island, but he had never met it. 'He doesn't seem to like wizards much,' Tom commented.

'Do you know where we are?' asked the warlock. 'No,' answered Tom, 'but I have a sneaking feeling that we are not in Dorset anymore.' **'No we're not, we are in the realm created by the council of magic to dump all the creatures they didn't want in their world.'**

Tom had heard about this from the Yeti while he studied in Tibet.

How wizards, witches and warlocks had gotten together to cast the biggest spell ever, and so rid the world of Dragons, giants, and a whole lot of other creatures that they considered to be evil, or just spoiled their peaceful existence.

Leaving the ogre behind them, still shouting obscenities, they continued along the shoreline until they rounded the headland into the next bay. Tom remembered from his holiday that it was called Lulworth Cove. Only that was in his realm, in this one there was no fishing village, just a massive castle.

It was built of a black rock, and it made Tom shiver just to look at it.

This was obviously home to the warlock master and his followers.

The boat grounded on a pebble beach, and they got out. Tom could hear footsteps approaching. He looked up to see a teenager about the same age as him rushing down a path to the beach.

'Welcome back master,' he said, bowing deeply. **'John, this is Tom, take him up to meet the rest of the brotherhood, then come to me in my quarters.'**

Tom followed as John led him up to the castle. 'What is this place?' Tom asked as they walked under the portcullis into the keep.

'This castle was built by the goody goodies that created this realm.'

Tom stopped walking, 'So this was built by the grand coven?' John laughed, 'I don't know about grand coven, more like a load of old fogies. They banished all those creatures, just because they ate a few worthless humans, but when we free them, we'll be the ones who will rule the world.'

John was slowly working himself up into frenzy, then as quickly as the look of fanaticism shone in his eyes, it evaporated. Shaking his head as if to clear it, he said to Tom, 'We're here.' Looking around Tom took in the vast dormitory. There were twenty beds placed against the walls down each side, in the centre stood a long wooden table and sitting on chairs, some reading, some just lolling around were nine young men, who Tom assumed to be the brotherhood.

'You'll have to introduce yourself to the others. I must go to the master.'

And rightaway John left. As Tom walked over to the table some of the brotherhood looked up, others ignored him.

'Hi, my name's Tom,' he said to the room in general.

One of the Brotherhood, who looked as though he was in charge stood up from the table and walked over to Tom.

'Another lamb to the slaughter,' he said holding out his hand. 'I'm Simon Gray, welcome to the home of the Warlock Master.'

'Does the "Warlock Master" have a name?' asked Tom. Simon sneered 'He has, and if he thinks you worthy, he will tell you it.'

'And if he doesn't?' Tom asked. 'Well in that case it won't matter, you'll be dead. Only those privileged enough to belong to the brotherhood ever learn his name.'

THE OGRE

Tom had been at the castle for a week and in all that time he had not had any contact with the Warlock Master. 'He has work to do,' was all he could get out of any of the brotherhood. As he stood looking out of a window at the cliffs and beach of the mainland, he could hear floating over the water the voice of the ogre calling insults and threats at the castle, his favourite being 'death to all wizards,' followed by invitations to 'come on over if you think you're hard enough,' or words to that effect.

Tom knew that the boat he had arrived in was still on the small beach next to the castle, so he decided to take it over and talk to the ogre. If, that is, he wasn't killed first, but that was a risk he'd have to take. He needed someone on his side, and if the ogre really hated wizards, Tom hoped that he could persuade him that not all wizards were his enemy.

Not having a staff like the warlock, Tom had to use the oars that he found in the boat. He ran it onto the beach a short distance from the ogre's cave. The creature saw him approaching. 'Come to take me on, have you? I think it only fair to inform you that I am the most powerful ogre there has ever been, so if you don't want to meet a nasty end, leave now or you'll regret it for the rest of your life, all two seconds of it,' the ogre shouted at Tom.

'If you are indeed such a powerful ogre, why not just kill me where I stand, why give me the chance to leave?' Tom asked.

The ogre started to splutter. 'Well I'm not in the mood to kill anyone today, but I will if I must,' he threatened.

Tom smiled to himself; the ogre appeared to be all talk. 'Maybe I can use this to my advantage,' he thought.

'Well thank you for sparing my life, I would not like to go up against such a powerful ogre, maybe we could just talk.' 'What about?' the ogre enquired. 'Well', said Tom, 'we could start with why you hate wizards so much.'

The ogre snorted, 'Oh that's an easy one, but it's not just wizards, I hate witches and warlocks too. All those who trapped me alone in this realm parted from my friends and family.' Tom was confused, 'I'm sorry but weren't all creatures like you sent here?' The ogre shook his head, 'Don't know your history very well, do you?'

The look he gave Tom reminded him of his old primary school teacher. 'I'm sorry but I don't know a lot about that time in history.' 'Well pull up a rock and I'll enlighten you.'

Tom sat down and listened as he was told how the ogres had been deemed to be of no threat to the humans, so were consequently allowed to remain in their realm, Tom was confused. 'If all the ogres were left in their realm, why are you in this one?' 'It's all that bloody troll's fault, the ogre spat with all the hatred he could muster. He had captured me for his lunch.'

Tom thought, 'He must have been very hungry indeed to consider an ogre for lunch.' The one he was looking at was green, very fat and covered in warts and boils.

The ogre continued, 'He was carrying me back to his cave when the spell was cast and the next thing I knew, I awoke in this realm. Luckily I had awoken before the troll and was able to escape. It took me a while to find out what had happened. One day while trying to avoid all the other creatures that wanted to eat me, I stumbled upon this cave. It must be because of its closeness to the portal to your world, but here I feel close to my brother. Sometimes I can almost hear his wonderfully grating voice, but then I think it's only wishful thinking.'

Tom had an idea. 'Does your brother live in a cave too?' he asked. The ogre gave Tom that teacher look again. 'All ogres live in caves, it doesn't take a genius to work that out.'

Tom smiled, 'Ok, how about this? Does he live in a cave on an island off the coast of Scotland?' The ogre looked stunned. 'How do you know that?' 'Well,' said Tom, 'it just so happens that a friend of mine owns the island, and he told me about this ogre that lives there.'

'Well, you're not as stupid as you look.'

Tom was not offended, coming from an ogre that was as close to a compliment you were going to get.

'I think if you help me, I may be able to get you reunited you with your brother,' he told the ogre.

'I will do anything to get out of this realm, even if it means helping a wizard.'

An hour later Tom was rowing back to the castle after he and the ogre had agreed on a plan of action.

'Where have you been?' The head of the brotherhood asked Tom as he brought the boat ashore. Tom didn't like or trust Simon Gray, he had told Tom on his arrival that he would be keeping an eye on him, because he thought that he was up to something.

'I got fed up with that ogre and his constant shouting, so I thought I would go over there and do something about it.' 'Did you kill it?' Simon Gray asked. 'No, I left him hanging from the roof of the cave. I told him I would give him some time to repent on annoying me, before I went back and killed him.' Simon Gray gave Tom a look of pure hatred. 'I don't believe you.' I think I'll take a trip over there and have a look myself.' Tom gave him a look that sent shivers up his spine. 'I wouldn't do that if I were you,' he told Simon Gray. 'Oh and what are you going to about it?' 'I've already done it,' Tom told him, 'before I left I put a curse on the entrance. Anyone trying to enter without the right password will be very sorry.' Simon Gray snorted, 'You don't frighten me.' But Tom noticed that he made no attempt to climb into the boat. He stormed up the ramp that led to the castle, shouting over his shoulder, 'We will see what the Warlock Master has to say about this.'

A TRIP TO SCOTLAND

Cuthbert now lived in his own cottage in the village of Thompson. It was painted in the brightest of greens, with the window frames being painted yellow. This was Cuthbert's way of paying homage to his favourite football team, Norwich City. He could often be seen on the terraces at Carrow road supporting the Canary's. (Norwich city's nickname)

Dressed in the green and yellow, Cuthbert looked subdued compared to his usual attire that consisted of gaudy Hawaiian shirts and Bermuda shorts, even in the depth of winter. Try as she might my wife Sadie could not steer him into something a little plainer. He loved colour and couldn't be dissuaded from his favourite wardrobe.

Friday nights were Cuthbert, Brandon and Jordon's film night. They'd stream a film to watch, along with the largest bag of popcorn each. Sadie worried about the boys' waistlines, but she need not have worried, for most of it was eaten by Cuthbert.

'I'm sorry boys,' he apologised 'but I've got to cancel our film night. I won't be here. I've got to go to Scotland.'

The look of disappointment suddenly disappeared when he mentioned Scotland.

'Are you going to the island?' asked Jordon. 'Yes, I received a phone call from Albert asking me if I could go up there as quickly as possible. Luckily, I had Shamus's mobile number, so I rang him, and he said he would be there in a few minutes.'

Out the corner of my eye I saw Brandon nudge his brother. 'Mum, can we go too?' 'Yeah,' Jordon said, 'we would like to see the unicorn again.'

Sadie turned her head so as the boys could not see her smiling. 'Don't you mean the girls?' I teased.

'Ignore your father,' Sadie told them. 'You can go on two conditions - one, that Cuthbert promises to keep you safe, and two, that he has you back here by Sunday teatime at the latest.'

I knew that Cuthbert could never promise to keep them out of trouble.

But I also knew that he would protect them at all costs, even if it meant him losing his own life doing so. Albert Stone, Safire and the girls stood on the lawn when they arrived. 'Girls, take Brandon and Jordon to see the unicorn, we have something to discuss with Cuthbert,' he said.

As soon as they were out of the way, Albert turned to Cuthbert, 'The ogre that's living in the cave down by the shore wants to have a word with you.' Cuthbert looked puzzled. 'Why me? We've never met, and trolls and ogres are not on the friendliest of terms at the best of times.'

Albert shook his head. 'I don't know, but he asked for you by name, so he obviously knows of you.'

Cuthbert made his way down to the beach. He had no trouble finding the cave, he could have found it blindfolded. You could smell it at a hundred yards, and the place had an odour of its very own, a combination of cesspit, dead fish and every other bad smell you could think of.

'Who is it?' a very grumpy voice shouted as Cuthbert neared the entrance to the cave. 'My name's Cuthbert. You asked me to come, said you had a message for me.' The ogre told him to enter.

As he went farther into the cave, the smell got worse. Finally he reached the back of the cave and there sitting on a heap of old bones, fish heads and several other things that Cuthbert didn't want to know about, sat the most disgusting creature he ever seen.

The ogre held up his hand, 'That's close enough.' Cuthbert couldn't have agreed more, 'I know you trolls have some terrible habits, but you are the first one I've met that smells so bad.'

Cuthbert was shocked. 'What do you mean smell? I had a bath before I came here.' (Cuthbert had a love of bathing, he had a large collection of bubble bath in his cabinet at home and would spend hours soaking in the tub, so to be told that he smelled, by an ogre, was laughable.

'I think it's a case of the pot calling the kettle black,' he told the ogre. 'Anyway, you asked me to come here, but if the smell is that bad, I would be happy to leave.'

The ogre waved his arms, 'No, no, don't go, please. I need your help to rescue my brother from the other realm.'

Cuthbert was taken aback. 'Do you mean the realm created by the wizard council to house all magical creatures not wanted in this world?'

The ogre nodded. 'Yes as you may know, we ogres were exempt from the spell, but my brother had the misfortune to be in the grip of a troll when the spell was cast, so he ended up on the other side.'

'What makes you think I would want to bring another ogre here?' Cuthbert asked. 'Your friend said that if we helped him, then you would help my brother,' the ogre told him. 'What friend?' 'My brother said his name is Tom.'

'We must go back to Norfolk now,' Cuthbert told the boys. 'But we've only just got here,' Jordon complained. 'I'm sorry but it's important. I must see your father on a matter of life or death.'

Safire said if it was alright with Cuthbert the boys could stay and she would look after them. Cuthbert said that it was alright with him if she rang Sadie and she agreed.

Shamus and Cuthbert arrived back and came straight to our house, where Sadie and I were having tea. Shamus left after promising to have the boys back by Sunday teatime.

'David, can I have a word with you in the garden?' Cuthbert asked. Sadie shook her head, 'Go on, if it's to do with the coven, I don't want to know.' Sadie had once been an apprentice witch, but after seeing Uncle Bert killed and then being kidnapped by Bella, she quit, to give the boys someone who was not magical in their lives.

Out in the garden I turned to Cuthbert and asked, 'What's going on? Why are you back so quickly?'

'It's Tom, he has contacted the Warlock master and will become a member of the brotherhood, if he can convince them he is evil, but now he is stuck in the other realm, Cuthbert informed me. We must call a meeting of the coven and fill them in.'

'I knew there had to be something. Tom would not leave the coven without good reason.'

Donna looked both happy and worried at the same time, if that was possible. Happy that Tom had not abandoned us, but worried for his safety. The coven was all crowded into Donna's small cottage, all that is, except Brandon and Jordon, who were still on the island of Haven with Albert Stone and his family.

Apart from myself and Cuthbert, there were Donna, Betty, Anne, and Dorothy, back from her travels abroad, Dermot and Hamish, the two wizards Cuthbert had persuaded Donna to let join the coven.

Shamus O'Brian had recently joined us to fill Tom's place in his absence, along with Adriana and Evangeline Mead, two promising young witches whom we had met on our last visit to the island.

Donna called for quiet. 'Now we are all here, will you please explain to us what it is that you and Tom have been up to?' she said to Cuthbert.

'First, I would like to apologise for not telling any of you about Tom's mission, but he swore me to secrecy, more for your safety than anything.'

He continued, 'Tom is on a top-secret assignment for the council of wizards.'

Everybody turned to Dermot and Hamish. 'Don't look at us, we know nothing of any assignment,' explained Dermot. 'He's right,' said Cuthbert, 'only the senior members of the council knew about it. Tom would not have confided in me if he hadn't needed my help.

'About a year ago there were rumours of a Warlock Master, who was forming a coven of wizards to search for the book of dark magic.

For those of you not familiar with the legend, five hundred years ago a group of scholars decided to compile two magic spell books. One would be the book of white magic, it would contain all good magic, spells to heal and help defeat dark magic.

'The other book would be a collection of all dark spell and curses. Obviously these learned folk had no idea of the damage that could be done by any wizard who had the book of dark spells in his possession.

When the council of wizards heard of this book, it was decided to destroy it. The only trouble was that any book with that much magic inside (be it good or bad) would be almost impossible to destroy.

'So, after several attempts in which a couple of wizards were severely singed, it was decided to hide it away where nobody could find it.'

STINKING CORPSE

'The stupid things won't walk in a straight line.' Brandon was getting exasperated. Safire had asked both the boys if they would bring the cows in for milking. Safire and Albert had taken to life on the small island of Haven, and loved the peace and quiet. They had decided to try and be as self-sufficient as they could, and Albert had been over to the mainland and returned with four cows and six goats. The milk from the cows would be enough for their needs, and with the goat's milk she was hoping to make cheese to sell at the farmers' market, held once a month on the mainland.

'Jade and Opal don't seem to have any trouble when they bring them in,' taunted Jordon. Brandon could not see that his brother was winding him up. He was getting angrier by the minute. Finally taking pity on his brother, Jordon explained, 'If you get the one with the bell around its neck going in the right direction, the others will follow.'

'Where are the girls anyway?' asked Brandon. 'They're helping their mother with the cheese making,' Jordon answered. Brandon held his nose, 'Rather them than me, that stuff smells disgusting. I hope they're not expecting us to try it.'

Brandon need not have worried; by this time Safire had finally admitted that her first batch of goats' milk cheese had turned out to be a complete disaster, as the boys found out on entering the dairy after bringing the cows in.

'Phew, what's that smell?' asked Brandon. 'It's goats' cheese, but it turned out a lot stronger than it was supposed to be.' Safire had tried to emulate her favourite cheese. It was called 'Stinking Bishop', and both she and Albert had a love for this very strong cheese.

Jordon peered into the vat containing the finished cheese.

'It's making my eyes water, and I think it's burning the hairs off on the inside of my nose.' As he looked closer, he could have sworn that the mixture was alive. 'It's moving,' he said. As he looked the mass in the vat seemed to have a will of its own, it reminded him of an old film called 'The blob' that he and his brother had watched on one of Cuthbert's film nights.

'I think it would be a good idea to keep a lid on this,' he told Safire.

She nodded. 'You could be right. I'm not quite sure what to do with it yet,' she smiled, 'there is no way it's fit for human consumption.'

On leaving the dairy Brandon and Jordon ran into a very flustered Albert Stone. 'What's the matter Mr Stone?' asked Brandon. 'You look upset, Albert sighed, 'It's that bloody ogre. Cuthbert asked me to go down to the cave and ask it if he had heard anything from Tom, but it wouldn't speak to me. Said I smelt disgusting, and would not let me in his cave. I wouldn't mind so much, but I had a shower this morning.' Jordon explained that everything we found beautiful and tasteful, the ogres found disgusting.

Knowing that any information they received from Tom would be vital in stopping the Warlock Master from retrieving the book of dark magic, they both volunteered to go down to the ogre's cave, first stopping off at the dairy for a present.

On approaching the cave, the boys heard the ogre shout in a loud voice, 'Who is it now, who has come to pollute the air with their revolting stench?' 'You don't know us sir, but my name is Brandon Johnson, and this is my brother Jordon, and we have brought you a gift.'

While he was talking, he had been taking the top off a container filled with Safire's cheese that they'd collected from the dairy.

The boys had come prepared; both had a large wad of cotton wool stuffed up their noses.

'What is that delicious smell? It's making my mouth water,' the ogre called. 'It's the present I mentioned earlier,' replied Brandon, 'and if you could see your way clear to allow us revolting humans into your cave, you can have it.'

The ogre knew that for something that smelled that good, he would let almost anyone in.

'Come in, come in young humans, you are most welcome,' Brandon and Jordon entered the cave, carrying the cheese at arm's length, and afterwards they both swore that it had started to emit a green vapour.

The ogre had a look of ecstasy on his face. 'If it tastes half as good as it smells, it will be delicious. What is it?' the now drooling ogre asked.

'Goats' cheese,' answered Jordon. 'But not any old goats' cheese,' added Brandon, 'it was made by the gargoyle woman up at the farm, and has been deemed too good for human consumption.'

'Has it got a name?' the ogre asked. The boys looked each other, then Brandon winked at his brother. "Yes, it's called 'Stinking Corpse".

A perfect name for such a delicious smell, 'Now let me taste it.'

By now there was a small puddle of drool on the floor in front of the ogre; and Jordon knew that however appetising their dinner was tonight, he and his brother would not be hungry.

Back at the farm, Brandon had just finished telling Safire that they had a buyer for the rest of her cheese, and an order for as much as she could make in the future.

'I can't believe it, you mean to tell me that the ogre thought that my cheese was delicious?' Safire had been on the point of throwing the whole disgusting mess away, only she could not think where. She thought of tipping it into the sea, but realised that the impact on the wildlife would be worse than an oil slick.

'We're as surprised as you' Jordon told her, 'but the ogre loved it. 'Watching him scoff down the tub full that we took him turned my stomach.' Brandon nodded, 'Mine too, but he loved it so much that he gave us this bag.' He said that he hoped it would be enough to cover the price of the rest.

Safire emptied the contents of the bag onto the kitchen table; there were ten gold coins. 'The ogre said that if it was not enough he would be happy to pay more,' Jordon informed her. She thanked the boys for their help in getting rid of the horrible cheese, 'But boys that wasn't the real reason for going down to the cave. Did the ogre have any news from Tom?'

Brandon and Jordon told her what they had learned in the cave and asked her to phone Shamus and see if he would take them back to Norfolk as soon as possible.

A NEW ARRIVAL

Donna called a meeting of the coven as soon as the boys had gotten back to Norfolk. Her small cottage was now full to bursting point, all the members of coven had turned up to hear news of Tom.

'I'd like to thank you all for coming at such short notice.' The room quietened, everyone was anxious to hear the boys' news.

'Tom was a lovely lad, and every member of the coven was fond of him, and thanks to the youngest members of our coven,' Donna turned and smiled at the boys, 'we now know that he has joined the Warlock Master and become a member of the brotherhood.'

A gasp went up around the room. 'There's no need to worry,' Donna told them. 'He's on a mission for the council of Wizards, his task is to find out what the Warlock Master is up to.

'Brandon and Jordon tell me that he is now in the realm that was conjured up centuries ago to take all the unwanted magical creatures that were banished from our world. Somehow the Warlock has gained egress to this realm and is now living in the castle that was built to house a team of wizards, whose job it had been, to monitor the spell, and to make sure that none of the creatures could get back to our world.

'After a suitable time, it was agreed that they were happy in their new home, so the castle was abandoned, and the portal sealed.

'Tom has made a deal with an Ogre, who lives in a cave on the beach overlooking the castle, and the boys have made friends with the Ogre's brother who lives in a cave on the island of Haven, so that way we can now exchange messages with Tom.'

Next morning Brandon and Jordon were trying to convince their mother that they had only the coven's interest at heart, when they volunteered to go to Scotland at short notice, even if it meant missing school.

'Nice try boys, but unless it is an emergency, it can wait until the weekend.'

Feeling disappointed the boys set off for school.

While walking through the village to catch the bus that would take them to Watton, Jordon mouthed to Brandon, 'We're being followed.' Brandon whispered back, 'Have you only just realised that? They've been there since we left home. Can you reach your wand?', Jordon nodded. 'When I say "now", spin around and be ready for anything.' The brothers looked at each other and Brandon said, 'Now!'

They both spun round, not knowing what to expect, it could have been a dark wizard or witch intent on doing them harm. But instead, there in front of them stood a beautiful young woman.

'Hello,' she smiled, 'you know it's not a very polite greeting, having two wizards point their wands at you.' 'How did you know they are wands?' Jordon asked, because like their lockets, they had altered the appearance of their wands, so to anybody watching it would look as if they were both pointing rulers at the young woman.

'I used to change the shape of my wand, too, when I was your age.

So, you see if I wanted to harm you, I could have done so at any time,' the girl said. 'The thing is I need your help. I'm looking for my boyfriend Tom, and I was hoping, you two could tell me where he is.'

'Excuse us a minute,' Brandon led his brother a few yards away. 'I never knew Tom had a girlfriend, did you?' Jordon shook his head. 'No, there was nothing in his letters about her.'

All the time they had been talking, Brandon had been keeping an eye on the girl over his brother's head; she wasn't making any threatening movements. She just stood there smiling at them, but he knew that she had an agenda, and he had an inkling that she was not to be trusted.

Turning back to the girl he said, 'Hello my name Brandon Johnson and this is my brother Jordon.' The girl smiled. 'Yes, I know. Tom told me all about you and the coven of the talisman. I've come a long way to see Tom. Would you take me to him? she asked. Brandon put his arm on his brother's shoulder, 'Sorry, we have to catch the bus for school, but if you go through the village, you will see a cottage painted green with yellow windows frames. Inside you'll find Tom's friend Cuthbert, he will be only too glad to help you.'

The boys walked off to catch the bus leaving the girl standing on the road.

Brandon stopped and turned around, 'You know our names, what's yours?' 'My name's Sienna,' she replied, walking off.

'You know bro, I don't think we've seen the last of her,' Brandon told his brother. Jordon grinned, 'Yeah, you wish.'

Cuthbert was halfway through his breakfast pizza, (even thought my wife Sadie had tried to wean him off pizzas, and on to other food, he still clung to his love affair with them) when the phone rang. It was Jordon telling him about their meeting with the young girl claiming to be Tom's girlfriend.

If Sienna was surprised by the door to the cottage being opened by a short round man wearing Bermuda shorts, a Hawaiian shirt, sandals, and a Norwich city scarf, she didn't show it. 'Hello, are you Cuthbert?' Cuthbert nodded, 'Yes'. The young girl held out her hand, 'I'm Sienna, Tom's girlfriend.'

'That's strange. He never mentioned you in any of his letters.' Sienna smiled, 'We haven't been going out long, I have only just started studying with the Yeti, and we take the same class in meditation.'

Cuthbert knew that Sienna was lying, because the Yeti only took on one student at a time.

'If you are looking for Tom, I'm afraid he's not here now. Is there anything that I can help you with?' asked Cuthbert. Sienna shook her head. 'No, it must be Tom.' She looked so lost that Cuthbert wanted to put his arms around her. 'You can stay here with me until he comes back, if you'd like,' he offered.

'Why would you do that?' Sienna asked. 'Well as the old saying goes, "Any friend of Tom's, is hopefully a friend of mine".' (Also, he was hoping to find out who this girl was and what she wanted with Tom). 'Well, as I have nowhere else to go, I would be only too happy to take you up on your kind offer.'

'That's settled then, come in. I was just having breakfast. I'm sure there's a slice or two of pizza left, if you're hungry.'

Later that afternoon Brandon and Jordon got off the school bus. They had spent most of the day dodging the school bully. Like all bullies, he only picked on people who he thought were weak and could not fight back. Even though the brothers could have made him break out in boils, or turned his hair bright pink, they knew that they were not allowed to use magic on other children, no matter how obnoxious.

'I still say it wouldn't have mattered if we'd have turned his trousers into a ballet skirt, nobody would have known it was us,' Jordon complained. Brandon shook his head. 'I know how you feel bro, but we can't risk it. If anyone found out that we were wizards, we'd be outcasts. They don't believe in witches and wizards anymore, they'd either call us freaks, or lock us in the loony bin. 'Yeah,' Jordon had to agree with his brother. 'I know, but I don't have to like it.' Brandon promised him that they would find a way to get even with the bully, without resorting to magic.

By this time, they had arrived at Cuthbert's house. Usually at this time of day he would be watching his favourite quiz show, and tucking into afternoon tea, which consisted of ham sandwiches, and a whole sponge cake, (the only meal that didn't include pizza). This afternoon was different. The television was turned off and sitting with him and eating cake was the young witch from that morning.

Cuthbert greeted the boys and asked them to join him and Sienna. 'You found Cuthbert alright?' said Brandon. 'Yes, and he was nice enough to invite me to stay here with him until Tom comes back.'

After tea, Sienna went for a walk around the village. As the door closed behind her, Brandon and Jordon erupted. 'You don't believe all that rubbish about her being Tom's girlfriend, do you?' asked Brandon.

Jordon joined in, 'We don't trust her.' Cuthbert held up his hands. 'Boys, boys, calm down. Like you I don't believe she's Tom's girlfriend. She is here looking for something, and I intend to find out what, and also keep an eye on her. What better way is there than having her staying here?'

ANOTHER NEW ARRIVAL

I got home just as the boys arrived back from Cuthbert's. Jordon came running into the kitchen. 'Dad, there's a strange motor just pulled up outside. It's all bright colours, with flowers painted all over it.'

The image of this old ex-army wireless truck disappearing out of my life came to mind.

'Does it have, "make love not war," written across the front?' I asked. 'Yes, dad' he replied. 'Then I think I know who it is.'

Walking outside, I did indeed recognise the vehicle, just as I recognised the old man who was talking to Brandon. Seeing me coming, he stopped talking and turned to me, 'Hello son, good to see you again. How about giving your old father a hug?' Apart from looking twenty years older, he was dressed the same as the day when he walked out on my mother and me.

My mother always said that he was stuck in the sixties, and looking at him now, I had to agree with her, for he was dressed in bellbottom trousers and a flower power shirt, so bright that it would have Cuthbert green with envy.

Making no effort to go forward for a hug, I just held out my hand.

Taking my hand, my father shook it with a strength that his painfully thin body belied. 'Well, we'll build up to that hug,' he said. Turning back to Brandon he asked, 'Is this my grandson?' 'One of them,' I answered. 'His name is Brandon, and this is his brother Jordon.'

Both boys were subdued in greeting their grandfather. 'You have two fine boys, you must be proud of them.'

I think at this point I should explain about my father. As I said before he is still living in the sixties. Growing up I was the only boy in school whose father was a hippie.

My mother had also been a hippie, but unlike my father, she moved with the times. 'Oh hell, I thought, how am I going to tell her that he's back?'

'If you don't mind me asking, why are you back? The last thing I remember is you getting in your truck, saying that you had to go and find yourself, that was twenty years ago, had any luck?' I asked sarcastically.

'I know how you must feel son, but it was something I had to do. There was someone who wanted to kill me, and I wasn't going to put my family in danger. You see I was on my own, I had no one to turn to for help, and so I disappeared, knowing that you and your mother would be safe if I was absent.'

All the time my father was talking, Jordon was pulling the leg of my trousers, trying to get my attention.

'What?' I snapped. 'Can't you see I'm busy?' He pulled me down so he could whisper in my ear. 'Dad did you know that grandfather's a wizard?'

I stood back up and looked at him again. I don't know how I'd missed it, because I had once seen a Gargoyle in his true form. But I suppose I had been so shocked at the sudden appearance of my father, that I missed the aura that surrounds all magical creatures, that includes witches and wizards, that was one of the perks to wearing the locket that I had around my neck.

I could not bear to call him father, 'So George, my boy tells me that you're a wizard, is that why you left?'

My father looked shocked. 'How did he know that?' he asked. 'So he's right then,' I said. 'Not only are my boys very clever, but they are also wizards and like me they belong to one of the most powerful covens there has ever been.' By now he had gone way past being shocked.

'B-but how? When I left the only person around here with magical powers was that old crone Mistress Clarke, and she was useless, just good for potions and scaring your kids. I could not contact any other wizards, and I knew that I would not be able to defeat the Warlock Master on my own.'

My father must have noticed the shock on my face. 'You've heard of him, I could tell by the look on your face that the name is familiar to you.' 'Yes,' I admitted. 'But how did you come to have anything to do with him, George?' He shook his head. 'I do wish you'd call me dad.'

I told him not to change the subject; I wanted to know how he came to know the Warlock Master.

He said that before he'd met my mother, he was apprenticed to a wizard called the venerable one, who lived in the village of North Elmham, along with a quiet lad named Cyril. Cyril had a voracious appetite for knowledge and had soon learned all old wizards had to teach him, but that wasn't enough. He then started reading books on dark magic.

At first the venerable one tried to persuade him to concentrate on good magic. When that failed, he asked Cyril to leave. I didn't see him again for fifteen years. By that time, I had married your mother and she'd had you. He just turned up one day and told me he had been taken on by a very powerful warlock.

That he was now a warlock himself, and his mentor had been killed on a quest for the book of dark magic, and that he had taken over the quest from the warlock.

He told me that he was going to form a brotherhood of wizards to help him, and that he wanted me to join. I told him that I had a family and there was no way I was going to leave them to go on any stupid quest.

He said that if I wasn't with him then I was against him, and now I knew of the quest he couldn't let me live, but he gave me a day to think on it and change my mind.

After he'd gone, I knew I could not protect you and your mother, so I left knowing that was the only way to keep the two of you safe.

'That was twenty years ago. Are you telling me that there was no way in all that time that you could have come back, even if it was only for a visit?' George looked so sad, that I almost forgave him for deserting my mother and me.

'I'm sorry son, but I just couldn't risk it. Other wizards I'd met on my travels had told me of the Warlock Master and his growing band of followers. They all said the same thing - that he was after the book of dark magic. But the first thing on his list was to find and destroy me, so you see I had no choice if I wanted to keep you both safe.'

Grudgingly I understood George's decision, having two boys myself. I knew that I would do anything to keep them safe.

'Ok,' I told him, 'I can see why you have stayed away all this time, but why are you back now?'

'Well, there has been a lot of talk in the magical community about this, "Coven of the Talisman", and how they fight dark magic. And I'm tired of always looking over my shoulder, so I thought that if they were half as powerful as folks say, I could kill two birds with one stone. One, maybe they could protect me from the Warlock Master, and two, I could get to see my wife and son again.'

I promised I would speak to the coven on his behalf. I didn't tell him about Tom or his mission, or that we knew where the Warlock Master was.

Like Sienna, I knew he was also not telling us everything, and it felt strange that two people should just turn up on the same day - one a witch and the other a wizard with an interest in the coven or one of its members.

Without delay George went off in his hippie wagon to see my mother, now that was one reunion, I didn't want to be a part of. My mother had said on many occasions that she would wring his neck if she ever set eyes on him again.

My boys stood staring intently at me. 'Dad why is it that we have never met your dad before?' asked Brandon. 'Let's go inside and get a drink, and I'll tell you all about it.'

At the same time as the boys and I were sat in our kitchen in Thompson talking, Tom was in the great hall of the castle that the Warlock Master was using as his headquarters. Now the coven was complete; and the final wizard to pass the test and been initiated into the brotherhood was Tom, so the Warlock Master began explaining his quest to the assembled wizards. *'Now we finally have a full coven, we can begin, but before I tell you my plan to retrieve the book of dark magic, let me first warn you all, I will not tolerate failure. Anyone who fails me, will pay with their lives. But if you think that's harsh, you'll find that it is nothing compared to the punishment for anyone who betrays me.'*

Tom sat off to one side of the great hall, listening to the Warlock Master explaining exactly what he would do to any of the brotherhood that earned his wrath. When he was finally sure that they all understood the cost of failure, he split them into four groups of three, and gave each group a task. Tom found himself grouped with Simon Gray, the only wizard to talk to him properly since his arrival, and the last wizard to join the brotherhood before Tom, a surly young wizard who said that his name was Death.

Tom had met this sort of wizard before; they thought that they could make up for a lack of talent with a name that they thought would make them sound dangerous. Tom wasn't intimidated by a name and couldn't stop himself asking him where he kept his scythe. Obviously Death had no sense of humour, because the words had hardly left Tom's mouth, when he found himself looking down the length of Death's wand.

'Think yourself funny, do you? Say something else so we can all have a laugh...'

Simon Gray, who was standing next to the young wizard, put his hand on his arm, and pulled his wand down until it was pointed to the ground.

'We don't have time for this crap, we've been given a job to do, now which one of you two is going to tell the Warlock Master that we didn't complete our task because we were too busy fighting amongst ourselves.'

Death gave Tom a look of pure hatred. 'We'll finish this later,' he spat the words at Tom. Tom smiled, 'I'll be looking forward to it.'

The groups got into four boats and headed back through the portal in Durdle door. The boat containing Tom, Simon Gray and Death was the last to reach the beach, the other groups had already disappeared on their given missions. Only the Warlock Master remained on the beach. As they alighted, he called them over to him,

'Before you go I have a special task for you three. You must do this before you complete the other mission I gave you. An old adversary of mine has just emerged from hiding, he must be dealt with before we go any further. If he gets wind of our quest, he knows enough to be able to make our task very difficult, if not impossible. Handing Tom a piece of paper with an address written on it, he ordered, **'You are to kill this man. His name is George Johnson and he's hiding in the village that I've written on the paper I gave you, now go and don't fail me.'**

Instantly, he turned round and walked off down the beach.

Tom looked at the paper he'd been given, and his blood ran cold. All it said was, the wizard's name and Thompson, Norfolk...

'What's it he wrote?' asked Death looking over Tom's shoulder. Tom handed him the paper and walked over to the path that led back to Lulworth cove. As he walked along his mind was racing, how was he going to warn the coven that three members of the brotherhood were heading their way, and who was this George Johnson?

TROUBLE COMES TO THOMPSON

Cuthbert was not his usual cheerful self. I met him next morning on my way to work. Normally you could hear him coming a mile off, he had this rather loud whistle that could shatter glass on the high notes, but this morning he was silent, and looked deep in thought, so deep in fact, that he would have walked over me if I hadn't move to one side.

'Morning Cuthbert,' I called as he walked by. 'You look troubled. 'Anything wrong? I asked.

He stopped walking and looked up at me, 'Sorry David, I was miles away.' Smiling at him, I said, 'Yes, I know, you nearly walked through me.'

'What's bothering you?' I asked. He shrugged his shoulders. 'I don't know, I woke up this morning with this feeling that something very bad is heading our way. 'Do you think it has anything to do with Tom?' I asked. He shrugged again. 'I don't know, maybe. I'm on my way to see Donna, maybe she's heard something.'

I promised him that I would go and see Donna during my lunch break. In the meantime, I would phone the other members of our coven and see if they'd heard anything.

Luckily, I had a hands-free kit in my tractor, so I could phone and work at the same time. Nobody I spoke to had knowledge of any trouble brewing. But, they all said that they had this feeling that something was heading our way, and none of them felt it to be friendly.

When it was time for lunch I headed to Donna's cottage, only to find it full of people. It seemed that after my phone call, each member of the coven had decided to head for Donna's.

It was Cuthbert who was addressing them as I walked in, 'We have to be extra vigilant,' he was saying as I sat unnoticed in a chair, 'I know we have nothing concrete to go on, but we all feel it, a cold feeling inside, that's getting worse.'

I know I'm not a wizard, but sitting there I suddenly had this feeling of dread come over me. It felt as if someone had covered me in a cold blanket. I found it hard to breathe, the room started to get dark, and I felt myself leaving Donna's cottage. It felt as if I was floating down a long dark tunnel, I could see nothing. But as I peered into the darkness, I could just make out a light in the distance.

'David, David,' I awoke back in Donna's cottage, being shaken roughly by a worried Cuthbert. 'It's alright Cuthbert, I think it was Tom trying to get a message to us, everything went dark, but I could hear voices. One of them was Tom, the other two made my skin crawl when they spoke.

From what they were saying it seems that they are heading here, and that they are looking for my father, and have orders from the Warlock Master to kill him as quickly as possible.'

Everybody suddenly started asking questions, mostly who my father was and what had he to do with the Warlock Master. Knowing this meeting would last longer than my lunch break, I asked Betty if she could tell the Major (my boss, her husband) that she needed me to work for her for the rest of the day. When he protested that he needed me to finish what I'd started and asked her what was so important that it couldn't wait until tomorrow, she said was that it had to do with her stuff, apparently that was all he needed to know.

The Major's philosophy was that if he didn't hear the words, "coven businesses" then he didn't have to admit that his wife was a witch.

Having filled everyone in on all I knew of my father's connection to the Warlock Master, I left Donna's cottage to look for him. Cuthbert accompanied me, just in case Tom and the dark wizards turned up.

'Where are we going to look first,' he asked. I replied that when I'd spoken to him earlier, he said that he was going to see my mother, so hoping that she hadn't wrung his neck as she always said she would, he will still be there.

When we arrived at my mother's house, the hippie bus belonging to my father was parked outside. 'Hello son,' my mother said as she opened the door. 'You'll never guess who's turned up,' pointing at the brightly painted bus parked in her drive. I said 'I don't need a guess. Is George in?' She shook her head. 'He's your father, show him some respect.' 'I don't want to argue mom, but I'm giving George all the respect he deserves.'

I could see that she was hurt, so not wanting to upset her anymore I asked if we could go in.

'He's in the lounge,' she told us. 'David, you've come to see your old dad, and brought a friend too. Are you going to introduce me?' I sighed, he's not going to give up with this dad crap, I thought.

'This is Cuthbert. Cuthbert, this is George my father.'

'I've heard a lot about you, half troll from what I hear,' holding out his hand, he said, 'pleased to meet you. What can I do for you boys?'

George took the news of the imminent arrival of three dark wizards bent on his destruction quite well. Luckily my mother was in the kitchen at the time, making us all a pot of tea and hadn't heard a thing.

'How did he know I was here?' asked George. Neither Cuthbert nor I had any idea. 'It's puzzling,' I told him, 'you only arrived three hours ago' 'and as far as I know, only mother and I knew you were here.'

'Did you tell anyone where you were going?' I asked. He shook his head. 'No, it was a last-minute decision. I suppose somebody could have followed me.' His face dropped. After a while he spoke, but it was more to himself than the others. 'I did tell someone, but it can't be her, she seemed such a nice girl.'

I looked at Cuthbert and he nodded as if to say that he was thinking the same as me. 'It wouldn't happen to be a witch by the name of Sienna, would it?' he asked George. A surprised look appeared on his face. 'Yes it would,' he answered. 'How did you know that?'

Cuthbert told him about the young girl who had turned up a few hours before his arrival, and who was now staying with him in his cottage.

We all agreed that it was time to go and have a talk with this young witch.

When we got to Cuthbert's cottage, George had a look of ecstasy on his face. 'Did you choose the paint scheme,' he asked. Cuthbert beamed with pride. 'Yes it was all my own work, they're the colours of my favourite football team.' Cuthbert now had a friend for life, George had been a Norwich city fan since his father had taken him to see a game when he was ten years old.

I knew I had to change the subject, or those two would be talking football for hours. 'We came here to find this young witch, not form the "Norwich City appreciation society".

'Sorry David,' Cuthbert apologised as he opened the door. 'Come in, I'll see if she's here. Sienna, are you there?' he called as we walked in. 'I'm in the kitchen,' she answered. 'Do you want a cup of tea? I'm just making one.' Cuthbert replied that that would be very nice, and could she make two more as he had friends with him.

Suddenly the noise of crockery breaking reached our ears. 'She's making a run for it,' shouted George. We dashed into the kitchen, in time to see Sienna disappearing out of the window.

'Leave me alone. If you don't let go of me, I'll put a curse on you.' It was then that George and I noticed that Cuthbert was not in the kitchen. On hearing the noise, he had gone in the opposite direction to George and me.

As we came around the corner of the cottage, we found Cuthbert standing under the kitchen window, with Sienna tucked neatly under his arm.

Let me go, she shouted. 'Only if you promise not to run,' Cuthbert told her. Sienna gave him a smile that would melt an iceberg. 'Ok, I promise,' she said, but no sooner had her feet touched the ground, than she was off across the lawn.

Cuthbert and I were taken by surprise, by the speed of her escape, but not so George, she had not gone ten yards before he had hit her with a spell that stopped her dead in her tracks.

As she lay lifeless on the lawn, we both spun round to confront George.

'I only stunned her,' he said 'she will wake up in a minute, and apart from a headache she'll be alright.'

Cuthbert went over and picked up the young witch and carried her into his cottage, where he placed her on the sofa. By this time she had started to come around. 'Ww-what happened to me?' she asked. 'You were running away, so I stunned you,' George told her.

'I thought you were my friend,' she shot back.

George smiled at her. 'Friends don't run away when you come to see them,' he replied.

You could see her brain working overtime, trying to come up with an excuse for her behaviour. 'I didn't know it was you, I thought the dark wizard had come for me.'

Getting more confused by the minute I had to butt in, 'Would I be right in assuming that you two know each other?' 'Yes son, you would. This is my apprentice Sienna.' Turning back to her he asked, 'What are you doing here? I thought I told you to stay out of this.' A look of defiance crossed Sienna's face. 'I'm not sitting at home while you go out and fight the Warlock Master and his brotherhood. I don't see why you should have all the fun.'

George shook his head. 'I knew she'd be trouble when I took her on,' he told me. 'So why take her on?' I asked. 'Putting everything negative aside, she and her sister are two of the most gifted witches I've ever seen. They can perform spells that I haven't managed to master in forty years of being a wizard,' he admitted. 'Anyway, where is Paris?' 'Oh, she's gone off looking for some old manuscript to help her with her study of magic.'

'Wait a minute,' he said, 'how did you know that I would be coming here?' Sienna smiled, 'Don't be angry at me. Before you left, I put a location spell on you.' 'What's a location spell?' he asked. 'It's like having a global positioning marker on you. All I had to do was to close my eyes and concentrate and I could see where you were.'

A thought entered my mind. 'Could anyone else access this spell?' I asked. Now it was Sienna's turn to look worried. 'I suppose if someone knew about the spell and if they were powerful enough, it might just be possible to see what I see.'

When we explained to Sienna that three dark wizards were on their way, with orders to kill George, she was devastated, and couldn't stop apologising, 'What can I do? To make up for bringing them here,' she asked. 'Well for a start you can turn that damn tracking spell off,' George ordered. 'No,' Cuthbert butted in, 'leave it. I have an idea.' George didn't look overjoyed at this. 'Let me guess, you want to use me as bait.'

With George muttering to himself, we went about setting a trap for Tom and the dark wizards. When I say "we", I mean I made the tea while George, Cuthbert and Sienna turn Cuthbert's cottage into a prison that would hold three dark wizards until the coven met to decide what was to be done with them.

'Well, that's it, if we can entice them in here, they'll never get out unless we let them go,' George boasted.

Cuthbert wasn't so sure. 'They are very powerful dark wizards, but we only need to keep them locked up long enough to talk to Tom.

Once we find out what tasks the Warlock Master has given the brotherhood, we can come up with a plan of action.' George was obviously confused, we filled Sienna and him in on Tom's mission for the council of wizards. 'But shouldn't you know all of this?' I asked Sienna. 'After all, you are his girlfriend.' She looked at me sheepishly. 'Yeah, well, about that, I'm not really Tom's girlfriend. As a matter of fact, I've never met him. I only said that so you would trust me and not be suspicious.'

GEORGE HAS TO DIE

Tom, Simon Gray and Death landed their brooms on the outskirts of Thompson, 'Right let's get this over with, then we can get on with our mission,' grumbled Simon Gray. Tom shook his head. 'Not yet, we have to do some reconnaisance first. Death was just as impatient as Simon Gray, 'Why? It's only one wizard, we can easily deal with him.' Tom gave him a stare that made him step back a pace 'Yes we can kill him with no trouble at all, if he's on his own, but this is the home of the Coven of the Talisman, and if he has gone to them for help we could find ourselves up against all of them.'

Although the others were full of bravado, Tom could see that the mention of the Coven of the Talisman had removed any urge to go charging in.

Tom suggested that they go and have a drink at the local pub, while he looked around. Knocking on Cuthbert's door Tom was at a loss as to how he could continue with his mission for the Warlock Master, without killing this wizard.

The door opened, but instead of a gaudily dressed half troll with a massive grin on his face, there stood a very pretty, young girl. 'Hello,' she smiled, and Tom's legs went to jelly. 'You're Tom, aren't you? she asked. 'I'm Sienna, come in.'

Tom blindly followed her into the lounge, where Cuthbert sat wearing the brightest shirt Tom had ever seen. He sat down in an oversized armchair, 'Am I glad to see you guys, I was hoping I'd run into you before it all kicked off.'

Tom looked exhausted. 'The brotherhood has been split into four groups of three, he told them, and each group has been given a task to complete. Our task was to locate a map to the first clue; it is hidden in an artefact that's on display in Norwich castle museum.

'But before we steal it, he has given us another more important job, we were told to kill a wizard by the name of George Johnson.' He turned to face George, and asked, 'Are you he? And would you by any chance be related to David?'

'About time, we were going to come and look for if you weren't back soon,' a grumpy Simon Gray told Tom as he walked into the pub. Tom could tell by the way he slurred his words that Death and he had been hitting the bottle rather hard in his absence.

'I wouldn't have any more of that,' Tom said, pointing to their glasses, 'you will need all your wits about you when you go up against the Coven of the Talisman.'

'What have they got to do with it?' Death asked. 'Well, it seems that he is related to a member of the coven, and they have offered him their protection, so what I want to know is, are you boys prepared to take them on? Or should I call the Warlock Master and ask him for reinforcements?'

Simon Gray sneered at Tom, 'That won't be necessary, we can handle them on our own.' 'Yes,' agreed Death, 'we're more than a match for a gaggle of old witches, just tell us where he is, and he'll soon be dead.'

Tom told them to follow him. They left the pub and walked to Cuthbert's cottage. As they approached, he explained that it belonged to a half troll, who also had given George Johnson his protection. 'We're not afraid of a full troll, so a half troll is no problem,' Simon Gray bragged. 'Ok, said Tom 'but watch out, he may not be alone.'

Taking out their wands, the three of them charged into the cottage.

As they entered the lounge they found George and Cuthbert and myself sitting drinking tea, Tom shot a spell at Cuthbert, who collapsed back on the sofa. 'What's going on?' asked George. 'We are here on orders of the Warlock Master,' Simon Gray told him. 'He wants you dead, and he has given us the job of killing you, and we're very good at our job, so this is the part where you die.' George held up his hand, 'Before you kill me, would you tell me why he wants me dead so badly?'

Death looked enquiringly at Tom and Simon Gray, 'Do either of you know why?' he asked. Simon Gray looked at George. 'I don't believe it myself, but according to the Master, you have the power to stop us using the book of dark magic,' he told him, and before any of us could move, Tom raised his wand and shot a spell, which hit George in the chest.

'Don't try anything,' he warned a very groggy Cuthbert, 'we have no quarrel with you, but we will kill you if we must.'

I went over to my father and cradled his head in his arms. 'He's dead,' said Cuthbert. I turned to Tom with a look of hatred on my face. 'I will kill you for this,' I spat at him. 'I wouldn't try that if I was you, we know you have a wife and two young sons, we would hate for them to have an accident, or some other misfortune to befall them.'

Speaking to the other dark wizards, he said, 'Let's get out of here, we have our task to complete.' They left without delay, with their wands trained the whole time on Cuthbert, and me.

As the door slammed behind them, George opened one eye 'That was some good acting, son, you almost had me believing I was dead myself.'

Back at Donna's, we were explaining to the rest of the coven, all that we had found out from the dark wizards. 'Why did they leave you two alive, why not kill everyone, why leave witnesses?' Donna asked. 'Tom said that they had been given the order to only kill George, and not in any circumstances were they to harm any member of the Coven of the Talisman.' 'Why do you think that is?' asked Betty. I told her that Cuthbert and I had been wondering that ourselves. There are two reasons that we can think of, one, that he doesn't think he and the brotherhood are strong enough to take us on at the moment, or two, the more likely one, is that he has plans for us. Whichever one it is, it will not end well for us.'

Norwich Castle

'I remember this place, I was here a long while ago,' Cuthbert told Betty, Sienna and me as we stood looking up at the castle. It is a very impressive structure standing high above the Norwich skyline. It was built after the Norman conquest of 1066, when it would have dominated Norwich and the surrounding countryside; it was originally built as a royal palace and the centre of Norman administration.

'How long ago?' I asked Cuthbert, he shrugged his shoulders. 'I'm not very good at remembering dates. After you have been alive for a couple of hundred years, it all seems to become a blur.' (A couple hundred years, I should be so lucky!) But he carried on, 'I do remember that they were still building it.'

That would mean that Cuthbert had been alive for over a thousand years. When I informed him of the fact, he said that at certain times in his life he had gone into a type of hibernation. If life had gotten too dangerous, or if he had lost someone dear to him, he would find a secluded cave and sleep for a hundred years or so.

Upon entering we split up, our intention was to search the castle from top to bottom, so between Cuthbert in the dungeon, Sienna on the roof and Betty and I searching the floors in-between, we had the whole place covered. We had agreed to try and locate any of the dark wizards, but not take them on. If we found them, the idea was to contact the rest, while keeping an eye on them until we all got there.

We had no idea what it was that they were looking for, so we must wait for them to steal whatever it is, and then try and capture them. We were all wearing our lockets, which meant we could communicate telepathically. Donna had lent Sienna hers, so we could also hear her thoughts.

'David,' Cuthbert's voice echoed in my head, 'I've had an idea, I think I can find out just what it is the dark wizards are after. Hang on a minute and I'll come to you.'

A short while later a very out of breath Cuthbert came panting up the stairs. By that time I had also been joined by Betty and Sienna. 'What have you got in mind?' I asked him.

Still bent over with his hands on his knees and breathing like a marathon runner who had just finished twenty-six miles, he held up one hand 'Give—me—a—minute,' he panted.

After a while he stood up. 'Those stairs are a killer,' he complained. 'Why didn't you take the lift?' I asked. 'There're lifts? Bugger, why didn't I see them?' I put my arm around his shoulder. 'I'll show you them later, but first, how are we going to find out what it is the dark wizards are looking for?'

Cuthbert took the eye of the lava troll out of his pocket. 'With this,' he answered, 'we can use it like you'd use a metal detector to find hidden treasure.' He explained, 'I've noticed lately that if it's put near to my locket or anything with magic properties it vibrates just like a mobile phone, so all I have to do is walk round the museum until my trousers start to vibrate.' (Hard as it was, I refrained from making any comment).

So off we went, we searched the castle from the dungeon upwards, but we found nothing. At last we came to a large open room in the keep, it had beautiful arches that had been built in Victorian times to support the new roof that was being fitted. They also put in a wooden floor that wasn't there in Norman times. It was as we walked around the different displays that Cuthbert said, 'It's here the eye is going mad, it must be something very powerful.' By this time we had arrived at a glass cabinet with two items in it. Both were shrines from medieval times, the one on the bottom shelf was eighteen inches long, by ten wide and ten high, carved in ivory, but the one that Cuthbert was looking at was smaller, it was a silver gilt casket in the form of a church about half the size of the ivory one.

As we stood looking at it, a young woman in her twenties approached us, 'Don't even think about it, it is protected by a very powerful witch, whose job it is to stop scum like you from stealing it.'

'I take it that you are the "very powerful witch",' I told. She gave us a look totally lacking in fear and said, 'Yes, so be on your way?'

We explained to her that we were from the coven of the Talisman, and we were in fact there to stop the casket being stolen by three dark wizards, who were at that moment heading for the castle with the intention of stealing it for the Warlock Master.

This information shook the young woman. 'What am I going to do? I can't take on three dark wizards on my own.' Cuthbert told her that we would help. 'But first,' he asked, 'what's so special about the casket?'

The young woman whose name was Alisha said that she was not told what the casket contained. All she was told was that it held something very dangerous, and on no account was she to let it fall into the hands of dark wizards or witches. Before she could elaborate any further Cuthbert butted in, 'They're here, I can feel that Tom's close by, and if he's here the other two can't be far behind.'

I asked Alisha if there was anywhere, we could hide. 'Hide? I'm not going to hide when there are thieves about to steal the one thing that I am here to protect.' I explained that they were only there to case the place, and that they would be back to steal the casket when there were less people about.

Reluctantly she took us through a door that had a sign that said, "Staff only" on it, and not a moment too soon, because as we closed the door Tom, Death and Simon Gray walked up the stairs and over to the display case that held the casket. Making certain that it was the artefact they were looking for, they spread out to search for any hidden cameras or anything that might set off an alarm. Finally they met up near the door behind which we hid, and with the door slightly ajar we could hear them discussing the plan. 'We'll come back tonight,' Tom was saying, 'we can land our broomsticks on the roof and make our entrance through a skylight. I will cast a spell to disable the burglar alarm, then we can get the casket and escape before anyone even knows we were here.'

Alisha was livid, 'If you think I'm just going to stand by and let three dark wizards steal the one thing I was put here to protect, well you can think again.'

I explained to her that we had to let them get the casket, so we could track it to the Warlock Master and stop him getting the book of dark magic.

'Alright I'll go along with your plan, but only if you let me join your coven until we have the casket safely back in its display case.'

Later that night Betty, Sienna and Alisha hid on the roof of an office block overlooking the castle. 'Where is Cuthbert?' asked Alisha. Betty explained that neither Cuthbert nor I could fly broomsticks, so it was up to the three of them to follow the dark wizards, but that we were not far away. At that moment we were sitting in Betty's range rover two streets away, waiting in case they needed help.

Another realm

Cuthbert and I were speeding down the M3 towards Dorset. The plan had worked. Tom and the other two dark wizards had stolen the casket containing whatever it was that they needed to find the book of dark magic. The three witches then followed Tom and his cronies to the beach overlooking Durdle Door, they just had time to hide before the Warlock Master appeared, to ferry the three wizards through the portal to the other realm.

Betty and the girls found a dingy farther along the beach, and had attempted to follow, but had found their way barred by a spell that none of them could break.

'Why is there never a Leprechaun about when you need one?' complained Cuthbert. We had tried to contact Shamus O'Brian, only to be told that he was at a spiritual retreat and could not be disturbed. After a lot of arguing with his housekeeper, she finally admitted that he and his brother had gone to a Star

Wars convention in Las Vegas. It turned out that they were both in the films, Shamus played an ewok, and his brother Michael, a droid.

I tried to calm Cuthbert down. 'Never mind, we'll be there soon. I have phoned the pizza shop in Weymouth, and there'll be three of their fifteen-inch specials waiting for us when we arrive at Lulworth cove.'

The thought of three of his favourite pizzas, cheered him up, but it was nothing to the joy that the news that Cuthbert was back in Weymouth had given the owner of the pizza parlour. He had visions of his profits doubling overnight.

We met Betty and the girls on the beach. 'We're glad you're here,' Betty told us. 'We tried to get through the portal, but we couldn't break the spell.' Sienna looked happy for another reason. Cuthbert had not yet finished eating. 'Is that pizza?' she asked. 'Ye--s,' he answered, looking worried. 'There wouldn't by any chance be any left, would there?' 'Only we haven't had anything to eat since we left Norfolk.'

Normally Cuthbert was generous to a fault, he would give you his last penny, give up his bed for you, even stand in the way of a dark spell aimed at you, but what I had never seen him do was share his pizza. He would rather buy you one, than give you a piece of his. I could see a look of panic cross his face, and after a moment he knew he was beaten.

'Here you are girls,' he said, handing over the box. I put my arm on his shoulder to comfort him. 'That was very kind of you,' I told him. 'I bet that came hard, giving away the last of your favourite pizza.' 'You'll never know,' he said, 'you'll never know.'

After the girls had eaten, we all tried to think of a way of getting through the portal into the other realm. 'We tried spells and charms,' said Betty, 'nothing we did had any effect on it.' Cuthbert shook his head. 'The spell that stopped you getting in was put there by a very powerful dark wizard, nothing you can do will even dent it. What you need is this,' he said holding up the eye of the lava troll, 'not being big headed, but this is far more powerful than any witch magic." (He may not have meant to, but it came over as being big headed).

So, we set off in the little boat towards Durdle Door, as we got closer the hairs on my arm stood up. 'Can you feel it?' I asked. 'Oh yes,' giggled Sienna. When I looked, I noticed that both the young witches' hair was standing on end. 'It's as if the air was full of static electricity.' When we arrived at the portal it was like looking into a pool of still water, but when I touched the surface it sent out ripples.

Cuthbert held the eye against the surface and said something in troll, nothing happened for what seemed like ages, then his arm disappeared, and slowly we began to be dragged through. In seconds we were on the other side. 'Grab an oar, David,' ordered Cuthbert grabbing the other one, 'we have to get to the beach before anyone sees us.' We rowed for all we were worth, expecting at any moment to hear shouts from the castle, but we made it without being spotted. The Warlock Master must have been totally confident in his magic and never thought that anybody would be able to gain entry to his lair.

'Oh no, not more smelly humans,' was the greeting we got when entering the Ogre's cave. 'I've only just got the stench of the last wizard out of my nostrils, and if that's not bad enough, you went and brought a troll with you, I think I'm going to be sick.'

'God this place smells almost as bad as the Ogre's cave on Haven,' moaned Betty.

The Ogre refused to let us wait in his cave until Tom contacted us, but he did say we could stay in a cave down a tunnel that he used as his larder, on condition we didn't steal any of his food.

There were piles of dead fish and a heap of decaying meat. All three witches had their hankies held to their noses. 'Isn't there some spell you could cast to get rid of this awful stench?' I asked.

The witches went into a huddle. After a brief discussion they set about casting spells. Betty's turned the stench from that of rotten fish into that of a summer garden, while Sienna and Alisha conjured four comfortable armchairs, and some colourful throws to hide the heaps of rotting food.

We were not as lucky as we had thought, someone had seen our arrival.

The wizard who called himself Death was stomping around the battlements; he had just suffered through ten minutes of the most humiliating dressing down in front of his fellow members of the brotherhood.

Tom had been giving his account of the killing of George Johnson, and the subsequent theft from Norwich Castle. As Tom gave his account the Warlock

Master walked round them. When he got to Simon Gray, he sniffed the air, Death could see the look of panic on Simon's face, he then turned to Death, and the young wizard felt as if someone had tipped a cup full of ice cold water down his back.

The Warlock Master held up his hand, and Tom stopped talking.

'Let me get this right, you went straight to Thompson, killed the wizard, stole the casket and came back here.' 'Y-y-yes m-master,' stuttered Death.

Tom could see that both Death and Simon Gray were shaking with fear; both had seen the Master in one of his legendary tempers. He had once gotten so angry with a young wizard who had brought him the wrong power that he killed him in front of the Brotherhood. The wizard had not done his research and did not know that that particular power died with the creature it belonged to.

'Then please tell me how come it is that I can smell alcohol on you and Simon Grey?'

Tom could see the look of terror on their faces as they turned to him for help. 'That would be my fault,' admitted Tom, 'I knew the area, so I told them that they would be less conspicuous if they stayed in the pub until I had finished my reconnaisance. As it happened it was a good idea as I ran into one of the old crones from the coven of the Talisman, luckily I was able to convince her that I was there to visit the troll that lives in the village.'

'Why didn't you just kill the old crone?' 'I thought it best not to draw attention to ourselves until we'd finished the task you'd entrusted to us.'

'In future you are to stay together, I don't trust you, that's why I sent you out in threes, to stop any of you from betraying me.'

After being threatened with a horrible death if he or any of the others failed him in any way, Death needed some air, and it was while he was walking the battlements that he spotted our boat coming through the portal. 'If I were to capture them, the Warlock Master would reward me,' he thought to himself.'

So, he took a boat and rowed over to the beach without telling anyone.

'What was that?' asked Sienna. 'I thought I heard a scream.'

The scream was Death torturing the ogre. 'I hate wizards,' screamed the ogre. 'I won't tell you anything,' he shouted at the wizard. 'Then you are going to die in agony, but until you do, you are going to tell me everything I want to know. Now again, where are the people who came through the portal?' as he spoke he pointed his wand at the ogre.

I never thought that I could feel pity for an ogre, but nobody, even a totally disgusting creature as the one who was cowering in fear on the floor in front of the wizard Death deserved to be treated like that.

But before the wizard could torture the ogre again, Sienna crept up behind him and introduced the back of his head to a four-foot-long piece of driftwood that she'd found lying around.

'Why didn't you just stun him with a spell?' I asked. Throwing away the length of wood she answered, 'He didn't deserve anything as gentle.'

Walking over to the ogre she asked, 'Are you alright? 'He gave her a haughty look. 'I've had worse treatment than that from wizards, you need not have come to my rescue. I would not have told him anything. I hate all wizards, but I hate that lot over there in the castle even more.'

Betty performed a memory spell on Death and sent him back to our realm, to Donna's cottage with news of where we were and what we had found out. We gave him a note for Donna telling her to keep Death with her until we got back.

Simon Grey didn't like giving his Master bad news, but he had drawn the short straw. 'Master, Death has gone missing, we have searched the castle from top to bottom and there is no sign of him,' he confessed.

'He's most probably off somewhere sulking.' 'That's what we thought, but we cannot feel him Master.' The Brotherhood had a connection like the one experienced by the Coven of the Talisman, they could feel where each other were, and if any of them were in trouble.

The Master cast his consciousness into the ether. **'You're right, he's either been killed, or someone is blocking our ability to locate him.'**

The Warlock Master was worried, not about the young wizard Death, but about the fact that someone had managed to kill or disable one of his disciples. Not only that but they had done it right under his nose, and in his realm too.

'Gather all the brotherhood together in the great hall,' he ordered Simon Grey. **'We have unwanted visitors,'** he told the brotherhood now assembled, *'one of our number is missing. He has either been kidnapped or murdered. We do not have the time to search the whole realm for these intruders. We are too near our goal to waste time on wizards who cannot stop us. Anyway, it is no more than an inconvenience, because we now have to find a replacement to make up the number for a full coven, but first we have to retrieve the first clue to the whereabouts of the book of dark magic, and thanks to the casket from Norwich castle we now know where to look.'*

From our vantage point inside the ogre's cave we watched as the Warlock Master and the Brotherhood exited the realm back through the portal in Durdle Door.

HOME AGAIN

Donna's little cottage was full to bursting point again, not only with the coven of the Talisman, but members of the council of wizards, Gargoyles, leprechauns and the newest arrival, a very tall white being whom I recognised from descriptions I'd read.

He introduced himself as Abraham Whitefang, he stood at least seven feet, but there was no way to be sure as he could not stand to his full height in Donna's little cottage.

I think by now you will have worked out for yourselves that he was a Yeti. He was Tom's mentor, at the retreat for gifted witches and wizards hidden high in the Himalayas.

He had come to offer his help in defeating the Warlock Master and after hearing that the Warlock master and the brotherhood had come through the portal back into our realm, I knew that we would be silly to turn down any help that was offered.

'Now that we've gotten the introductions out of the way,' said Donna 'perhaps we can get down to the reason that we are all here, namely, to find a way to defeat the Warlock Master and destroy the Book of dark magic.'

'The problem is,' interrupted Betty, 'we have no idea where he is, and just what it is that he is going to do next. I think it would be a good idea if you all were to go back to your homes and speak with as many of your friends and anybody of the magical persuasion you know and see if they have heard anything that might give us a clue to his whereabouts.'

With the meeting over, it was decided that Abraham would stay with Cuthbert. Donna would quite happily have let him stay at hers, but he had only been there for a couple of hours and he had already banged his head four times. Cuthbert's house being newer than Donna's had much higher ceilings. The only problem was how were we going to get him there in broad daylight? The solution was simple. I borrowed George's hippy van, but even that was a tight squeeze, the van was not built with the transportation of Yeti in mind.

Cuthbert was happy; he had at last found another person who had the love of tea that he had. His teacup as you might remember was a pail with handle riveted on the side. Luckily, he had a spare, because five minutes after we had delivered the yeti to Cuthbert's house, saw both with a pail of tea in one hand and a whole fruit cake in the other.

At the same time as Cuthbert, his house guest and my two boys were settling down for their weekly movie night, Tom was flying over water, heading out to sea with the Warlock Master and the brotherhood.

'Where are we going?' Tom asked the wizard on the broomstick next to him.

'You'll find out when we land,' came the terse reply.

As the night came to an end, and the sun began to make an appearance, Tom could see an island in the distance. The Warlock Master signalled for them to land on a remote beach. **'There's a fisherman's hut just up the beach. We'll stay there until dark, we can't risk flying in daylight.'**

The hut was tiny, outside hung some old nets and heaped up against the wall were a pile of old crab pots. It looked as though nobody had been there for a long time.

The Warlock Master entered first. Tom wondered how the thirteen of them were going to squeeze into such a small hut, but on entering he could see that the Warlock had been busy. Instead of a cramped hut, there was now a large room with beds around the walls, and a long table piled high with food stood in the middle.

'Get yourselves some food, then get some sleep, we have a busy night ahead of us.'

Tom had little to eat, and even less sleep, now that they had left the other realm, he had no way of contacting anyone; he was totally on his own.

Back in Thompson, Donna and Betty were having the same thought. 'I hope Tom can find some way of getting in touch with us,' Donna said. Betty nodded her agreement. 'Yes, I feel so helpless, he could be in mortal danger and there's nothing we can do to help.'

George (I still couldn't bring myself to call him father) lay asleep on the sofa in my mother's lounge. 'How long has he been like this?' I asked.

My mother gave me a worried look. 'All afternoon,' she told me. 'He usually has a nap after his lunch, normally only an hour or so, but it's been four hours and I've even shook him hard, but he won't wake up. I tried shaking him myself, but to no avail, so I called Donna for help.

She informed that he was not sleeping; he was in deep meditation and would only wake when he was ready.'

Tom was pretending he was in a deep sleep, when he was roughly shaken by a member of the brotherhood, 'Rise and shine sleepy head,' he sneered, 'it's time to earn your place in the brotherhood.'

Tom was taken to the Warlock Master. *'I have an important task for you, achieve it to my satisfaction and you will become a full member of the brotherhood,' he told Tom. 'We are on the island of Jersey. The casket you retrieved from Norwich castle contained a clue to a map that is hidden somewhere here. There is an underground hospital built by the Germans during the Second World War. You must pose as a tourist and buy a ticket for a tour of the hospital. When you come to a section of unfinished tunnel, you must find a way into it. Somewhere inside you will find a box that contains a map to the hiding place of the book of dark magic.'*

Tom was half way through the tour. The guide explained how the hospital had been built by prisoners of war. It had taken the lives of a great many of them to build it, but it was never used. It had a strange effect on him. It was not only the suffering of the poor men who died there, but he could also feel a much older sorrow, as if something terrible had happened there even before the hospital tunnels were dug, and it got more pronounced as the tour arrived at the unfinished part of the tunnels.

Nobody noticed as Tom slipped away from the tour. As he looked through the wire mesh that blocked off the entrance, again he had a feeling of immense sorrow.

Finding a spot where the mesh was not as securely attached as the rest Tom forced his way into tunnel. The Warlock Master had given him a spell to use. Tom recited it and a small red ball of light appeared out of the end of his wand, it hovered in front of him until Tom commanded it "locate" and watched it float off down the tunnel.

After a while the ball of light suddenly turned right and disappeared through the wall. When Tom placed his hand on the spot where the light had passed through, it felt as if he was pushing his hand into jelly. Suddenly something started to pull him and after a few seconds he was on the other side of a portal guarding the grotto that he was now standing in.

He could see no light source, but the grotto was filled with a soft glow that seemed to emanate from the walls, the only thing of interest was a pillar of rock about four feet high, and sitting on the top was a box covered with ancient runes, that Tom could not read.

Back at the fishermen's hut, Tom handed over the box to the Warlock Master. **'You have done well young wizard.'** Staring at the box he asked Tom, **'You haven't opened this, have you?'** Tom shook his head. 'You told me only to retrieve it, and that's what I've done.'

The Warlock Master didn't look convinced but said no more.

Taking out his wand, he placed the end into the lock and uttered a spell in the old language. The lock popped, and the Warlock Master opened the lid. Inside lay a piece of parchment that looked so old that it would crumble if anyone tried to pick it up. That didn't worry the Warlock Master. He snatched it up and shouted with a look of triumph on his face, **'We have it, now nothing can stop us finding the book of dark magic.'**

THE RACE IS ON

Cuthbert ran breathlessly up the lane towards me. 'They are back in the other realm, and they've found a map that shows them the way to the book of dark magic.' I held up my hand, 'Get your breath back, then tell me all from the start.'

After a few minutes of being bent double, Cuthbert could eventually relay to me what had been passed to him by Shamus O'Brian, the leprechaun who was now based permanently on the island of Haven to relay messages between the ogres in their respective cave in the two realms.

Tom had been tasked to find entry to a grotto hidden in a half-finished tunnel on the island of Jersey. The tunnel was excavated by the German military during the Second World War. This tunnel was the last to be started and therefore not finished before the end of the war.

But what the Germans didn't know was that there was a very old structure deep inside the hill that they were tunnelling into.

Many hundreds of years earlier, a wizard named Wishbone had volunteered to go into exile to guard the map to the book of dark magic.

He had found the grotto and turned it into a magical fortress, vowing to protect the map with his life. The only way anyone could get to see it was with permission from the council of wizards.

Luckily Tom was able to prove that he was on a mission for said council.

Anyone who had the map could find the book. That is why he was able to look, but nobody was allowed to take it out of the grotto.

The old wizard told Tom that the map not only gave the hiding place of the book, but also held a spell to defeat one of twelve charms placed on the book to stop anyone stealing it.

Unknown to the Warlock Master, Tom had talked the old wizard into letting him make a copy of the map, minus the spell that is.

'So apart from Tom's fake map, there is nothing to stop the Warlock Master gaining control of the book of dark magic?' I asked Cuthbert.

He stared at me with a worried look on his face. 'We must call an

Extraordinary coven, the like of which has not been seen since the great coven convened to cast the spell to create a realm for the creatures not wanted in this realm.'

Donna's cottage was not big enough to hold all the witches, wizards, and an assortment of magical creatures, all volunteering their services in the upcoming war with the Warlock Master.

Betty had persuaded her husband to go away for a week's fly fishing in Scotland. He complained that he had a lot of work to get through and couldn't spare the time. She told him that that was alright, but she would be using the library for a meeting of "her kind" and she just thought that he would be better off in Scotland. Agreeing with her wholeheartedly, he went straight upstairs and packed a bag and headed off at great speed.

Even the great library of the manor house that Betty and her husband called home only just about held all the magic folk that had turned up to help in our fight with the Warlock Master and the Brotherhood.

Betty called for order and Donna rose to address the room, 'First we would like to thank you all for coming. We have a terrible battle ahead of us, and for those of you who are not up to date with what's been happening so far, I will fill you in.'

As Donna was going through how we'd first come to hear of the Warlock Master, and subsequent events, I took the time to look around at the folk assembled there. A lot of them I had met before, such as the Gargoyles, the leprechauns, and of course the obligatory witches and wizards.

They all had one thing in common; they were all totally engrossed in Donna's tale of how we came to be where we are now.

That is, all except one creepy individual, who seemed to be more interested in my father, George. The news had been going around that the dark wizards had killed him, and as far as we knew there was nobody in this room that had ever met him.

Betty was stood to the left of me, I tapped her on the shoulder and asked, 'Who's that chap over there?' 'I haven't the foggiest,' she replied. 'He said he was from Dover and his name was Bilious Wormgay, and told me that the Warlock Master had killed all his family except him in a fight over a family heirloom that he claimed he needed to find some magical artefact or other. He said that he had only just managed to escape, and that the Warlock had been chasing him ever since.'

I turned to Cuthbert who stood to my right, and noticed that he also was studying the same man that I'd just been asking about. 'Your feelings are spot on David, there is something wrong about him. He's not glued to Donna's every word like the rest of them, and I don't think he has taken his eyes off your father since he arrived.'

Slowly, without drawing attention to ourselves, we both tried to sneak up on him from opposite directions, and we would have made it, but for an old wizard by the name of Oswald Greybeard, who grabbed my arm with one hand and my hand with the other. 'David, I can't tell how nice it is to meet you again,' he said in a rather loud voice, while shaking my hand with great vigour. Wormgay looked towards the noise and saw me looking at him. He knew he had been sussed, so he tried to make a break for it, but he was not quick enough. Heading for the door at great speed he had the misfortune to run headlong into Cuthbert's rather large fist.

The look of surprise on Wormgay's face when he came around to find himself tied to a chair was priceless.

'What's going on?' he asked. 'You invited me to this meeting, and then you assault me for no reason at all.' Cuthbert shook his head, 'Betty is very meticulous, she made a list of all the people invited, and I know what you are going to say - it says on the invite that you can bring along anyone wanting to help - but we have asked everyone, and do you know what? Not one of them claims to know you.'

After an hour of questioning him, the wizard had not told us anything.

'What are we going to do with him?' Betty asked. Donna shook her head. 'I don't know. We can't just let him go, because if he is working for the Warlock Master, he will go straight back to him.'

Bilious Wormgay awoke from the stunning spell that had been aimed at him when he had refused to answer our questions. Looking round the room he now inhabited, he realised that he was locked up in a prison somewhere. 'I'll soon break out of here,' he thought 'and find my way back to my master. And when I tell him that the wizard called George Johnson is still alive, I will be rewarded with a place in the brotherhood.'

What he did not know was that he was not in a prison as such, he was in fact in the cavern below Donna's cottage. The cavern as you may know was originally a spell that had been conjured up to rid the world of dark magic. It started to gather spells, when it became aware and decided it was on the side of good. In the beginning it was held in a locket, but as it gathered more and more spells, it ran out of space and enlarged a cellar under Donna's cottage, which now was so huge that it covered at least an acre. Among other things it held the locket it had grown out of. It also held a multitude of objects collected since its beginning.

The cavern seemed to know what we wanted, because as we carried the now unconscious Bilious Wormgay down the steps, a prison cell started to emerge out of the wall, it looked just like the real thing, (not that I've ever been in one, honestly!) 'He'll be alright in there, until we deal with the Warlock Master,' Cuthbert smiled, 'he looks as if he could do with three meals a day. Looking at the body lying on the bed I had to agree with him, Donna had promised to take care of our guest until we had defeated the Master and his followers.

'The Master wants to see you in the great hall,' called Simon Grey as he passed Tom's room, 'and I wouldn't keep him waiting if I was you. I don't know what you've done, but I've never seen him in such a foul mood before.' Simon Grey had never liked or trusted Tom, and you could see by the look of glee on his face that he was hoping it was something serious.

Instead of just walking into the Warlock master's presence, Tom decided to try and find what he wanted him for.

A raised gallery ran around the wall of the great hall, and it was from that vantage point that Tom looked down on the gathering below, all the brotherhood was assembled there as Simon Gray walked in.

'*Where is he?*' asked the Master. 'He's right behind me. I didn't want him to suspect anything, so I let him come alone.'

'Good thinking, I don't want him to be prepared when I hit him with the torture curse. I knew that map was fake as soon as I opened the box. That's when I tried to read his mind, but he is more powerful than I thought, so I'm going to have to get the information I need by torture.'

Tom knew then that he had to get out of that realm as soon as possible, and he was going to have to take someone with him.

'Oh it's you, what do you want now?' moaned the ogre. 'Well, that's nice,' said Tom 'after I've come to take you to see your brother.' The ogre studied Tom to see if he was lying. After a while he could see no deception in his eyes. He asked, 'And how are you going to do that?' Tom explained that because the ogre could hear his brother's voice coming through from the other realm, there must be a conduit between the caves. All Tom and the ogre had to do was make the conduit large enough for the two of them to pass through.

'Oh, is that all?' said the ogre sarcastically. 'I know,' said Tom 'but we must try. Any minute now there will be several rather pissed off wizards heading in this direction.'

'Oh great, so no pressure then.' (Ogres really are the most miserable of creatures).

Safire was in the dairy when Tom walked in. 'Hello, I don't know if you remember me, we only met once, a long while ago.' Safire smiled. 'You're Tom, I remember you. But I thought you were with the Warlock Master. Tom explained about his hasty retreat and the reason for it.

Safire shook her head. 'So you're telling me that I now have two nasty smelly ogres living in the cave on the beach.'

'I apologise,' said Tom. 'But look on the bright side. Now you have twice the orders for this wonderful cheese I've heard so much about.'

'Would you like to try some?' offered Safire. Tom declined. Just one look into the vat, at the heaving mass of cheese that seemed to be giving off a green vapour was enough for him.

Shamus O'Brian, our friendly taxi service, brought Tom back to Thompson. 'I can't stay long,' Tom told us, 'the Warlock Master won't be far behind me, and

I have to get back to Jersey and see if I can talk Wishbone into letting me have the real map. Now that they've found out that I gave them a fake, it won't take them long to realise that the original is still in the grotto in Jersey. That will be their second priority after first killing me that is.'

'Why didn't you just go straight back there?' asked Sienna. 'I would have done, but there's something I need and I'm hoping that the Talisman can help me.'

Ten minutes later saw Tom, Cuthbert and myself in the cavern, heading towards the pile of treasure that Cuthbert had left there hundreds of years ago. 'Here we are,' announced Cuthbert. 'What are we looking for?' 'I don't know, it's something that belonged to the witch named Gwen that Wishbone loved, and who was killed by the Warlock Master. He went to pieces after her death. That's when he volunteered to guard the map. He wanted to get away from the world and mourn his beloved Gwen.'

'How do you know it's here? Whatever it is?' I asked. 'I don't. Only, Wishbone told me that he had once owned a painting of Gwen that was housed in a gold frame, and that it was stolen from his house after her death, so seeing as this is the largest haul of ill-gotten gold in the world, I was hoping that it might be here.'

The heap started to move as if something was trying to burrow its way out, then as if the Talisman knew what we were looking for, a golden frame with the painting of a beautiful woman emerged from the pile.

'What are you doing back here?' asked Wishbone. 'I told you the last time that I could not help you anymore.'

Tom explained that his plan to trick the Warlock Master into believing that the copy he'd given him was the real map had backfired. 'He knew as soon as he looked at it that it was a fake, and I don't think it will be long before he comes looking for the original. When he gets here he will not be alone, he will have a whole coven of dark wizards with him.' The wizard looked very old and confused. 'What am I going to do?' he asked.

'The only way to stop the Warlock getting the map is to let me take it with me. I promise you I will guard it with my life, or if needs be destroy it before he can use it.'

Wishbone gave over the map into Tom's keeping and wished him luck. Tom tried to persuade the old wizard to go with him. 'You'd be a great addition to the coven of the Talisman,' Tom told the old wizard. 'As much as I would like to even the score with the warlock, who killed my beloved Gwen, when I took this job, it was on the understanding that I would never grow old as long as I never left the grotto, but if I did leave all my years would come back to me and I would die.'

Before he left, Tom gave the old wizard the painting of his Gwen that we'd found in the cavern.

Wishbone sat in the grotto looking at the painting that the young wizard had given him. All through the years that he had been the guardian of the map, he had thought of Gwen and his love for her. As he sat staring at the painting, he could almost hear her voice calling his name. As he sat there, he imagined it getting louder.

When he looked in the direction of her voice, the grotto wall started to shimmer and the shape of a woman appeared. 'Gwen? Is that you?' 'It's me, Wishbone, you have discharged your duty. Now it's time for us to be together again.' She held out her hand and said, 'Come my love.'

'There's nobody here, Master, the place is deserted,' called Simon Gray *'Yes, I can see that for myself, the Warlock Master replied. 'Tom has it. Put the word out, I'm offering a reward for the whereabouts of this traitor. Make it so large that we'll have all of the magical community looking for him. Until we have that map we cannot find the book of dark magic.'*

The meeting at the manor was in full swing. Betty's husband was still away so he didn't have to pretend that the magical beings now entering the library were ordinary folk, (something he was finding harder to do). The room was bursting at the seams with folk wanting to help.

Betty called the meeting to order. 'We are here to form a plan of action. Now that we have the map to the book of dark magic in our possession, we must decide if we should destroy it or find the book of dark magic ourselves.'

As with many such gatherings, some wanted to burn the map, and some wanted to find it, but it didn't stop there, there were those who wanted to use the book to wipe-out dark magic, and those who wanted to destroy it.

After a lot of arguing, it was time to vote on it.

'We have counted all the votes,' Donna informed everyone, 'and the majority of votes were for a group of seven made up of one from every group here to find the book and destroy it. So Oswald Greybeard will represent the wizards, Donna for the witches, Sandstone for the gargoyles, Liam Delaney for the leprechauns, Cuthbert representing the Trolls and last but not least I would be going for the humans.'

I know I said seven and so far there was only six, but George insisted on coming, because he said that he knew the Warlock Master and what he was capable of. Not only that, he had a score to settle. A row then broke out. 'It was agreed that only one from each group would be allowed,' shouted one of the gargoyles, 'if he goes there will be two wizards.'

George said that he was going as a representative of the hippies.

As silly as it sounded, we knew that if we told him he couldn't come, he would just follow us, so reluctantly he was allowed to join our quest, making seven in all.

THE BATTLE OF THOMPSON

It didn't feel right going off in search of an old book and leaving my wife and sons behind. I knew that I had no powers, I'm not a wizard like my boys Brandon and Jordon. The only thing slightly magical about me was the locket I wore. It was one of eleven that had been conjured up by the Talisman for our coven, it gave the wearer the ability to feel if any of the coven were hurt or in danger. It also magnified the wearer's spells, but seeing that I had no power to cast spells, the Talisman used me as a conduit though which to cast spells and inform the others of its wishes.

I looked at my wife's face and saw fear in her eyes. 'Why do you have to go? Can't someone else take your place?' she asked me. 'Sorry love, but for some reason I must go. I think Donna knows why, but she's not saying.'

I turned to my boys, 'Take care of your mother until we get back.' They both nodded. 'Don't worry dad, we won't let anything happen to mum,' promised Brandon. 'Why can't we come with you?' asked Jordon. I explained that they had to stay in case the Warlock Master came looking for Tom. 'You are getting to be very powerful young wizards, so Donna and Betty tell me. That's why you have to stay. If we took all our most powerful people with us, who would we have left to take care of those without magic? You know that the Warlock Master would destroy Thompson and everybody in it if he thought the map was still here.

You and those remaining may have to take on the Brotherhood and their master, so you see, you have a very important task to perform for the coven.' They both looked at me with determination on their faces. 'We won't let you down, dad,' they said in unison.

I knew that the rest of the coven and assorted magical folk now assembled at Betty's would not put my family in any danger. My wife and boys would not be allowed to come to any harm.

That night Betty's house was full to breaking point. 'It's a good thing my husband is still away,' she told Sienna, 'he's not comfortable around magic folk.

He calls them, "my friends". He's not prejudiced or anything, it's just he doesn't know how to act around magic, so he acts as if everything's normal. He once came upon me flying my broomstick in the garden. The only thing he said when I landed was, "Don't the roses look lovely in the moonlight?".'

Just then the door to the lounge burst open. 'They're here,' said a rather out of breath Leprechaun, 'Right now they're trashing Donna's cottage.'

Every window and door of the manor was being guarded by at least one wizard, witch, gargoyle or leprechaun. Betty, Alisha and Sienna were roving about ready to prop up any weak spot should the need be. 'We must give the seven enough of a head start that will allow them to find the book of dark magic before the Warlock Master,' Betty shouted.

'What are we doing down here in the cellar?' asked Jordon. 'Yeah,' agreed his brother, 'they're not going to break in through here.' Sadie put her arms around both the boys. 'Everybody knows that you've become powerful wizards for your age. But you are not yet powerful enough to take on a whole coven of dark wizards, let alone a warlock.'

'I want them alive,' the Warlock Master said to the brotherhood. **'Someone in there knows where the map is, so don't kill all of them. But don't underestimate them, most of them inside are members of the Coven of the Talisman.'**

'Here they come,' called Alisha who was on lookout in the master bedroom. This was quickly confirmed by shouts from other parts of the house, and by shattered glass from the windows blasted apart by spells from the dark wizards.

Betty just managed to pick herself up off the floor, when a dark wizard appeared at the opening where a hundred-year old window had been, 'You-come-into-my-home-to-destroy-my-family's-heritage. How-dare-you?' Betty punctuated each word with a spell that drove the dark wizard out of the window he had just entered by, and on the word "you" she hit him with a stunning spell that blasted him ten feet across the lawn.

Betty was now on a mission, she went through the house like a hurricane, stunning any dark wizards she came across.

'They're more powerful than we thought,' Simon Grey informed the Warlock Master. *'You still have this knack for stating the obvious,'* the master sneered, *'call everybody back. I'll handle it.'*

The red mist in Betty's head started to disperse. There were no more dark wizards to take her rage out on. All had gone quiet, and as if from a long tunnel she heard a voice, 'Betty they're gone, Betty snap out of it.' She then realised that Sienna was talking to her. 'Talk about a whirling dervish, you went through them like a dose of salts.'

After a search of the manor, not one of the dark wizards could be found. 'They must have taken the stunned and wounded with them,' Sienna told Betty. 'We beat them,' bragged Sienna, 'we kicked their backsides.' 'No, butted in Betty, 'they left for a reason, and I don't think we can celebrate quite yet.'

'Master,' one of the Brotherhood came running from the direction of Donna's cottage. 'I've found Bilious Wormgay, and he says that he has something important to tell you.' *'Take me to him.'*

Bilious Wormgay sat in an armchair as the Warlock Master walked into Donna's cottage.

'I thought you were dead.' 'That's what they wanted you to think, but they locked me up in a cell under this cottage. It was weird. The walls glowed and although I never saw anyone, my meals would suddenly be there when I woke up, or I would look at my tray and it would be empty. But if I turned away for a second, when I looked back my food would be there. *'That's all very interesting, but how does that help me find the map?'*

'Well at first I thought that I was going mad because I could hear voices. It didn't take me long to realise that I was hearing conversations from the cottage above, and the last thing I heard was the location where the first clue to the book of dark magic is hidden.'

'We're going to have a look about outside,' Sienna told Betty. 'It's been three hours since we've seen any sign of the dark wizards.' 'Ok but take care.' Sienna and Alisha sneaked out through the kitchen garden, and returned half an hour later the same way. 'We've searched everywhere, there's no sign of them. We also checked the cavern and found the prisoner was gone, the only thing we can think of is that he had overheard someone talking about the whereabouts of the first clue. And he has told the Warlock Master.' Betty looked troubled.

'There is nothing we can do now. I only hope that we gave the seven enough of a head start.'

'How are we going to find the cave where the book is hidden?' asked Oswald Greybeard. Cuthbert opened the map. 'It's all written down here, what we must do is follow the instructions and decipher the clues that will lead us to it.'

'The first clue says, "Find where a giant lay asleep under a blanket".

It goes on "only one who is the opposite will with luck find the next clue". 'I know where we must go,' said Liam Delaney. 'I am the opposite in stature to a giant, and nobody has more luck than a Leprechaun.' Promptly, he called up a rainbow and invited us to follow him.

Stepping out at the other end, we found ourselves standing on the seashore, but it was not your normal seashore. Instead of a beach or cliffs, we now stood on thousands of odd shaped columns. 'I know where we are,' said Betty, 'this is the Giant's Causeway. My husband brought me here on our honeymoon.' The Gargoyle named Sandstone, who had now taken on human form, and said his name was Mr Stone, was down on one knee touching the strange columns that covered this part of the coast. 'This is Basalt,' he said reverently, 'it is very magical. It comes from volcanos where the original trolls lived, and it is unique in that there has never been a Gargoyle composed of Basalt.'

'That's all very well, but how does that help us find the next clue, and what has this to do with a sleeping giant?' asked Oswald Greybeard.

Liam Delaney asked us to sit. This goes back to the time many years ago when a giant named Finn McCool built the causeway to Scotland so he could reach his enemy Benandonner. Now here versions differ, but the one our clan adheres to, is that Finn got half way over to Scotland when he got tired and fell asleep. His wife saw Benandonner coming, and also noticed that he was twice the size of her husband, so she covered him with a blanket and told him that Finn was actually her baby. Benandonner thinking that if this was their baby, her husband must be ginormous, so not wanting to fight such an unbeatable foe, he turned back to Scotland breaking up the causeway as he went.' 'Well that explains the first part, so we know we're in the right place. Now what?' I asked. Liam said something in Gaelic and a cauldron full of gold coins appeared at his feet. Taking one he threw it into the air. 'May we be lucky in our endeavour,' he shouted.

The coin hovered in the air for a few seconds, and then floated off to the left of us. We followed it for a hundred yards until it came to a standstill.

'What now?' enquired Cuthbert, but as we looked it dropped down and landed on one of the columns. The coin grew till it covered the top of the column. It then rose into the air, leaving a hollow space in which sat a wooden box with runes carved into the lid.

'They were here Master,' and it looks like they found the clue. **'Again Simon you demonstrate your talent for stating the obvious, and it's getting rather annoying.'** 'Sorry Master,' Simon Grey apologised, 'but what are we going to do now?'

'He hasn't moved for an hour,' Bilious Wormgay observed, and it was true, the Warlock Master had gone into a trance when he found out that the seven had beaten him to the first clue.

Suddenly the Warlock turned to Simon Grey, **'Assemble the Brotherhood we're leaving.'** 'Where are we going?' asked Simon, **'To Cheddar Gorge'.**

Already in Cheddar Gorge, (a beautiful gorge cut through the hills of Somerset over millions of years by the flow of water) the seven were heading to a place called Gough's cave, a tourist attraction halfway up the gorge. 'Have any of you got any money?' Oswald Greybeard asked. 'What do we need money for?' The old wizard looked at Mr Stone (the gargoyle) and sighed, 'You have to pay to enter the cave. Can't we say we're on a mission of great importance?' Mr Stone carried on. 'Tell them you are a wizard, and they might let us in for nothing.' Oswald shook his head. People don't believe in us anymore, we'd more likely be put in a mental institution. No, the easiest way is just to pay the admission. I'll pay,' offered Cuthbert, getting out his platinum credit card (how the other half live).

The cave was full of tourists. 'Even if we find the next clue, how are we going to retrieve it without all these people seeing us?' Donna asked, 'Let's find it first, then we can worry about that later,' I told her.

As we walked on, I noticed that Cuthbert had the eye of the lava troll in his hand. Suddenly he stopped, and I noticed that the eye was emitting a pulse of light.

'There is something magical in here,' Cuthbert muttered more to himself than anyone. 'Who has the parchment?' he enquired.' 'I have,' said Donna, giving it to him.

A typical looking American tourist, wearing shorts, white socks, up to his knees and with the obligatory camera hanging around his neck looked over Cuthbert's shoulder. 'Gee that looks old. Martha,' he called, 'come and see what this young gentleman has here.' straightaway a rather large lady came over. 'That's fine honey,' she gushed. 'Is that a treasure map?' she enquired.

Cuthbert gave the pair his biggest smile. 'Yes, it is,' he confirmed. 'It is said that the highwayman Dick Turpin stashed his ill-gotten gains somewhere in this very cave.'

There must have been a bus load of Americans, because before you could say McDonalds, a crowd of similarly dressed people had surrounded Cuthbert. While he went on telling his story of the highwayman's life and his treasure, he managed to pass the parchment to Donna, who signalled us to follow, then set off further into the cave. 'Now that Cuthbert has given us some privacy, we can get on with the job in hand.' The first clue had led us to the cave we now stood in, the second would lead us to the next clue, it says: "I'm looking down at myself looking up". Then it went on: "Only one of my kin will succeed". Everybody looked at each other with the same look of bewilderment. 'Ok, let's start with the first line, the only things that looks down in a cave are – one, bats and stalagmites,' said Donna, 'and I don't see any bats in here, so we have to start looking at all the stalagmites and see if one fits the bill.'

So, we all went off in different directions. As I looked, I could still hear Cuthbert regaling the Americans with his totally made-up stories of Dick Turpin.

'I think I've found it,' called George. When we had all gathered around him, he pointed to a stalagmite hanging down from the roof of the cave.

'Why is this one different from all the others in here?' asked Oswald Greybeard. George invited us all to "look down". Below the stalagmite was a dish worn out of the floor by thousands of years of water dripping off the stalagmite. The dish was half filled with water, so you could see the reflection of the stalagmite in it. 'That's it," cried Donna. "Looking down I can see myself looking up". Oswald Greybeard stood shaking his head. 'No it's not what we are looking for, I don't even think we're in the right place, the first clue could mean anywhere, afterall there are lots of other gorges in Britain, if it's even in Britain. No I think we should go back to Thompson and consult with the wizards' council before we go any further.

It seemed to me that the old wizard was trying to put doubt in our minds.

'No,' said Donna 'this is the right place, and you know it. Now let's get on before the Brotherhood turn up.'

Getting out the parchment, she read the second line, "only, one of my kin will succeed". 'Only one of my kin,' she repeated. 'I'm stumped. What could ever be related to a stalagmite?' We heard someone answer. 'Um, I think that would be me,' said Mr Stone. He went on to explain that as a gargoyle he was born from rock, and he would become rock again when he died, so you see I am related to all things mineral.'

'Yes, yes, that's all very well, but how does that help us with our quest?' said a rather grumpy Oswald Greybeard.

While the old wizard stood mumbling to himself, Mr Stone went over to the stalagmite. 'I'm going to try something.' Instantaneously, he turned back to his true form, and put his stone like hand into the puddle of water below the stalagmite. 'It's deeper than it looks,' he said. By now he had his arm in up to his elbow. 'There's something down here, it feels like another box.' And when he took his arm out, that's exactly what it was, only this time the box was made out of stone.

Simon Grey couldn't help himself. 'We've missed them again master.' Luckily, he had quick reflexes, and ducked as a stunning spell meant for him hit the American tourist who had stayed behind to look for Dick Turpin's hidden loot after the rest of his tour had gone on to the next cave. 'Sorry master, it won't happen again.' But the Warlock Master had gone into a trance and had not heard a word.

'I know where we are,' called George as we emerged from the rainbow.

'This is the Manor Oak, the biggest oak tree in Britain. It has a girth of 33ft and a spread of 92ft, weighs an estimated 23 tonnes. It is over 800 years old and stands in the middle of Sherwood Forest.'

'How do you know all this?' I asked him. 'Google, how else?' he answered.

Unlike the other clues, this had only one line to decipher. All we had to do was to be holding the parchment that we'd found in the stone box. The one line written there read: "open my heart with part of me". 'Ok, so it stands to reason that one of us is capable of retrieving the next clue,' said Donna, 'the first clue was found with Leprechaun's gold, the second needed a Gargoyle, so that means that one of us five has part of that oak tree on them.'

Again, Oswald Greybeard became the voice of doom. 'How can we be sure that it has anything to do with this tree? As I said before, I don't even think we are on the right track. We should go back and start again.'

Donna flew at him, 'What's gotten in to you? All of a sudden you've become all doom and gloom. It's as if you are trying to sabotage this quest.' The old wizard went red in the face and started spluttering, 'How, can you say such a thing? I've always been loyal to this quest. I—t's just that there is so much pressure on us to succeed, that I just want to get it right.'

Cuthbert, George and I were watching this exchange from a way off. 'I get the feeling that the old boy has an agenda of his own.' Cuthbert and I both nodded to George that we agreed with him. 'We had better keep an eye on him,' Cuthbert added.

'If there are no more of you wanting to go home,' glared Donna, 'we should surround the tree and find its heart.' We found it harder than we'd thought. 'There are dozens of hearts,' called Mr Stone. Lovers had been carving hearts with their initials entwined on the trunk of the tree for almost as long as the tree had been there.

'I've found it,' called Donna, 'it's not a carved heart.'

We all gathered where Donna stood, pointing at a heart shaped knot on the trunk. 'It's where a branch has been cut off hundreds of years ago, and the tree has grown over the cut to form a heart.' 'Now we must find out which of you five has part of this tree in your possession.' 'You can rule me out,' I told Mr Stone. 'Me too, I have nothing made of wood on me,' added Cuthbert. 'That leaves you, Donna, George, and Oswald. And I know you have wands and a staff made of wood.'

'My wand's made of birch,' said Donna. 'And mine's hickory,' added George.

'Well that just leaves you, Oswald, and from here it looks like your staff is made of oak,' Donna observed.

Oswald Greybeard tried to drag his feet again. 'Very observant. Yes, my staff is oak, but I don't know how that helps us.' Donna shook her head. 'Listen, you doddering old fool, you read the parchment, tap the centre of the heart with the end of you staff.'

He knew better than to argue with Donna when she was angry, so he hit the heart with his staff and jumped back as if expecting a dragon to fly out.

Nothing happened for a while, then we heard creaking as though a tree was falling. As we looked, the heart started to enlarge until it was big enough to walk into. 'What now?' I asked. 'Do we all go in, or is this for Oswald alone?' The old wizard took a step backwards. 'I'm not going in there on my own, one of you will have to come with me.' Cuthbert volunteered. 'I'll go, and you two can come as well,' he said pointing to George and myself.

As we walked through the heart shaped door, we entered a large area. 'I can't see a thing,' moaned the old wizard. 'There, is that better?' said Cuthbert holding up the eye of the lava troll that was now glowing bright enough to illuminate the entire inside of the tree.

'Ok, everybody spread out and find the box with the next clue in it.' We all did as Cuthbert asked, and after searching everywhere, we came up empty handed. 'I don't think this clue is going to be as easy to find as the others.' 'No David,' agreed Cuthbert, 'it stands to reason that the clues are going to be harder to find the closer we get to the book of dark magic.'

We spread out again, this time to look for anything that seemed out of place. The inside of the tree looked just like the outside, everything was covered in bark, and it was as though the tree had been turned inside out.

We all met again in the centre. 'There's nothing,' George said what we all thought. 'What about that?' Cuthbert said, pointing to the floor. 'It's just a knothole,' moaned Oswald Greybeard. 'Then why is it on the floor?' asked George. 'You'd normally find one on the trunk. Anyway, there seems to be a hole in the middle that goes down a long way. Put your staff in it, and let's see what happens.' The old wizard shook his head. 'No, I've had this staff for sixty years, and I'm damned if I'm going to lose it now.' I knew that he was going to need persuading, so I asked, 'Do you want me to get Donna in here so you can tell her "no"?

My question had the desired effect. 'No, that won't be necessary.' He pushed the end of his staff into the hole. It slid in about a foot then stopped. We all stood back waiting to see what happened next. We didn't have to wait long, because as we watched, from the staff branches started to grow, then leaves, followed by flowers, It reminded me of one of those wildlife programmes where they used time lapse photography. Then from the flowers fruit began to grow, eventually there waswere five yellow apples and on the end of one branch hung a roll of parchment.

Cuthbert was the first to move. 'George, find something to put the apples in while I get the parchment.'

Oswald Greybeard was on his knees, 'My lovely staff, how am I going to cast spells now?'

I felt sorry for him, but we needed the clue to find the book before the Warlock Master.

As George plucked the last apple off the tree, it slowly reverted to the old wizard's staff.

The Warlock Master and the Brotherhood had just arrived next to the Manor Oak. **'If you say one word Simon Grey, it will be your last,'** but Simon Grey had learnt his lesson, he would not be stating the obvious again. **'We are getting closer. Every time they use magic, I can detect them quicker. Eventually we will arrive before they can move on.'**

'There won't be nearly enough room for all of us to sleep there,' moaned Oswald Greybeard.

'Are you sure you have never been here before?' asked George. 'No, never,' spluttered the old wizard.

I took George to one side 'Why do you think he knows this place?' I asked. 'Well, I'm sure that the Warlock Master has been here recently, and I don't trust that old wizard.'

On entering we found that what looked like a small fisherman's shack on the outside, had been magically changed on the inside. 'This must be the place where they stayed while Tom retrieved the clue from the underground hospital in Jersey.'

As I looked around, I could see that someone with magic had been there, the shack was at least five times bigger on the inside than it was on the outside.

'You didn't look the slightest bit surprised when you entered, it's as if you were expecting to see it like this,' George watched the old wizard to gauge his reaction.

The old wizard sighed, 'Alright, you win.' He slumped down into an old armchair. 'Yes, I was a member of the brotherhood, and yes, I have been here before, and before you could say antidisestablishmentarianism (look it up) everybody in the room had their wands or whatever magical device they used pointed at him.'

Being the only one without magic, I took it on myself to calm things down.

'Everybody please lower your wands. Let's find out if Oswald is still working for the master.' The old wizard put his head in his hands and started to sob. Donna went over and sat on the arm of the chair. 'Why don't you tell us what's going on?'

Oswald took his head out of his hand and looked at Donna, 'I didn't want to do it, but he said that he would kill my daughter if I didn't help him. She's all I've got. I was old and stupid and he promised me that when he got the book of dark magic, he would be able to perform any spell there was, including one to make me younger. As time went on I came to realise that all he wanted the book for, was to satisfy his own agenda. He has no regard for his disciples, he would sacrifice them all to get the book.'

'So why are you still helping him?' I asked. 'Ok, I'll put it another way, why are you hampering our efforts to find the book?'

'For that I am very sorry. I thought that if I could stop anybody getting it, you would all give up and the book could remain hidden, but now I realise that the master will never stop looking for it, so I've come to the conclusion that the best way to stop him is to help you. On one condition.' 'What's that?' I asked. 'You have to find my daughter and keep her safe until this is over.' Oswald promised to send wizards from the council to hide his daughter until this was over.

After much discussion, it was decided that it would be a good idea to have Oswald with us where we could keep an eye on him.

'Now that we've sorted that out, can we have a look at the parchment?' Donna enquired.

Cuthbert unrolled it on the table. 'Ok, who's got the suntan lotion?' 'Why do we need suntan lotion?' enquired Donna. 'Well, if you'd ever been to Tenerife, you wouldn't ask that question,' said Cuthbert.

'I've always wanted to go to Tenerife,' Sadie shouted at me, 'and here you are going without me.'

We had gone home to Thompson to inform the rest of the coven on our progress and to have a quick shower and change our clothes.

'Yes I know darling, but it's not a holiday, this is coven business. I don't think you had being chased by a dark coven and a Warlock Master on our itinerary. I promise you when all this is over I will take you there for the holiday of a lifetime.' 'I'm going to hold you to that,' was the last thing she said as she left the room.

We exited the rainbow in the square of a town on the coast of Tenerife; in front of us was a tree that looked as if it had been there since the time of the dinosaurs. 'That,' said Liam Delaney, 'is "El Drago" the dragon tree. Local legend has it that it is at least a thousand years old, but the truth is that it is between two hundred and fifty and three hundred and sixty-five years old.'

'That's all very interesting,' I commented, 'but what has this to do with our next clue?' Cuthbert took out the parchment, 'It says here that we are to find the oldest living and ask it for help.'

It was lucky that we had arrived on the island at 5.30 in the morning, because the sight of our little group arguing over how we were going to ask a tree for help would have sent most of them for counselling.

Getting inpatient I waved them all to stop talking. 'Look we can argue this until we all grow old and not agree, so why don't we just do as the parchment says and ask for help?'

Grudgingly they took my advice. 'Ok David.' Cuthbert turned to the tree and asked in a loud voice, 'We need your help, we are looking for the book of dark magic before a coven of dark wizards can get it, so if you have any knowledge of its whereabouts, we would be grateful for any help you can give us.'

Two or three of our group looked at each other as if to say, "He's lost it".

But before they could say anything, a voice said, 'and what would you be a doing with the book of dark magic? I ask myself, yes what would they be doing with it?'

The voice took us all by surprise. 'Um, hello my name is Cuthbert, and my friends and I are members of the coven of the talisman. We are looking for the book to stop it falling into the hands of dark wizards.'

After a few seconds' contemplation, the tree spoke again. 'Why are your hands any better than the dark wizards? You both use magic. Why is your magic any better? Yes, why is yours any better? Shut up, I'm doing the talking, I'm the oldest.'

I turned to Cuthbert and whispered, 'Either that tree is schizophrenic or there is more than one person, creature, or whatever, hiding in there.'

Cuthbert nodded his agreement. 'Who do I have the privilege of addressing?' he asked. 'He's very polite for a troll, yes very, but our question is still the same. What do you want with the book of dark magic?'

Cuthbert replied, 'The only reason we are trying to gain possession of the book is to put it somewhere where it can never be used for any dark purpose.

'The warlock master has an agenda of his own. We are not privy to that agenda, but we know that whatever it is that he's planning, it will not be good for the rest of us magical creatures.'

We could hear whispers coming from the dragon tree. 'It sounds like there is a whole group of whatever they are in there,' I said to Cuthbert. He nodded. 'I think I know what it is we are dealing with. The oldest thing on Tenerife is not "El Drago". I think what we have here is a colony of tree sprites.'

'Oh no, not bloody tree sprites,' Liam Delaney lamented, 'this could take forever.' Cuthbert nodded. 'He's right, the colony has no leader, no chain of command. They must agree totally, or nothing gets done. So, as you can imagine they'll talk about things for so long that at times they forget what it is that they were discussing in the first place.'

Suddenly it went quiet, every sprite stopped talking. 'It looks as if they have come to an agreement,' Donna whispered. 'Yes, it's unusual for them to decide so quickly,' said Cuthbert.

As we watched what looked like a piece bark about three feet high detached itself from the side of the tree. We then realised that it was a tree sprite, and as if it was a signal, the rest of the tree sprite colony appeared out of nowhere.

'My name is "The Oldest",' he told us in a voice that sounded like the rustle of dry leaves. He then went on to introduce the rest of the colony, who had names like "The Youngest" "The Fattest" "The Wisest" and so on.

They were more descriptions than names, but they all seemed to fit.

After Cuthbert had introduced us, we got down to the business at hand.

The Oldest asked us all to sit down, so as he could see our face as we talked. 'Please to explain to us why we should help you.' Donna then went on to explain who we were and how we came to be looking for the book of dark magic.

After that the tree sprites went into a huddle, and thirty minutes later, The Oldest who if not their leader, was at least their spokesperson (or spokes sprite), said, 'We are not the keepers of the book of dark magic.' 'But we do hold a key to its hiding place,' he carried on, 'what we were charged with hundreds of years ago, was that we were only to give up the clue if the book was in danger of being found by someone who would bring darkness to the world. What we are asking is, is this warlock the person we were warned of?'

'Yes, I believe he is,' Donna answered.

The Oldest looked deep in thought, and kept turning to face others of the colony, as if he was talking to them. 'They can communicate telepathically,' Donna whispered, and as if to prove this, The Oldest said, 'We have need of more proof. Is there anyone here that has had any contact directly with this warlock master?' Oswald Greybeard stepped forward. 'I have,' he said, 'I was once a member of his coven.'

The Oldest asked Oswald to sit on the ground in front of him. 'Is this going to hurt?' asked the old wizard. The tree sprite shook his head, 'No, I'm only going to search your memory to find out if this warlock is as bad as you say he is.'

He placed one bark covered hand on either side of Oswald's head.

'Is he alright? I asked Donna, who sat with The Oldest in her arms. He seemed to go into a trance along with Oswald.

After a minute, they started to come around, 'W-what happened?' asked Oswald. 'I'll tell you later, right now the sprite's waking up.'

The Oldest opened his eyes, stood up and walked over to colony. After a heated discussion, (telepathically), The Oldest came and addressed us, 'We've seen through the old wizard's memories the evil that is the warlock master, and we have agreed for the first time in a hundred years. So, we will give you the next clue, and we wish you all good luck.'

Any luck that Simon Grey had left, had just run out, his mouth had been in overdrive, again! While his brain was still in neutral, his last words before a killing spell from the warlock master had hit him was, 'They've beaten us to the clue again.' Unfortunately the colony of tree sprites had fared no better, the ground around the dragon tree was littered with what looked like tree bark but was in fact the bodies of the colony.

'John,' warlock master beckoned the young wizard to him, ***'you are now my second in command. Don't fail me, unless you want to end up like Simon Grey.'*** 'Thank you, master.' John wondered if it was a good career move or not. Simon Grey was the third second in command to incur the master's wrath. **'Now pick up Simon Grey's wand and let's get out of here.'**

'Well,' enquired my wife as I walked into our kitchen, 'is Tenerife as beautiful as it looks in the holiday brochures?' 'Darling, we were there for only half an hour. All I got to see was a large square with a beautiful dragon tree in it, and some strange little creatures called tree sprites. We got what we needed and came straight home.'

After promising my wife that when all this was over, I would take her for a holiday there, I set off down to Donna's cottage.

On arrival I was greeted by Tom. 'Where the hell have you been?' I demanded. 'We could have done with your help finding the clues.' Tom smiled, 'From what I've been hearing, you've all done brilliantly without me. You know I would have given anything to have been with you all, but there was something I had to do that was vital for the success of our endeavour.'

We shook hands and I told him that it was good to have him back. Just then Donna called the meeting to order. 'As you all know by now David and the others have retrieved what we think is the last clue to the whereabouts of the book of dark magic. We think that it is hidden in the catacombs under the city of Paris.

'Many hundreds of years ago the outskirts of the city were riddled with mine tunnels from which most of the stone used in the construction of Paris came from.

'When the mines were no longer needed, they were used as ossuaries.' 'As what?' enquired Liam Delaney. Donna gave him that "shut up and let me finish look" that we'd all come to know.

'An ossuary is depository of bones. These hold over six million of them, and somewhere in amongst those bones is hidden the book of dark magic, and we must find it before the warlock master.' 'Oh,' smiled Oswald Greybeard, 'is that all? And if I may ask, how many of us are going on this suicide mission?' 'Only me,' answered Tom.

The room erupted, half were relieved, the other half were outraged that Tom was leaving them out.

Donna waved her arms and brought the melee to a conclusion. 'Why are you not taking anyone else with you?' she demanded. Tom looked around at us all and said, 'While you were out hunting the clues, I have been down in the cavern meditating. I know that the Talisman is not alive as such, but it holds so much accumulated knowledge and wisdom, so I thought that if I tried connect with it, some of that wisdom might just rub off on me. And it did.' Again Tom stared at all of us. 'I'm going to ask you all a very big favour,' he said tipping the apples out of Donna's fruit bowl. 'I want you all to give me the copies of the Talisman that you were given when you formed your coven.' Everyone looked shocked. 'But why? I asked. Tom put his hand on my shoulder. 'From my time in the cavern, 'I got the distinct feeling that when the final battle for the book occurred, there would only be two wizards involved. I also got the impression that the master would not be needing the brotherhood for much longer.

'So, I'm going to need all the power of the Talisman to defeat him.' Everybody grudgingly handed over the necklace that had become such a big part of their lives.

The last to hand theirs over were my sons Brandon and Jordan. 'Do we have to give you ours?' asked Brandon. 'We not powerful wizards yet, there can't be a lot of magic in them,' continued Jordan.

Tom looked at the boys with pity in his eyes. 'I'm sorry but what I haven't told any of you is that for the last ten minutes the Talisman has been draining all the magic out of you all.'

As we looked on dumbfounded, each Talisman belonging to every member of the coven began to turn to liquid. 'What's happening?' I asked 'You'll see,' said Tom as he lowered the original Talisman into the bowl.

At the same time in the castle of the warlock master, the brotherhood was stood in a semicircle facing the master. *'Now I want you all to hold out your wands, so the tips are almost touching mine.'* 'What for?' asked John the new second in command. *'Don't question me John, I am your master, and you will do as you are told.'*

Without further questions the brotherhood held out their wands as ordered, with John holding out his and the late Simon Grey's as well.

The Warlock Master began to mutter a spell in a low voice. After a few seconds a beam shot off the end of his wand and connected with all the others. John began to feel very strange. 'What are you doing master?' he asked. *'I will need all the power I can muster if I am to beat the coven of the talisman and retrieve the book of dark magic, so I'm afraid I am going to have to drain you all of your magic. But don't worry, you were not that good as wizards anyway. It would only be a waste of time letting a bunch of morons like you loose with something as powerful as the book of dark magic.'*

At that moment the beam ceased, and the brotherhood collapsed to the floor.

At the same time, back in Donna's cottage the original talisman was absorbing the liquid from the bowl. 'What do you mean draining our magic?' demanded Betty. Tom looked at each member of the coven, there was great sadness in his eyes, 'I'm sorry it had to come to this, but I need all of your magic if I'm to beat the warlock master. 'I promise you all that as soon as this is over, I will return your magic to you.' Turning to Shamus O'Brian. 'Your magic is derived from a different source than witchcraft, and I have no control over it, so I ask you one last favour. I need to get to Paris now.'

Tom was painfully aware that he was totally on his own; he had to defeat the warlock master, find the book of dark magic, and all he had was the talisman, a very powerful wand and five golden apples (and he still had no idea what he was going to do with them).

A small globe of light floated along in front of Tom as he walked through the ossuary. He looked around at millions of bones, he knew that somewhere in amongst this vast collection was hidden the book of dark magic.

In another part of the catacombs, the master was having the same thoughts, **how am I going to find one book in all these bones?**

'Hello,' the master spun round, **'who are you?'** he asked a very thin, old man. 'I'm the guardian, pleased to meet you,' he replied punctuating the last word with a loud and smelly fart. **'What are you the guardian of, may I ask?'** 'You know very well that I am the guardian of the book of dark magic, and before you ask, no, you can't have it.'

The master couldn't understand how someone so old and smelly could have disappeared before he even had time to raise his wand.

This time it was Tom's turn to hear the word, 'Hello,' followed by the loudest and smelliest fart. 'I take it that you are the guardian of the book,' he enquired while trying his hardest not to breathe. The old man smiled. 'Sorry about that, but when all your diet consists of is rats, it plays havoc with your digestive system. What I wouldn't give for some fruit?' Tom smiled to himself. 'Well, maybe we could help each other. I'm looking...' 'Yes I know, you're looking for the book of dark magic, and if you didn't already know, I am the guardian of said book.'

Tom told the guardian everything, how he was on a quest to stop the warlock master from gaining control of the book and plunging the world into a realm of dark magic.

Smelly listened to all that Tom had to say. 'I understand what you say and I agree that if the book falls into the wrong hands it could mean the end of good in the world, but I'm here, charged with the duty of stopping anybody getting their hands on it, but, if you were to have, say, some fruit about your person, I may by prevailed upon to point you in the direction of someone who might be able to help, if you can put forward a strong enough case.'

Taking off the rucksack, Tom took out two of the golden apples they'd found inside the Manor Oak and held them out to the guardian. 'How can I eat them, they're solid gold,' but as he looked the apples turned from gold to golden delicious, Tom's favourite apple.

Obviously, the guardian could smell the fruit, because much to Tom's disgust he started to dribble. 'Do you know how long it's been since I've seen an apple, let alone tasted one?' 'Well help me, and both will be yours,' Tom offered.

Watching Smelly devour the first of the apples had put Tom off fruit for life.

'You could search these ossuaries your whole life and never find the book. It was here, but it's been moved. It's now in the realm of dragons, so if it's a choice between you and the other guy it's no contest. I will open a portal to the home of the dragons, where hopefully you can enlist somebody's help to find the book of dark magic.'

THE DRAGON REALM

After walking through the portal, he found himself somewhere completely the opposite to the catacombs. Tom looked about, no roads, no cars, no houses, no people, no animals, except for one humungous dragon, and one very attractive girl about Tom's age.

'I wouldn't make any sudden moves if I were you. Firefly and I are not used to strangers, and she might mistake you for lunch.'

'Hello, my name's Tom, and if you don't mind me asking who am I speaking to, and where am I?'

'I'm Poppy, and as I said earlier this beautiful creature is Firefly, and as to where you are, are you telling me that you have no idea of your location?'

'Look,' the last thing I remember is being in the catacombs below the city of Paris, France with a very smelly old man.'

Poppy looked confused. 'You are lying, there is no Paris, France in this realm.'

'Ok, let's start again. Hi, my name's Tom, and would you be so kind as to tell me exactly where I am?'

Poppy gave Tom the look you'd give a confused child. 'You mean to tell me you have no idea that you are in the Dragon realm? I'd have thought that the sight of Firefly would have given it away.'

'I'm in the realm created long ago by the council of wizards for all the unwanted creatures in our dimension.'

'You're not too quick at catching on, are you? Yes, you are in the Dragon realm.'

'And yes, this is where the council disposed of all the things they didn't want in yours, and yes there are a lot of horrible beings here, but there are also some very beautiful things too.'

'Look, I'm sorry, I didn't mean to offend you. The spell that brought me here must have scrambled my brain. Tell me, how is it that you come to be in this realm, and how do you come to have a pet dragon?'

Tom knew as soon as he'd said it, that he'd offended Poppy.

'Firefly is not my pet, she's my friend, she's my soul mate, and when we fly together, we become one. Now, if you've finished insulting me, Firefly and our realm, perhaps you'd be good enough to tell me what you're doing here.'

Tom then explained about the coven of the talisman, the warlock master, and how they were both looking for the book of dark magic.

'And what will you do with the book if you find it?' asked Poppy.

'Well, if the coven finds it, we will hide it somewhere it can never be found.'

'And what will the warlock master do with it if he finds it?' asked Poppy

'Nothing good,' said Tom. 'We caught a couple of his followers, but even they had no idea why he was looking for it. Only that he'd do anything to get his hands on it. He's already killed several people, and magical creatures to collect their powers to make himself even more powerful.

So, you can see why we must find it first and hide it so he can never use it.'

'And you think this book is here in my realm?' Poppy mused.

'We have no magic book hidden here, and even if we did, how are you going to find it?'

Tom looked worried. 'Are there any other people besides you in this realm?'

Poppy smiled, 'Yes, of course there are. When the council of wizards announced that they were going to send all unwanted creatures into another realm, all the dragon riders and grooms elected to accompany them; ok, we put up with odd troublesome troll or ogre, but usually they keep to their part of the realm, and we keep to ours.'

'Poppy, would you mind taking me to the person in charge?' asked Tom.

'Person in charge,' laughed Poppy, 'we have no ruler, no king. We have no one telling us what to do, we live our lives how we want, if we need advice or help, we ask the Wise one.'

'Well, in that case, can you take me to the Wise one, please?'

'Yes, Tom, I think he will be up from his afternoon nap by now.'

Poppy smiled at the look on Tom's face. 'He needs his afternoon nap, after all, he is five hundred years old. I don't think your council of wizards thought it out when they conjured up this realm. They magicked this beautiful place, perfect in every way, except they forgot to add one thing.'

'And what was that?' asked Tom.

'Time,' spat Poppy. 'Oh don't get me wrong, we have a year, we have spring, summer, autumn, winter, trouble is we have the same spring, summer, autumn, winter, the same year that they had while they were conjuring up this realm.

'The same year, repeatedly. Luckily it took a year. If they'd managed it in a month, we'd all be dead, but we have a year, so we can grow crops and feed ourselves.

'The downside is that no one ever gets older. We all look the same as we did on the first day, so although the Wise one looks seventy, he is in fact five hundred years old.'

Poppy could see the next question that Tom was going to ask.

'And no, before you ask, I'm not going to tell you my age.'

'That's ok, but I must tell you that I've always had a thing for older women.'

Poppy smiled, 'You've never met one as old as me, I'll bet.'

Changing the subject, Tom asked, 'How far is it to the wise one?'

'Only about two hundred miles, as the crow flies, luckily, we have Firefly and she's a lot quicker than a crow.'

'Um, we're flying there on your dragon, is it safe?' asked Tom.

'Well, we could walk, but it would take five days, that's if we survived attacks from trolls, or ogres, or any other dangerous things, that want to kill you, or eat you, or kidnap us for ransom, or maybe just because we're in their territory.'

'Ok, ok,' Tom capitulated, 'you win we'll go by dragon.'

Poppy led Tom over to Firefly, the dragon bowed its head, so Tom's head was level with its eye, although Tom was looking more at the row of very large teeth.

'Don't worry, she's just a big softie,' said Poppy, stroking the dragon lovingly.

Tom believed "big", but he was not so certain about the "softie".

'Alright, let's go.'

Before we go, you must be introduced to her and Tom you will have to ask Firefly if she will take you to the wise one.

Tom approached Firefly, my name is Tom, and I'm on a mission to find the book of dark magic.

The dragon looked at Tom, then lay down. It was then that he noticed that Firefly had what looked like a leather sofa strapper on its back.

'I think she likes you; she wouldn't let just anyone ride on her back,' Poppy told him, 'follow me.'

Finally seated after a long climb, Poppy asked Firefly, 'Please my darling, take us to the Wise one.'

Taking flight by slowly flapping her massive leathery wing, they gracefully climbed higher and higher, until they could see the Realm of Dragons stretching out below.

'Wow, I've flown in a plane before, but this is better than looking out of a tiny window.'

How does one explain an aircraft, to someone born hundreds of years ago, Tom thought. 'I'm afraid it would take too long to explain it to you,' he apologised.

'That's ok,' because they were descending towards a very familiar castle.

'I know this castle, I've been here before, but then it belonged to the Warlock master.'

'It never belonged to that evil warlock! He took it over, driving the Wise one out,' spat Poppy with such hatred, 'after that he told everyone to keep clear. Only the Wise one and me kept watch on what he was up to. I saw you, but the Wise one said that you were not one of them, that you were there to gather information and find out what he was doing.'

'How did the Wise one know this?' asked Tom.

'Well, he is the Wise one,' laughed Poppy, 'and not only that, he also had a spy nearby.'

'You don't mean that smelly, obnoxious ogre that lived in the cave nearby, and kept shouting insults at everyone?'

'Yes, that's him, he is a friend of the Wise one, Tom! You said "lived"; does that mean that the warlock killed him, like he always threatened? I know he was smelly and obnoxious, but he was also kind and helpful, and he knew healing spells for sick dragons."

'Don't get yourself upset, Poppy, he's quite safe. I found a way to send him back to our realm. He now lives in a cave on an island owned by a gargoyle family. He's sharing a cave with his brother, and he also has a regular supply of the most disgusting cheese, so he and his brother are in ecstasy.'

'Thank you, Tom, now let's go and see the Wise one.'

The warlock master had been searching around the catacombs under Paris for two days, and he was getting very frustrated. He had been thwarted at every turn by the smelly old caretaker, and to make him even angrier, all his followers had suddenly appeared.

'What are you morons doing here? I told you to stay at the castle until I needed you.'

'Sorry, master, it wasn't safe to remain there any longer. We were all in the main hall, when suddenly this enormous dragon appeared, flying around, shooting fire everywhere. On its back rode a girl and an old wizard, who kept firing spells at us. You told us we had the entire realm to ourselves. We were not prepared for battle with a wizard and a dragon, so we left and came to find you, master.'

'You idiots are not able to take on even the lowliest of wizards. If I didn't need you for the final spell to open the book of dark magic, I'd would have destroyed you all long ago. Now, spread out and find me the portal to the book of dark magic.'

'Master,' one of the young men held up his hand, 'I've been thinking. What if the book is hidden in the realm we've just left.'

'You have surprised me, I didn't think any of you could think. You can hardly follow orders, but maybe you have redeemed yourselves this time.'

After twenty minutes of pacing up and down, the warlock turned to the young man, **'You may have a point, what better place to hide the book, than somewhere there are no humans.'**

'But there are humans, at least two, and a huge dragon,' blurted out the follower.

The warlock master rounded on the lad.

'I think that I can handle one dragon and old wizard, don't you?'

'Yes master,' they all agreed.

'Your confidence is inspiring,' he sneered.

'Now back to Durdle door and we'll see if your hunch is right.'

The dragon circled the castle slowly flying lower and lower until they landed in the courtyard.

'How was that compered to your plane?' asked Poppy.

'A lot colder, but with a better view. You see,' explained Tom, 'you fly in a plane, not on one. Maybe one day I will get to take you in one.'

Poppy led Tom across the courtyard and into the castle. It had changed a lot since he was there with the warlock master. It was a lot cleaner, and a lot brighter. Where before there were drab walls, there now hung colourful banners, and tapestries depicting hunting scenes.

The door at the far end of the hall opened, and the Wise one entered.

Despite his five hundred years, he still had the look of someone in their seventies. He was tall, losing his hair, and had a belly that many men of his age sported. He also had a kind face. With a broad smile he walked towards Tom with his hand held out.

'Hello, my name's Richard, and Poppy tells me that you are Tom and are here on a mission for the council of wizards,' all the time shaking Tom's hand continuously.

'Yes,' said Tom, trying to shake some circulation back into his hand, 'a warlock and his followers are trying to get their hands on the book of dark magic, and I'm here to stop them.'

'How do you intend to do that?' he asked.

'By finding it first,' answered Tom. 'And what are you going to do with it when you find it?' 'Destroy it, so no one can use all the evil spells in it.'

The wise one (Richard) shook his head, 'My dear boy, you can't destroy the book of dark magic, because if you did, you'd also destroy the book of good magic. They are both sides of the same coin, you can't have good without evil, it's the law of nature.'

Tom sighed, 'It seems then I must return to the coven of the talisman and seek their advice, but before I go, can you tell me if the book is even here in this realm?'

'No, I have sworn an oath to the council of wizards never to divulge the location of the book, but I will tell you this, you have good instincts, follow them and you will find what you're looking for, good luck.'

The wise one held out his hand, 'Goodbye Tom.' Tom smiled, 'I think I'll give it a miss the time.' I've only just got the circulation going from the last handshake.

Back to Norfolk

Back in Thompson, the coven had convened in the cavern under Donna's cottage. It couldn't have been held anywhere else, because the quest for the book of dark magic had gathered so many wizards, witches, gargoyles and several other magical entities, all wanting to help.

Tom brought everyone up to date with what had been happening since he last saw them. He finished by saying that in his opinion the book of dark magic was hidden in the realm of dragons.

'Well-done young wizard, you've done a good job so far, but now I think it's time for more senior wizards to take over.' This came from a rather pompous, self-important looking wizard. 'If you don't mind me asking,' said Donna, 'who the hell are you?'

'My name's not important, all you need to know is that I represent the council of wizards, and we are taking over the search for the book of dark magic, so, you can go back to whatever you ladies do and leave the important work to your superiors.'

'And where were you superiors when we vanquished Bella and her coven, as they tried to steal the Talisman a couple of years ago?' shouted Dermot an Irish wizard who'd helped us to beat Bella and her coven and stopped her gaining control over the Talisman.

'You didn't need our help to take on a gang of second-rate witches and wizards. To be honest, nobody on the council even believes that there is such a thing as this all-powerful Talisman. We think that it's something you've dreamed up to make your coven seem more important, so, I suggest you go back to making your potions and casting spells to cure warts and verrucae's and leave the more important work to the council of wizards.

'And as for the rest of you,' he sneered at those non-human magical entities that had offered their help, which included gargoyles, leprechauns, and two very smelly Ogres, 'crawl back under your rocks and stay out of council business.'

Immediately, there was a blinding flash of light and the council wizard disappeared.

Tom looked shocked. 'I never knew that any wizard had gotten that powerful, he must have been a warlock, to vanish like that.' 'I don't think he did,' mused Donna, 'think where we are, what's the most powerful thing in here?' Tom thought for a moment. 'The Talisman,' he answered. 'No, it wasn't the Talisman, it was me,' and from the back of those assembled there, two young girls came forward.

'Well! If it isn't my girlfriend Sienna,' said Tom sarcastically. 'Get over it, Tom, I only pretended to be that so I could find out what had happened to my mentor George.'

'She's telling the truth,' said an old man dressed like he'd just travelled forward from the sixties, in bell bottom trousers and a multi coloured shirt that had "make love not war" printed on it. She is my apprentice, as a matter of fact both girls are. As you've already heard, the older one is Sienna and the younger is Paris.

At that point there was an uproar among the witches. 'Wizards are not allowed to train witches,' shouted one witch. 'It's against the law,' called another. 'Quiet!' The shouting suddenly ceased. 'They are right,' Donna told George, 'the law was brought in after the magical conference convened to banish all unwanted creatures to the realm of dragons. Witches were allowed to train only witches, and wizards were only allowed to train wizards and warlocks.'

'Yes, you are right,' Donna, 'but the rules don't apply in their case. You see, I'm not training them to be witches, they are already too powerful for that, no, with the full permission of the council of wizards, I've started to train them to be the first female wizards.'

Now it was the turn of the wizards in the room to cause an uproar. 'It's blasphemous,' shouted one old wizard, 'it's unnatural,' called another.

George held up his hands for quiet, 'I know this goes against all the rules, but this has been sanctioned by the council.'

'If he has the council's blessing, why did she make that pompous ass disappear?' asked Donna.

'The thing you should know about Sienna,' George explained, 'is, not only is she abnormally gifted in the magical arts, as is her sister Paris, but Sienna is also autistic, so some of her spells are just a reflex, if something, or in this case, someone, upsets her she reacts.'

'I'm sorry,' Sienna apologized, 'it's just that I couldn't stand to listen to that idiot waffle on any longer.' 'If you don't mind me asking,' enquired Donna, 'what have you done with him?' 'Well, I thought he needed to cool down, so I sent him to a small island off the coast of Scotland. He'll be alright, there's a pub, and a ferry calls once a week.'

Tom called for quiet, 'Ok everybody, let's get back to the reason we're all here.'

After a long and heated discussion, it was decided that everybody going was a bad idea. Tom, it was agreed would lead a party of seven. After another long debate, the chosen consisted of, Donna, Betty, and for some reason one of the smelly ogres, Tom, Cuthbert, Sienna, and for some unfathomable reason me (David).

Well, that's settled then, said Donna, the seven of us will head for Dorset first thing in the morning.

'Don't you mean the eight of us,' said a small voice. It came from the other of Goerge's apprentices.

Thereafter, Sienna's sister, Paris marched forward, 'My sister's not going without me.. Our mother told me to stick with Sienna and if she needed my help I'd always be there. So! If she goes, so do I.'

I held my hand up, 'Excuse me, as I've said before, I'm not a wizard, so why do you keep putting me in these situations?'

'Oh David, don't be afraid, you're our lucky charm, we always come out on top if you're with us, and besides we need someone to drive the minibus down to Dorset.'

Dragons, dark magic and sorrow

After a five-hour drive with several stops at a certain burger establishment for Sienna and Paris, we finally arrived at Lulworth cove, Dorset and set out along the cliffs toward Weymouth until we reached Durdle door where we climbed down to the beach and uncovered a small boat that we had hidden in the old ogre's cave. This, not being big enough to take all across, we had to take two trips to get to the Realm of Dragons, as we rowed through the portal, and landed on the beach. We looked around and apart from the massive castle, everything looked the same.

'Welcome!' shouted an elderly man, 'to the realm of dragons. I'm known as the Wise one, but you can call me Richard, and this beautiful young lady is Poppy, and this magnificent creature is Firefly.'

'What creature?' asked Betty. Poppy smiled, 'She'll be here as soon as she realises that you are not going to hurt her. Ah here she comes.'

Suddenly a large head appeared above the parapet at rear of the castle, followed by the rest of an enormous dragon.

'It's alright, Firefly, no one's going to hurt you.'

'Hurt him? It's more likely that he'll be the one hurting us,' said a nervous looking Cuthbert.

Poppy laughed, 'Three things you should know about Firefly is - one, he's, a girl, two, she's very placid, and three, she only eats fish and the occasional sheep.'

Sienna walked up to the dragon and stretched out her hand, 'Hello my name's Sienna, will you be my friend?'

Everybody held their breath, as Firefly lowered her head until it came to rest on the ground next to the young witch.

'You are a very beautiful dragon, and one day I hope you will let me ride on your back.'

Firefly lifted her head, so that her nostrils were level with Sienna's head, opening her mouth. We all thought that she was going to either eat Sienna or burn her alive.

But to the contrary, she just exhaled a long breath at her, and apart from blowing her hair all over the place, nothing happened.

'That means she likes you,' Poppy told her. Sienna let out a sigh of relief. 'I wouldn't like to see what she'd do if she didn't like me,' laughed Sienna.

'I hate to break up this little 'getting to know you' party, but we will have a lot of warlocks and wizards here before long, and some of us will have to delay them, and the rest will have to find the book of dark magic, because if they get their hands on it the whole world will suffer,' shouted a rather grumpy Wise one, now let's get settled in the castle, there's food and drink ready for you, and we can discuss what we are going to do over dinner.

The great hall was, as Tom remembered it. Only when he was with the warlock master, he and the rest of his followers had to cook their own meals, but now the long table where they ate was overflowing with a delicious looking selection of dishes.

'Take a seat and dig in, there's more if you need it.' As if to prove his point, the wise one filled his plate to overflowing.

Everyone was catered for, even the smelly ogre, who had a table of his own, set well away from everybody else, had his own favourite food, which included a very smelly cheese, apparently a delicacy among ogres.

'Well, that was a wonderful spread you put on for us,' Cuthbert complimented the wise one, 'I was wondering how you managed it, I haven't seen any staff since we arrived.' 'Oh they're about, it's just that if I had introduced them to you beforehand, I doubt you'd have eaten your meals. You see it wasn't only creatures that the council banished to this realm, they also exiled people they considered undesirable.'

'What gave them the right to exile people? This realm was meant for creatures only,' shouted Cuthbert, 'that's why I never trusted them, too much power in the hands of a load of geriatric old morons.'

The Wise one smiled, 'I'll have you know that I was one of those geriatric old morons.'

Cuthbert looked shocked. 'Um, ah, I'm sorry I didn't mean to offend you.'

'No need to apologise. You're right, there was too much power given to too few people and I think it went to our heads. By the time I realised what we'd done it was too late to stop it.

'The reason I haven't introduced you to them is that they are zombies. Unlike the ones you see in films and books, most are gentle caring souls that have gotten trapped between life and death. Those that live and work here, keep the castle clean and cook when we have guests. Ok, occasionally you may find the odd finger in your stew, but that's just the price you have to pay for good food.'

A groan went up around the table. 'I'm sorry, I couldn't resist it,' laughed the old man. 'You don't have to worry, the food's perfect, they wear gloves when they are preparing and cooking meals.'

After everybody had eaten their fill, the wise one led us to a smaller room, just off the main hall.

'This is my office, where I'm writing a history of the realm of dragons. Whatever clues you need, to lead you to the book of dark magic, you'll find in here.

'I've scoured this land from one end to the other, noted down every anomaly and strange occurrence, unusual caves, rock formations and anything I've found out of the ordinary.'

After hours of sifting through reams of material, we narrowed it down to half a dozen places, we thought needed looking at. Dividing up into teams of two, we got ready to set off. Three of the sites were a couple of days' walk, so the fittest gather the supplies and camping gear needed for a two day hike and set off with a map given to them by Richard (the wise one), Cuthbert and Tom to a cave near a lake to the south, myself (David) and Sienna to the east, a reluctant Betty and the smelly Ogre towards a large mountain, visible, to the north east.

That left Donna and Paris, they were to check out two places farther away.

Donna wasn't happy. 'Why is it that we must go the farthest?' she complained. 'And on top of that, we'll be checking out two sites when the others only get one.'

Poppy smiled, 'The reason you were chosen, is because you are the most qualified, and because Paris is the least qualified, we feel that she would far safer with you, and as for the distance, the others will be walking, whereas you two will be going by dragon.' This calmed Donna down, but that was not the case with Paris. Nobody heard her muttering under her breath, 'Least qualified! I'll show them.'

'Follow the stream for one day until you'll find a flat piece of rock with a standing stone at the end, camp there for the night.' Sienna complained, 'I don't know why we must walk all the way.' Well, we've got another day's trek tomorrow,' I told her. 'If only I'd remembered to bring my broom, I hate walking.'

'You'll feel better after a good night's sleep, now help me get the tent up.

If I must,' she said. Taking out her wand, she waved it over the bag with the tent in it. The poles and canvas floated out of the bag and the tent erected itself.

Apparently, she had worn herself out erecting the tent, so couldn't manage to conjure up dinner, so it was down to me. After a meal of beans and sausages, we climbed into the tent which was divided in two by a wall down the middle. 'Is this your idea?' I asked Sienna. 'Yes, and my side's sound proofed, so you can snore all you want.'

Cuthbert and Tom were having a great time. 'I love being out in the countryside,' said Cuthbert. Tom agreed, 'It's also good not having to worry about all that's going on, at least for a couple of days.' 'Now, according to the map, we are to stop for the night in the small wood up ahead, but we have at least another three hours of daylight left. Why not carry on?' asked Cuthbert.

Tom shook his head, 'No, the map says we are to set up camp, here, so we camp, here. I get the feeling that it is all planned for us to arrive there at precise time.'

'Ok, let's get a fire going and find out what food they packed for us,' said Tom opening his rucksack. 'I don't suppose there's any pizza inside, is there?' asked Cuthbert. 'Sorry mate, only beans and sausages.' (Cuthbert had a varied diet, he would eat vegetables, fruit, meat, but only if it was on a pizza base with mozzarella).

Betty and the smelly ogre had reached the place marked on their map. 'I'm afraid we will have to share,' Betty told the ogre, 'there's only one tent.'

'You have the tent, I'm not sure if I could put up with the smell of a human all night, so I'll sleep out here.' 'Please yourself,' said a very angry Betty, 'if you think us humans smell bad, you should try smelling yourself. Anyway what do you want to eat?' The ogre spat on the ground, 'I'll not be eating that disgusting stuff that you humans eat, no, I'll find my own food.'

'This is great,' shouted Paris, as they soared high above the ground on the back of Firefly.

Donna on the other hand, wasn't as impressed, 'I don't like flying, I'll only use a broomstick if there's no other alternative.'

'Don't worry, we're almost there,' Poppy informed them. 'How many people can say that they've rode on the back of a dragon?' asked Paris. 'Well, here's one who would gladly forego the pleasure,' moaned an unimpressed Donna.

Five minutes later Poppy landed Firefly on a level stretch of ground next to a large boulder. 'This is it,' said Poppy, pointing to the boulder, 'the wise one told me that this rock doesn't belong here. He says that there is no other site in the realm where you can find this type of rock.'

Donna and Paris walked around the boulder. 'I don't see what's so special about this rock,' Paris told Donna, 'I mean there's no markings or anything, it's just an old rock.'

Moving closer to it, Donna placed her hand on the boulder. 'It's warm, warmer than it should be on a cool day like this, I think that there has been a spell placed on it.'

Donna took several paces back, took out her wand and pointed it at the boulder and said, 'REVEAL'. (Witches never used long complicated words when performing magic).

The boulder became covered in a blue fire, and an eerie voice boomed, It's not here, I've looked. So, I suggest you leave this realm, pack up and go back to your herbs and potions or I will destroy you and your coven, you have been warned.'

As the two of them watched, the blue fire died away. 'Who the hell was that?' asked Paris. 'I think you'll find that was the Warlock master,' Donna told her. 'Well that proved one thing, the book of dark magic is still hidden.' 'How do you know that?' 'Well, Paris, for one thing - if he'd found it you would feel it, because he would not be able to resist using it, and two, he'd have no need to warn us off if he already found it.'

THE END OF DAY TWO

Tom and Cuthbert followed their map to the cave that they'd been asked to investigate. Having arrived at noon they decided to check it out then, instead of the following morning. Finding their torches, they headed off to the cave entrance leading into the hillside. 'I hope it isn't inhabited by an ogre, their caves are disgusting,' commented Cuthbert. Much to his surprise, the cave was clean and hardly smelled of anything bad.

'Hello,' came a voice from the rear of the cave, 'welcome to my home.'

Tom, by now had taken out his wand, and was pointing it in the direction of the voice. Cuthbert also had the eye of the lave troll at the ready.

'Now boys, there is no need for that, I mean you no harm.' 'In that case show yourself,' Tom told it.

It! Turned out to be a female troll!!

Cuthbert's jaw dropped. 'I-I-I thought I was the only troll left,' he stammered. 'How long have you been here?' 'Ever since those damn wizards cast that spell to create this realm,' she replied. 'You're a bit small for a troll,' she smiled, 'but cute. Very cute.'

'Um, excuse me, have you lived in this cave all that time?' asked Tom. 'Yes, this has been my home for as long as the realm has existed.' 'And in that time have you had any contact with any dark wizards?' 'No,' was the answer to Tom's question.

Leaving the two trolls talking, Tom headed further into the cave to discover if there was anything hidden by magic, or any clues to the whereabouts of the book of dark magic.

Sienna and I make a friend.

Sienna and I (David) also arrived at our destination early, it being a wildflower meadow with a small wood at the end.

'Ok, Sienna, you're the witch, what are we looking for?' 'All it says on the map is, "seek what's not there". 'O---K, now why couldn't they have just written, go to the tree with the big X on it or something like that, why do they have to be so cryptic?'

But Sienna wasn't listening, she'd walked off into the meadow. Taking out her wand, she walked round in circles, chanting something that I couldn't understand. With nothing else to do I followed her. 'What are you looking for?' I asked. "Something that's not there", she replied. Let me know when you find it.' After that I left her to it and found a fallen tree where I sat with my back to the trunk and dozed off.

I was awakened by a loud explosion. 'What the hell's going on?' I shouted. Looking around I spotted Sienna standing next to a smoking crater. Her face was red, and she was shaking. 'There's nothing here,' she shouted to nobody in particular. 'I've been searching from hours, and I can't see anything, and the only thing I could hear was you snoring,' she said glaring at me.

Trying to calm her down, I suggested we both walk around one more time and see if the adage ,"two heads are better that one" (or in this case four eyes are better than two), worked. So, we set off walking around the meadow.

After an hour we still hadn't found anything. I could see Sienna was getting angry and frustrated. 'Let's go and look in the wood. If we don't find any clues there, we'll give up and go back and see if the others have had any luck.'

Taking a deep breath, the young witch walked toward the wood. 'Maybe,' she smiled, 'we will find that tree with the X on it that you wished for.'

'Do you mean that one?' I asked her. Sure enough, a hundred yards into the wood, there stood an ancient oak tree with an X carved into it.

'It doesn't make sense, the map says, "Seek what's not there".'

'I can see what's not there, can't you?' I asked. 'No, I can't. What's not there, Mister Clever Dick? Please enlighten me.' 'Calm down, Sienna, if you look at the tree again it will come to you.' Pointing her wand at me and looking very angry she warned me, 'I'm coming very close to turning you into something you wouldn't like.'

'Look young lady, I know it's against wizards' and witches' law to harm non magic folk.' She gave me that smile of hers that made me think that she was only smiling on the outside.

'Yes, --- but there are only you and I here, so who's to know what I do?'

She smiled again, only this time her smile reached her eyes, and I knew she was toying with me.

'Sorry David, I just couldn't resist it, but enough fun, tell me what you see that I don't.'

Taking her to the oak, I pointed at the X and said, 'What has the rest of the tree got, that the X hasn't?'

'Bark, --- why didn't I see that? So, we've solved the clue (we) now all we need to do is find out what it means.'

'Look David, there's a knot directly where the two lines dissect.' As I looked, she placed the tip of her wand onto the knot. Slowly it started to grow until it took up all the X, then it collapsed in on itself, leaving a hole big enough to put your arm in.

'Let's see what you're hiding, shall we?'

'Whoa, wait a minute, young lady, we don't know what's in there. It could be a trap.' 'Obviously, it's a trap David, but how else are we going to find out if it's a clue to the book of dark magic without looking?'

'In that case I should be the one to risk it. You have the wand, and know magic. So, if I get into trouble, you'll be there to help me out. Not only that, but you are also not tall enough to reach the hole.'

As I lifted my arm to insert my hand into the gaping hole, I heard, 'No, no do not place arm in hole. No, bad idea, yes, bad idea, very bad, yes.'

'Who said that?' demanded Sienna. 'It was I said that. Yes, I it was. 'And who and where are you?' Sienna asked. 'I am me, yes me, and I am here.' 'Why can't we see you then?' 'Because, you have wand and I am frightened, yes frightened, no man has no magic, no, no magic, but you have magic. Might hurt me, might kill me, yes, might kill me. Better stay invisible, yes, better stay alive, not want to be dead, oh no.'

I knew the voice was emanating from the oak tree. 'Sienna, put away your wand, you're frightening it,' I told her.

'Not it, no, not it, I am guardian, yes guardian. Was sent here by the council of wizards long ago. Yes, very long ago, given task of caring for realm of dragons, yes. And when dark book was hidden here, charged with keeping it safe from any who might want to steal it.'

'So, you know where it is then?' I asked.

'Yes, we know, we know. But not tell, no not tell, never tell.'

'You said, "We", 'does that mean that there are more of you in this realm?'

'Yes, many of us, but we will not tell. No, big secret, swore oath, never tell. Die first, yes die.'

Betty's solo trek

'I've had enough this,' spat the smelly ogre, 'it's not only that you smell terribly, but your food is disgusting. So, I'm going to find myself a tasty half rotten carcass and a lovely fungus covered cave and never see another disgusting human ever again.'

With that he stormed off, muttering to himself.

Betty was surprised that he'd lasted this long, it had been a day and a half of listening to the ogre complaining about everything. Betty walked too slow, smelled bad, the food was according to him inedible, plus a dozen other things he found annoying; the most annoying thing turned out to be Betty's singing.

Betty always thought of herself as a good singer, but for some reason to the ogre it sounded like fingernails on a chalk board.

Betty decided that she would be better off on her own, so when they began their day two trek, Betty sang all her favourite songs, at the top of her voice. It was getting towards noon when the ogre finally cracked. 'Will you stop making that terrible noise? It sounds like you're strangling a troll, and not in a good way.' 'Don't you like my singing, people say that I have quite a lovely voice. As a matter of fact I feel so good I think I'll keep singing for the rest of the day.' That's when the ogre stormed off.

Now she had rid herself of that awful creature, Betty continued the quest to find out what was at the end of the map. She was glad the ogre had left when he did, as her throat was sore, and she didn't think she could go on singing all afternoon.

On the map was an arrow pointing to a pool of water, and under it the words "answer truthfully" were written.

Betty could see water in the distance, at the foot of a snow-covered mountain. 'This must be the place,' she told herself. Walking up to the pool, she looked into the crystal-clear water. She could see her reflection staring back.

Her face in the pool started to shimmer, until it suddenly it wasn't her face anymore, but the face of the warlock **'You're too late, you witches are no match for the warlock master. I have two clues and you have none. Tell the rest of your so-called coven of the talisman to go home, or I will destroy you all.'**

Suddenly, Betty was hit by a beam of intense light, and was thrown ten feet from the pool. Slowly coming around, Betty's head was throbbing, and her eyesight blurred. 'You were very lucky, could have been killed, yes killed.'

Slowly Betty's eyesight came back into focus. She realised that a metre in front of her stood the strangest looking creature she'd ever seen. It was about two feet tall, covered in hair, or fur, she was not sure which, and nothing else.

'What are you?' she asked.

'I am a guardian, yes, a guardian. We care for this realm and all in it.

I could not stop you, no, was not quick enough. No, sorry, very sorry.'

Betty studied the small creature, it was like nothing she had ever seen, nor heard, or read about in any magical writings.

'How did you come to be a guardian, and how many of you are there in this realm?' 'Many, yes, many. We were brought to life by the council of magic to guard this realm and all who live in it.'

'Brought to life? Are you saying that you were the result of a spell?'

'Yes, we are truly magic creatures, born of magic, a collection of abilities from many species. Can cast spells, become invisible, change shape, but not do harm. No, not hurt, no, not hurt anything.'

'So, you're like the magical version of Frankenstein's monster.'

'No, not monster, no. We kind to all, never harm anyone, even if they harm us.'

Betty knew she'd said the wrong thing as soon as the words left her mouth.

Holding up her hands, trying to calm down the very irate guardian, 'I'm sorry, I didn't mean to upset you, please forget I said anything.'

Trying to calm things down, Betty invited the guardian to share a meal with her.

Lighting a fire (this amazed the little fellow, he'd never seen wood burst into flame as if by magic - 'You must be a very powerful witch to be able to produce fire whenever you want to.') She tried to explain the concept of a match, but finally gave up, and cooked beans and sausages.

The guardian tucked into his plate full, with gusto, and asked for seconds.

Finishing off the last of the food, he sat back and let out a long burp.

'Did you enjoy that?' Betty asked. 'Very much, yes, very, very, much, had nothing like it before. In this realm, only fruit, vegetables, and herbs.' Betty thought that the burp was long and loud enough, but as a full stop to his sentence, he let off the biggest and smelliest fart she'd ever had the misfortune to be present at.

Tom is saved by a guardian.

Searching farther into the female troll's cave, Tom couldn't find a thing. There was no sign of any magic being used, nothing out of the ordinary, so he headed back to the cave entrance. 'Wait a minute,' he said to himself. 'I didn't notice that on my way in, a section of the cave wall to my right was shimmering. Well, what have we here?' Walking towards it Tom realised that it was about the size of a door.

Tom was trying to decide whether to investigate it himself, or fetch Cuthbert to help.

But before he'd made up his mind, a voice nearby said, 'Do not enter, no, a trap it is, yes, a trap.' 'Who said that?' asked Tom. 'And where are you?' On a ledge three feet from where Tom was standing, stood a strange looking--- he didn't know what, all he could see was that it was two feet tall and covered in hair.

'I am a guardian, yes, a guardian am I.'

'A guardian of what?' Tom asked. 'Of this realm, yes, this realm. We have been tasked with protecting good from evil.'

'You say "we", how many guardians are there?' 'Many, yes, many. We watch, we see evil warlock searching the realm for book of dark magic. He collect clues to hiding place of book, nearly find book, we knew where book was hidden by wizards. Wizards think they so clever, think nobody find it, but not so clever, warlock nearly find it. So we take it, hide in place where no one find it. No, nobody find it.'

Paris's second day

Donna was not feeling well when their second day arrived. 'I don't think I'll be of much help today,' she told Paris. 'Ever since that boulder lit up and we heard the warlock master's voice, I've felt weak and unwell. I wonder if there was a spell on it? How are you feeling?' she asked Paris.

'I'm fine, but then I wasn't as close to it as you,' Paris looked at Donna, and was worried by what she saw. 'You stay in bed, I'll go with Poppy. You get some rest.'

Before she and Poppy set out, she found the Wise one and asked him to look in on Donna.

'Where are we going today?' Paris asked Poppy. 'Well, according to this map it's a cliff on the coast at the farthest part of the realm. I'm afraid we will be camping out tonight, as it will take us most of the day to reach, but we'll be alright. I've packed the tents, and plenty of food.'

Unlike Donna, Paris loved flying over the realm on Firefly's back. 'You have the best job in the world,' Paris told Poppy. 'To be able to fly on the back of a dragon whenever you like, must be the best feeling in the world.' Poppy smiled, 'Yes, it is quite wonderful, but, sometimes I miss the other realm. Maybe now there's a way to leave, I could take a holiday back there once in a while, but I could never leave my darling Firefly. 'We are soul mates, once a dragon has allowed a human to ride on them for the first time, their hearts become one. If one of them dies, the other also dies, that is how strong their bond is.'

They had been flying for hours. Paris had fallen into a deep sleep, dreaming about having her own dragon, and flying off on it, to faraway places and fighting dark wizards.

'Wake up Paris, we're nearly there.' Sitting up, and shaking her head to clear her mind, Paris could just make out a coastline ahead. Instead of landing, Poppy flew out over the sea, turned around and headed back in land.

Firefly landed on a pure white beach with massive cliffs of black rock.

'Well, we're here, what exactly are we looking for?' asked Paris. 'Your guess is as good as mine. You saw the map same as me, all it said was to come here. So now were here, it seems it's up to us to find a clue, and we can start by checking out what that is over there,' pointed Poppy.

On the beach, up against the cliff there appeared to be a small bundle of fur. 'It looks like some sort of animal. What do you think Poppy?' 'I've never seen anything like it in all the time I've been here, but it looks more humanoid than animal,' Poppy told her, 'and judging by the burns on its body, it was tortured before being killed. This was done by magic.' 'Magic!' cried Paris. 'Who would torture anything with magic? It's one of the first rules you learn, never harm another soul with magic. I think that whoever done this, they were beyond rules. I have a feeling that this was the work of the warlock master.'

The girls split up and went in opposite directions along the cliff to search for clues. After thirty minutes or so they met back where they started. 'Any luck?' asked Poppy. 'No just bare rock. And you?' asked Paris. 'Yes, there's a section of the cliff that looks like it had drawings on it, but it's been totally obliterated by blasts of magic.'

They both decided it was time to return to the castle and report their findings to the others, but first it was only right that they bury the remains of the poor creature they'd found.

A sorrowful return

As Firefly circled the castle before landing, the girls saw the wise one waiting for them. 'Something's wrong,' Poppy told Paris. 'He's looking worried, 'something must have happened.'

As soon as Firefly landed, the girls jumped off and ran to the wise one. 'What's the matter?' they said in unison. 'Come with me, I'll explain on the way. As you know Donna wasn't feeling too good when you left, and despite my best attempts to find a cure for whatever is making her sick, I've had no luck. She's getting worse by the minute.'

When they arrived at Donna's room, they were both shocked by the sight of her, it was as if she'd aged a hundred years in one day.

'Is there nothing you can do for her?' asked Poppy. 'No, I need to know more about her, like how old she is.' 'That depends,' said Poppy, 'on whether you mean her actual age or how long she's been in the house at Thompson?'

'You're going to have to explain yourself, Poppy.'

It took a while for her to tell the story of the talisman, and how she and her sister, Bella had volunteered to keep the powerful relic safe from any dark wizards who would use its power for evil. They took it in turns, one guarding it while the other was put under a spell that stopped them aging a day for a hundred years at a time while they slept.

'So, you see, there's no way of telling her age. She could be in her eighties, or she could be four hundred and eighty.'

'Oh dear, now I see what's going on.' 'What?' Poppy asked the old man. 'She's dying, and there's nothing we can do about it,' the wise one sat down and put his head in his hands. After a minute he raised his head, he now had tears running down his cheeks. 'That evil swine put a spell on the boulder that would remove any enchantment that had been placed on anyone to protect them.'

'Poppy, we need everyone back here as soon as possible. Could you and Firefly go and fetch all the teams we sent out and bring them back here? Maybe with the power of all of them, we may be able to reverse the warlock's spell and save Donna.'

First on Poppy's list to pick up, was Tom and Cuthbert.

The guardian suddenly stood up and started to scan the sky. 'Dragon coming, oh yes, dragon.' 'I can't see anything,' said Tom. 'Cannot see, no, but feel it, yes, feel it.'

As if to prove the little fellow right, off in the distance, Tom could just make out something on the horizon. 'There it is,' he called 'and it's coming this way.'

Five minutes later Firefly landed near the female troll's cave and Poppy jumped off and ran over to them. 'Donna's very sick, the wise one thinks she may even be dying. He wants everybody back to the castle, in the hope with all of us there, maybe we can find a cure to the spell that the warlock master placed on her.'

Cuthbert said his goodbyes to the female troll, promising to come back to see her when this was all over.

'Wait a moment, where's the guardian gone?' said Tom. 'I am here,' said a voice beside him, 'here I am.' 'Poppy is my friend, neither she nor Firefly will hurt you,' said Tom. 'Who are you talking to?' asked Poppy.

'Why don't you show yourself? Nobody's going to hurt you.'

The little creature appeared at Tom's side, holding on to his trouser leg for dear life. 'Poppy this is a guardian.' 'Hello guardian. My name's Poppy. What's yours?' 'I am a guardian, yes, guardian. We are all guardian, no more. Just guardian.' Poppy went down on her knee and held out her hand, 'Pleased to meet you.' A look of fear came over the guardian's face as he crept around behind Tom's leg. Bending, Tom lifted the little fellow up and held him close to him, he could feel him shaking.

'You are safe with us, I promise.'

Back at the castle Poppy dropped the three of them off and set out to pick up Betty and the ogre.

On landing at Betty's camp site, Poppy found only Betty and a guardian. 'Where's the ogre?' she asked. 'He told me that he'd had enough of humans, so he went off to find a cave, saying, he hoped to never see another human ever again. And I could not have been happier. I lost a very smelly ogre, but I've made a new friend, this is a ----'. Poppy finished Betty's sentence, 'a guardian. I know, he's the second one I've met today.'

Seeing as there were only two (one and a half really,) passengers, Poppy decided to carry on and pick up Sienna and me on the trip back.

Sienna sat by the tent talking to our new little friend, when suddenly he stood up, 'Dragon, yes dragon coming, must hide. Do not want to be eaten. No, must hide.' Sienna placed her arm around him, 'It's ok, Firefly won't hurt you. She's very friendly, and Poppy, her rider will not hurt you either.'

With us all finely aboard Firefly, we headed back to the castle.

The mood on our arrival was very sombre. The wise one asked all of us to convene in the great hall.

'Now, for the benefit of the late arrivals, let me explain what's going on. Donna has been cursed by a spell cast by the warlock master. It removed an enchantment placed on her hundreds of years ago to prolong her life so she could guard the Talisman in her cottage in Thompson.

'This was made worse by the fact that she no longer had any magic in her, because she had surrendered her power, so Tom would be strong enough to fight the warlock when they met.'

Tom was distraught. 'Is there anything I can do? I mean, I have all this power, and I have the talisman. Surely one of you know of a spell that can reverse the curse.'

'I'm sorry Tom, this sort of magic is way beyond any of us.'

'She must leave this place, yes leave.' 'Who said that?' from one of the what we thought to be empty chairs around the table that we all sat at, a guardian got to his feet, 'I said that, yes, it was I.' Judging by the way he spoke and his nervousness I realised that this was the guardian that Sienna and I had come across.

'Quiet!' The other two guardians had stood up on their chairs and were shouting at the one who'd spoken. 'You have no right to speak, you are not whole, you are no longer guardian.'

'Why is he no longer a guardian?' asked Sienna. 'He was captured by the warlock master, tortured by him. When you become a guardian you take oath, swear to die rather than betray any secrets that you have promised to keep. The coward told the warlock where to find the next clue, the evil one tortured that guardian, but he would not betray his oath and died keeping our secret.'

Poppy stood up and addressed the two guardians, 'Paris and I found the body of your fellow guardian on the beach near a part of the cliff that had carvings on it. It had been blasted so as no one could learn their meaning.

We buried the body at the top of the cliff and left a heap of stones to mark the grave.'

The guardians bowed and sat down.

As the meeting went on, nobody came up with any solution to our problem.

As someone came up with another idea, and everybody interrupted with whether it would work or not, I felt something tugging my trouser leg. Looking down I saw that our little friend was back. He motioned me to follow him, taking me down a corridor which led to a small room. 'Must listen to me, yes listen, must take lady home, yes must. She must not die here. No, never find peace, if she die here. Will be too much evil. Realm cease to be, realm made for good. Since warlock and his coven, nothing but evil, weaken spell, humans not meant to be here, no, not here.'

'I agree with you that Donna should go back to her cottage in Norfolk. If she's going to die then I think she would prefer it to be in her own home, but, we have no way of getting her there. The journey would be too long, and I don't think she'd survive it.'

'Please don't tell others, I told you. But, could ask The Guardian, the Guardian has powerful magic, yes, very powerful magic.'

'Are you telling me that all you guardians have a leader?'

'Yes, big secret, yes, not allowed to tell, no, mustn't.' 'Then why are you telling me?' I asked. 'No more guardian, no more, so am free to help you, yes, free.'

'If you are no longer a guardian,' I asked 'what shall I call you? What's your name?' 'Have name, only guardian, no other name.' I thought for a while and decided that he looked a lot like a very well loved and played with teddy bear I had as a child.

'Ok, if it's alright with you, from now on I shall call you Ted.' The little chap bowed, 'Thank you master, I am honoured, yes honoured.'

'Why do you call me master? I'm not your master.'

'You named me. That means I belong to you, master. I am yours to command.'

'We'll talk about this later, Ted. Right now I want you to tell me how to get into contact with the guardian.'

'I will call him, yes, maybe he kill me, yes kill me, but will help you, my master.'

I assured Ted that I would not let that happen.

It was as if Ted went into a trance, after five minutes his eyes opened, 'Is coming, oh yes, he is coming.'

When we arrived back in the great hall, everybody was still debating what to do.

'Excuse me everybody, but I must tell you that we are expecting a guest at any moment,' I told them. Right on cue, at the end of the table the air started to shimmer, and a much larger version of our little friends appeared and at the same time Ted disappeared.

The wise one got to his feet. 'My good friend, it's so great to see you again. What's brought you here to us?'

'I was summoned here by the one who is no longer a guardian. He says you need my help. Before I do anything, you must bring him to me, so he can be punished. He has betrayed his oath and caused the death of another. Where are you? Show yourself, you traitor.'

I knew Ted was near me, as I could feel my trousers vibrate. I looked down, Ted's head appeared, there were tears in his eyes and a look of terror on his face.

The guardian was at least three times the size of Ted and a lot scarier.

Getting to my feet I said, 'I haven't met this warlock master, but from what I hear he scares the life out wizards and witches alike.

So, I can understand why such a little thing as Ted broke under the warlock's torture. I know that he's devastated by what happened to the other guardian. I just hope you can see it in your heart to forgive him.'

The guardian glared at me, 'Who are you? And who's this Ted?'

'My name's David and I'm a non-magical member of the coven of the talisman.'

Lifting him up and standing a shaking Ted on the table, 'This is Ted.'

A very angry guardian looked as if he was about to attack. 'You will not harm my master,' shouted Ted. Only now he was shaking with rage rather than fear.

'My master saved me, yes saved me, and gave me a name. He thinks I'm worthy of a name, so I am Ted. Yes Ted, I will obey my master, I will protect my master, I will die for my master, yes, die.'

The guardian looked at me and sneered. 'You can keep this coward as your pet, only don't bring him near myself or any of the other guardians.'

'Now we've sorted that out, we can get down to the reason we called you,' said a very relieved wise one.

'Ted, I think it would be better if you made yourself scarce while the guardian is here.' 'Yes master.' instantaneously he jumped down from the table and became invisible.

'Would you like to come to my rooms where we can discuss this in private,' the wise asked the guardian. 'Only if you've still got some of that fiery brandy left.'

He must have had some, because half an hour later they both looked a lot happier when they arrived back in the hall.

'My good friend and I think we have come up with a solution to our problem (hic). First the guardian will make temporary doorway into our realm (hic) then we must find a spell to make Firefly and her passengers invisible. Then she will fly Donna and Betty back to Thompson.'

'The guardian has assured me that the book of dark magic is here in this realm and under his protection. When we've gotten Donna safely home, then we will meet up again and decide what is to be done about it.'

It took two days to come up with a spell to make Firefly invisible. When everything was ready and the door to our realm was open, Firefly, Poppy, Betty and Donna, slowly faded as the spell took effect.

The rest of us made a more mundane trek back to Norfolk.

A sad return

After a seven-hour drive we arrived back at Donna's cottage. As we drove up the lane, my wife Sadie, and my boys, Brandon and Jordon, were waiting. All looked as if they had been crying. 'She's near the end,' were the first words my wife said, before they all came and hugged me. 'She wants to see you alone.'

I shut the bedroom door behind me and walked to her bed. The difference in appearance from the last time I'd seen her was terrible. Her hair was pure white, and her skin looked like ancient, like a mummy. 'David, I'm so glad you got here before I pass on to my next life.' 'You think that there's something after death?' I asked.

She smiled at me, 'Yes, I don't think magic has done with me yet, but before I go, I have a gift for you. Take my hand.' I reached over and held her hand in both of mine. Her skin felt like parchment, I thought that if I squeezed too hard, it would crumble to dust.

Donna's voice hardly audible, said, 'Close your eyes and don't open them until it's done.'

Her hand became warm, and I felt as if something flowed from Donna into me. After what felt like an hour, but was probably just a minute or two, the warmth began to dissipate and I felt Donna pass. Placing her hand by her side and closing her eyes, I went outside to tell the others.

Two days later the coven of the talisman and all her magical friends gathered at Donna's cottage for the wake.

Tom clapped his hands and asked for quiet. 'Ladies and gentlemen, in accordance with Donna's wishes, she will be interred in the cavern under her cottage, so, those of you that wish to say your goodbyes, please follow me.'

On entering the cavern, we noticed that Donna's body was laid out on a raised platform made of the same material as the walls and floor of the cavern.

The wise one had made the journey from the other realm to preside over the ceremony. 'I didn't know Donna long, but she soon became my friend. She was kind, liked by all, fiercely loyal, and I know like me you'll miss her greatly.'

As he was talking the platform began to sink into the floor of the cavern, taking Donna's body with it, until there was nothing left but the floor.

It was decided that we of the coven of the talisman would remain in Norfolk for a couple of days and Poppy, Sienna, Paris and the wise one would head back to the other realm.

As I walked back home with my wife and boys, Betty joined us. 'David, I think it would be wise if I stayed here when you go back to Dorset. I don't like the idea of leaving Donna's cottage unguarded.' I agreed, 'Ok, in that case I'll take George back in your stead.'

As we walked along, I suddenly felt a now familiar tug of my trouser leg. 'Ted, is that you?' 'Yes master.' 'Dad, who are you talking to?' asked Brandon. 'Wait till we get home, and I'll explain everything.'

As we entered the house, everybody started talking at the same time. 'Quiet please, and I'll answer all your questions, but first, Ted show yourself.'

After that, Ted became visible. Rather than the sight of Ted frightening them, Sadie said, 'Isn't he adorable?' and in chorus my boys said, 'Can we keep him dad?'

'No, but he can stay with us till we get this sorted out. Just remember, he's a sentient being, not a pet.'

'What are you doing here?' I asked. 'Ted, go where master go, do as master say, ride here on dragon with sick lady, to be with master. Yes, not like to fly, make Ted sick, get here for when master arrive.'

'Why do you make the little fellow call you master?' asked Sadie. 'It's not me,' I told her. 'I'm not the one who's making him call me master. He says I saved him and gave him a name, which is a very big thing in his world.'

'Yes mistress, to have a name is very big honour. To say to someone, "hello, nice to meet you, my name is Ted," that means I am someone, not just one of many.'

Cuthbert then arrived. 'David I need to talk to you.' 'Why don't we discuss this over tea?' Having Cuthbert over for tea meant "pizza" so Sadie put three fifteen-inch pizzas in the oven.

Cuthbert and I sat at the dining table while the boys took Ted upstairs to show him their rooms.

'The guardian has told us that the book of dark magic is hidden their realm.' 'Yes Cuthbert I know, what's your point?' 'My point is, is it safe there? The warlock master has already killed one of the guardians, and tortured another. Eventually one of them is going to break and tell him everything.'

I had to agree with Cuthbert, the more people who knew, the greater the chance of someone revealing the hiding place.

'Master, it must be brought to the dead lady's cottage and placed in the cavern.'

'Did you hear that?' I asked Cuthbert. 'Hear what?' 'Ted,' he said the book needs to be brought here to Donna's cottage and placed in the cavern.

'I never heard a thing, but I've been thinking that for a while now. When we've dealt with the warlock master, we can place the book of dark magic and the talisman in the cavern, then find another witch or wizard to guard it.'

Sadie announced that the food was ready, and we were deafened by the sound of what should have been a herd of elephants, but was in fact Brandon, Jordon, and Ted charging down the stairs.

It seemed that Ted shared Cuthbert's love of pizza. Me, Sadie and the boys shared one of the pizzas, Cuthbert, as usual, had a whole one and Ted was munching his way through the third one all by himself.

'Are you enjoying the food Ted?' 'Yes master, very much, no pizza in my realm, no, lovely scenery.' 'Nice creatures, mostly, but terrible food.' I then noticed that his stomach had doubled in size.

I watched in awe as Ted finished off his pizza and the crusts that the boys left, plus a slice given to him by Cuthbert.

Return to the realm of dragons.

Again, I drove a minibus full back to Dorset. Only this time instead of Donna, my father George was with us. It took two trips in the rowing boat to ferry all of us through Durdle Door into the realm on the other side.

When we were all gathered in the great hall of the castle, the wise one called the meeting to order. 'Welcome back, and not a minute too soon. Things have gotten worse in your absence. The warlock master is back and he knows that the book of dark magic is here. The bodies of two more guardians have been found tortured to death. The guardian tells me that neither of them betrayed their oath, and died to keep the hiding place of the book secret, but he fears that it is only a matter of time before someone cracks under torture and gives away the location of the book. So he says that it's up to us to find somewhere safe to hide it. Also it will require a very powerful witch or wizard to guard it.'

Cuthbert stood up and addressed the room, 'I can't say where now, but I think I have the perfect spot. But before we do anything, first we must deal with the warlock master, once and for all. We must lure him away from this realm.' 'Why?' asked the wise one. 'Simple,' Cuthbert explained, 'this realm was created by magic. If too much dark magic is used, it could destroy the spell that holds this realm together. And if that happens, all the things that were put here from our realm would suddenly be back in the world of men.'

Poppy stood up, 'Can you imagine the panic if people came face to face with ogres, dragons, and all manner of creatures that they had thought of as just myths. Firefly is the only tame dragon, there are those in this realm who'd regard humans as dinner.'

Everybody believed we should do all we could to preserve the realm of dragons. Where we differed was, in the way we should go about this.

Some thought we should keep the book hidden in this realm, others said we should take it back to our realm and hide it there, but all agreed we should stop the warlock master getting his hands on the book.

It all became a moot point, when the guardian suddenly appeared, and after a quick conversation with the wise one, he called us to order. 'The guardian has just told me that another two guardians have been tortured to death by the warlock master. He is asking us to take the book of dark magic back to our realm as soon as possible, before he loses even more of his people.'

The warlock master was regretting taking all his coven's powers. Yes it made him a lot more powerful, but now he was only one man, and he could only look in one place at a time, and he'd come up blank again. This time the little strange creature that called itself a guardian had seen him coming and disappeared.

'Hello, Cyril, haven't seen you for years,' the warlock master spun around. **'Who's that, where are you? Show yourself.'** 'You've changed, I remember you as this snivelling little kid, always had a runny nose, always wiping in on the arm of your coat. Thought you were the greatest wizard, but, could never do the simplest of spells.'

'Yeah, well all that has changed. I am now the greatest warlock master alive today.' 'Master, master of who? As far as I can see, you're here alone.'

'There are at least fifteen of us, we were also looking for the book of dark magic. But as of twenty minutes ago, we now know where it is, and it will be in our hands before you and I have stopped talking.'

The warlock took out his wand and started throwing killing spells in all directions, trying to hit anyone nearby. The air around him turned to flame, which engulfed the warlock, but no sooner had the flame reached him than it was replaced by a wall of water.

'It will take more than a fire spell to beat me,' boasted the warlock. 'Ok how about a dragon then?' Firefly, now visible, roared so close to the warlock that his robe blew out around him.

Glaring at George sitting on the dragon's back, he shouted, **'You, you're a dead man.'** And disappeared.

Poppy turned to George, 'You know him, how's that possible?'

George told her all about his early days when as young man he trained with an old man called Oswald Greybeard, a very powerful wizard.

All went well until he was asked to take on another apprentice by the name of Cyril Jones, a weedy little chap, with an ever-running nose and never a hankie in sight.

George noticed at the time that he only seemed interested in learning dark spells, and when their master's book of forbidden spells went missing, their master knew who'd taken it. He told them both, that if the book was returned before morning, nothing more would be said about it.

Morning came and there was no sign of the book or Cyril.

'It seems he's come a long way since then.'

Now we had better get back and inform the others what we've learned.

While George and Poppy's encounter with the warlock master was taking place, back at the castle things didn't go as smoothly as anticipated.

The guardian had changed his mind and was refusing to reveal the location of the book of dark magic.

The wise one was getting very frustrated. 'You know that if the warlock master uses too much dark magic it could mean the end of this realm,' he told the guardian. 'Yes, my friend, but it was entrusted to me. I swore an oath to protect it, or die in the process.'

The air in the middle of the table shimmered as one of the smaller guardians materialised. 'Sire, another of our brethren has been killed and had this message pinned to his chest with a dagger.' Handing him a piece of blood splattered paper, he left.

'What does it say?' asked the wise one. The guardian handed it to him 'Read it out loud.'

The wise one looked at the note and went pale, 'It says that the warlock master will kill every guardian he finds, unless we hand over the book of dark magic.'

'That settles it then, we must take it out of this realm, and as soon as possible.'

Talking the guardian into letting us have the book of dark magic was not as easy as we had thought. Even though some of his people had been killed, he said that he'd sworn an oath to guard the book and keep anyone from getting it. Finally, after hours of discussion, he agreed that it would be safer if taken out of the realm of dragons, but, only if a guardian went with it. Only then would he feel that he still had a connection to it.

He wasn't pleased when I told him that we already had a guardian in our realm. He was even more displeased when I told him it was Ted. 'You took one of my guardians out of my realm without my permission.' 'Not really,' I explained 'he stowed away on the back of Firefly when she ferried Donna back to Norfolk.'

'Where is he now, David?' he demanded. 'He's at my home guarding my wife and children.'

This seemed to placate him somewhat. 'Well I hope he does a better job of that, than he did guarding the book.'

'So,' asked the wise one, 'where is the book of dark magic hidden?' The guardian smiled, 'It's here, in the castle.' 'You mean to tell us that while the warlock master lived in this castle with his coven it was under his nose the whole time?'

'Yes, David. As a matter of fact he'd been sitting on it.'

The guardian pointed to the chair now occupied by the wise one.

The chair was a very ornately carved oak throne rather than a chair. 'Is there a spell or a chant to reveal the hiding place?' I asked.

'No not really.' The guardian took the leather padded cushion off and lifted the seat. In the recess below was a very old tome with the covers held together by an ornate clasp. Carefully taking it out, the guardian placed it on the long table. 'Don't any of you try to open it, there's a very nasty spell on it and if you don't know how to remove it, it could kill you.'

The next problem we had, was how to transport it back to Norfolk.

We couldn't take it back in the mini bus, we couldn't risk Firefly getting attacked flying it back. In the end we decided to take it back through Durdle Door and get one of our leprechaun friends to take us all back via rainbow.

After two trips and a lot of rowing on my part, we all gathered on the beach near Durdle Door, to be met by our old friend Dermot, the leprechaun. 'This is going to take more than one trip to get you all to Norfolk,' he informed us.

'At least you don't have to worry about me,' I told him. 'Somebody must drive the minibus back.' 'And I'll go with you, as long as we can stop in Weymouth for a pizza or two for the journey.' 'Of course we can, Cuthbert.'

'Well, in that case, if one more of you will go with David, I can take the rest of you in one trip.' 'I'll go with them,' volunteered George, 'it will give me time with my son. If it's alright with you David.' I reluctantly agreed. (As you may remember I still have not forgiven my father for leaving my mother and me when I was a boy).

The trip back home was uneventful, my father and I managed to come to terms with why he'd left, and although I'd not forgiven him, as they say, eventually, hopefully, "time heals all wounds".

On arrival back in Thompson, my first call after George and Cuthbert were dropped off at Donna's cottage was to check on my family, which now included Ted.

I guessed this when I opened the door to be met by him in blue trousers, a red waist coat and a baseball cap. 'Well, don't you look smart!' 'Thank you master, the young masters gave me these wonderful clothes, and the mistress said that I can stay as long as I like.'

'You told him he can stay as long as he likes?' I asked Sadie. 'And you gave him clothes?' 'Well we couldn't have him walking about naked, could we?'

'And where did you get the outfit from?' I asked. 'You remember that big teddy that your mother gave Jordon when he was little?' 'You mean the one that made him cry every time you got it out? The one your mother made the clothes for in the hope that he'd come to like it?' 'Yes that's the one dear, and if you remember, you put it up in the attic, when her plan backfired and he was even more afraid of it?' 'Yes I remember, it was the most grotesque teddy bear I'd ever seen. I don't know where your mother got it from, I often wondered if it was made for some horror film.'

'Well, I had to do something,' my wife told me. 'I know he's covered in hair, but underneath he's naked, and it freaked me out. Luckily, I remembered the teddy in the loft, so I got the clothes down and they fitted him.'

I know this might sound a little sexist, but I can never work out a women's logic.

(Maybe, I'm not supposed to).

Anyway, the five of us then made our way down to Donna's cottage.

As we arrived, we were greeted with pandemonium. 'Well, somebody must have it,' shouted Betty, 'we all saw the guardian place the book in the box before we left, so where is it?' 'What's going on?' I asked. 'It seems, David that somehow between all of us seeing the guardian place the book into this crate and arriving here, the book of dark magic has disappeared.'

'Quiet please, can I have your attention please?' I looked round and noticed that my father had entered the cottage, and for some reason he was still carrying the suitcase he'd brought with him from Dorset.

'I'm sorry to have deceived you all, but the book of dark magic was never in the crate, it's been in my keeping the whole time.'

'I didn't know if the warlock master had a way of spying on us in the castle. After all, he'd lived there for several months and he'd want to keep an eye on his coven. Cyril never was a very trusting sort.'

'Who the hell's Cyril?' demanded Betty. 'That's the warlock's name. Does that mean that you know this warlock?' 'Yes I do, Betty, but that's a story for another time.' 'Ok then, how about you tell me how the book got from the crate into your suitcase?' 'That was me,' confessed Sienna. 'I cast a transference spell on the crate, so that anything put into it would instantly be transferred to George's case.

'From what George has told us over the years he's been teaching us, my sister Paris and I have built up a profile of the warlock master (Cyril). The things we've learned are. Taking it in turns to speak the two sisters laid out their conclusions -

'He doesn't consider non-magic folk worth a thought, also any lower species,

Anything below witches, who, by the way he thinks of as minor magical forms, who should stick to curing warts and flying around on broomsticks.'

That last observation came from Sienna, who at that moment was being restrained by Paris. 'Can one of you please take Sienna's wand away from her before she blasts something?' begged Paris.

As I walked over to Sienna, I noticed a faraway look in her eyes, 'How dare he say that about witches?' As I got close enough to reach for her wand, I noticed that he eyes now had a look of hatred in them, 'He's here, and he's not alone.'

The battle of Thompson

On the outskirts of the village, a motley crew of thugs were assembling. The warlock was scraping the barrel with this lot. His new coven consisted of second-rate wizards just along for the money.

'Ok, listen up, we are here to destroy the coven of the talisman and anyone else standing with them. Wipe them out, all of them, no one leaves that wood alive.'

'Um, excuse me, but you never said anything about killing anyone. I didn't sign up to murder a load of old witches.' A beam shot out of the end of the warlock master's wand hitting the speaker in the chest, blasting him backwards.

'Anyone else, having second thoughts?' asked the warlock.

The rest of the coven took that moment to study the ground around their feet, while muttering 'No master.'

'Sienna, Sienna snap out of it,' I said shaking her gently by the shoulders. Her eyes cleared, and she came back to us. 'Sorry I got carried away, I was in the mind of one of his thugs. Not a very pleasant place, especially when you're watching the warlock kill one of his men for having second thoughts.

'He has told his men that none of us are to get out of here alive. Not only does he want the book of dark magic, he now wants the talisman and all the power that this place holds.'

The only way into Donna's cottage was up the pathway through the wood. Cuthbert, Tom, and George would be in hiding in the bushes on either side.

Sienna, Poppy, Paris and Betty would be in the house, in case they got past those outside.

As they waited, Cuthbert, Tom and George discussed how they were going to cope with an influx of wizards, who were intending to wipe out the coven of the talisman and steal the book of dark magic.

'We could do with some help, we are outnumbered at least three to one,' Cuthbert told the other two. 'Everybody we contacted were either too frightened to take on the warlock master, or could not get here on time,' George explained.

'It seems like we are on our own,' Tom added.

'We've got company,' George whispered. As they listened, they could hear voices coming up the lane. 'Why must we kill a load of old biddies,' said one voice. 'Because that's what the warlock master is paying us to do,' came another. 'But why isn't he here with us?' 'If it's going to be that easy, why doesn't he do it himself?' chirped another. 'You heard him, he's giving us the easy task, has a score to settle. Once he's killed his old enemy's family, he'll join us here.'

George's blood ran cold, he knew that the warlock master hated him. He always blamed him for being expelled from the teaching of Oswald Greybeard to whom they were both apprenticed.

'I've got to go,' George whispered to Tom. 'You go and protect your family, 'we'll handle this lot.' Luckily Tom had given everybody in the coven back the power that he'd taken, back before the warlock and his mercenaries had arrived.

Meanwhile, totally unaware of what was heading our way, myself, Sadie, my mother and our two boys were sitting down to our evening meal.

My mother let out a scream, as Ted suddenly appeared on the table, 'Master, evil comes this way, yes evil.' I could tell that Ted was frightened. Since coming to live in our realm he no longer punctuated each sentence with a "yes or a "no" but now he had reverted to his old ways.

'Boys, please take nanny up to your room and explain everything to her.'

As the boys disappeared up the stairs, I could hear my mother saying, 'Why is your old teddy talking?' Sadie poured a large brandy, 'I'll take this up to mum, I think she's going to need it.'

I turned back to Ted, 'Now tell me everything.' 'It's the warlock. I heard him tell his coven to keep the others busy while he came to kill you and your family to punish your father for something he'd done in the past.'

'Does anybody else know he's coming here?' 'No master, they are all protecting the book and the talisman.'

'Can you go to the cottage, Ted and tell my father what's going on?' 'Yes master.'

Upstairs my boys and Saidie had finally calmed my mother down. (I think the brandy helped as well).

Taking Brandon and Jordon to one side I explained what was heading our way, 'I know that you're only apprentices, but is there anything you can do to slow him down until help arrives?' Jordon looked at Brandon, 'What do you say bro?' 'I think we might have a few surprises in store for him.'

'Don't go putting yourselves at risk, just keep him occupied until the others get here.'

'Yeah dad, we'll be careful.' That and several more assurances could be heard from the boys as they raced out of the door and disappeared into the garden.

A warm welcome

Tom and Cuthbert had taken up positions on either side of the lane. As the coven drew level, Tom shouted. 'That's far enough, we're going to give you this chance to turn around and leave. We are a peaceful people, we don't want to harm you, but, we will protect what we guard with our lives, even if it means taking yours.'

Tom knew that they were outnumbered, and there was no way that they could defeat this many.

Tom and Cuthbert both had the strangest feeling, it was as if someone was tugging on both of their trouser legs. Looking down, they both saw a guardian on either side looking up and smiling. 'We have come to help,' said a voice in their heads 'yes, we have, but we are not alone, no, we have brought a friend, a big friend.'

Without delay they vanished, Tom suddenly realised who the "big friend" was.

Gary Gray was not up for all this killing people and fighting other witches and wizards, but he needed the money that the warlock had promisedHe had hung behind and was now the last one. 'Beggar this,' he thought, 'I'm off.' he ran back down the lane as fast as his old legs would carry him.

The others had not the sense that Gary Gray had.

'I think it should be you who are the ones to leave, but first, give us what we've come for, and we promise we will let you go unharmed.'

Tom and Cuthbert walked out of the wood. 'This is your final chance. Turn round and go, or suffer the consequences.' The wizard who thought of himself as the leader laughed, 'There's only two of you, there's eleven of us.' 'Actually there's ten of us,' said a voice from the back, 'Gray's done a runner.' 'Ok,' snapped the leader, 'but ten against two is still good odds.' Tom said, 'Excuse me, there are another five out here and some more in the cottage.'

'Well, if there are five out here why don't they show themselves?' sneered the wizard 'Guardians will you please show yourselves?' The air in front of Tom and Cuthbert shimmered and the guardians appeared. 'What's this, an army of teddy bears?' the coven burst into laughter.

Tom held up his hand, 'Don't be fooled by their appearance, these are guardians from the realm of dragons, but I see that you are not overly impressed by them, so maybe you will be more impressed by the last member of our little group.' 'Ok, and where is this person we're expected to be frightened of? 'Don't tell me, you've got him in your pocket,' laughed the wizard.

'No,'she's not in my pocket, she wouldn't fit, as a matter of fact she's standing right behind me. Firefly would you be so kind as to show these gentlemen what a beautiful lady you are?'

Nobody laughed when Firefly appeared. The coven stared in terror at the dragon, then as one they tried to turn round. Tried, but nothing happened because while their attention was focused on Firefly, the guardians had tied their legs together.

The thing about the guardians is not only can they become invisible, but they are incredibly quick and extremely intelligent.

Before most of the wizards had even hit the floor, the guardians had tied their hands together also. The ones they missed found that they couldn't sit up, because there was a little hairy creature sitting on their chests.

Tom and Cuthbert helped secure the last of the wizards, they dragged them all down to the cavern under Donna's cottage.

Once this was done, Betty said that she and the girls would guard the prisoners, then told Tom and Cuthbert to hurry over to my cottage and help stop the warlock master.

'Master, he's out there?' 'How do you know?' I asked. 'I've felt the evil that he gives out before, in the realm of dragons.'

I then remembered that my boys were out there also. I didn't know how, but I knew that I had to find them and keep them safe. Just as I reached the door, I found Ted barring my way. 'No master it's too dangerous, you have no magic. But don't worry help is coming.' This did not stop me wanting to rush outside, but I found that I could not move, it was as if I'd come up against a glass wall. 'What have you done to me, Ted?' 'It's for your own safety master.'

Outside Brandon and Jordon were in position either side of the path leading to our cottage. 'Here comes trouble bro.' 'Yeah, I see him, doesn't look all that powerful to me.'

If you are wondering why the warlock master didn't hear the boys talking, it was because they had learned to talk telepathically. 'Yes, I know, but our job is to delay him long enough for the others to get here.' Jordon was always the sort to dive into any situation head first, while Brandon liked to think things out, before acting, but not this time. 'You are not welcome here, leave while you are still able.' Not to be left out Jordon added, 'We are two very powerful wizards, we don't want to hurt you, but we will if you don't leave.'

The warlock master laughed. 'Your threats don't frighten me, you're just two kids playing at being wizards, but he soon stopped laughing when a pair of stunning spells hit him. 'Well you have been practising, they might have been good enough to stun an ordinary wizard, but not someone as powerful as me.'

Ted's voice could be heard in both the boys' head, 'Young masters, your grandfather is nearly here. Just keep him busy for a few moments longer.'

'Listen bro, we can't match him magically,' Brandon told his brother. 'So let's do what we do best.' Jordon chuckled, 'You mean wind him up?' 'Yeah bro.'

'Are you really that powerful, or is it all just hype to frighten people?' 'I bet you're not as good as our granddad George, I'll bet he's twice the warlock you are.'

That must have hit a nerve, because the warlock master began throwing out curses in all directions.

'Cyril, Cyril, Cyril reduced to anger by two young wizards!' 'Don't call me Cyril, I'm the warlock master, the greatest warlock ever.' 'Oh Cyril how did you become so deluded? When we were apprenticed to Oswald Greybeard, you could hardly manage even the easiest of spells.'

'That's because he would only let us cast good spells, but when I left, I found a new teacher, one who taught mainly dark magic. With him I found out that I was very good at them, hence I became a warlock.'

While Cyril was explaining how great a warlock he'd become, George had signalled to the boys to go indoors and leave Cyril to him.

'Tell me old friend, why are you here at my son's cottage?' The warlock master's face had a look of pure evil, 'I'm here to punish you for turning Oswald Greybeard against me. I'm going to kill every member of your family and finally you.'

What the warlock hadn't noticed, was that Tom, Cuthbert and the four guardians had arrived and were now surrounding him.

'I didn't turn him against you, you done that all by yourself. Always wanting to learn how to hurt others. All our master wanted us to learn was how to care for magical creatures, and to turn into the sort of wizards that did good in the world.'

'Yeah well, the master I ended up with, taught me that the only thing worth learning was how to gain more power. You can never have enough power, he used to say and that's why you are going to hand over the book of dark magic. If you do, I promise you that I will not harm you or any of your family.'

'You never were a very good liar, Cyril.' The warlock master shrugged his shoulders, 'It was worth a try, but I promise you if you give me the book, I'll make you and your family's death quick.'

'You always did like the sound of your own voice, Cyril, while you've been waffling on, you've given some of my coven time to get here, so it's no longer just the two of us. If you'd care to look behind you, you will see what I'm talking about.'

While keeping his wand trained on George, he looked over his right shoulder and then his left, catching sight of Tom and Cuthbert. 'I'm powerful enough to handle the three of you.' 'Look again,' said George.

This time the warlock took more care in scanning his surroundings.

'Those things,' he spat, 'they have no magic. I've tortured and killed several of them in the other realm. What have they got that can beat me?' 'Speed, my old friend, speed. Now!' shouted George, and before he could raise his wand, the guardians had pounced on him and had him hogtied on the ground.

'See Cyril, you don't always need magic, sometimes all you need is speed.'

What George hadn't noticed was that the warlock still had his wand in his hand. Before anybody could take it from him, he cast a killing spell that hit George in the chest. 'You always underestimated me, George, that's why I'm the greatest warlock ever, and you're just dead,' shouted Cyril.

I'd witnessed all that had gone on from inside our cottage and rushed out to my father, resting his head in my lap, I looked into his eyes, 'Help's on the way, dad.'

He smiled up at me. 'Nothing can help me now, son, I can feel the magic leaving me, but at least I got to hear you call me "dad". Does this mean you have forgiven me for leaving all those years ago?' 'Water under the bridge, dad. Being a part of the coven of the talisman has giving me an idea of what made you leave, you were only trying to keep your family safe.' 'Thank you son, I can rest easier knowing that there is no animosity between us.' He motioned me to come closer and whispered in my ear. 'Yes father, I will, I promise,' and then he was gone.

It was then I realised that Cyril was ranting about how he was the greatest warlock ever, and that once he had escaped his bonds, he was going to kill all those who had anything to do with his capture, but only after he had tortured us, so that we begged him for release.

I'm not a violent person, but I gently laid my father's head down, walked over to the warlock. As I looked into his eyes, I could only see madness. Obviously something had snapped in his brain. I had come over to hurt him badly, but I realised that there was nothing left to hurt.

Parting of the ways

The next few weeks were hectic to say the least. I kept my promise to my father and had him buried in the church yard in a double grave so my mother could join him later, the next part of the wishes that he'd whispered to be a lot harder to bring about.

The warlock's band of hired thugs were handed over to the council of wizards for punishment, but we made no mention of the book of dark magic or that it was in our keeping.

The wizard in charge of the coven that were taking the prisoners away was the same wizard that had come to tell us that he was taking over the search for the book from us and ended up on a Scottish isle, courtesy of Sienna. He obviously hadn't learned anything from his trip to Scotland. 'I've told you lot before to stay out of council business, this is your last warning. Anymore meddling in things that should be left to your superiors, will be dealt with most severely.'

While he was speaking, he hadn't noticed Sienna walk up behind him, 'I hear that Antarctica is quite nice at this time of year,' she whispered in his ear.

The wizard jumped out of his skin, 'You, you're the one who sent me to that island. The ferry broke down and I was stranded there for three months.'

Sienna smiled, 'I don't know what you're talking about, but if you would like a trip to the South Pole, I'm sure I could arrange it.'

'That won't be necessary, I think our business here is concluded.' he made a hasty retreat thereafter.

Gary Grey, the wizard who was one of the crew that the warlock had hired to kill the coven of the talisman and steal the book of dark magic, and then had chickened out, was sitting in the village pub sipping a pint in the beer garden and regretting his choices and praying the council wizards didn't know about him.

'I think he's one of the dark wizards, yes, I do, no, I see him run away, yes, I did. So if he run away, why he still here? Why? Maybe he thirsty. I know I am, and hungry.' 'You always hungry.'

Gary Grey could hear voices all around him, but the garden was empty. 'I know someone's there I can hear you, show yourselves,' he demanded.

One minute he was alone and the next there were five creatures standing in front of him, four covered in hair, one also with hair, but wearing a small bib and brace overall. Gary looked at his glass and wondered, 'How many of these have I had.' 'What are you?' he asked. 'We were guardians,' said the one with clothes, who seemed to be in charge, 'but we are having so much fun here that we don't want to go back to the realm of dragons. Not only is it no fun there, but also there is no pizza.' 'We love pizza,' they all agreed.

'So, if you're not going back, what are you going to do in this realm?' As one they answered, 'We are going to be, the magic police. If anyone tries to steal the book of dark magic, we will be there to stop them.' 'Hang on a minute. Are you telling me that the book of dark magic is here in this village?

There was mayhem among the five. 'We should not have told him. He is on the side of evil,' said one. 'He will tell all the dark lords, yes, he will,' said another.

'Please,' said Gary Grey. 'I'm not evil. I only went along with them because I needed the money, but as soon as I realised what they were up to I got the hell out of there.'

'Ok,' said Ted. 'We might believe you if you were to get us one of those drinks each.'

If anybody was to venture out into the beer garden, they would have been surprised to see an old man sitting alone at a table covered in empty beer glasses.

'Beer is the best thing ever,' said one. 'No, pizza is the best thing ever,' said another. 'No,' chipped in a third, 'beer and pizza is the best thing ever.'

Poppy had taken Firefly back to the realm of dragons. Paris had also gone, she was frightened the whole time at Donna's cottage and wanted somewhere to study the history of magic. Unlike her sister, she was a scholar not a fighter.

The rest of us gathered at Donna's cottage to discuss what should happen next. Betty brought the meeting to order, 'The first and most important thing is what we are going to do with the book of dark magic.' Tom agreed, 'We must find somewhere to hide it, somewhere no one will ever find it.' Cuthbert asked, 'Where's it hidden now?' 'It's in the cavern,' said Betty, 'but we can't keep it there. It's the first place anyone will look, and I don't want Thompson turned into a battlefield.'

Down in the cavern we all gathered round a chest that had appeared out of the floor. 'It's not there,' cried Betty, as she opened the lid. Everyone started to panic. 'It was in there, you all watched me put it in,' Tom exclaimed.

I looked into the chest. 'What's this?' I said taking a piece of paper from the bottom of the chest and handing it to Betty. 'What's it say?' asked Cuthbert. 'I don't know who it's from, but it says "I have taken the book of dark magic and hidden it in a safe place".' There was then a lengthy discussion about who it could have been, and how had they gained access to the cavern. Only those of us now in the cavern had known that the book was in there. Betty carried on reading, 'I am not one of you. You don't know me, but do not worry I have only done this to stop you being plagued by dark wizards trying to gain access to the book. Please do not look for it as you'll never find it.' It was signed, "a friend".

The end of the coven of the talisman

A lot happened after we found out that the book of dark magic had been taken. The last few left of us from the original coven of the talisman held a meeting to decide what to do next. Eventually, after many hours it was decided that Donna's cottage would be sealed back into the wood for another hundred years, in the hope that witches and wizards would be more enlightened by then. (Me, I had my doubts).

Tom and Sienna also went back to the realm of dragons, Sienna to study under the wise one, and Tom to see Poppy. Once there, Sienna would finish her studies to become the first female warlock. The council of wizards were totally against this. The head of the council had come to the realm to personally inform the wise one that it would not be happening. 'You are not to break council rules, and you are, young lady,' he sneered, 'not to get ideas above your station. Young ladies like yourself are to be trained as witches and that's it.'

And that was it, because there was a flash of light, and the wizard was gone.

'Where to this time?' asked the wise one. 'Well he looked a bit pale, so, I thought that a bit of sun would do him good, and I hear that Australia is nice this time of year.'

The portal through Durdle Door was changed so that only people invited could enter, which meant that Brandon and Jordon would be going there to be apprenticed to the wise one.

'Why so sad?' Sienna asked Tom. 'You know that Poppy and I are a couple.' 'Yes, you'd have to be stupid not to notice that so what's the problem?' asked Sienna.

'The problem is that I want to take her to Tibet to meet the yeti and lots of other places that she's never been to.' Sienna smiled, 'So? I'm sure she would be only too happy to go.' 'She would, but she has nobody to look after Firefly while we're gone.' 'Problem solved, I'd love to look after Firefly while you're gone.' 'Are you sure, Sienna?' 'Yes, I'm sure.'

Cuthbert was also in the realm; he had come to see the female troll he'd met while looking for clues to the whereabouts of the book of dark magic.

'Hello there, if it isn't that cute little fella who was here before? I didn't think I'd be seeing you again,' Cuthbert blushed (which is not an easy thing to do if you're a troll). 'W-well I-I couldn't stop thinking about you, s-so I-I had to come and see you again.' 'Well now you're here, you can tell me all about yourself over lunch.' 'Do you have any pizza?' asked Cuthbert. The troll looked at him, 'What's pizza?'

Back in Thompson, Ted had brought the four other ex-guardians to live with Sadie and me. 'What are you five going to do? You are welcome to stay with us for a while, but eventually you'll have to find your own place.' Ted looked at me, 'We are going to stay here in the village of Thompson, 'we are going to guard the book of dark magic, and stop anyone stealing it. We even have a name for our group.' He stood up and proudly exclaimed, 'We are MI5.'

'What?' Yes, David, MI5, it stands for magical investigators five.

We are working on adding another member to our team. He is a bit reluctant to join at this moment because he was a member of the coven that attacked us.

Only he couldn't go through with it and fled. He has a home in the village which would make a great headquarters, but he is frightened that you all will hold that against him.'

'Why don't you bring him to Donna's cottage to meet what's left of the coven, so we can see what kind of wizard he is?'

Later that afternoon a rather nervous Gary Grey, led by Ted and the rest of the MI5 joined us down in the cavern.

'Don't look so worried Mr Grey. We asked you to meet us down in the cavern because it's easier to detect any dark intent on your behalf down here. But so far, the floor hasn't opened, and swallowed you up, so you must be ok,' Betty informed him. 'Well, that's good to hear,' said a rather less worried Gary Grey.

A lot of things happened over the next few weeks. Cuthbert came home from the realm of dragons, but not alone. He had persuaded the female troll to join him as his wife. Luckily female trolls are a good deal smaller than the males, but even so, she was nearly twice the size of Cuthbert.

The troll equivalent to a marriage service was to find a female whom he thought suitable, hit her over the head with something handy and drag her back to his cave.

Cuthbert on the other hand, being only half troll and having been living with humans for the last three hundred years, was a bit more civilised. He had asked the female if she would like to come to our realm and live with him, and she said "yes".

One afternoon there was a knock at the door, I answered it to find Cuthbert standing there, and towering over him was the love of his life, 'David, I'd like you to meet Petal. The name given to her by the trolls is unpronounceable, even for me, so, as she reminds me of a lovely flower, I call her Petal.'

Well, I thought, if the petal is over six feet, I can only imagine the size of the flower.

I invited them in, and over the next hour Sadie and I got to know Petal. For one so large, she had a soft voice, and we soon came to like her. 'Petal's coming to live with me,' he told Sadie. 'She knows no one, or how to act around humans, so maybe you could be her first friend and show her around.'

Sadie said, 'I'd love to.' Smiling at Petal, she said, 'I'd be only too happy to show you around, Petal, and introduce you to my friends.' Petal beamed, 'I've never had a friend before. I think I'm going to enjoy living here, you're all so very kind.'

Cuthbert's surprise

Before we sealed up the wood and concealed Donna's cottage for another hundred years, Cuthbert called us all to the cavern under the cottage.

That included the wise one, Poppy, Sienna, Paris, me, Tom, Betty, two ancient looking Gargoyles and even the MI6 (as they now called themselves).

Cuthbert called for quiet. 'I've asked you all here to discuss a problem we all have, and that's money. Wise one, you want to turn the castle in the realm of dragons into a refuge for any magic folk in trouble and a place of learning for any who want it, am I right?' 'Yes, the Guardian and I have agreed that the fate of the realm of dragons should no longer be decided by the council of wizards. In time we will form a council of our own from wizards and witches who only have the realm's interest at heart.'

'Tom, you want to take Poppy on a tour of all the magical places you've visited. David, you would like to take Sadie away on a long holiday. Paris, I'm told that you want to be a magical historian.' 'Yes, I've always thought that the history of famous witches and wizards should be recorded for all to read. All their successes and failures, so as to help some, or deter others from making the same mistakes.' 'MI6, you have vowed to protect the wood when it's sealed again.' 'Yes,' Gary Grey answered, 'the former guardians have asked me to be the head of MI6 and their spokesperson. We have taken an oath to protect the wood from all who wish to gain entry.'

'Betty, your farm has been in your family for six generations, has it not?' 'Yes, and my husband hopes it will be for another six, at least.'

'And finally, we come to Sienna. Your ambition is to become the first female warlock, is it not?' 'Yes,' and I will, the wise one has offered to continue my learning as far as he can.' 'Yes, then what?' Cuthbert asked. 'Then I will have to find another master to further my learning.'

'The problem you're all going to have, is finding enough money to achieve all your ambitions. Well, I've come up with a solution. I don't know if you are aware of the fact, that I once lived in this cottage with the first woman I ever loved, my Beth. This was her home, and when I rescued her from being eaten by an ugly troll, we came to live here. I was the one who dug out this cellar, as it was at the start, to hide all the treasure that the troll had stolen. We buried it down there and forgot about it, and that's why these two gentlemen are here.'

Cuthbert waved the two Gargoyles forward. 'I'd like to introduce all of you to Mr Flint and Mr Stone. Mr Flint is expert in rare metals and gems, while Mr Stone is the manager of the largest private investment bank in the world. They will explain what we've been doing with all the treasure that I hid here all those many years ago.'

Mr Flint cleared his throat, 'Ladies and....' Looking around he could see that "gentlemen" would not cover it. 'Sorry, I mean folks, Cuthbert contacted me a month ago and asked me to value the mass of treasure he'd hidden down here many years ago. After nearly a week of cataloguing all the artifacts, I came to a rough estimate of its value, and I must tell you that the amount it came to exceeded my wildest dreams. Some of the hoard was just gold plates and goblets, these only had a scrap value, so were melted down and sold as bullion.

'This alone came to several million pounds, which was petty change compared to the remainder of the hoard consisting of jewellery and crowns, also boxes of gems and chests of gold coins, all of which are being sold off slowly so as not to flood the market and draw any attention back to anyone of us.'

Everyone seemed to be flabbergasted by enormity of what the gargoyle had said, but it was nothing compared to what Mr Stone was about to tell us.

So as not to miss anyone out, Mr Stone started his explanation with. 'Friends, I will attempt to simplify my part in all this. After Mr Flint has sold a part of the hoard, he will deposit the money, less his commission, in my bank, where I will invest some of it and the rest along with the profits from those investments, less of course my commission, are sitting there waiting to be spent.'

I think I must have been the first one to gather my thoughts. 'Cuthbert, what does all this mean? 'Well, David, it means that no one in this room will ever have to worry about money again.

'Mr Stone has started a company, and you are all shareholders in that company. Before we leave, we will all be given credit cards in the company's name and a salary will be paid into you bank monthly.'

The next two weeks went by quickly, Donna's cottage and the wood was now covered by rhododendrons as it was five years ago.

Cuthbert and Petal had settled in together. Petal had made several friends in the village. She joined the women's institute where she learnt to cook and even changed Cuthbert's eating habits.

Brandon and Jordon had gone to the realm of dragons, to study under the wise one along with Sienna who was looking after Firefly as well as studying.

Tom and Poppy had gone to Tibet to see the yeti.

Sadie and I were packing our bags. I'd promised her that when this was over, I'd take her to Tenerife, but thanks to Cuthbert we could do it in style, so we were off on a month-long cruise of the Canary Isle.

Betty was quite happy to stay at home on the farm with her husband.

MI6 were also happy to stay in Thompson, they had set up a ring of magic that surrounded the wood and patrolled around the perimeter daily.

It was a good thing that they could become invisible, even though they had gotten themselves clothes. The sight of five two-foot-high little hairy creatures wandering about the village would have caused some consternation.

There was already talk over the amount of beer and pizza that was being delivered to Gary Grey's house.

And somewhere in Australia the wizard sent there by Sienna, had given up magic for a metal detector and gone on a search for gold.

Finally, you may be wondering what happened to Cyril the warlock master. Well, it seems as if he lost his mind, as well as his ability to perform magic and had to be put into a nursing home. There he started telling everybody he met that he was the most powerful warlock ever, and that his coven would be there soon to rescue him.

Well, that's it, everything's peaceful in the village at this moment in time.

But if anything happens in the future, I'll let you know.

DAVID.

Milton Keynes UK
Ingram Content Group UK Ltd.
UKHW051511290924
448926UK00007B/45